BLOW DOWN

THE PLUMBER'S MATE MYSTERIES FOUR

JL MERROW

D0925559

RIPTIDE PUBLISHING

Riptide Publishing
PO Box 1537
Burnsville, NC 28714
www.riptidepublishing.com

Blow Down

Cover art: Christine Coffee, coffeecreatescovers.com
Editor: Carole-ann Galloway
Layout: L.C. Chase, lcchase.com/design.htm

ISBN: 978-1-62649-726-9

Second edition
March, 2018

Also available in ebook:
ISBN: 978-1-62649-725-2

BLOW DOWN

The Plumber's Mate Mysteries Four

JL MERROW

RIPTIDE PUBLISHING

This book is dedicated to the late Roger Margason, aka Dorien Grey, author of the Dick Hardesty mysteries, who sadly passed away while I was writing Blow Down. *His words will live on.*
With grateful thanks for all their help to Josephine Myles, Pender Mackie, Kristin Matherley, Susan Sorrentino, Jennifer Bales, Victor Banis, Rachel Jeffrey, and everyone at VWC.

TABLE OF CONTENTS

PROLOGUE

She was still warm—and yeah, I knew who it was the minute I touched her. Had known all along, really—so I made myself feel for a pulse, for signs of breathing, anything. Just because the vibes had felt like death didn't mean she was *actually* dead, right?

Right?

Wrong. There was something around her neck, making it hard to find a pulse point, but her slender wrists were bare, and neither of 'em had a pulse. Should I try to loosen the thing round her neck, give her a bit more room to breathe? Yeah, I know, messing with the evidence—but what if she was still saveable?

I scrabbled at the stuff round her neck, gagging when it came away bloody from where it'd sunk into the skin. I recoiled again when I realised what it was.

There was no sign of movement or life from the body I'd just been manhandling.

Woman-handling? Corpse-handling?

I shuddered. Should I try CPR? You weren't supposed to do mouth-to-mouth anymore, were you? Vinnie Jones said so in that TV ad.

"Staying Alive" thudded through my brain, and I wished I'd been paying more attention to the telly at the time rather than having a quick grope with Phil.

Christ, what I wouldn't give to be back on my sofa with my bloke right now.

Then again, I imagined the woman I'd just fallen over might have felt pretty much the same.

CHAPTER ONE

These days, when my big sister phones me, I don't expect anything worse than an invite to lunch and the latest gossip, so I hit Accept Call that night without even a hint of a suspicion of foreboding.

Just goes to show, this being-psychic lark really isn't all it's cracked up to be.

"'Lo, Sis. What's up?" I held the phone to my ear with my left hand while I stirred the pasta sauce with my right. Phil was coming round for tea but wasn't sure when, so I was doing something I could leave on a low heat to keep warm if need be.

"Oh, hello, Tom." Cherry paused. "Um, how are you?"

I sighed. The only time she ever opens with *How are you?* is when she's desperate to ask for a favour but thinks it'd be rude to launch straight in without a bit of chitchat. "What is it?" I asked, resigned to doing another job for mates' rates for someone who was no mate of mine.

At least, I hoped it was a job, not anything family related. Especially seeing as my family had recently got a bit more complicated.

"Amelia Fenchurch-Majors," Cherry said. "She asked me to ask you to do a job for her. She's based in St. Leonards—I know it's a bit further afield than you'd usually go, but honestly, you'd be doing me a *huge* favour if you could go over and see her. At your earliest convenience."

From the sharp tone in Cherry's voice, I guessed (a) she was hoping I'd focus on *earliest* rather than *convenience*, and (b) she'd been getting her ear bent by Mrs. Double-Barrelled Shotgun. "Friend of yours, is she?"

"She's not a *friend*. We just happen to know one another."

"Let me guess—through Greg?"

Greg is my big sister's unfeasibly reverend fiancé, canon of St. Leonards cathedral. Mrs. Fenchurch-Majors sounded like the sort of person he had over for sherry all the time. She was probably a drill sergeant in his army of grey-haired old dears who'd outlived their husbands by twenty years or more and now seemed to worship the ground under Greg's unusually large feet. I could see her now, barking orders at the twinset and pearls brigade to *Crochet faster* and *Don't put those flowers there, put them THERE.*

"Not exactly. The bishop held a garden party over the summer, and we were introduced there. Amelia was *very* interested to hear about you. Well, of course she heard all about your heroics at the Dyke."

I winced. Not only was all this well embarrassing—they'd put a picture of me in the paper and everything—but several months down the line, I was still having nightmares about that night. Only in my dreams, I didn't get there in time. So I wasn't too chuffed to be reminded about it.

"Oh yeah? So exactly what did you tell her?"

"Nothing." Cherry sounded hurt. "Although I don't see why you're so keen to have everyone forget about it all. It's hardly something to be *ashamed* of."

"I'm not ashamed. Course I'm not. It's just, well, you know they put that bit in the paper about me having psychic powers, yeah?" I wasn't sure who'd blabbed—hopefully not one of my mates, but then I hadn't exactly sworn anyone to secrecy, which was beginning to look a bit short-sighted of me. Then again, it wasn't beyond the bounds some disgruntled copper had made an off-the-cuff remark about me being DI Southgate's tame psychic.

"So?"

"*So*, I've had everyone and his bloody dog asking me all kinds of crap ever since, up to and including 'Will it rain tomorrow?' and 'Can you just fill in this lottery form for me?' ta very much."

"That's just silly. You can't do anything like that." She paused. "Can you?"

"Sis, I live in a two-bed semi in Fleetville. What do *you* think? But try telling them that. Everyone seems to think 'psychic' means whatever they bloody well want it to mean."

Look, I've just got a bit of a knack for finding things, that's all. Hidden things, that is, and I have to be fairly close to them to start with, although Phil's constantly on the lookout for ways of extending my reach. All the better to help him make a killing in his chosen profession and retire early on the profits. I used to think he was onto a loser, but ever since the fire at the Dyke, I've been starting to wonder. Something about that night amped the vibes up way beyond anything I'd ever felt before—and no, I'm not talking euphemisms here, 'cos by the time we'd made it home, we were too bloody knackered for anything like that.

Phil, of course, had various theories as to what exactly might have sharpened the old spidey-senses: the danger to yours truly; the way a couple of people I cared about were also at imminent risk of getting toasted; even the heat counteracting moisture in the air (water messes with the vibes, which is handy when you're trying to locate a leak underground but not so much the rest of the time). Fortunately, Phil's caseload had been busy enough over the summer to take his mind off too much experimentation with my dubious talents.

Well, *that* sort of experimentation. We'd managed to find time for a few experiments of a different sort. But yeah. Not your all-purpose psychic. My so-called gift doesn't hold with multitasking. "It's like they think it's some kind of one-size-fits-all thing," I muttered down the line.

There was a weird sort of breathy sound down the phone. "I suppose that'd be *medium*, then. The size."

"I literally can't believe you said that," I told her after a healthy pause to let her know just how much I meant it.

Sisters.

"So what's the job?" I asked before she could come up with any more comedic gems.

"She didn't say. I gave her one of your cards and suggested she call you direct, but she seems to have this bee in her bonnet that you'd be more likely to accept the job if it came through me."

"Right, gimme her number and I'll give her a bell."

There was a pause. "They're ex-directory, and she doesn't give out her number. You'll have to go round."

"You're kidding, right? Seriously?"

"Look, she's very persistent," Sis said, which was an admission of defeat if ever I heard one. "*Please* just go round? You can come over to Gregory's for tea afterwards. We've got some very nice cakes." Translation: the cathedral ladies had been baking again. Come to think of it, I wasn't sure they ever stopped. Maybe they took a short break every now and then for knitting bedsocks and crocheting jam-jar covers, that sort of thing.

"Are you actually living there now?" I asked, because Sis had her own house in Pluck's End, a village not far from St. Leonards, but every time she invited me and/or Phil anywhere lately, it'd been to the Old Deanery, currently occupied by the Youngish Canon.

(I nearly said the Middle-Aged Canon, seeing as how Greg had to be in his midforties, but since reaching this side of thirty, I'd gained a whole new perspective on the subject. Funny, that.)

"No, of course not," Cherry said as if the very idea was ridiculous. "That wouldn't be at all proper."

"Course not. What was I thinking of? Fine, I'll go and see this pushy old biddy of yours. Tell her I'll be round Friday afternoon—I've got a couple of hours free then."

There was another of those breathy sounds.

"What?" I asked.

"Nothing," Cherry said brightly, and reeled off the address.

Just as I finished writing it down, Phil walked in followed by his adoring public, otherwise known as Merlin and Arthur, my two cats. "Emergency call-out?" he asked after I'd hung up.

"Nah, just an extra job for tomorrow," I told him, expertly dodging the cats so I could give him a welcome snog and a grope of that magnificent arse, which he returned with interest. "Nothing serious," I muttered into his shoulder.

Like I said, Nostradamus I am not. If anyone was daft enough to hand me a crystal ball, I'd see bugger all. And then drop it on my foot.

Mrs. F-M.'s gaff on the outskirts of St. Leonards turned out, when I got there the following afternoon, to be your actual Grade II listed farmhouse, and she had plenty of acreage to go with it. I felt like a right pleb parking the van on a posh, red-brick driveway only slightly less extensive than the M25 and going up to knock on a front door built to withstand siege, battering ram, and revolting peasants.

It didn't help there was a choice of two doors with nothing much to distinguish between 'em. I went for the slightly larger one, in the end, on the basis I was doing the old girl a favour, so I was buggered if I was going cap in hand to the tradesman's entrance.

Hey, I might actually *be* a tradesman, but I doff my cap to no man. Or woman, as it might be. Metaphorically speaking, obviously. Hats and me have never really got on. You'd think putting something on your head would make you look taller, but I just end up looking like the sort of stable lad who wants to be a jockey when he grows up.

The door was opened by a young woman who could have been a model, if that hadn't been something only common people did. Well, she was a bit on the short side—her sharp green eyes were on a level with mine—but otherwise, she'd have made a pretty good showing on the cover of *Vogue*. She even had the expression down pat—that one where they glare at the photographer like he or she's something they just scraped off their shoe. God knows how fashion photographers cope with all that negativity shoved in their faces day in day out. Give me happy-smiley wedding pics any day, or those ones you see mums queuing up for in Boots, with the baby poking its head up out of a flowerpot.

"Tom Paretski?" she said, sizing me up with one unhurried glance and not bothering to crack a smile in welcome. "I'm Mrs. Fenchurch-Majors. Do come in."

I blinked. *She* was Mrs. F-M.? I'd taken her for some kind of PA, hired by the lady of the house to deal with tedious and/or unpleasant matters like correspondence and talking to members of the working classes.

No wonder Cherry had laughed when I'd called her an old biddy.

"Cheers, love," I said, mostly to annoy her.

She winced and glanced pointedly at the doormat, despite the fact it wasn't raining outside, so I obligingly went through the motions.

And no, I hadn't missed the fact I got a first name and she didn't. I bet if I was lucky enough to get a cuppa, it'd be made with the second-best tea bags and come in a chipped mug kept 'specially for workmen and other oiks.

"Right, love, what's the problem?" I flashed Mrs. F-M. my best smile.

She didn't return it. "Less of the endearments, please. I am not your *love*. This way, please."

She click-clacked ahead of me on sky-high heels, and I swear I heard the ancient timber floors groan as she approached. And who wears stilettos in their own house, anyhow? Speaking of which, her skirt and blouse were tight and tailored, more like a posh version of office wear than something you'd wear to clean the bathroom. Or show the plumber where the problem was, for that matter. So maybe I shouldn't have been surprised when she led me not to a bathroom, downstairs loo, or even the kitchen or utility room, but right up several flights of creaking stairs to an attic bedroom. The door was locked, but she had a key.

Which made me wonder a bit, because this clearly wasn't Mrs. F-M.'s bedroom. Despite the double bed, I was fairly sure it was a single woman's room, and there was ample evidence the occupant was several clothing sizes larger than Mrs. F-M. To be perfectly frank, it looked like an explosion in a TK Maxx. Designer handbags and shoes littered the floor and the furniture indiscriminately, and there was a pile of frocks on the bed that could keep the Chelsea Oxfam shop going for a month.

As you've probably guessed, it was a pretty big room, as attics go. I mean, when most people talk about attics, they mean the space under the roof like I've got in my house where you can just about manage to shove a few suitcases and your Christmas decorations so they're out of sight, out of mind. Or maybe, if you're lucky, put up a couple of starving artists and a mad first wife for similar reasons. This was definitely more at the luxury loft conversion end of the market, with large dormer windows and more floor space than my whole upstairs.

There was also a distinct lack of plumbing anywhere I could tell. And trust me, I can tell. I was starting to get a bad feeling about this one.

"So what can I do you for, love?" It slipped out. Honest.

Mrs. F-M. looked like she'd just been served a glass of wine with bits of cork in it, but at least she didn't tell me off again. "I need you to find my necklace."

Despite the loud *clunk* as my heart plummeted into my boots, I played dumb. "What happened to it? Down the loo? Plug hole?"

"I doubt it. I'm sure the little *darling* is keeping it quite safe somewhere." The way she said *darling*, you'd be forgiven for thinking it had only four letters and rhymed with *blunt*.

"Not sure I follow you," I said a lot more breezily than I felt. I mean, I should've known. I really should've known. So much for all the years I'd spent training in my chosen profession, getting my City and Guilds and all that bollocks.

"Don't be obtuse." Yeah, I could tell she was a mate of Cherry's. "I need you to do that *thing* of yours. Remote viewing. Divination. Whatever you like to call it."

I'd never called it either of those things in my life. "Uh, did Cherry say something to you about, you know?"

"*Obviously*. Now, can we please get on with it? I presume you charge by the hour. And I have an appointment at four."

I was going to kill Cherry, I decided. Beat her to death with a couple of bloody dowsing rods. Or strangle her with a pendulum. For a mo, I seriously considered telling Mrs. F-M. where to shove her flippin' necklace, but, well, I'd have felt like a right bastard if Sis had ended up getting yet more grief over it all.

Which I know doesn't exactly fit with the whole wanting-to-kill-her thing, but that's family for you.

"You do realise, once I start looking, I'll come up with all kinds of stuff, yeah?" I said, admitting defeat. "I mean, there might be stuff you don't want me to find—"

"Then you'll just have to focus, won't you? Now, it's a simple pendant. Eighteen-carat gold, with a central, heart-shaped pink diamond surrounded by white diamonds. Quite delicate. Antique. *Extremely* valuable."

"And you're sure someone's hidden it? I mean, if it's just lost—"

"*Quite* sure. Alexander's little *poppet* has hated me since the minute we met—of course, nobody should dare to take the place of her sainted mother—and you should have seen her face when he gave it to me as a wedding gift. I wasn't a bit surprised when it went missing two weeks ago."

I was beginning to have a lot of sympathy with Little Poppet-darling. Mrs. F-M. didn't realise how lucky she was that it was only the necklace that'd disappeared. Sod it. What was I supposed to do now? For starters, I only had Mrs. F-M.'s word for it the necklace actually belonged to her. And I really didn't like the thought of helping her go behind her stepdaughter's back.

Mrs. F-M. strode through the room, grinding a silk kimono casually into the carpet with her heel as she went, and flung open a door at the far end. "You'll need to search in here too," she said, switching on a light.

I'd thought the bedroom, large as it was, was cluttered. The space beyond, which was almost as big, looked like it held fodder for a whole series of *Cash in the Attic*, and several episodes of *Antiques Roadshow* besides. Not to mention *Hoarders*. No wonder she'd wanted to call in an expert to find anything in there.

Didn't make me any happier about being the expert she'd called. "Well, it doesn't always work . . ." I tried.

She gave me a sharp look. "Cherry said you had an excellent success rate." Something told me Cherry'd be in for a right ear-bashing if I didn't at least give it a go.

Course, she'd be in for one from me whatever, but that was different. That was family, that was. "Fine. I'll just . . . Um. You mind leaving the room?"

It was nothing to do with the vibes. I just didn't like her breathing down my neck all the time.

She gave me a different sort of look then, and her tongue darted out to wet her upper lip, which creeped me out a bit—I mean, I could imagine her doing that on purpose, thinking it was sexy or something, but it looked totally unconscious. Sort of like a python while it's considering whether it's really got room for a whole goat. "No, I think I'll stay."

Flippin' marvellous. "Uh, it's easier if I'm on my own. Might take a bit longer with you here." Well, she *had* said she had an appointment.

She smiled wide enough to show a bit of fang. "Then you'd probably better get started, hadn't you?"

Great. "Well, could you go over by the door, at least?" I did *not* want her literally looking over my shoulder the whole bloody time.

She sent me a cool stare, then glided over to where I'd asked her to, somehow managing to make the sway of her hips look sarcastic.

Or, you know, maybe I was just a bit on the oversensitive side right then.

Once she had her back against the wall, I gave myself a brief shake, then *listened*.

I mean, not with my ears. For the, you know. Vibes.

Then I blinked. Whoa. Little Poppet-darling was one seriously secretive young lady. The room was buzzing with bright vibes, all tangled up like a plate of spaghetti. Forking any one particular meatball out of that lot wasn't exactly going to be a picnic. There was a bitter taste to it all too, while we're on the food metaphors. Or similes, maybe. Whatever. Whether it was all directed at the evil stepmother, I wasn't sure, but there was definitely something—

Then the door swung open to hit the wall with a crash, I jumped halfway to the ceiling, and a loud female voice shouted in my shell-like, "What the *hell* are you doing in my room?"

CHAPTER TWO

I turned and gave Little Poppet-darling a weak smile while my heartbeat calmed down to nonlethal levels. At least I hadn't been standing where Mrs. F-M. was. Another six inches closer to the door and she'd just have been a nasty stain on the wall by now.

"Plumber?" I said, my voice cracking just a little bit. "Thought you might have a leak in your pipes."

She was a big lass—like her stepmum, she was about my height, but unlike Mrs. F-M., she had a healthy amount of padding on her bones. Same taste for tight, tailored clothes, but what came across as cool and professional on Mrs. F-M. looked downright racy on Poppet-darling, maybe because like the frocks on the bed, her blouse and skirt were definitely on the vivid side of the colour palette. *Subtle* clearly wasn't a word she had any truck with if she could help it, and pastels were for pushovers. She looked like the sort of girl who liked a drink and a laugh, and would be up for a kebab or a bag of chips at the end of the night.

We'd probably have got on all right if we'd met under different circs, but right now her mouth was still narked at me and one of her eyebrows was telling me plainly it thought I was mental. "What pipes?"

"Well, you know these old places. Never find the plumbing where you expect to, do you?" God knows why I was covering up for Mrs. F-M., 'specially since she'd yet to say word one in our collective defence. Guilty conscience, probably, for going down the path of least resistance and not telling her to do her own sneaking around. "Tom Paretski, by the way. You must be, uh . . ."

"Vi. Vi Majors." I noticed she didn't bother with the double-barrelled bit. "And this is *my* room."

She swung her gaze around the room, probably to check for what I might've nicked, and noticed her stepmum for the first time. "*You*."

Mrs. F-M. peeled herself off the wall and stepped forward fearlessly. "Tom was just giving me a hand here."

"Oh, I'm *sure* he was, and you can keep it out of my bloody bedroom. Your latest bit of rough, is he? Does *Daddy* know he's here?"

"Oi, I'm not—" I spluttered, just as Mrs. F-M. snapped out an outraged, "Don't be *absurd*," in a tone that was less than flattering to yours truly. "Tom's here to help me find something. You know how so many of my things have been going missing lately, don't you?" There was a definite implication that Vi also knew *why* and *where to*.

"You know what?" I said, edging around Vi's ample figure. "I'm just gonna let myself out. Let you and your stepmum catch up and all that."

Mrs. F-M.'s lip curled. "Oh, *dear* Violet and I have said all we have to say to one another, I think." She turned and stepped delicately out of the room, leaving me on my tod with an irate Vi.

Cheers, love.

"I can't *believe* that cow. I could bloody *kill* her." Vi turned to me. "Tell her I haven't got her bloody earring or whatever it is she's lost this time, and when she finds it, she can take it and shove it right up her—"

I made it out of the room, thank God, and shut the door behind me quick. Yep, definitely not much love lost in this happy little family. Course, these two were only related by marriage, so the whole blood-is-thicker-than-water thing didn't really apply.

Then again, blood's not the only thing that makes people family. And I'm speaking from a position of personal experience here.

Mrs. F-M. was waiting for me at the far end of the landing, head on one side and an eager look in her eyes. She didn't seem fazed in the slightest by the hatred coming at her from Vi's direction. Maybe that was why her skin was so pale and clear: she had antifreeze instead of blood running through her veins. "Well? Did you find it?"

"Didn't exactly have a right lot of time in there, did I?"

"But did you get anything? Any sense of it at all?" She click-clacked closer.

"Weeellllll . . ." Shit. I really wasn't comfortable with this. 'Specially after Vi had made her feelings on the matter so bloody clear. "Sorry. It was all a bit vague."

"But there *was* something?"

"Um. Maybe?"

"I knew it." She didn't exactly purr. It was too reptilian for that. "You'll have to come round again. I'll call you."

I made a mental note to call-screen from now on.

"In the meantime, there's something else you can do for me. As you're no doubt aware, I'm organising this year's Harvest Fayre. I'm sure I can count on your support?"

"Uh..."

She smiled, all teeth and no sincerity. "Excellent. I'll be in touch with further details. Now, I'm sure you have work to do." She didn't actually say *chop-chop*, but axes were definitely implied as she chivvied me out the front door.

Flippin' marvellous. I stomped down the drive to the van, wondering just what I'd managed to sign up for without ever, at any point, saying yes. Hopefully it'd just be a stint manning the barbecue or working the beer tent. I could handle that, particularly the latter. Just as long as it didn't involve me having to put on any sort of themed costume and make a prat of myself.

Oh God. Harvest Fayre? She'd better not be expecting me to dress up as some kind of humorous vegetable. A leek, maybe? It'd better sodding well not be a pea.

I slammed the van door a bit harder than I needed to and shoved the keys viciously in the ignition. This was *not* turning out to be my day. Still, at least I'd be able to console myself with a few rounds of cake at the Old Deanery. And maybe wring Cherry's neck while I was at it for putting me through all this. I switched on my phone to check the time—Sis had said come round at four—only to find a text from her saying, *Dont come rnd sprise bishp.*

After a moment's head scratching, I took it to mean she'd been surprised by a visit from the imperial overlord and didn't want me coming over to show her up. Rather than, say, she just didn't want to see me and was suggesting I go play pranks on His Right Reverendness as an alternative activity. Great. So now I wasn't even going to get any cake. As I watched, a second text pinged through with a belated, *Sry*.

I wasn't in the best of moods after that, so seeing as it was Friday, it was around teatime, and it was a nice day and all, I popped in at Phil's office on my way home to see if I could persuade him to knock off early too and go grab a pint.

Alban Investigations Ltd. (director and sole employee, Phil Morrison, Esq.) has its registered address on Hatfield Road, St. Albans, above a firm of no-win-no-fee lawyers of the sort my barrister big sis likes to look down her nose at. It's a cosy little place, by which I mean cramped, but then all he really needs is a desk and a couple of parking spaces: one for his shiny silver VW Golf and one for clients. Or, as might be, my van. I slotted it in neatly and rang the bell for him to buzz me up.

Phil had a file open on his desk when I walked in the door, but I was fairly sure that was just part of the window dressing to impress any potential clients who might drop in unannounced how busy he was. 'Specially seeing as he also had the paper open to the puzzle section and a cup of tea by his elbow. He gave me the raised-eyebrow treatment when I walked in, but I could tell he was pleased to see me.

"Fancy a pint down the Cocks?" I asked, dropping into one of his client chairs, because it'd been a while since I'd had a good swivel.

Ye Olde Fighting Cocks is a pub down by the park in St. Albans. Despite the name, it's not a gay bar with a particularly violent rep, just your average watering hole with an extra bit of history.

It claims to be Britain's oldest pub and to have been serving beer since around the time Vikings first made the happy discovery that monks in Lindisfarne didn't fight back, but if you ask me, any place that feels the need to put "Ye Olde" in its name is definitely calling its authenticity into question. Normally I'd prefer the Devil's Dyke in Brock's Hollow, but it was presently undergoing major renovations on account of having been gutted by a fire back at the start of the summer. The landlady, Harry Shire (who'd also been pretty gutted about it all), was keeping her business going out of the downstairs room in a local restaurant, but on a sunny summer evening, you want a beer garden, don't you?

Harry would understand.

Well, maybe not, 'cos I wasn't planning on being daft enough ever to mention it to her, but, well, in principle she would. Probably.

"Some of us have to work for a living," Phil muttered. Still, he closed the file.

"Hey, does that mean I get to be a kept man when we tie the knot?" I grinned at him. We'd got engaged the day after the fire, which had happened to be my thirtieth birthday, and the ring he'd given me still felt a bit weird on my finger. In a good way, mind. Definitely in a good way.

"In your dreams." He smirked. "People are always telling me there's a load of money in plumbing. Maybe I'll be the kept man."

"Yeah? Which people are those, then?" I mean, I'm not on the breadline or anything, but if plumbing's the way to make your fortune, I've been doing it wrong all these years.

"Jase, mostly."

"Like he knows his arse from anyone else's elbow." Jase was Phil's brother, and a first-class graduate of the school of talking bollocks. We'd only met a couple of times so far. He seemed to like me for some reason, but I can't say the feeling was all that mutual.

"Yeah, well, that's not the only thing he's been mouthing off about. I got a call from Mum this morning." Phil imbued this dire pronouncement with the gravity it deserved, which was more than you'd think. "Something you want to tell me about?"

"Uh, right." I tried to look like it'd genuinely slipped my mind. "You mean, like me bumping into Jase the other night down the supermarket, and him noticing the ring?"

I'd been a bit surprised Jase had realised the significance at the time, seeing as I was wearing it on my right hand—the plan was to switch it over to the left when we were official. Then again, maybe that's what Phil had done when he got spliced to the Mysterious Mark?

That not being a subject I was too keen on thinking about, I preferred to speculate that Jase just wasn't too hot on the difference between left and right.

Phil grunted. "That might be the sort of thing I was thinking of, yes. So I got a right ear-bashing from Mum, and we're going round on Sunday for a bit more of the same."

I winced.

Look, it wasn't like we were keeping the engagement a secret or anything.

But, well, relationships between mine and Phil's families had never been much cop, owing (a) to the fact they'd had bugger all in common apart from sons the same age attending the same school, and (b) to a certain incident when we were seventeen, when I'd ended up under the wheels of a Chelsea tractor under circumstances that might, to some people, have looked like it was sort of Phil's fault.

Which it wasn't, all right? It was just one of those things. An accident. My mum and dad threatening to sue had been well out of order.

Now, all that was over a dozen years ago, and chances were Phil's mum wasn't still bearing a grudge or anything. But anyway, me and Phil had both agreed we weren't in a hurry for any cosy family get-togethers.

"Oh, and she knows who you are," Phil added. "Jase finally twigged."

Jase hadn't seemed to cotton on I was *that* Tom, when I'd first bumped into him way back in January, but I s'pose he'd had plenty of time since to remember why the name Paretski had seemed a bit familiar. "Uh, yeah, I thought he might have, the other night. You know, from the way he kept staring at my hip. You oughtta tell him, some gay blokes might take that the wrong way."

Phil gave me a look. "*You* want to tell Jase it looked like he was eyeing you up? Just don't expect me to bring you grapes when you wind up in hospital."

"You mean you wouldn't leap to my defence? I'm crushed."

"Not half as crushed as you'd be if Jase really got into it with you. He used to beat the crap out of me when we were kids. Course, I reckon I could take him easy now." He looked grimly satisfied at the prospect. Looked like he might have a few scores to settle there.

Which would really add spice to our Sunday lunch with the folks. Great.

"So were you serious about having to work, or can we go and get that drink? 'Cos I reckon I need one now."

"Got a client coming. In about twenty minutes, so if you're parked up back, you'll need to shift the van." Phil at least had the decency to look regretful.

"Yeah? What sort of case?" I hoped it wasn't another cheating wife/husband/significant other. Phil's inner cynic didn't, in my considered opinion, need any more encouragement.

"Some woman claiming identity theft and refusing to pay her bills. Client reckons it was her all along."

"What do you reckon?"

"Don't know yet, do I? That's what I'm supposed to be investigating—after he's given me all the details. Anyhow, you'd better get that van shifted. Just in case he's early. Tell you what, though—walk back up in an hour or so, and we can go out for that pint."

"Or you could drive down and pick me up."

"More chance of making it before closing time if you come up here, the way this bloke goes on. He spent half an hour on the phone just making the appointment."

"Fine, I'll come and save you from the mouthy client. Don't worry about me having to drive home and then slog all the way back up here." All right, it was only a five-minute walk, ten if I stopped off at Vik's shop en route for a Mars Bar and a natter, but it's the principle of the thing.

Phil smirked. "Help stave off the middle-age spread, won't it?"

"Oi, I just turned thirty, not fifty!"

Unsympathetic git.

CHAPTER THREE

Cherry rang again that evening, just as me and Phil were getting cosy in front of the telly with the cats, having decided we couldn't be arsed to go out after all.

"Did you go to see her?" she demanded.

I heaved myself off the sofa and walked into the kitchen so Phil could carry on goggle-boxing in peace. Merlin, the eternal optimist, padded after me to give his empty bowl a pointed look. Arthur, being a lazy sod and cynical to boot, stayed where he was, purring on Phil's lap. "Yeah, I went. You know she only wanted me to search her stepdaughter's room, right?"

Sis made some kind of noise that didn't translate at all well over the phone. "Oh, I was afraid of that. Sorry."

"Yeah, well, you might have warned me."

"Would you have gone round if I had?"

"What do you reckon?" All right, I probably still would've, but no need to let Sis know that.

"Which is why I didn't warn you. Look, I know she's tiresome, but please just humour her. For my sake?"

I rolled my eyes at this blatant attempt to appeal to my brotherly feelings. It was safe: she couldn't see me. "Who exactly is this Mrs. F-M., and why's she got you over a barrel?" I asked.

Cherry tsked. "She's friendly with the bishop. *Very* friendly. She's only been living in St. Leonards for less than a year, but she's already running half the activities of the diocese."

I took that with a pinch of salt. There's a whole team of high-up church types at St. Leonards, and I've never been sure exactly what all of 'em do. Canon Greg, although definitely a big shot compared to your average parish priest, seemed to be a fairly minor firearm in the cathedral's arsenal. Which, as usual, seemed to directly translate as "did all the work." At any rate, he was a fair way below the bloke with the shepherd's crook and the pointy hat, who Cherry had her heart set on officiating at her and Greg's wedding.

God knows why. I mean to say, if anyone's going to upstage the bride on her wedding day, it's got to be a bishop. Unless Cherry went for the full-on puffed-up meringue look—which, being her, I was pretty sure she wouldn't—no way was her frock going to be prettier than his.

"If she hadn't just got married to Alex Majors," Cherry went on, "I'd suspect her of having set her cap at the bishop. He isn't married, you know."

"Yeah? This your *surprise bishop* who ate all my cakes?" Merlin gave his bowl one last disappointed sniff, then tried winding himself round my legs in case I was up for a bit of emotional blackmail.

"Toby. Yes. We don't have any suffragan bishops at St. Leonards."

Whatever those were. I focussed on the bit I understood. "You call the bish *Toby*? Isn't that, I dunno, disrespectful or something?"

"What do you expect me to call him? *My lord*? Nobody's that formal these days. And at least I don't refer to him as *the bish*. He came round to talk about carbon footprints with Gregory. And before you come up with some *hilarious* joke about Gregory's shoe size, please *don't*."

"Wouldn't dream of putting my foot in it like that. Hey, if Greg and the bish are all chummy already, why are you so worried dear old Amelia's gonna put you in bad with him?"

"They're not. That's the problem. You know Gregory's been castigated—"

"Sounds painful. Is the wedding still on?"

"—for speaking out in support of gay clergy? Well, the bishop is something of a traditionalist, I'm afraid."

"Great. Still, he's not likely to refuse to marry you for something like that, is he?"

"This isn't just about the wedding. Gregory's career is at a very vulnerable stage. He doesn't want to be a canon all his life, you know."

"Oh, I see. Got your eye on a bishop's palace, have you? Fancy Greg in purple?"

"Don't be silly. I just want what's best for Gregory. And the position of dean could be becoming vacant soon."

"So we need to keep the bishop sweet at all costs. Got it."

"Not at *all* costs." There was a breathy noise down the phone. "I'm not really asking *that* much of you, am I?"

"No, but . . . I dunno. Just doesn't seem right, sneaking around behind the daughter's back." Talking of which, I felt an arm sneak around my front as Phil stealth-cuddled me from behind. I leaned back into him, smiling at Merlin, who'd finally abandoned all hope and was sitting on top of the fridge. He gave me a frankly worried look, leapt down, and scarpered. "*And* she's roped me into her Harvest Fayre, whatever that is," I went on. "Has it got a *y* in it? I bet it has. You've got to have a *y* in it, or people start expecting fairground rides and dodgy hoopla stalls."

"I think she's planning some of those as well," Sis said drily. "And it's not *her* Harvest Fayre, or at least, it never used to be. It's an annual event in St. Leonards, to raise funds for the needy."

"I s'pose it's a bit better than just getting all the kiddies to turn up to church with an out-of-date can of Heinz soup from the back of the cupboard. Or a couple of wormy apples from the tree in the garden." Which was the sort of thing I vaguely remembered from my long-off Sunday school days.

"Exactly. So what's she got you doing? I'm running the cake stall, of all things." Cherry's tone said it all. My sis doesn't bake. Ever.

"Didn't say. When is it, anyhow?"

"The last Saturday of the month. *This* month, so don't forget. Although I'm sure Amelia will give you very precise instructions nearer the time." There was a certain tightness to her tone.

"Voice of bitter experience, that, is it?"

"It wouldn't be right of me to say anything disparaging about someone who's done so much for the cathedral," Cherry said in the sort of voice that meant she really, *really* wanted to. "Anyway, I know it's short notice, but why don't you and Philip come over to Gregory's for Sunday lunch this weekend?"

I gathered that was a peace offering. "Sorry, can't. We're going round to Phil's mum's."

"Oh." There was a pause. "Is this the first time you'll be meeting her?"

"Yeah. Well, you know, since school." I mean, chances were I'd at least seen her around at some point, but to be honest I couldn't have picked her out of a police lineup. It wasn't like me and Phil had been mates in those days.

"Oh. Well, good luck." She made it sound like I'd need it.

"You, um, remember Phil's family?" I was very conscious that the bloke himself was currently wrapped around me and could hear every word I said.

"Oh yes." Another pause. "Call me Sunday night if you need to."

Cheers, Sis. Way to make me feel optimistic and all.

Saturday, both me and Phil had work to do in the morning that managed to stretch on to midafternoon. We met up for a late lunch—well late—and decided it was way too nice out to just veg in front of the sport on the telly, 'specially as in mid-September you know the weather's not gonna hold forever. So we took a walk down to Verulamium Park, where we wandered around the old Roman ruins, had an ice cream from the van, and ended up down at the Fighting Cocks like I'd wanted to the previous evening.

The beer garden there isn't huge, and it was full of people, like us, trying to stretch out the summer just that little bit longer. In fact, we got out there with our pints just in time to nab the last couple of seats—they'd set up a big screen out there to show the England rugby match that night, and laid on a barbecue as well. Now, rugby's not really my thing—bit too public school for me—but it was England, yeah? You've got to cheer on your national side. And I've gotta say, there's a lot to be said for what rugby does to a man's thighs. So we settled in for the evening, and a very good evening it was too.

See, the thing about football—proper football, I mean, played with a round ball like God intended—is, it's like an art form. The clever footwork, with eleven men playing as a team, dodging and, all right, sometimes diving. Tactics. They call it the beautiful game for a reason, don't they? It's, well, it's elegant. Poetic, even. The players are athletic, yeah, but it's all about the skill too. Not just the brute force.

Rugby, now . . . Well, it's just a bunch of big bastards getting up close and personal with each other, innit? Sort of like wrestling, only not faked, with intervals of some bloke built like an armoured car grabbing the ball and legging it, trying to make it to the other side of the pitch before fifteen other blokes, some of who're built like Chieftain bloody tanks, throw themselves on top of him. And, all right, there's a bit of skill involved too, but mostly there's a raw physicality about it that I didn't have to be into the game itself to appreciate.

I wasn't alone there, as it happens. I was trying to grill Phil a bit about his family, get some tips on how best to make 'em like me—or at least, to not piss them off too much. I mean, I did okay with Jase, but this was Phil's mum. It was important, yeah?

But every time I tried to bring up the subject, some bugger with legs like beer barrels would make a tackle, or score a try, so I s'pose it wasn't surprising Phil kept getting distracted. I mean, who wouldn't?

Couple that with the testosterone boost of our side winning, well . . . I'm sure you get my drift. Not that me and Phil were all over each other while we watched or anything—Phil's not into public displays of affection, and neither of us is into getting gay-bashed—but let's just say we had a very good night after we got back to mine.

Waking up slowly on Sunday morning in the arms of my fiancé was pretty good too. At least, until I got a look at Phil's expression and had a moment's panic it was Monday. "Oi, what's up? Merlin wake you up by biting your toes again?" Serve him right for being so bloody tall his feet stuck out the end of the duvet.

Phil made a low, grumbly sound. "Forgotten what today is, have you?"

"Sunday. I checked. Day of rest, peace, and goodwill to all men—no, wait, that's Christmas. So what's got you all pissed off before you've even got out of bed?"

He *hmph*ed. "You do remember where we're going today, don't you?"

"Well, yeah. Your mum's. But that's hours off, innit?" I tried to snuggle into his side, possibly—all right, definitely—with a view to getting a bit frisky, but it was like trying to cuddle a block of granite.

"One o'clock, Mum said. She's doing a roast." Phil glowered so hard at one particular spot on the ceiling, I was worried the plaster would crumble.

I could feel my sex life going the same way. "Okay, you wanna tell me why you're looking so bloody miserable at the prospect? What is it—lumpy gravy, overcooked meat, what?"

Phil almost smiled at that, and shook his head. "Nah. She's not a bad cook. It's just . . . Mum stopped doing Sunday lunch after Dad died. Said it was too much of a faff, and none of us lot ever appreciated it anyway. Half the time, Jase was at work, Nige was away, and Leanne was still in bed sleeping off her hangover."

All right, it wasn't that early in the morning, but it was still too early for me to read subtext. "You're gonna have to spell it out. What is it—sad memories of your dad?" I hadn't thought he missed the old guy that much, but still waters sink ships and all that. Maybe recent developments in my life had brought it all up in his mind. Dredged up long-buried emotions, that sort of thing.

He huffed. "Nah. It's you."

"Me? What did I do?"

"It's not what you've *done*. Pulling out all the stops, isn't she? Just you wait. There'll be napkins on the table and forks with the pudding spoons. She'll probably even turn the telly off while we eat."

"Hang on, I thought you said she remembered me?"

"Yeah, as that posh kid whose family were planning to sue us."

"Come off it—you know I'm not posh!"

"Yeah, you are. Compared to my family, anyhow." At least he said it without getting visibly shirty. My Phil's always had a bit of a chip on his shoulder about his council estate origins, but I like to think I'm doing my bit to wear it down. Phil would probably be the first to agree I can have an abrasive effect at times.

"You don't act posh," he added grudgingly.

"Yeah, well, the polo pony got a flat, and my top hat's in the wash."

He laughed. "Never seen you dress posh, for that matter. Not since Gary and Darren's wedding, anyhow."

"Leave all that to you, don't I?" It at least made him an easy bloke to buy presents for, which I appreciated, seeing as he had a birthday coming up in October and him proposing on *my* last birthday had set the bar a bit high. All I'd have to do would be take out a second mortgage and buy him another sweater. "Oi, I don't have to dress up for this, do I?"

"Christ, no. Just wear what you want. Well, not your actual work clothes or they'll think you're taking the piss. And maybe give the joke T-shirts a rest."

"Okay, you wanna stop before you rule out my entire wardrobe?"

"Don't worry. *I* might think you look best naked, but I don't reckon it'd go down too well with my mum." Then he huffed to himself. "Either that, or it'd go down too bloody well."

We eventually dragged ourselves out of bed—there's only so long you can ignore the pointed miaowing of a couple of cats convinced they're about to die of starvation—and grabbed a light breakfast of toast and coffee. Well, you've got to make sure you leave plenty of room for a roast dinner, haven't you? Mortally offending Phil's mum by refusing her Yorkshire pud probably wouldn't be the best way to make a good first impression.

I'd thought maybe Phil would actually dress down for the occasion, but he just put on his usual gear of designer shirt and trousers so smart that if *I* wore 'em, I'd be pretty much guaranteed to spill gravy all over the front. I kind of liked that—like he was saying, *This is how I am now, and I'm not gonna change for anyone.*

Course, he might also have been saying, *Look how far I've come, losers.* Like I said, there's a bit of a chip on those broad shoulders of his.

I dithered a bit, then put on a new-ish pair of black jeans and a dark-green shirt Gary reckoned brought out my eyes. Phil gave me a look.

"What?" I asked, narked.

He smirked. "Thought you weren't gonna dress up."

"Shut up. Are we going or what?"

Phil gave me a look like he wanted to say *Or what*. Then he squared his shoulders, took a deep breath, and headed down the stairs.

I'd be lying if I said there weren't one or two butterflies flitting around my insides as I followed, but Christ, how bad could his family be?

CHAPTER FOUR

Phil's mum still lived in the house he'd grown up in, which was on the Cottonmill council estate at the bottom of St. Albans. The estate had a bit of a bad rep locally, but it's all relative, innit? A bad postcode round here was still dead posh compared to any of your inner-city no-go areas. Phil's childhood home was one of a row of terraced houses with white-painted siding and a blocky entrance hall-cum-porch stuck on the front like a spare building block chucked there by a giant-sized toddler.

"Home sweet home, eh?" I asked as we marched up the garden path.

Phil coughed. It sounded a lot like *Fuck off and die.*

"Come on," I said. "One meal, then we're out of here. How bad can it be?"

Phil just looked at me.

I rang the bell. There was a short pause during which I'm pretty sure Mrs. M. hurriedly put on her lipstick, if the wonky line of it when she opened the door was any guide.

Not that it mattered, as she proceeded to leave most of it on Phil's cheek and then turned to bung the rest on mine. I tried to wipe it off under cover of handing her the big bunch of flowers we'd brought. (Phil had tried to talk me out of them, but my mum brought me up proper.)

"Oh, love, that's so sweet of you. And it's lovely to meet you *at last.*" That was directed at Phil. "Come on in, love, don't stand on the doorstep. The neighbours can bugger off and make their own entertainment, that's what I always say. Come on, straight through to the living room while I sort out dinner. And call me Tracy, love."

By the time I'd finished thanking God she hadn't asked me to call her *Mum*, she'd shepherded us inside and closed the door behind us.

Phil might have been right about his mum preferring me naked, at that. I was guessing Mrs. Morrison—sorry, Tracy—fancied herself as a bit of a cougar, judging from the amount of leopard print she was wearing. It was a long top that clung tightly to her curves, of which she had an ample amount, and was low-cut to show about three times as much boob as any of the female members of my family would have thought it suitable to put on display.

Then again, if you've got it, why not flaunt it? Even if the only people around to flaunt it at are either (a) related by blood or (b) demonstrably gay. Still, for all I knew, she'd be off out merry-widowing this evening. She was a lot younger than my mum, after all. Phil had told me she'd been twenty when she had her first kid, and there weren't that many years between any of 'em, which made her . . . Blimey. Midfifties, I'd say. Yeah, plenty old enough to be my mum, but still young enough for *my* mum to be *her* mum, at least theoretically speaking, which was all kinds of weird.

Still didn't make it any easier thinking of her as *Tracy*.

The hall leading from the front door was narrow and cramped, half-full with shoe racks, recycling bins, and coats hanging six-deep on pegs. There was a strong smell of air freshener. It was a bit of a relief to get out into the living room, which was rectangular and boxy, with a squashy sofa in front of a large flat-screen telly at one end and a small, rickety-looking dining table already laid up for dinner at the other. God knows how Phil's mum and dad had brought up three strapping lads and a daughter in a place this size. Maybe they'd eaten in shifts?

There were napkins on the table. And forks for dessert, and the reason I noticed all this particularly was because I was putting off paying attention to the other end of the room and, specifically, the sofa. Not that there was anything wrong with the sofa, mind. Unless you counted its occupants.

Jase, Phil's brother, was sprawled across two-thirds of it reading the *Daily Mail*. He looked up briefly to say, "All right, mate?" then looked back down without waiting for an answer. The girl curled up at the other end with her nose in a magazine didn't even go that far to acknowledge our presence.

The telly, as Phil had predicted, was off. I got the feeling Jase and Leanne weren't any too chuffed about that.

I caught a barely there sigh from Phil's direction. "Leanne?" he said loudly, and waited.

She looked up with a sulky teenager expression on a face at least a decade too old for it. "Oh. You got here, then."

"Leanne, this is Tom. My fiancé."

There was a noise from Jase's direction. It sounded a lot like a snort. Leanne twitched her lips up for a fraction of a second.

I sent her my best difficult-housewife smile. "Lovely to meet you, Leanne. Can't say I notice a family resemblance between you and Phil"—this was true—"you're way prettier than he is."

That was a bare-faced lie. But it did the trick. Leanne uncurled her legs from the sofa and stood up. In her bare feet, she was a little shorter than me, with bleached-blonde hair pulled up into a big donut shape on top of her head that made her look like a ballerina doll. She had tattooed-on eyebrows and liked her makeup even more than her mum did. She hadn't put any of it on wonkily, though. "You never said he was *nice*," she told Jase accusingly.

"What? I said he was all right. You know, for . . ." Jase trailed off under the force of Phil's glare.

"You just said he was better than the last one." Leanne's curled lip indicated just how little of a compliment *that* was.

There were rumblings from Phil's direction, so I jumped in quick. "Phil never mentioned what you do for a living, Leanne."

She smiled a bit more genuinely this time. "Beautician. You know that new salon in Pluck's End?" I didn't, but I nodded anyway. "That's where I work. Dead posh, innit?"

"Nothing but the best, eh? My sister lives in Pluck's End," I added.

Leanne looked panicked. "I can't do her a discount. I only just got taken on."

"Nah, that's all right. Cherry doesn't go to that sort of place anyway."

Now she just looked narked.

"Allergies," I said quick. "She can't wear makeup and stuff."

You'd think I'd said she had something terminal. Leanne's heavily mascara'd eyes went wide. "Oh my God, poor woman. That must be so awful. Still, she could have her nails done, couldn't she? I get my nails done there." She spread out her hands for my inspection. "Good, ain't they?"

I gave 'em a good look, and did the pursed-lips-intake-of-breath thing. They were the fancy sort, all right, with several colours, little sparkles in and everything. Cherry, I wouldn't mind betting, would rather do a Lady Godiva through the streets of St. Leonards than be seen dead with anything like that on her fingers. "Couldn't get away with those in my line of work, love. But yeah. Dead smart. Like the bling."

"See?" Leanne slung in Jase's direction. "*Some* people appreciate them."

Jase gave a more audible snort this time. "Lee, nobody gives a toss about your bloody nails. He's just being polite."

"Not like anyone else around here ever is, is it?" she snapped back.

Jase growled and put his paper down.

"Jase, mate, how's work going?" I threw in a bit desperately.

That brought on a rant about effing bloody useless customers, which kept us safely occupied until Tracy came in to tell us dinner was ready and she wasn't carrying it all in by herself so we could all shift our lazy bleeding arses, guests excepted, obviously, Tom, you just sit yourself down.

I sat myself down. At least the table was round, so I didn't have to worry too much about sitting in the wrong spot. Phil, who still hadn't said more than three words since we'd got here, sat next to me instead of trooping into the kitchen with Jase and Leanne. Fair enough. If the size of the rest of the house was anything to go by, it was probably chock-full even without his shoulders in there.

The meals arrived already plated, which was only sensible given the size of the table, but meant I got a lot more roast parsnips than I was entirely comfortable with. Also a lot more roast beef, Yorkshire pud, carrots, broccoli, and gravy.

I mean, I like my food, but I also like to be able to move after meals.

Jase was looking disgruntled at his dinner too, and seeing as I reckoned it was for the opposite reason, I swapped 'em quick when Phil's mum optimistically went back out to get more gravy. "Think I got your plate, here."

He grinned and gave me a thumbs-up. Phil huffed beside me, but I ignored him. I'd already checked, and he'd had at least as much on his plate as I had.

Leanne had brought her own plate in, with only lean meat, carrots, and broccoli, I noticed. She didn't bother with the gravy either, just added a smear of mustard. Even then, she just picked at it all. I guessed she was trying to avoid taking after her mum's admittedly well-rounded figure, but I was surprised she wasn't giving the diet a day off seeing as her mum had made all this effort.

"Phil's told you about our Nigel, I take it?" Tracy asked once she'd sat down. Jase was already tucking in, scooping up roast spuds with his fork like there was no tomorrow and no such thing as table manners either.

I swallowed my mouthful of gravy-soaked carrots. It was pretty tasty. "Yeah. Working on the oil rigs, isn't he?"

"It's good money up there. As certain other people could take note," she added, with a pointed look at Jase.

He glared back at her. "Make enough to pay you rent, don't I?"

"Living at home at your age. Some people'd be ashamed. You ought to get yourself a nice flat like Phil, here."

Jase glared at Phil, who gazed back stonily.

"And Tom here's got his own house, or so I hear," she added.

Great. Now Jase was glaring at me. "It's nothing much. Just a two-bed semi in Fleetville, but it's home, innit?" It came out a bit more apologetic than it really deserved to.

"Yeah, but his folks always were loaded, weren't they?" Jase muttered to his gravy.

"Hey, I pay for my house through the sweat of my brow," I said breezily to hide the fact I was a bit narked.

Jase waved a roast potato at me. "Betcha had a bit of help with the deposit, though, dintcha?"

"Oi, you, stop getting on Tom's case," Leanne said snippily, surprising me. "At least *he* don't go on about all his posh uni mates all the time." She smiled at me. "*And* I bet you won't screw around on Phil neither, not like the last one did."

"Leanne!" Her mum snapped it almost loud enough to cover the ominous scrape of Phil's chair—but Jesus, that'd been well out of order. I turned Phil's way so quick I got a crick in my neck, and put a hand on his arm in the hope it'd stop him walking out. Not that I'd have blamed him. His jaw was so tense you could crack a walnut on it, and he was visibly making an effort not to explode, breathing deeply and staring straight at the wall.

"What?" Leanne was saying. "We all know he did."

"Yeah, see," I said awkwardly. "Me and Phil, we don't tend to talk about our exes all that much."

Leanne went bright red and looked down at her plate. "How was *I* s'posed to know he din't know?" she muttered.

I coughed. "So, you lived in this place long, Tracy?" I asked brightly.

She didn't fumble the catch, thank God. "Oh Christ, yes. Ever since I got married. Well, not quite, but I don't count that flat we had until Nigel was on the way. Proper disgrace, that was. Cockroaches! Never seen so bleeding many, not even when I was in South London. Knocked 'em down after we got moved, they did. It's mine now, this place. Me and Phil's dad got it under the right to buy. Course, I could probably retire if I sold it and downsized somewhere smaller. These ex council places, they go for a fortune nowadays."

Round here? I doubted it. Then again, fortunes are relative too.

"Yeah, uh, Phil said you work at Sainsbury's, right?" They had a big store not far from here, next to a Homebase and a Matalan and a few other big shops that were subject to change without notice.

Tracy nodded. "Gets me out the house. Course, I never had a chance to learn a trade like you or Phil, here."

"And me," Leanne piped up. "I got my City and Guilds."

"Yes, love." It came over as well dismissive. Poor Leanne. "How are your parents, these days? Still going strong?"

"Yeah, they're, uh, all fine." Okay, there might have been a bit of a wince at the *all*.

Leanne looked up from her dry meat and boiled veg. "'All'? Why, how many you got?"

Shit. Phil hadn't told them? I sent him a panicked glance. Was now *really* the time to announce my mother's infidelity to the world?

Phil coughed and put down his fork. "Since when have you been the family grammar Nazi, Lee?"

She flushed. Jase laughed. "It's them courses she been doing, innit? Creative bloody writing and English fucking literature, like anyone gives a toss about all that bollocks."

His mum glared at him. "You leave your sister alone. At least she's *trying* to better herself, unlike *some* lazy arses I could mention."

"Where are you studying?" I asked quickly. "Local college, or Open University?"

Leanne looked at her plate. "College. I mean, I'd like to do OU, but it's expensive, innit?"

"What, you with a degree?" Jase was off again. "Be like—"

"Shut it," Phil said before we could find out what it'd be like, in Jase's very limited imagination.

Jase slammed down his fork. "Oh, for fuck's sake. What'd I even say?"

"Jason Aaron Morrison, I will *not* have that language at my dinner table."

Jase opened his mouth. Tracy glared at him until he shut it.

"More gravy, Tom?"

"Yeah, that'd be smashing," I said, and faked a smile so hard my cheeks hurt.

CHAPTER FIVE

We eventually got out of there, but not before I'd earned Jase's and Leanne's undying hatred by offering to wash up. Tracy refused to hear of it, so Jase and Leanne got the ear-bashing from their mum about how *some* people had proper manners, and then had to wash up as well.

Me and Phil had to sit on the sofa—telly *still* off—and try to make polite conversation with Tracy to the backdrop of them bickering in the kitchen. Every so often, she'd break off to yell at them to *Shut up, Christ, and act your bleeding ages*.

Phil was quiet as we walked back to his car. My eardrums were honestly enjoying the peace and quiet, but I didn't like to think of him brooding. "Look, about what Leanne said," I started.

He didn't ask what I was referring to. "What? Want to know if it's true? Yes, all right? He screwed around on me."

Shit. "That wasn't what I was gonna say. None of my business, yeah?"

"So what were you going to say?" he ground out.

"I was gonna say, I'm sorry you had to go through that. Her coming out with it, I mean. That wasn't right. Doesn't matter whether it was true or a complete load of bollocks, she shouldn't have said it."

It was only as Phil visibly relaxed beside me that I realised just how tightly wound up he'd been. He took a deep breath. "Sorry. Didn't mean to take it out on you."

"No worries. It's family, innit? Didn't some posh bastard write a poem about how they fuck you up? Far as I'm concerned, it didn't happen, okay?"

'Cept it wasn't okay, not really. Because it *had* happened, and now that I knew . . . I really, *really* wanted to know more. Like, f'rinstance, why, if the Mysterious Mark had been a cheater, had Phil kept his photo around long enough after the bloke had died that I found it on a windowsill first time I'd visited his flat? It hadn't looked like he'd been using it for darts practice.

I couldn't ask him, though.

Like I'd said. None of my business.

I forced a cheery tone. "So, it's Sunday afternoon, all the shops are shut, and I'm too full of your mum's gravy to even think about going for a pint. Wanna slob out in front of the sport at mine?"

Phil was silent a moment. "I'll drop you off. Got stuff to do at the flat."

Great. Still, at least now I knew why Phil was so bloody emotionally constipated. Turned out it was his mum's cooking that did it. "Urgent stuff, is it?"

"Don't start."

"Would I?" I sighed. "Look, feel free to come round later, yeah? Or not. Whatever you want."

He nodded, which I took as a reasonably positive sign.

I wondered, after I'd let myself into my cold, empty house—all right, my comfortably warm, cat-occupied house—if he'd really thought things through before asking me to tie the knot. I mean, we hadn't talked about dates or anything, but judging from a few things he'd let slip, I wasn't the only one assuming he'd move into mine sooner or later, and at any rate after the wedding. So what was he going to do then when he wanted to come over all Greta Garbo and indulge in a bit of solitary brooding?

I laughed as a thought struck. I could always build him a shed down the bottom of the garden.

Phil didn't come round on Sunday evening. Not that he was supposed to. I mean, I'd made it clear it was up to him. So it wasn't like I went to bed pissed off at him for not turning up or anything.

Yeah, right. Anyhow, I just happened to be down Brock's Hollow way around lunchtime, so I called Gary up and dragged him out for a pub lunch. Not that he needed a lot of dragging, mind.

Gary's my best mate. He's some sort of IT consultant who works from home and does well enough to keep Julian, his Saint Bernard, in sirloin steak and Bonios. He's the camp-'n'-cuddly sort—Gary, I mean, not Julian, who has an air of sober and stately masculinity despite the vet's attentions—and rings the bells at St. Anthony's church in Brock's Hollow. I don't get to see as much of him as I used to, since his wedding, which was another reason to meet up for lunch. Evenings, him and Darren come as a job lot these days.

The Dyke being out of commission, and Harry's arrangement with the local restaurant not, unsurprisingly, extending to competing for the lunch market, we went to the Four Candles. Gary's choice, not mine. It's a chain-owned pub down by the river. It's all right, I guess, but every time they redecorate the place, they take a little bit more of the soul out of it.

"You have glum-face," Gary told me as we sat down in the bar area. I swear that gets smaller every time I go in, as more and more tables get co-opted for diners. "Tell Uncle Gary all about it. What *has* the nasty man done now?"

"Nothing. Seriously." I shrugged. "We just went round to his mum's for Sunday lunch yesterday, and it was a bit of a mare."

"Ooh, go on."

I hesitated. It didn't seem right spilling the beans about Phil's cheating ex. "Oh, you know. The usual family arguments. His mum having a dig at the kids every chance she got, playing 'em off against each other. She even brought me into it a couple of times. You know how it goes."

Gary stared at me in polite incomprehension. "No, but I'm *fascinated*. Do go on."

Right. Gary was the only child of hippy parents who were still daft for each other. He'd probably never observed a full-on family row in the wild. "Uh . . . It was just a bit tense. That's all."

He pouted, cheated of juicy details. "You're no fun."

"Yeah, neither was that lunch, which is why I don't wanna talk about it." I hesitated. "Listen, have you ever had an ex you just couldn't get over, no matter how much of a shit they were to you?"

"I hope we're not talking about your fiancé, here."

I gave a shaky laugh. "No."

Gary raised an eyebrow. "Hmm. Well, personally, no, but I have observed the phenomenon in others. It's The One That Got Away. The Grass That Is Always Greener."

Don't ask me how Gary manages to pronounce capitals. He also does a nice line in quotation and exclamation marks.

"What, you reckon it's not the bloke at all, just the idea of 'em?"

"How unusually perceptive of you, Tommy dearest. Yes."

Great. So I wasn't up against a memory of a cheating bastard. I was up against a memory of an *idealised* bastard.

Gary patted my knee. "But don't worry. I'm sure he loves you more."

I gave him a weak smile of thanks. Then I blinked. "Oi, I said we weren't talking about Phil."

"I know, darling." Gary took a sip of his martini, smiled, and set down his glass. "But I'm not silly enough to believe you."

The week went by without any further skeletons toppling out of closets, for which I, for one, was bloody grateful. Phil got over himself—by which I mean his family—and came round to mine for tea more often than not, although he was busy a couple of nights with work.

We didn't talk about the Mysteriously Cheating Mark. To be honest, I was still struggling to get my head round it myself. I mean seriously, if you had Phil waiting for you at home, would you really bother looking around for a bit on the side? Depending, obviously, on your personal orientation. Me, well. Don't get me wrong, if anyone asked, I was totally up for a thirty-two-some with the England rugby squad. But as for anything remotely likely to ever happen, what'd be the point? Phil was tall, built, and gorgeous, and what's more, he knew what I liked. And, well, I loved him, didn't I?

I nearly asked Phil about moving in a couple of times, but the moment never seemed quite right.

It wasn't that important, anyhow. We'd sort it all out once we'd got a bit further with planning the wedding.

The day of the Harvest Fayre dawned bright, sunny, and warm, with the prospect, so the girl on the telly told me, of clear skies all day.

It was the sort of British summer's day it would have been nice to have in the actual summer, instead of tacked on in the autumn when the kiddies were back at school and the shops were already starting to get their Christmas stuff in. I'd have suspected Greg of having had a word with the bloke upstairs if I hadn't thought it more likely Mrs. F-M. had performed some arcane ritual of her own. At any rate, there was no chance of me getting out of whatever she had planned for me now.

All right, I *could* have simply not turned up. I just wasn't certain Cherry would ever speak to me again if I didn't go along to do my bit for the needy of St. Leonards and, more importantly, Greg's career.

"So what is it you're doing at this thing?" Phil rumbled in my ear, his arms around my waist while I buttered a slice of toast. He'd stayed over Friday night.

"Buggered if I know. S'pose I'll find out when I get there. With a bit of luck, it'll just be an hour or two manning the bar, and then we can skip off together. Unless you've got a secret passion for Morris dancing? I mean, there's got to be Morris dancers, right? Big event like St. Leonards Harvest Fayre, there might even be competing teams having a dance-off." A stray thought struck me. "Oi, your surname's Morrison, innit? So does that mean, way back in the mists of time, one of your ancestors was a Morris dancer?"

Phil gave me a look. "I'd have thought you'd be the last person to make assumptions based on anyone's surname."

"Fair point. But were they?"

"If they were, they had the decency to keep quiet about it so as not to embarrass the descendants, all right?"

"What are you saying, here? It's a very manly pursuit, Morris dancing. Some of 'em have really big sticks."

"Like a man with a big stick, do you?"

The conversation sort of degenerated even further after that, which is my excuse for rolling up at the Harvest Fayre a good hour or so after the official start time of twelve noon. Well, if dear old Amelia had needed me there earlier, she should have said so. Or, you know, said word bloody one to me. *In touch with further details*, my arse.

The fayre was being held on the St. Leonards playing fields, which had the advantage over the cathedral grounds of (a) being bigger, (b) having a lot more space to park cars, and (c) not being filled with gravestones, which could have put a bit of a damper on the general festive atmosphere. Or maybe not, who knows? Maybe some people would have liked to think Grandad and Great Auntie Mary had some part in the proceedings, even if it was only as a convenient spot to perch with your picnic.

Phil parked the Golf at the end of a long, wonky line of cars, as directed by a beaming volunteer in a straw hat and what I presumed was a olde-worlde farmer's smock, although it looked an awful lot like the white robe things the cathedral choir had been wearing over their red frocks that one time Cherry had tricked me into coming to evensong. Then we strolled over to the fayre, which was in full swing. The air was full of the smell of barbecuing meat, mixed in with the spicier aroma coming from a brightly coloured bunny chow stall that seemed to be doing a roaring trade over by the ice cream van.

I was beginning to regret having had a proper fry-up for breakfast. Still, we'd be here for a good few hours; plenty of time to work up an appetite.

"Why d'you reckon they call it bunny chow, anyway?" I asked idly as we passed the South African stall. "It's not like there's any actual bunnies in it. I checked, that time they had the food fair in St. Albans."

Phil shrugged. "It comes with rabbit food on the side? It's served in a bun? What am I, Wiki-bloody-pedia? Anyway, hadn't you better find this Fenchurch-Majors woman and find out what your duties are before you get stuck into lunch?"

"Killjoy." I looked around. Besides the stalls and the bouncy slides and stuff for the kiddies, there was a large area in the middle of the field that'd been fenced off with bunting and hay bales, which were doubling as seats for spectators. Not that there were all that many of them for the current act. You had to feel sorry for the poor girl, although to be honest, if I'd been planning to put on a hula hoop display—or any other kind—I'd definitely have brushed up on my skills beforehand.

There was a small gazebo set up at one end, with audio equipment that was currently blaring out hula-girl's music to the crowd. "She's probably up there somewhere. Wanna come, or shall I catch you later?"

Phil huffed. "You're on your own. I don't fancy getting roped into anything."

"Hey, it's all for a good cause, you know. Food for the needy and all that bollocks. Anyone would think you wanted people to starve."

He smirked. "Nice try, but I'll be doing my bit by putting my hand in my pocket going round the stalls. See you later." He disappeared off to the right, probably to grab a beer and put a quid or two on the ferret racing. Lucky bastard.

I sighed and followed the call of duty.

Course, I didn't see any particular reason to hurry. Might as well have a look around first.

I soon spotted the Morris dancers. There was a team of 'em (or do I mean a troupe? What's the word for a bunch of Morris dancers, anyhow? A jingling?) leaping around already over by the Dogs Trust stall. They had their own music to compete with the stuff blaring out over the speakers, courtesy of a bloke with an accordion. When you got close enough, it was actually pretty good at drowning out the piped stuff.

There were a couple of familiar figures among the onlookers, so I veered that way. Well, it was only polite to say hi, wasn't it? The fact it would put off, for just that little bit longer, getting lumbered with whatever duties dear old Amelia saw fit to dump on me was just a fringe benefit.

"Gary," I called out once I was in hailing distance of him and Julian. Which was closer than you'd think, given the racket that accordion was making. "What brings you out all this way?"

"Tommy, darling." Gary greeted me with the usual hug/smooch combo—he's been leaving off the playful little grope part ever since becoming, in his own words, a staid old married man. Although seeing as how him and Darren had hinted more than once they'd be up for a foursome with me and Phil if we fancied it (we *really* didn't), I reckoned *staid* was a relative term. "Isn't it obvious?" He waved at the blokes in bells currently capering on the grass in front of us.

I looked. Then I looked again, in a classic double take that had Gary chortling into his bunny chow. "Bloody hell, is that Darren?"

It was, too: all four foot nine of him, done up in whites and bells and those funny-coloured tassel things they wear, and with a straw hat on top. He was currently banging sticks with a bloke around twice his height.

"Doesn't he just look so *virile*?" Gary gushed.

"That's . . . one way of putting it." To be fair, he was probably the best-looking one of the lot, most of whom had clearly been working on the middle-aged spread for a while now. You'd think all that jumping around would keep 'em a bit trimmer, but then again, from what I hear Morris tradition tends to include the odd pint or six after a show. "How long's he been doing this, then?"

"Oh, he used to do it all the time, but he's only recently taken up his staff once more. Fortunately the St. Leonards Stompers dance Cotswold style, like his old side. You can't just learn those dances at the drop of a hat, you know. It takes *intensive* training."

Especially for a bloke whose staff was as tall as he was, I wouldn't mind betting. "He's kept that quiet."

"He does like to be a dark horse. Although not literally."

"What? Oh." Gary's remark was explained as a bloke wearing a giant black papier-mâché horse's head with a big cloak attached ran in with a whinny and started prancing around among the dancers. "Yeah, I wouldn't fancy his job, either, not with all those staffs flying around." I winced as one of 'em missed his pointy ears by a whisker.

"Staves, Tommy dearest, staves. Like in music."

And there I'd been all proud of myself for not calling them sticks. The dance ended, and we clapped. Darren nodded to me, but stayed with his fellow dancers as a bloke in a waistcoat it looked like he'd made himself collected up the sticks—sorry, staves. Then it was hankies aweigh as the accordion player struck up the next dance.

From the suspiciously moist gleam of husbandly pride in Gary's eye as he watched, the dancers had better watch out or he'd be stealing their hankies to have a good blow. "Got to go, mate," I yelled in his ear.

"Going to prepare yourself for your big moment?" Gary nodded wisely. "Say no more. I'll see you later. Wouldn't miss it for the world."

"Uh, yeah." I was starting to have a bad feeling about this. Maybe I did ought to hurry it up a bit and find out exactly what Mrs. F-M. had me in for.

I tracked her down, as expected, under the gazebo up by the speakers. Amelia was dressed today in a chic floral silk frock I wouldn't mind betting she normally kept 'specially for garden parties, polo matches, and days at the races. Her shoes were still sky-high but were strappy wedges rather than stilettos, a note of practicality I wouldn't have expected given what she was willing to do to her own wood floors.

She fixed me with a look of calm disapproval. "*There* you are. You missed the bishop's opening address. It was very inspirational. Oh, and who was that man you came in with? The tall, well-built blond?"

She'd seen us all the way across the field? The woman had eyes like a hawk. I glanced down, and yeah, she had the red-painted talons to match. "Phil. My fiancé." Still felt weird saying it.

She raised an eyebrow. "Really? Well, tell him I need him at four. We're short of a few strong men for the tug-of-war."

Heh. I was looking forward to telling Phil he hadn't escaped after all. "Yeah, no problem. He'll be glad to help you out," I lied through my teeth. Then a thought struck. "Uh, I'd volunteer myself, yeah, but you know. Dodgy hip."

The second eyebrow joined its mate. "Oh. No, I wasn't planning to ask *you*."

Ouch.

"But I hope you're all ready for your demonstration."

"Uh . . . my what now?"

"Your *demonstration*," she said ultra-distinctly for the clearly hard-of-thinking. "We've just put you down as *Psychic*, as you didn't give me any further details of what you'd be doing." There was a note of disapproval in her voice.

The bottom dropped out of my stomach. It threatened to drop out of my bloody bottom too. "Wait a minute. You're expecting me to put on a show? Like some cut-price Mystic Meg? No way. No *way*."

Mrs. F-M. smiled. It was all teeth. "You assured me I could count on you."

"Yeah, to lend a hand with the barbecue or something. Not to go on stage like a bloody performing monkey."

Her smile didn't falter. It was well creepy, given the venom in her tone. "If you didn't want to do it, you should have made your feelings known earlier. We can't change the programme now. You're down for the arena at three, after the birds of prey."

She'd put it down in the programme and all? I could *kill* her.

Maybe I could borrow a raptor from the birds of prey people to do it for me.

"What the bloody hell am I supposed to do out there?"

"A demonstration, obviously." She shrugged, somehow making it look fake even though I was pretty sure the indifference was actually genuine. "*Find* things. You're only on for half an hour. I'm sure you'll think of something."

She turned away. Subject closed. Put up or shut up.

Christ. I reeled away from the gazebo feeling in dire need of a bit of moral support, possibly of the liquid variety.

No, scratch that. This was serious. I needed moral support of the tall, blond, and broody variety.

At least with his height, he was easy to spot. Phil was over by the cake stall talking to Cherry, who was looking harried as she tried to stop little kiddies putting their fingers in the buttercream and nicking the smarties off the top of the cupcakes. "That's fifty pence, please— no, fifty pence *each*. Thank you. Tom. *Finally*. I was beginning to worry you weren't going to turn up."

"Yeah, well if I'd known what bloody Amelia had me down for, I sodding well wouldn't have." I glared at Cherry so she'd know that yes, I did bloody well blame her for all this.

"What's that?" Phil put in around a mouthful of cupcake. Typical. He's always going on about *me* liking my food too much.

Cherry gave him a hard stare. "I hope you've *paid* for that."

Phil looked a bit embarrassed and pulled out a handful of change.

"She only wants me to go on in that bloody arena and do tricks like a bloody performing seal, that's what."

"Well, I hope you're going to clean your language up a bit when you go out there," Cherry said with a sniff and a nod towards an elderly customer who was busy giving the fruitcake a critical squeeze and didn't look in the least offended by my so-called profanity.

"I'm not going out there!"

Cherry picked up a cake knife. She didn't exactly wave it threateningly in my direction, but the potential was definitely there. "Tom, you can't back out now. The bishop is here."

"I know. His opening address was very inspirational. Or so I've heard. But what the bloody hell's that got to do with the price of fish? What's he gonna do—excommunicate me?"

"You're *my* brother. How's it going to look if you embarrass everyone like this?"

"Oh, I like that. It's fine for *me* to make a giant tit of myself doing something I never even agreed to in the first place, but perish the thought anyone else might be mildly inconvenienced!"

"Oh, for heaven's sake. Stop making such a drama out of it. We all have to do things we don't want to." Cherry looked daggers—or at least pastry knives—at yet another sticky-fingered tot. "If you're not going to buy it, please don't touch. Just look at it as a promotional opportunity for your business."

Me and the kiddie exchanged confused glances as we tried to work out which bits of all that were meant for who. Then while the tot handed over a grubby fifty-pence piece, I grabbed up a fayre programme Cherry had shoved under a plate of shortbread. I flicked past all the local tradesmen's ads (actually, come to think of it, why hadn't I got an ad in there? That was the sort of promo opportunity I wouldn't mind getting behind) to the middle. "Three o'clock . . . *Psychic demonstration.* Great. It hasn't even got my name in. What sort of bloody promo is that?"

Phil huffed a laugh down my collar, and I turned to glare at him. "What's so bloody funny?"

"What were you expecting—*The Great Paretski*? You'd have been well pissed off if she'd put that in there."

"That's not the point," I muttered, narked at him for being right. "What the hell am I supposed to do? They're going to be expecting some stage magician with a load of patter and tricks like Derren Brown. I can't do any of that crap!"

Phil shrugged. "Just give 'em some guff about the dowsing side. Tell 'em water divining is an ancient and honourable art. All that bollocks. Then give 'em a quick demo and call it a day."

"A demo? Just how am I supposed to do that? Get someone to bury a bottle of Evian?"

"You can't go round digging up the playing fields," Cherry put in earnestly. "The parish councillors would be furious. *No*, fifty pence *each.* Thank you."

"We could get someone to hide something somewhere on the field, but not too far from the arena," Phil suggested. "It'd have to be someone above suspicion of collusion."

"Right, Cherry'd better go sweet-talk the bish, then." I gave her a significant look.

Sis reddened. "I'm really not sure he'd think it was theologically sound. And Gregory and you are too closely connected," she added, heading me off at the pass.

I sighed. "Bloody marvellous. All right, how about your dear chum Amelia, then? Seeing as all this was her idea in the first place?"

"*I* can't ask her," Cherry complained. "Who'd look after the cake stall?"

"Phil can do it," I said with a smile. "He won't mind."

"He won't, will he not?" Phil asked. "And what are you going to be doing while all this is going on?"

"Me? I'm going to be on my phone. Trying to memorise the Wikipedia article on bloody dowsing."

Despite throwing me a clear *do I have to?* face, Sis agreed to sort something out with Mrs. F-M. and headed off. "And make sure she steers clear of the hook-a-duck pool," I shouted after her, garnering a few odd looks from passersby.

All right, it was only a kiddies' paddling pool filled with water and some faded plastic ducks, but it could still mess with the vibes.

I grabbed a cupcake and headed round the back of the tent to do my homework.

CHAPTER SIX

ome half past two, I'd crammed in enough info about dowsing to bore the pants off anyone daft enough to turn up to my so-called psychic demonstration. *I* was certainly falling asleep, although the pint that'd turned up courtesy of someone I'd never seen before (Phil showing his talent for delegation, I reckoned) and the warm sun were probably at least partly responsible.

And I know what you're thinking, all right?

You're thinking, how come I didn't know all this stuff already? How come I hadn't already tried to find out all I could about my so-called gift?

Thing is . . . Thing is, I did, all right? Once. It was just after I'd got back on my feet after my little disagreement with a four-by-four when I was seventeen . . . Actually, it must have been a fair bit later than that, seeing as I'd already started my City and Guilds at the local college. S'pose I was in the studying mode. Thought it'd help me in my chosen career, whatever. Can't honestly remember now. What I do remember is finding out about a local group of dowsers and deciding on the spur of the moment to go along on a Saturday afternoon and give 'em a try.

It was a total, cringe-making nightmare. For a start, they were all at least three decades older than I was. Most of 'em had beards. Some of the women, even. And this was back in the early 2000s, so beards? Not cool.

But I reckoned, seeing as I was there, I might as well give it a go. See if I could learn something from them. I mean, they were all so much older than me. Surely they had to know something I didn't?

Did they bollocks. It turned out their brains were as woolly as their chins. They all just kept rambling on about mystical crap, and it didn't sound anything like the way my spidey-senses worked.

The killer, though, was at the end, when everyone got in a line to walk a local field and see what we could pick up. Some of 'em had forked sticks; some of 'em had divining rods. In fact, one lady insisted I borrow hers as I'd come without. So I got in that line and marched up and down that field with the rest of 'em, while they wittered on about tingles in places where, trust me, there was nothing to get tingly about, and to a man missed an underground stream three feet wide. I felt like a right tit.

And that was before I heard someone call my name, and looked up from those fucking useless rods to see three of the lads from college laughing their arses off at the whole sad lot of us. Took me years to live that one down.

So yeah. After that, I pretty much decided anything anyone else said about dowsing wasn't worth listening to. How was I supposed to know I was going to be facing an exam on it all a dozen years later?

Anyone tempted, at this point, to say something along the lines of *Because you're psychic* can leave now. I'm serious. Please *do* let the door hit you on your way out.

I still hadn't had lunch, but somehow my appetite seemed to have done a runner. Right then, as I headed back up to the arena like a condemned man trudging to the scaffold, I seriously considered following its example.

Halfway there, I spotted Vi Majors—squeezed into a short, strappy, bright-red sundress, she was pretty hard to miss—and I ducked out of sight behind a woman with a hat. The last thing I needed was for her to come and have another go at me for sneaking around in her bedroom. I was a bit surprised to see her, to be honest. I'd have thought she'd be the last person to come along and support anything her stepmum had organised.

Shit. I hoped she hadn't just come along to heckle.

There was another familiar figure up by the hay bales, so seeing as I was well early, I thought I might as well join him. Maybe he'd have some words of spiritual comfort for me—God knew I could do with them. Greg, dressed in crumpled linen and dog collar like a vicar from an Agatha Christie show on the telly, was watching the birds of prey with a worrying glint in his amateur taxidermist's eye. "Tom! Good to see you. Cherry was a little concerned you might not turn up, but I told her we could count on you."

"Yeah, course," I muttered, feeling guilty for having thought about bailing on them.

"A truly magnificent specimen, don't you think?" He beamed up at the Harris hawk currently soaring above the field, blissfully unaware it was being sized up for a wire frame and a couple of glass eyes.

"You want to watch what you say," I warned him. "If any of those birds turn up dead in suspicious circs, you're gonna be first on the list of suspects."

Greg guffawed and clapped me on the shoulder so hard it bloody well hurt. "Rest assured, I should never dream of harming one of God's creatures merely for my own amusement. Are you all set for your own demonstration?"

"No, and I never bloody will be," I muttered, feeling a bit like the day-old chick currently being chomped up by our *magnificent specimen*, now returned to earth.

"I'm sure it will be splendid. You're a person of some note these days, as I'm sure you're aware. People are agog to see you demonstrate your talents."

Great. No pressure, then.

The birds of prey mangled their last baby chick and went off, which I took as my cue to nip around to the gazebo smartish. Dear old Amelia had disappeared, and there was just a grey-haired old bloke fiddling with the speakers, and what had to be the bishop.

He didn't look much like a bishop to me. Well, yeah, he had on the purple shirt and the dog collar, and a nice bit of ecclesiastical bling in the form of a huge gold cross hanging on a heavy chain around his neck. And there was a hint of Friar Tuck about that well-padded belly. But from the neck up, he looked more like an Italian gangster, with jet-black hair—what was left of it; if he had been a friar, he wouldn't have had to bother with any head-shaving—and matching goatee.

Sort of like a Tony Stark who'd got religion and gone to seed, or a jollier, churchier version of the old-style Master from *Doctor Who*. There was a gap between his two front teeth that, once I'd noticed it,

I couldn't stop staring at. I tried to pull myself together and look him straight in his twinkly dark eyes. Did I say twinkly? I'd have called them that at first, but now I thought about it some more, I wasn't sure the laughter lines around them weren't just camouflage.

Course, current circs might've shaped my impressions of him a bit.

He gave me a questioning look as I stepped into the shade of the gazebo. "Uh, I'm Tom. Paretski. The, um, psychic." I couldn't help a wince as I said it.

The bishop smiled, in a manner scarily similar to his dear chum Amelia. "Ah, yes. You know, I'm not at all sure I should approve." He chuckled. "It's perhaps just as well that the church tends to frown on witch-burning these days."

Only *perhaps*? Nope, nothing twinkly about those eyes. He didn't invite me to call him *Toby* either.

"I hear you're Gregory's future brother-in-law," he went on. "It was really *quite* a surprise to all of us to see him choosing to marry so late in life."

"Uh, really?"

"Of course, celibacy isn't for everyone. Even St. Paul recognised that. A viewpoint I understand you agree with."

"Yeah?" I was rapidly getting lost here.

"Cherry tells me you and your, ah, *partner*, I believe the common term is, are planning a civil ceremony?" The way he said it got my hackles right up. Like he reckoned gay people were another species or something, and registry office weddings didn't count.

"We're getting married, yeah," I said shortly. One thing was for certain, the bish wouldn't be getting an invite. I s'pose I should've expected the attitude, after what Cherry had said about him getting on Greg's case about speaking up for gay rights, but well. It *could* have been all about not rocking the boat, rather than actually being bigoted.

Here's a word puzzle for you: change the word *bishop* to *bigot* in three easy steps.

Or, you know, don't bother.

Suddenly I felt a lot more invested in Greg's career taking off if it meant he might get to topple blokes like this from their bloody high horses.

Rather than look at his smug face any longer, I sneaked a peek out the front of the gazebo. The birds of prey had gathered a pretty big crowd, nearly all of whom seemed to have decided either through boredom or sheer bloody inertia they might as well stick around and see what the psychic could do.

They were going to be well disappointed.

The bishop stepped up to the mike stand in front of the gazebo. "Now, in the absence of our dear Mrs. Fenchurch-Majors, who has gone to prepare a vital part of our next entertainment, I'd like to invite you all to give a last big round of applause, please, for Swan Bottom Birds of Prey!" He paused, beaming paternally while everyone clapped. "And now, my dear friends, ladies and gentlemen, boys and girls, please welcome—" he stopped and looked down at a scrap of paper "—our very own local celebrity and hero, Tom Paretski, who is going to give a demonstration of his amazing psychic powers!"

Yeah, right. I was well amazing, me. Clearly the bish thought so too, as he managed to make it sound like he couldn't quite believe what he was reading.

He handed me the mike, and I cleared my throat. Amplified by the sound system, it echoed around the field, probably drawing even more attention. Great. "Thanks, um, Bishop." Shit. Should that have been *your lordship*? "So, um. Yeah. Dowsing. Water divining. It's, well, it's been done for centuries. Longer, even." I desperately tried to remember that Wikipedia article, which five minutes ago I would have sworn I could have recited backwards while standing on my head.

Someone yelled, "Are you going to get your rod out, then?"

I looked. It was bloody *Darren*, standing on a hay bale and surrounded by Morris men. "Uh, good point," I said, wishing his bloody bells would drop off. "See, some people use tools like rods, or . . . or pendulums to tap into the, um, the vibes. I mean, I don't, but there's a, uh, theory they just sort of amplify movements made by your subconscious. I mean, um, your subconscious is, like, sensitive to the vibes and it makes your hands twitch, so if you're holding a rod, you twitch more?"

Oh God. This was terrible. People were starting to drift away at the edges of the crowd. Lucky bastards. I was stuck here in the metaphorical spotlight, sweating bloody bricks. My palms were so slippery, I was going to drop the mike any minute now.

"So what you're saying is," Darren piped up again, "if *I* held your rod, it wouldn't twitch?"

There was laughter from the more beer-infused of the crowd. Some kiddies joined in despite not having a clue what they were laughing at.

At least, I hoped they didn't have a clue. Then again, you never know with kids these days.

Christ, my face must be redder than the baby chick innards still strewn over the grass where one of the birds of prey had been a messy eater. "Uh, yeah. You've got to be, um, sensitive."

I cast a desperate glance behind me for Mrs. F-M., for the bishop, for *anyone* with the sense to realise this was all going tits-up and come and put us all out of my misery. No such luck. The gazebo was completely free of floral frocks and dog collars, and even the old bloke tinkering with the speakers had buggered off somewhere. I was on my own.

"Right, well. Think we'll move on to the finding-stuff bit of the demo, yeah?" I hoped Mrs. F-M. had got a shift on with hiding whatever it was I was supposed to be finding. Too late, it occurred to me I'd have a better chance of (a) finding it and (b) convincing the punters I knew what I was doing if I actually had the first bloody clue what the hell I was looking for. What if it was just, I dunno, a hat or something? Everyone would reckon someone had just lost it and I'd taken advantage. Still, no use crying over spilt milk. All that liquid would play merry hell with the vibes.

"Okay, I want everyone to be quiet for this bit," I said into the mike. "Something's been hidden somewhere in the grounds here, and I'm going to find it. But I need to concentrate." There was no noticeable effect on the general noise level, but at least I didn't get catcalled by Darren.

I shut my eyes and *listened*.

Then I shivered, despite the warm sun.

There was something very weird about the vibes. Yeah, I was getting *hidden* and *Mrs. F-M.* and all kinds of other stuff, but it just didn't seem right for a half-arsed dowsing demo. It was way too strong, for one thing—either dear old Amelia was *really* into hiding stuff for me to find, or I was picking up on some other trail. A sickly bright trail, with undertones of savage anger, satisfaction, guilt—and oh shit. Malice, of the deadly variety.

Oh, bloody hell. Had some sick bastard decided it was a lovely day for a bit of gratuitous violence and stashed the victim somewhere on the fields? The weird—*scary*—thing was, I was almost certain this was all the same trail. Not two mashed up together. Which meant . . .

Which meant I'd better get a bloody shift on and follow it, for Mrs. F-M.'s sake if nothing else. I opened my eyes, blinked in the bright sunshine, and immediately started to doubt myself. Maybe it was, I don't know, nerves or something? I'd never liked finding stuff for an audience, even when it was people I knew. Maybe I was just picking up on emotions, or the crowd's excitement, or something?

'Cept, to be honest, most of the crowd looked only mildly entertained, if that.

I was starting to get a *really* bad feeling about all this. Suddenly, standing up in front of a crowd and looking like a right tit didn't seem all that bad a fate. "Right, coming through," I said and, in the absence of anyone to hand it to, stuck the mike back on its stand.

People moved out of the way as I followed the trail out of the arena, even getting up off their hay bales to traipse after me like I was the bloody Pied Piper of St. Leonards.

I wished they'd bugger off.

The trail led through curious crowds and around stalls to a tent just off to one side that had apparently had reptile . . . stuff . . . going on earlier. I hoped they hadn't left any behind. I pulled up the flap and stared into the darkness, pitch-black after the bright sun outside.

It was shouting at me now, and I had a horrible feeling I knew what I was going to find.

I swallowed.

Some bloke behind me was saying loudly, "Well, of course it's in the reptile tent. It's the only logical place to hide something." It was mixed in with the chorus of younger voices with variations on *What is it?* and *Move over, I can't see.*

I turned. "Look, nobody's to come in, all right?" Ignoring the moans, I let the tent flap fall closed behind me and waited until my night vision had started to kick in and I didn't feel so blind.

Then I stepped forward and literally fell over the body.

CHAPTER SEVEN

I scrambled onto my knees next to what was left of Amelia Fenchurch-Majors and had my little mini meltdown over whether she was still alive and how the hell I could keep her that way.

Great, Paretski. Way to contaminate the crime scene.

Course, it didn't *have* to be a crime, did it? Maybe they *had* been a bit careless with the reptiles and left something poisonous behind that'd fancied a bite out of dear old Amelia for its dinner. Maybe she'd tripped and knocked her head on a tent peg. Maybe she'd just keeled over from all the excitement. I mean, it did happen, right? Even young people had heart attacks sometimes.

Trouble was, I clearly remembered how she'd looked earlier. I knew damn well she hadn't been wearing a scarf—and in any case, my night vision was getting better all the time. I could see now that what was wrapped around Mrs. F-M.'s slender neck wasn't something she'd ever have willingly put there. Whoever had done for her had used a length of bunting, so Mrs. F-M.'s attacker was either opportunistic or had a nice sense of irony. Or both.

I tried to get it loose, just in case there was still some hope, but no dice. The swollen ridges of her skin hugged it tight, and all I got for my pains was the certainty that if I didn't stop I was gonna hurl, which would *really* make a mess of the crime scene.

Shit. She needed someone who had the first bloody clue what they were doing. I lurched to my feet and made for the exit, almost tripping over Mrs. F-M. again en route. Blobs of colour from the blinding sunshine danced over a sea of expectant faces when I poked my head outside. I blinked frantically. "Somebody get a doctor. Quick."

Nobody moved.

"For fu—flip's sake, get a doctor!" It was probably my voice breaking on the last word that convinced 'em it wasn't all part of the act. After that, it all got taken out of my hands, thank God. St. John's Ambulance, who'd been having a nice natter by the beer tent, were scrambled, and a team of green-shirted volunteers swarmed over to start doing CPR on Mrs. F-M. and hand out shock blankets to anyone who stood still long enough.

"Bloody hell, I can't take you anywhere, can I?"

I'd never been more glad to hear Phil's voice in my ear. Or to feel the warmth of his arm around my shoulders. "Yeah, I reckon Mrs. F-M. went all out for this demo, didn't she?" I gave a shaky laugh, which shows you the state of my nerves right then as it really, *really* wasn't funny.

They'd looped up the side of the tent to let the St. John's lot in, and I'd got a good look at what I'd stumbled over. It wasn't pretty. *She* wasn't pretty, not anymore, which is more or less what you'd expect when someone's been strangled—or do you call it garrotted when it's not just bare hands? Not sure.

You never get used to it. Death, I mean. At least, I haven't, and I sincerely hope I never bloody well will. It wasn't just the way she looked, her face all swollen and dark. She'd have been well upset if she could see herself. It was the fact that this person, only minutes ago, was alive and doing stuff and talking to people, and now she wasn't and never would be again, and how the hell was that even possible? It just didn't seem right.

I mean, I hadn't even liked the lady, but seeing her now—it was just wrong.

A tall, thin, grey-haired bloke I vaguely recognised as the one who'd been tinkering with the speakers earlier barged in, even pulling one of the green-shirts aside, which didn't go down too well. "Amelia," he kept saying in a tone I found myself thinking of as *strangled* and then really wished my subconscious hadn't gone there.

There was a chorus of *Please let us do our job, sir*, from the St. John's mob, but it was Vi Majors who eventually managed to haul him out of the way. "Daddy, you've got to leave them to it."

Daddy? This was Alex Majors? I couldn't help staring as he stood to one side, Vi's arms around him like she was still having to physically hold him back. I reckoned she could do it and all, looking at her dad.

I dunno what I'd expected, really. Someone aggressively businesslike, probably. Granted, this wasn't the best of circs to meet him under, but the word that sprang to mind when I looked at Alex was *faded*. With his flat grey hair and deeply hooded grey eyes, he looked way too old and tired to be married to Mrs. F-M. His light-grey summer-weight suit was obviously expensive, but it hung on him like he'd lost weight recently. And trust me, he didn't have a lot of weight to spare. Blokes like Alex seem to have been invented to make spiders feel less conspicuously leggy. Course, maybe he'd taken up marathon running in his spare time. Or the new missus had been giving him a regular workout in the bedroom.

Didn't look like that was going to be a problem from now on.

Alex's eyes were glued to his wife's body as the St. John's lot kept on trying to bring her back to life, but there was no hope in his expression. Poor sod. Having married a woman around twenty years younger than he was, he couldn't have expected to outlive her. Vi, on the other hand, looked *furious*. All I could think was that she was mad at her stepmum for upsetting her dad, which seemed a bit heartless, but there you go.

We all had to clear out when the emergency services turned up. The police were first in, closely followed by the real ambulance lot. They shepherded us over round the back of the tent, by the hedge, which meant I ended up not six feet from Vi and Alex. She shot me a poisonous glare but clearly decided looking after Daddy was more important than tearing me a new one right now.

Then we just had to wait until they were ready to deal with us.

Of course, me being the one to find the body meant I was the number-one attraction for the local plod.

We weren't by the reptile tent any longer, thank God, so I didn't have to try to wrestle my thoughts into some kind of order while the scene-of-crime bods did their stuff with the late Mrs. F-M. in the background. The police had commandeered the local tennis clubhouse, which was off to one end of the playing fields, for their on-site interviews, so we were sitting on plastic chairs around the table-football table in the main room. One side of it was all windows, looking onto the tennis courts, now cleared of players. The other walls were covered in notices, tournament tables, and motivational posters, including the one of that girl in the white frock scratching her bum.

"So you arranged with Mrs. Fenchurch-Majors beforehand that she'd hide something in the tent?" The lady copper was young, mixed-race, and aggressively keen. She'd given tennis girl's poster a disapproving look, unless it was the one right next to it of Roger Federer with his shirt off she didn't like. Personally, I'd have found that one well motivational if I'd been into tennis.

"Not in the tent, specifically. Just, she was supposed to hide something somewhere." I swallowed. Not being totally daft, I had a fair idea how it must look to them. "Look, I hardly knew her. She just asked me to do a turn to entertain the crowd, and it was part of the show, her hiding something."

"You had something of a disagreement with Mrs. Fenchurch-Majors earlier on today, didn't you, sir?"

You know you're in trouble when the plod insist on calling you *sir* in that steely tone of voice. "Well, yeah, but nothing I'd have strangled her over. It was just about that demo she had me doing. Been a bit of a communication failure, hadn't there?"

"Tell me, Mr. Paretski, what *would* you consider sufficient grounds for murder?"

You get the drift.

Cherry, being my self-appointed legal representative, had insisted on sitting in, which didn't endear either of us to the long arm of the law. I made sure I thanked her for it in appropriate terms when they finally let us go home. "Cheers, Sis. Way to make it look like I've got something to hide."

"Oh, don't be silly. They don't seriously suspect you. They're just following procedure."

"If that's the case, why'd I need you?"

"Well, excuse *me* for wanting to give some moral support to my baby brother. Oh, look, there's Alex over there, poor man. We must go and offer our condolences."

"Uh, not so sure about that . . ." I started, seeing as Alex Majors was with his daughter, who still looked ready to lay into someone given the slightest excuse. I'd already given her plenty, so I didn't rate my chances of coming out alive.

"For heaven's sake, Tom. He's just lost his wife. Come on." She slung her arm in mine and practically frog-marched me over with no consideration for my dodgy hip.

Not that it was actually hurting at the time, as it tends to do okay in warm weather, but it's the principle of the thing.

The bishop was over with Alex and Vi, so a less charitable brother might have concluded this was more about gaining brownie points with the bish than consoling Alex for his loss. He didn't even glance our way as we approached. The bereaved husband himself was looking greyer than ever, although fair dues, I'd probably have looked pretty grey if the bish had been getting physical with me like that. Dear old Toby was holding Alex's hand and patting it gently, murmuring what were presumably words of spiritual comfort.

"Alexander, Violet," Cherry began. "I can't begin to tell you—"

Vi cut her straight off, while giving me a look like I'd just crawled out of her drains dragging half the contents with me. "The police asked me if I'd noticed any suspicious characters hanging around Amelia lately. I made sure I told them all about the creep sneaking about in my bloody bedroom."

Great. When your name's Tom already, the last thing you need is to get a rep for peeping into ladies' bedrooms.

"Oi, she asked me to do that!" I glanced around nervously. The plod had already decided I was a person of interest, without her making me sound like some weirdo stalker.

"*Tom*!" Cherry was clearly wishing she'd offloaded me somewhere before coming over.

Alex finally looked up. "What? You were in my daughter's bedroom?"

"Look, it was your wife, yeah? She wanted me to find, um, something she'd lost." On the subject of diamond necklaces I decided it was probably least said, soonest mended.

Alex frowned. "But what were you doing in Vi's *bedroom*?"

Cherry made a high-pitched, exasperated sound. "Oh, for heaven's sake, Violet, Tom's as gay as a maypole. It wasn't as if he had any nefarious intent."

Vi gave me a considering look, and I expected her to ask what I'd been hunting for, but she didn't. "You're the psychic, aren't you? So go on, who did it? Who killed her?"

"Sorry, love. Not that sort of psychic," I said, just as Alex came out with a weak-sounding "Violet, *please.*"

"Well, we need to know, don't we?" Vi said bluntly. "Or the wrong person might get blamed." She had a fair point—my mate Dave, or DI Southgate as he is generally known, had as good as told me one time they always reckon there's a ninety percent chance it's the spouse/significant other what done it.

Cherry frowned. "And so that there's justice for poor Amelia," she said pointedly.

"Oh. Yes, that too."

We all shuffled our feet and tried to ignore the obvious insincerity there.

The bish clearly decided it was time for him to put his ecclesiastical oar in. "Oh, I think murder will out. And rest assured, even should the guilty party escape judgement in this world, they will face it in the next." Maybe it was just me, but there seemed to be a nasty little edge to his smile.

"Quite right, Toby," Cherry said firmly. "Now, *as* I was saying, Alexander, of course I'm most dreadfully sorry for your loss. If there's anything I can do—"

"What could *you* do?" Vi asked rudely. "And anyway, you didn't even like her."

"Violet!"

"Well, it's true, Daddy. Nobody liked her except you. And Toby and Uncle Arlo, I suppose. And Lance, maybe, but that's only because he *had* to." The sulky look on Vi's face turned stricken, probably 'cos her dad looked on the verge of collapse.

"Amelia"—Alex's voice broke on the name—"was a dear, dear soul and had a great many friends. I realise you and she have had a difficult relationship, but I hoped—" He choked up completely and couldn't finish.

Cherry looked like she felt she ought to give him a hug but was hoping somebody else would get in first. Luckily for me, after her maypole comment, I was pretty sure he wouldn't welcome it if I volunteered.

The bish squeezed Vi's bare shoulder, which, from her pissed-off expression, she found as creepy as it looked. "One should never speak ill of the dead, my dear. *They* may be beyond our censure, but the good Lord sees and hears all."

Vi shook him off with a hint of a shudder. "Come on, Daddy, let's get you home. If the police need to ask you any more questions, they can bloody well come and find us." She put an arm around her dad and led him off without so much as a fare-thee-well to any of us, her high heels aerating the playing fields with every step.

"Oh dear," Cherry said. "Death does have a terrible effect on people, doesn't it?"

Me and the bish just looked at her.

Our other halves, who'd been politely told to piss off earlier by the plod, turned up then, thank God. Mine and Cherry's, I mean, not the bishop's. I amused myself for a mo trying to imagine what sort of person would marry (a) a bishop in general and (b) this bishop in particular, then remembered the answer to (a) would be Cherry, given half a chance, and (b) this one was single.

Then I started wondering how he'd managed that if blokes in purple were such a catch in God-bothering circles. What, to be blunt, was wrong with him? I mean, personally I could think of plenty, but the sort of stuff I objected to was probably an enticement rather than a deal breaker for a lot of the women he came in contact with.

Greg slapped me on the shoulder. "I trust you've been ruled out of enquiries?" he said with a chuckle.

"Er, yeah, I think so." I'd have thought the laughter was a bit inappropriate in the circs.

Apparently I was in a minority, seeing as the bish joined in with the lols. "I do hope so, Gregory. I'm not at all sure I could in good conscience officiate at your wedding to the sister of a convicted murderer. After all, I might end up sitting near him at the wedding breakfast, and I hear there have already been some poisonings in the family."

I could feel Sis fuming beside me. Greg just beamed.

Phil coughed. "Don't worry. I'm sure the Lord will protect you." It was just on the inoffensive side of sarcastic. Just. "Are we getting out of here, Tom?"

"You must be the, ah, partner," the bish interrupted before I could say *God, yes please*. He thrust out a hand, which Phil inspected with narrowed eyes before giving it a short, sharp shake. "So interesting to meet you."

"Fiancé," Phil corrected, stony-faced. "And yeah, likewise. Come on, Tom."

"Sis? I'll call you, yeah?" I threw over my shoulder as we legged it.

CHAPTER EIGHT

"Jesus, I thought we'd never get away from there," Phil muttered as he put the Golf into gear. It'd been parked in the sun and was warm enough inside that if Cherry's stall had run out of cakes, she could have baked a few more in there no trouble. If, you know, the whole dead-body thing hadn't put a pretty final dampener on sales. Luckily, the air-con was already kicking in. I just wished it had some kind of accessory to help me chill inside as well as out.

"Me too. Where's Dave Southgate when you need him? At least when he's on the case I'm not suspect number one just 'cos of tripping over the body."

"You should give him a ring. Get him to put in a word for you." Phil swung out onto the main road, which was a relief. There's something about going faster that makes you feel cooler, even though in a car with air-con, it shouldn't really make a difference.

"Way ahead of you. It's about time I took him out for a pint, before he gets stuck in every night changing nappies." Dave and his wife had a nipper due any day now.

"Tonight?"

"Nah. Too knackered. All I wanna do is veg out in front of the telly with a takeaway." I paused. "You in?"

Phil sent me a look I'd class as fond but exasperated. "Course I'm bloody in. Not gonna leave you on your own tonight, am I?"

"Oi, I can cope. It's not like it's the first time I've found a body. No need to pass the smelling salts, ta very much."

Phil glanced my way again. There was more of the exasperated and possibly less of the fond this time. "Course you can cope on your own. You just don't bloody well have to."

"Why don't you move in?" I blurted out.

This time, he didn't look at me. Course, he was driving. He probably wanted to keep his eyes on the road. "You want—" He broke off and sighed. "I don't think that's a discussion we should be having right now."

"No. Course not." I looked out the window at fields starting to take on the barren look of autumn now the harvest had been gathered in, despite the bright sunshine and the heat of the day that could fool you into thinking it was still only August. But the nights were drawing in already, and it was only a month until the clocks would go back. I shivered, and Phil reached over to turn the air-con down a bit.

"What do you wanna eat tonight?" I roused myself to ask.

"Don't mind. Indian, if you're up for that. Nothing too adventurous."

"Yeah, sounds good. Chicken tikka, maybe some of that naan with the meat in it?"

Phil nodded.

Sometimes you just want a bit of same old, same old. Comfort food.

I called Dave as soon as we got back to mine.

Well, all right, as soon as we'd got back to mine *and* called the takeaway. It's a matter of priorities, innit?

It was a while before he picked up, which I took to mean he wasn't working today. "Dave? It's Tom. Fancy a pint tomorrow night?"

"Do I ever. Usual place?" That was the White Hart down Holywell Hill, your actual ancient Tudor coaching inn with oak-panelled walls, low beams in the ceiling that didn't tend to bother yours truly overmuch, and a skeleton in every closet, courtesy of the management.

"Fine by me." I paused. "Listen, I oughtta warn you, I sort of gave your name out as a character reference today."

Dave sighed. "Bleedin' hell, don't tell me. You've gone and dug up another body, haven't you? Jesus, I can't leave you alone for five minutes."

"Oi, there haven't been that many. And some of 'em *you* put me onto in the first place. But, uh, yeah. Over in St. Leonards. Wasn't *my* fault."

"I should bloody well hope not. Come on, spill. You were just walking down the road when this body fell out the back of a lorry, honest, guv?"

"Walking into a reptile tent, and no lorry, but yeah." I filled him in on the Harvest Fayre events but decided against giving him the background on the mother/daughter relationship. Didn't want to bias him or anything, and it wasn't like I'd mentioned it to the St. Leonards mob either.

Look, I felt a bit uncomfortable about it, yeah, but it wasn't like they'd asked me or anything, was it? They'd just wanted to know how I knew the victim, and I'd told them the truth: she'd got me in to do a job, through my sister, and it'd involved a bit of a hunt around the place. Wasn't my fault if they assumed it was a plumbing job, was it?

I mean, it wasn't like it was actually *relevant*. I hadn't even found anything, had I?

If I *had* made a point of telling the police about dear departed Amelia calling me in to search Vi's bedroom, it'd look like I was pretty much accusing Vi of killing her stepmum. Which, yeah, I didn't wanna do 'cos (a) I felt bad enough about sneaking into her bedroom and (b) if I ended up sending 'em on a wild-goose chase after Vi, the real murderer could get off scot-free.

Course, *now* it occurred to me they hadn't said anything to me about Vi grassing me up. So, say, me making sure I'd explained why I'd been in her room might have been seen as me having something to hide.

Sod it.

Dave listened, grunting at appropriate moments and asking the odd question, not all of which I could answer. "Right," he said in the end. "Scratch tomorrow evening. Make it Monday night, give me a bit more time to find out what's what with your latest murder."

"Oi, you're making me sound like a serial killer. And, hang on a mo, since when's policing been a nine-to-five, Monday-to-Friday gig?"

"The missus is dragging me out tomorrow. To Mothercare. Got to buy a pram, 'cept it's not called a pram these days, *oh* no. It's a bleedin' travel system and takes a degree in engineering to put together every time you want to nip down the shops. God knows where she's going to keep the bloody thing, what with all the changing tables, baby bouncers, and Moses bloody baskets she's filled the place up with. We never had half this stuff with the first lot. I tell you, soon as she drops that sprog, I'll be getting my marching orders 'cos the house ain't big enough for both of us."

"Ah, you love it really." I wasn't just saying it. There was a definite hint of fond fatherly pride buried in that little rant. "Anyhow, Jen's not gonna kick you out. Who'd change all the dirty nappies and get up in the night when it screams the place down? While we're on, me and Phil want to get you something for the little nipper—got any ideas?"

We'd already got the gag gift, mind. Gary found it online for us: a onesie with the slogan *Proof My Daddy's Not Gay*. Seeing as the same site also sold an identical onesie printed with *I Love My Gay Daddy*, I wasn't so sure about the logic, but I reckoned Dave would appreciate it.

Or, you know, not.

"Jesus, I dunno. Jen's already bought up more stuff than one kid could use in a lifetime. You save your money, mate. Use it to buy me a pint or six when the credit card bills come in."

We hung up, by which time Phil had got back with the Indian takeaway and opened up a couple of bottles of beer. I wasn't sure which of 'em I was gladder to see.

Not including Phil, obviously.

We sat down in front of the telly, food on the coffee table where the cats gave it a good sniff before stalking off, unimpressed. "Stop judging my taste in food," I told Merlin. "I saw you eat a moth last week. *And* it was still flapping at the time. You haven't got a paw to stand on."

Merlin gave me a disdainful flick of the tail, then settled down to wash his rear end, which is just what you want to look at while you're eating.

"I swear he does that on purpose," I muttered, sitting back with my plateful of bright-red chicken tikka masala and sag aloo, 'cos you've got to have a bit of green stuff in there so you can kid yourself it's not that unhealthy, honest.

Phil huffed. "What, you think it's possible to lick your own arse by accident?"

"Maybe. If you're a cat. He could be washing, I dunno, his leg, and forget to stop?"

"More likely he's looking for his bollocks, poor sod. Now shut up and eat your curry. Makes me nervous, seeing you with a plate of food in front of you and not shovelling it in like there's no tomorrow."

I stuck up one finger at him. And with the other hand, got on with shovelling down my food like there was no tomorrow. Just call me the king of multitasking.

I slept badly that night, despite Phil staying over, and not for any of the fun reasons either. I hadn't set my alarm, but still ended up staggering out of bed before eight. It could've been even earlier, but getting up before seven on a Sunday would've seemed like admitting defeat.

The cats must've thought it was Christmas, getting fed so early without any application of claws to sensitive areas. I wasn't totally sure I was hungry, myself, so I just made coffee—bunging an extra scoop of coffee grinds into the cafetière while I was at it—and chucked a couple of slices of bread in the toaster.

I still wasn't sure I was hungry by the time it was done, but seeing as the secondary purpose had been to lure Phil out of bed with delicious, toasty aromas, I counted it as a win when he stumbled, bleary-eyed and fluffy-haired, into the kitchen. "Do I smell breakfast?" he muttered, coming over to give me a half-awake kiss.

"It's yours if you want it," I said, getting out the marmalade.

I could tell how awake he wasn't by the way he didn't even smirk at the innuendo. "Cheers. Coffee?"

I handed him a mug. Phil leaned against the counter and yawned. Then he took a gulp from his mug and grimaced. "Bloody hell, are you trying to give me heart palpitations?" He grabbed for the milk and sloshed a load more in his mug.

"Uh, sorry. Fancied it a bit stronger this morning."

"Next time, warn me. Because believe me, I can think of ways I'd rather you got my heart rate going." He grabbed for me, but I sidestepped and crouched down to stick my head in the fridge instead.

"Fancy bacon and eggs for afters? Seeing as it's Sunday? Could grill up a couple of tomatoes to pretend it's healthy, if you like. Or there's mushrooms. Could make an omelette, come to that. If you like." I paused, realising the conversation had got a bit one-sided. "Phil?"

There was a sigh. "Didn't sleep well last night, did you?"

I shrugged, which felt a bit lopsided with one hand full of eggs and the other holding a packet of bacon. "Just a bit restless, that's all."

"Uh-huh. Wouldn't have anything to do with what happened yesterday, would it?"

"Dunno," I lied, turning to the stove and putting down the bacon so I could grab a pan. "So what's it gonna be? Fried, scrambled, or omelette?"

Phil's hands landed gently on my shoulders. "Could always let me cook if you're having trouble choosing. Pretty much cuts the options down to *scrambled*."

I smiled at the cooker hood, relieved he wasn't going to make me talk about it. "Nah, don't do yourself down. I can definitely tell your fried eggs from your omelettes. Well, most of the time, anyway. Tell you what, we'll have fried, and I'll show you how to do the yolks properly, yeah?"

He dropped a kiss to my neck. "Can't see the point of going to so much trouble, to be honest. They all taste the same smothered in brown sauce." I swear I could hear him smirking behind me, the palate-less git.

"The chickens that laid those eggs would be crying in their coops if they heard you say that."

"No, they wouldn't. We ate 'em last night, remember?" Phil's arms snaked around my waist, and he rested his head on my shoulder. "What you were saying yesterday. About me moving in. That what you want?"

He wanted to talk about it *now*? "I dunno," I said, slapping some butter into the pan and turning on the heat. "I mean, we haven't even set a date for the wedding. I wouldn't want to ruin your reputation."

"Stop evading the question."

"Hey, it's a valid concern for some people."

He huffed down my neck just as I was cracking an egg into the pan, and I nearly broke the yolk. "What, elderly spinsters of this parish?"

"Oi, don't you talk about my sister like that."

"Git." He paused. "Think you should give her a call and make sure she's all right? About that woman dying, I mean. They were friends, weren't they?"

I was touched, 'cos, well, Cherry and Phil hadn't exactly hit it off immediately when we started going out together. "Yeah . . . I reckon *friends* would be overstating it a bit. But I'll ring her later. After church." By which I meant, after *she'd* been to church, not me.

He nodded. "We don't have to talk about the other stuff right now. Let me know when you're ready."

"It's not—" I stopped. We both knew what I'd been about to say was a lie.

Phil kissed my neck. "Come on. Show me how you do those yolks."

So I did.

I seriously didn't deserve him.

I must have been a bit previous calling Cherry, as when she picked up the phone there were the unmistakeable sounds in the background of an after-church coffee morning going full swing.

"Want me to call back later?" I asked after we'd exchanged *hellos*.

"Oh God, no." It sounded a lot quieter on her end now. I guessed she'd nipped off for a bit of privacy. "It's horrible. All anyone can talk about in there is the fayre."

"I'm guessing you don't mean the ferret racing."

"I really don't know why Gregory didn't cancel coffees today. He said Amelia would have wanted us to carry on as normal and not make a fuss, which I *completely* disagree with. She'd have wanted there to be as much fuss as possible."

"You're not wrong there. Was it Greg's turn to do the service today, then?"

"No, but the bishop asked him to take over as he was too *distressed*."
There was a sarcastic edge to Cherry's voice on the last word.

"Yeah, he seemed to be coping just fine yesterday, didn't he?"

"Mm. Honestly, you have to wonder just why some people even join the church."

"Mi-*aow*."

"Oh, shut up. I've had just about enough of all the falseness her death's brought out. Everyone saying how *dreadful* it was, when they obviously only want to hear as many details as possible. It's just ghoulish, and it's horrible."

Okay, so Sis was definitely a bit more cut up about it all than I'd thought. "You want me to come over later? Or you could come to mine?"

There was a sniff. "Thanks, but we're having tea at Mum and Dad's later. I'd say come over and join us, but you know how they don't like too many people round at once."

I did. "Yeah, no worries. Say hi from me, though. And Phil, obviously."

"I'll give them your love."

"What, Phil's and all?"

"Of course. You're engaged now. Have you set a date yet, by the way? You know Mum will ask."

"Uh, no. Thought we'd get you and Greg hitched first, yeah?"

"Oh, Tom. A wedding takes a vast amount of planning. Don't leave it too late."

I'd been expecting a call from Gary all day, seeing as I hadn't spoken to him since the fayre and he's not normally the type to shy away from delicate subjects like yours truly falling over another corpse. So when the doorbell rang midafternoon, I thought it might be him.

It wasn't. A flash blinded me, and then some bland-looking bloke I'd never met before lowered his camera and asked if I'd mind answering a few questions about Mrs. F-M.'s death for the benefit of the local rag.

"Uh..." Actually, I did mind, and I was still trying to think how to say that politely but firmly when Phil loomed up behind me.

"He says *No bloody comment*, and you can quote me on that," Phil growled, and slammed the door in his face.

Fortunately he didn't have a foot stuck in the doorway, or we might have ended up with a few toes as a souvenir.

I turned to frown at Phil. "Oi, I could've handled that. You didn't have to be rude."

"Yes, I did. That's all their sort understand. Did he ask permission before he took your photo?"

"No. Shit. Is that gonna go in the paper?"

"Maybe. We didn't give him much of a story to go with it."

I didn't much fancy my customers finding out about my little habit of tripping over dead bodies. Funny how getting mixed up with a few murders can give people second thoughts about inviting you into their house. And I didn't need any more publicity for my psychic bloody talents, either. "Can we stop them printing it?"

Phil stared at me. "They print naked pictures of royalty. What do *you* bloody think?"

"Bloody marvellous. Great. So all I can do is hope for another sinkhole to open up and swallow a few houses this time."

Phil nodded, a half smile on his lips. "That'd knock you off the front page all right."

The next time the doorbell rang, I didn't bother getting up from the sofa, where Phil and me had been pretending to do paperwork while watching the motor racing on the telly.

"Don't answer that," Phil warned, presumably in case the old reflexes were just being a bit slow today.

"Wasn't gonna," I assured him.

Then a voice called through the letter box. "Yoo-hoo! It's only us."

Gary. And Darren, presumably. That was a relief. And not just because it gave me an excuse to leave off doing the VAT return for a bit. I opened the door and cracked a welcoming smile at them. "'Yoo-hoo'? Seriously?"

"Did the job, dinnit?" Darren stomped past me into the hall, carrying a six-pack of beer in each hand. I felt a sudden surge of affection for him. "How you doing, short-arse?" he carried on.

Ah, well, the affection had been nice while it lasted. "I'm good. Want to bung those in the fridge?"

"Cheers, mate. Got any crisps?"

"Nope. Sorry."

"Bleedin' 'ell." Halfway to the kitchen, he turned to Gary. "I told you we shoulda brung crisps."

Gary rolled his eyes at me—*after* Darren had disappeared fridgewards. "Husbands. What can you do?"

I grinned. "I've got some dry-roasted peanuts."

"Nah, cheers, mate, but I like my nuts just to taste of salt, like nature intended." Darren had reappeared and was now off to the living room. "Phil! How you doing there, mate?"

Phil said something I didn't hear, and Darren gave a loud cackle.

Gary beamed. "Isn't it lovely how well our other halves get on together? Now, if you ever reconsider on the foursome . . ."

"You'll be the first to know," I assured him. And it'd be sweater weather in hell, I didn't add. I wouldn't want Gary to take it the wrong way. Or even the right way, for that matter. "I've got some pizza in the freezer, or we could get a takeaway—"

"You're a treasure, but no. We're dining with Darren's family tonight. This is just a flying visit to see how you're bearing up. How *are* you bearing up? After all that unpleasantness yesterday."

I made a face. "Ah, you know. Wasn't great, finding her like that. Did you know her?"

"Only in passing. Which, I might add, I did as quickly as possible. One does hear things."

"Yeah? Like what?"

"Oh, only that she had something of a forceful personality. I wouldn't have wanted to be a keg of gunpowder anywhere near when she and her stepdaughter got going."

"Ever hear about her playing away from home?" I asked, 'cos that reminded me about what Vi had said about me being her stepmum's latest bit of rough.

Gary just shrugged. "Well, who could blame her? Alex Majors is hardly the sort to get anyone's juices flowing. Now, shall we join the boys?"

Phil shut his laptop, I shifted my files off the sofa, and we all sat down with a beer—well, all except Gary, who pulled out a mini bottle of piña colada from his jacket pocket. I got him a glass and some ice. What with the sleepless night I'd had, the beer went right to my head, but I wasn't complaining.

"So, are you officially consulting with the police on the murder?" Gary asked, while Darren munched on a packet of mini Cheddars Phil had found for him, which I'd have sworn we didn't have in the house.

I snorted. "No. I'm helping with their enquiries, which, believe me, isn't the same thing at all."

"Ah, coppers. Can't trust 'em as far as you can throw a panda car at 'em," Darren put in. "No offence, mate," he added to Phil.

"None taken." Phil was smiling, so I guessed it was true. "Tom's not about to be arrested. They just asked a few questions about his psychic demonstration."

"Ooh, that reminds me," Gary piped up. He looked at Darren. "The hobby. Shall you tell him, or shall I?"

The hobby? What hobby, and did he mean mine or his?

I wasn't even sure I *had* any hobbies, unless you counted the cooking. Oh, and slobbing out in front of the telly with my bloke.

"I'll tell 'im, pumpkin. See, Geoff, that's the leader of the Stompers, he was wondering if you'd be up for doing mates' rates on a job for us. Course, I told 'im I don't reckon it's your line, but I'd ask you anyhow."

I was getting a bad feeling about this.

Darren took a swig of beer, belched, and carried on. "See, it's our hobby. Some turd borrowed it while we was watching you do your stuff, and we found it shoved in the 'edge with a flippin' great dent in it. Geoff's hopping mad. So he was hoping you could do, like, a reading on it or something. Find out who done it."

"Okay, what? I haven't got a bloody clue what you're on about. What do you mean your hobby? And what do you want me to read, for God's sake?"

"He means the horse, Tommy," Gary put in. "Well, the horse's head worn by one of the dancers. It's called the hobby. From hobbyhorse?

Or maybe that's where hobbyhorse came from. Do you know, sweetie pie? Which came first, the hobby or the horse?"

"Hang about," I interrupted before the plot got totally lost. "What exactly do you expect me to do with a horse's head? And, oi, keep it clean. There's no Tory politicians round here."

"Spoilsport." Gary pouted and took a sip of his piña colada.

Phil put his beer down on the table. "He wants you to see if you can get any vibes off the horse costume. Anything that might tell you who damaged it."

I frowned at him. "That's not what I do. You know it isn't."

"Could be linked to the murder—if you saw someone wearing a papier-mâché horse's head, you'd assume it was one of the Morris dancers, wouldn't you? Might be a good way to sneak up on the victim without anyone knowing."

"What? It'd be a bloody awful way to sneak up on anyone. You think the witnesses wouldn't have *remembered* a six-foot-tall horse man?" And great, now my nightmares about stranglers were going to be even more colourful and disturbing.

"Might not hurt to see what you can get from it." Phil's tone was that careful *I'm not judging you* one he uses when interviewing people, so naturally enough, I got all defensive.

"It'd be a total waste of time. I don't get vibes off things unless they're hidden, all right?" Whose talent was this, anyway?

"Have you tried?" Gary asked.

"I don't need to try, all right? I know how it works. Hidden stuff. And water. That's it."

Darren shrugged. "'S all right. I'll tell Geoff you're not interested. No worries."

"I'm not . . . *not interested*. It's just not my thing, all right?"

"Yeah, 's what I said, innit? I'll tell 'im. Don't get your kecks up your crack." Him and Phil shared a look, which didn't make me any happier.

"Did you have any premonitions before you found her?" Gary said, leaning forwards.

"Not exactly," I said, just as Phil came out with a huff and a "He doesn't do premonitions either."

Everyone stared at me.

Great. "It wasn't like I knew anything was going to happen before it did, all right? It was just that the trail I was following felt . . . I dunno. Wrong. Nasty."

They all nodded solemnly.

"Do we have to talk about this all evening?" I said, picking up my beer and realising I'd finished it already.

"Course not," Darren said brightly. "So anyhow, you and Phil set a date yet? Got the venue sorted?"

Bloody marvellous.

"Ooh, yes." Gary beamed. "After all, you don't want to leave it—"

"Too late," I finished for him. "I know, all right? I *know.*"

CHAPTER NINE

I was glad to get back to work on Monday, if I'm honest. Had a mare of a job sorting out a blockage at one of those big, posh houses on London Road—God knows what the cowboys who put the original plumbing in were thinking. They put in some of the pipes so the water *literally* had to run uphill, and when I took off the bath panel to have a butcher's, there was all kinds of old crap they'd just shoved in there rather than clear up after 'emselves. Including—I kid you not—someone's greasy sandwich wrapper, still with a mummified apple core inside.

Mr. K. sent it a look of betrayal. "They seemed like such nice young men. Always polite. And they did the job so quickly too."

I did my best for the bloke—unblocked the pipe and tidied up a bit—but I told him straight, the same thing was gonna keep happening unless he had a total refit including raising the bath. I could tell he thought I was just trying to screw him for some extra work.

Maybe if I'd bodged the job so I could do it in half the time and thrown in a few *sirs*, he'd have given it to me.

The rest of the day was your bog-standard stuff, mostly involving, heh, bogs. New siphon on one and a leak on the other—sort of jobs I could do in my sleep, which was just as well considering my eyelids were a bit on the heavy side after the previous night. I had to stifle a yawn as I waited for Mrs. G. to write out a cheque in shaky old-lady handwriting.

"You look like you could use an early night, dear," she said as she handed it over. "New baby, is it?"

She was eyeing my ring finger like it meant something it didn't. And yeah, I guess it looked like I was wearing a wedding band, but seriously, did questions of right and left have no meaning to anyone these days? "Uh, no. I haven't got any kids. Just didn't sleep well, ta."

"No children? Well, don't leave it too late. You want to be young enough to enjoy them."

Cheers, love. Just what I needed—a reminder of another conversation me and Phil hadn't quite got round to.

Phil was busy on his identity-theft case, so I ate my tea alone. Even the cats had buggered off somewhere. They sloped back in just as I was on my way out to meet Dave, presumably to make sure I wasn't trying to sneak off without filling their food bowls, as if I'd do anything *that* daft. I prefer my legs skin on, ta very much.

I beat Dave to the White Hart by around thirty seconds, and we were both early. Not that *early* has to mean *desperate to get out of the house*, of course.

"You're lucky you caught me on a free night," he said as he parked his considerable arse on the barstool next to mine. "What with all the bloody antenatal classes and pregnancy massage and all that bollocks. I ask you, why's she got to bother with all that this time round?"

I shrugged. It wasn't exactly my area of expertise. "Dunno, mate. They changed the procedure since you had the first two?"

Dave and his wife married young and popped out a couple of kids in their early twenties. Dave and Jen, I mean, although come to think of it their kids were now also in their early twenties and therefore old enough to be this latest sprog's parents. Both had been living away from home for a few years now. Maybe I should ask Dave to give Phil's mum some tips.

I hadn't really thought about it before, but it must be weird growing up with your dad a copper. Must be like dad squared, when it came to underage drinking and the odd herbal cigarette. Not that I'd ever done a right lot of either, but I didn't kid myself I was in the majority here.

Dave laughed and patted his belly. There was a fair amount of it to pat. "Can't you tell? It's the dads what have 'em now, like bloody seahorses."

I grinned. "Your Jen not still giving you grief about the diet, then?"

"Too bloody knackered to give a toss. She's spent the summer with her feet up, going *Get this bloody thing out of me*. Says she'd kill for a rum and Coke too."

Cheers, mate. A flashback to Vi saying *I could bloody kill her* made me shudder, but I s'posed it was as good a way as any of introducing the topic of the day. "So are we gonna talk about this murder?"

Dave sighed. "Better buy me a pint, then, hadn't you? And a packet of salt 'n' vinegar, while you're at it."

A skinny barmaid with creepily perfect makeup and bleached-blonde hair took our order. "You new here, love?" I asked, 'cos I hadn't seen her before.

"Yes. Since two weeks." Her accent was foreign—German, maybe?

I caught Dave giving me a sly look. "Bloody foreigners," he muttered when she went over to the other side of the bar to use the till. "Coming over here, taking our jobs, impregnating our women—"

"Har bloody har," I told him, sticking up a finger and swivelling it gently at him.

Dave cackled, and the barmaid gave us a funny look. "Private joke," I told her, in case her hearing was sharper than Dave had given her credit for.

We took our pints over to a secluded table (not hard to find on a Monday night) and sat down.

"So, you spoken to your mates in St. Leonards?"

Dave nodded. "Yep. Rang 'em up and offered them the scoop on one Tom Paretski. Course, they were well disappointed when I told 'em you were a local bloody celebrity round our way, tripping over bodies both dead and alive left, right, and bloody centre."

"Oi, I'm not a celebrity."

"Course you bleedin' are. Front page of the local rag for saving that barmaid, weren't you?"

"Yeah, well, you'll notice we're not exactly being mobbed by people asking for my autograph. Anyway, so what did you find out?"

"One or two things." Cagey bastard.

"Come on, are you gonna tell me, or do I have to bribe you with a packet of pork scratchings?"

"It's a serious offence, bribing an officer of the law. Better make it worth your while by adding a pint as well. Nah, only kidding, my shout. Same again?"

I then had to wait half an hour while he heaved his bulk over to the bar, waved the barman over from the other side, ordered the drinks and the nibbles, and carried them back to the table.

"You did that on purpose, you bastard," I greeted him on his return. It wasn't exactly a leap of logic, seeing as we both still had half our original drinks left and he hadn't even touched his crisps.

He *still* didn't say anything until he'd opened his pork scratchings and scoffed a handful, the git. "You're fine. Never a serious suspect anyhow."

I stared. "That's it?"

He stared back. "What? I'm not gonna give you all the ins and outs of an ongoing police investigation. Be a breach of professional ethics, that would. I will tell you this, though. For what it's worth, my money's on a lover." Dave belched and wiped his mouth with the back of his hand.

"Why? I mean, do they know for certain she had one? I mean, she was a busy lady, fingers in all sorts of pies."

Dave snorted. "Oh yeah? Bit of a dyke on the side, was she?"

"Christ, not *that* kind of pie." I sent him a look I hoped conveyed just how unimpressed I was with his so-called sense of humour. "Least, not that I'm aware of. I was just wondering if she had the time for a lover."

"Who knows? But it's suggestive." Dave leaned forward, not without a bit of difficulty, and tapped the side of his nose. "Now, you didn't hear this from me, but there were definitely circumstances suggestive of a lover spurned."

"What circumstances? Which, obviously, I also didn't hear from you," I added as encouragement.

"Ah." Dave took a long swig of beer. "Well, they got a bit of a surprise when they cut her open for the postmortem. Prize in every packet, you might say."

"You what?"

"Whoever did her in shoved a gold necklace down her throat. Well, tried to, anyhow. Owing to the cause of death, there wasn't a right lot of room."

Suddenly I was ice-cold. "Diamond?" I asked, and could have kicked myself for it a moment later.

Dave stared at me. Then he put down his pint. "Bloody, bleeding bollocks." He shook his head. "You're going to be the death of me, Paretski, you know that, don't you? David Southgate, tragically taken from us in his prime, predeceased by his sodding career. Come on then, out with it. What do you know about that bloody necklace?"

Look, I didn't want to drop Vi Majors in it. But this was Dave. And, well, it was murder, wasn't it?

"I don't *know* anything," I started. "And I've never even seen the sodding thing. But, well . . ."

I told him all about my first meeting with Amelia F-M., which, when you say it like that, sounds like some posh radio station for genteel young ladies. I didn't reckon Vi would be caught dead listening to it, but then again, she wasn't really in their demographic. Posh, yeah. Genteel? A big, fat no.

Dave heaved a sigh. "Fine. You realise I'm going to have to pass this on? And they're going to want to talk to you again. Why the bleedin' hell didn't you tell them this to start with?"

"Didn't know it was significant, did I? Shit," I added as a thought struck. "Are you gonna get in trouble for telling me about the necklace?"

Dave stared into his pint for a minute. "Nah," he said at last. "We'll spin it that you and me were having a friendly chat over a pint, and you just happened to mention the victim hiring you to find a necklace. Whereupon I, seeing as how I knew stuff you didn't, was on it like a car bonnet and got you to sing like a canary what's won *The X Factor* and got top billing at the Royal Opera House." He sat back, his expression a lot like Arthur's after he's managed to sneak some of Merlin's dinner without getting caught. "That'll do. Just don't grass me up, and we're golden."

I gave him a sideways look. "So did you tell me about the necklace after I'd sung, or not?"

He sent back a look that was full-frontal and unimpressed. "Paretski, you're the world's worst liar, and believe me, I've met some fucking tragic ones in my life. Yes, I told you about the necklace, using my professional judgement to determine that sharing a confidence would persuade you a full confession was advisable. Happy?"

"Well, not with you calling it a confession. But yeah, I can work with that."

"Thank God. Pork scratching?"

I held up a hand to ward off the snacks of the devil. "No, ta."

He snorted and shoved the crisps in my direction instead. "Worried you won't fit into your wedding dress? How's all that going, anyway? The wedding preparations, that is, not your bleedin' love life 'cos I do *not* want to know. Have you even set a date yet?"

"Nah. Sometime next summer, that's all. Got to get my sister hitched first."

"Yeah, well, don't leave it too late."

"Christ, why does everyone seem to think time's running out for me?" Not that Mrs. G. had been talking about weddings, of course. Still, I was starting to get a bit paranoid, what with the way the whole world seemed to be singing the same tune.

"Bloody hell, when did you turn into such a drama queen? Jen reckons the best places get booked up two years in advance, that's all." He huffed at my look of surprise. "She's only planning the christening already. Wait until the baby's born, I keep telling her. Don't count your chickens. Will she listen? Will she bollocks."

What with my brother and sister both being childless, and most of my mates of the nonbreeding persuasion, I hadn't had a right lot to do with christenings up until now. "How much planning does a christening take? Don't you just turn up at the church, splash the sprog with a bit of holy water, and God's your uncle?"

"She wants a bloody *reception*." Dave shuddered, his belly doing a weird ripple thing. "Posh finger food and piano music. Like the baby's going to give a crap."

"Thought that was mostly what they did. That and the sleeping and crying."

"Eff off, or your name's going right to the top of the babysitting list." Dave took a long swallow of beer. "Ah, that's better. So you and Morrison, you planning to adopt or something?"

"Jesus, let us get hitched first, yeah?" I fixed him with a stern look. "And don't bloody tell me not to leave it too late, yeah? I've had about as much of that as I can stand."

Dave laughed, the bastard. "Mortality creeping up, is it? Christ, just wait till you get to my age. Everything sodding aches, and if it doesn't, it's 'cos it's bloody dropped off." Then his smile turned misty, which was disturbing. "It's gonna be good for us, this nipper. Me and Jen. Keep us from getting old and sad."

There was only one possible response to that, so I made it, Dave told me to eff off again, and then we got another round in. Good times.

I slept like a baby Monday night, despite (or maybe because of) being on my own. Well, like one of the babies in an advert for expensive, brand-name nappies designed by NASA, anyhow. Dave reliably informs me real babies aren't like that and prefer to spend most of the hours of darkness puking, pooping, and having a paddy.

Course, if they were *that* bad, he wouldn't be having another one, would he? I lay in bed for a mo in the morning and wondered what it'd be like having a kiddie of my own.

Then Merlin jumped on my stomach and Arthur gave my foot a friendly scratch, both of then miaowing fit to wake up the dead 'cos breakfast hadn't been served, and I reckoned I might have a fair idea already.

My phone rang just as I pulled up outside the first job of the day. (Washbasin down the road for the newly single Mrs. Z. She didn't volunteer how the last one had got cracked, and I didn't ask.)

"Paretski Plumbing," I answered breezily.

"Tom Paretski? This is Vi Majors. I need to talk to you." She was one of those people with a telephone voice that could carry across three continents without the need for 4G. I moved the phone further away from my ear.

"I'm listening," I said cautiously.

There was a barely audible *tch*. "Not on the phone."

Bloody hell, not her as well. "Yeah, see, I'm not sure I'm gonna be out your way for a bit—"

"I'll come to you. Where do you live?"

"Fleetville. St. Albans. But—"

"Where's that? Oh, never mind, I'm rubbish with directions anyway. Just give me your postcode, and I'll set the satnav. You'll be there tonight?"

I hesitated, not sure if Phil would be free to come round—I had a feeling this might be just his area—but sod it, she might be a big lass, but if it came down to a fight, I was fairly sure I could take her. And she *had* just lost her stepmum, never mind that she hadn't exactly broken down with grief last I'd seen her. Actually, that brought something else to mind. "What about your dad? Are you sure you should leave him? He looked a bit cut up about it all on Saturday."

"Oh, he'll be fine." She dismissed all five stages of grief with the airy confidence of someone who'd never lost someone they cared about.

Then again, Alex had been a widower before the advent of Amelia, hadn't he? So she'd lost her mum sometime in the past, and presumably she'd actually liked her.

Jesus, poor Alex. He must be devastated, going through it all a second time around. "Maybe he could come with?" I found myself saying, when I hadn't meant to agree to her coming round at all.

"God, no. I told you, he'll be fine. He's with Uncle Arlo."

There was that name again. All these *A*s were giving me a headache. "That's his brother?"

"*No.* Amelia's brother, as if that had anything to do with *anything.* Look, just give me your postcode."

I gave. I also told her not to come round before eight 'cos I'd be having my tea.

Then I rang Phil and offered to cook him pasta tonight.

CHAPTER TEN

I played it safe and didn't mention Vi was coming round until after we'd eaten (just a carbonara, with a rocket salad on the side, as I couldn't be arsed to do anything fancy), but Phil was still less than impressed with my plans for company for the evening. "Going for the record, are you—most murderers entertained in one living room? And what if I hadn't been free tonight? Hoping the cats would leap in to protect you?"

I leaned back in the sofa and nudged my plate to one side with my toes so I could put my feet up on the coffee table. It was all right. I had clean socks on. "Don't be daft. She can't have done it."

Phil leaned back too, but kept his feet on the floor. Probably just as well, seeing as Arthur jumped up on his lap a moment later. That cat could do serious damage by landing on unsupported knees. "Why not? She's got plenty of upper-body strength. Keen tennis player, from what I heard. And she rides."

"So? Nobody strangled the woman with their thighs."

Phil huffed. Arthur's ears twitched, and he kneaded Phil's legs with his paws. "Have you seen these horsey types? Spend more of their time slinging hay bales and mucking out stables than they do in the bloody saddle. Don't be fooled by the padding on those arms. She's probably got more muscle on her than you have."

"Oi, who are you calling a wimp?" I flexed my biceps in his general direction. You have to have a reasonable amount of strength in your arms, in the plumbing line. Course, legs are a different matter, but luckily it wasn't shorts weather anymore. "Anyway, she still didn't do it. Can't have, or she'd never have said what she did up at the fayre. You heard her, telling everyone she hated her stepmum."

"No, I didn't, and neither did you. We heard her saying everyone *else* hated her."

I thought about it. "S'pose you're right. All except Alex, some bloke called Lance, and Uncle Arndale."

"Arlo."

"Whatever. You're still not telling me that's actually a name. Not that Lance is much better, poor sod."

"Fit right in round here, though, wouldn't he?"

I frowned. "You what?"

"Arthur, Merlin . . ."

"What, you think it's actually short for Lancelot? Jesus, his parents must have hated him."

Phil shrugged. "It's not that bad. Makes a man stand out, get noticed, having an unusual name." He looked a bit wistful, in a grass-is-always-greener sort of way.

"Oi, I hope this doesn't mean you're planning on changing your name by deed poll to something weird and wonderful, like that nutter who called himself after the entire Arsenal football team. I mean, seriously, he could at least have picked a decent side." A thought struck. "Hey, we haven't talked about names, have we? After we get hitched, I mean. Are we gonna be Paretski-Morrisons? I don't reckon Morrison-Paretski would work."

Phil stared at me for a long moment. "You want to do that?" he asked at last.

"Don't you?" I countered, feeling a bit uncertain. As per bloody usual, neither his face nor his tone had given anything away as to how he actually felt about it. "I mean, we don't have to. It was just a thought."

Phil opened his mouth—and then the doorbell rang.

Bloody Vi Majors. She was twenty minutes late already. Couldn't she have stretched it another ten? I sighed and went to let her in.

Vi was in purple today, to match her name. She had on a silky blouse thing that gaped a bit at the buttons, a matching Alice band, and a pair of dark-grey tailored trousers. The outfit didn't seem quite *her* somehow, despite the trousers being the regulation size too small—maybe it was her idea of mourning gear?

"Find us okay?" I asked politely, gesturing her in.

She sort of shrugged and cast a glance behind her. "I hope the car's going to be all right, parked round here."

"Well, if you don't wanna stay . . ." I was a bit narked at her suggestion this was a dodgy neighbourhood. She should see the estate Phil grew up on.

Vi shook herself. "God, no, don't mind me. It's just, well . . . What happened. Makes you a bit paranoid, doesn't it?" She gave me a lopsided smile that made me like her a whole lot more. "Sorry."

"No worries. Come on in."

I led her through to the living room, where she gave Phil a suspicious look. He'd stood up to greet her, which Arthur must've been well chuffed about. Not. I was relieved to see my beloved's trousers were still intact, which boded well for what was inside them. Hey, I've got my priorities.

"Oh. The fiancé," Vi said flatly. "He's not staying, is he?"

My hackles were getting a proper workout this evening—up and down more times than a porn star's arse. Just to annoy Vi, I put an arm round Phil's waist and gazed up at him adoringly, sort of like Julian after Gary's just given him a doggy treat. "Oh, me and Phil don't have any secrets."

Vi looked like she was about to gag. "God, gay couples are the *worst*. Look, this has to be confidential, all right? I don't want any of it getting back to Daddy."

"Any of what?"

"Tell you what," Phil butted in. "You two sit down. I'll go make some drinks. Tea? Coffee? Something stronger?"

"Coffee, I suppose, since I'm driving," Vi said regretfully. She watched him go with a look of approval. Well, he did look pretty damn hot in those jeans.

We sat down, her at one end of the sofa and me at the other. Arthur plodded up to give her a sniff, but she ignored him.

"Not a cat person?" I asked, pulling him onto my lap. He showed his gratitude by digging his claws into my legs, then settled down to be pampered.

"No." She shrugged, suddenly seeming more human. "Don't really know what to do with them. We always had dogs. Well, until *Amelia* barged in and pretended she was allergic, and we had to put Lady and

Sebby into kennels. We could have them home again now," she added, brightening as if it'd only just occurred to her. Then she coloured. "I suppose you think I'm heartless, but she really was an utter bloody bitch."

I took it she was talking about her stepmum, not Lady. "Uh, well, grief's a funny thing," I said noncommittally. "So what was it you wanted to talk to me about?"

"I want to know what you were looking for," she said, leaning forward. "Not at the fayre. In my bedroom. She told you I stole something, I bet she did. What was it?"

"Uh…" Thankfully Phil got back at that moment with the drinks, which gave me a moment to think.

See, I was pretty sure Dave Southgate wouldn't look too kindly on me spreading the gossip about a certain diamond necklace. Then again, whoever was investigating the murder must have been asking about it, mustn't they? First up, you'd show it to the next of kin—suitably cleaned up and all that. I hope. *Do you recognise this necklace?* That sort of thing.

It couldn't be a coincidence Vi had turned up here desperate for a chin-wag the day after I spoke to Dave.

"Jewellery," I said, looking at her carefully.

She coloured again. "It was that *bloody* necklace, wasn't it?"

Phil coughed. "Which necklace?"

Vi turned on him. "Oh, don't be such a dick. If you and he *really* don't have any secrets, which I seriously bloody well doubt, but anyway, then you know perfectly well which one. Pink diamond. Gold. Found on my stepmother's body. Ringing any bells yet?"

That was interesting. *On* the body, not *in* it. Was that just her being imprecise, or were the police keeping shtum about that little detail in the hopes someone would incriminate themselves? "Maybe," I answered, as she'd turned back to me.

Vi grabbed her phone out of the designer handbag, thumbed through some photos, and thrust it under my nose. "This one."

It was round the neck of a lady of, well, I'd guess exactly Vi's mum's age, judging by the family resemblance and the shared taste for silky tops, although the first Mrs. Majors clearly didn't agree that pastels were for pushovers. What surprised me the most was the way the necklace looked. Not exactly my area, bling isn't, but I'd been expecting something, I dunno, more elaborate? This was just one big—but not *that* big—pink stone, cut into a heart shape and surrounded by little white diamonds—probably, although for all I knew they could have been glass—hung on a delicate gold chain. It looked like the sort of thing little girls went for, all shiny and sparkly. It didn't look real, or valuable, or even that expensive.

Then again, if that stone in the middle *was* real, it ought to be worth a small country. Not surprising Amelia had wanted to get her hands on the thing. I pictured it hanging around her neck. Then I pictured it shoved down her delicate little throat and shuddered.

"Classy lady, your mum," I said, handing the phone to Phil so he could have a proper butcher's.

Vi looked a bit startled. "Yes. She was."

She said it with a quiet sincerity that convinced me that yeah, she'd grieved for her real mum, all right. Course, it wasn't necessarily *because* she was her real, as in birth, mum. Maybe if Amelia had married Alex a lot earlier and been the one to bring Vi up, she'd have grieved for her, blood relative or no?

Maybe I was just trying a bit too hard to see the parallels between Vi's situation and mine.

"How long ago did you lose her?" Phil asked, handing back the phone.

"Three years now." She stared down at her hands, which were turning the phone over and over in her lap. "Daddy met Amelia last summer. Everyone called it a whirlwind romance when they got engaged a month later and married on St. Valentine's Day this year. *I* call it her making sure she got her claws into him as quickly as she could."

"You think she married him for his money?" Phil's tone didn't judge.

"Isn't it obvious? She was far too young for him. Even if she wasn't a total *bitch*."

"Age-gap relationships can be a success," Phil suggested.

She shot him an incredulous look. "God, you're naive. Men are just so bloody *stupid* when they get older."

I coughed and leaned forward. "So why d'you s'pose she thought you'd taken that necklace?"

Vi reddened. "Well . . . it wasn't the first thing to go missing."

"You'd been, um, borrowing her jewellery for a while?" I asked, because it seemed a bit rude to just come out with *So, you made a habit of nicking her stuff?*

"Not exactly . . . Honestly? It started because I just wanted to piss her off. So I'd take one of a pair of earrings. Make her think she'd dropped the other one somewhere. Or one of those designer scarves she's so fond of. I used to use them for dusters when I was poking around in the attic. And it was *fun*, watching her go mad trying to find where things had got to. You don't know what it's been like since she got her cheap talons into Dad. It's been horrible, no fun at all. She's such a c—" Vi stopped, her round face all screwed up. "Oh, bollocks, now I'm sounding like I did do it, aren't I? But I *didn't*. Anyway, it was all petty stuff. I'd never have taken something as valuable as the necklace. Although even if I had, it wouldn't have been *theft*. It was Mummy's necklace, and it should have been mine. But I'd never *steal* it."

Phil coughed. "How valuable was the necklace?"

Vi shrugged. "Oh, I'm not sure. Daddy paid three hundred thousand pounds for it"—okay, so maybe not a small country, but definitely a small house in the country, as long as you didn't mind a bit of a fixer-upper—"but that was years ago. It should be worth a lot more now. The diamond market's gone up like crazy in the last few years, and this is a top-quality stone. Superb clarity." Whatever that meant. "It was vintage, from the year Mummy was born, and Daddy had it reset for her. I thought it was so romantic when he bought it for her." She bit her lip, showing the first signs of any softer emotions I'd ever seen from her.

"You must have been upset when he gave it to your stepmother," Phil rumbled, his tone neutral.

Vi looked up sharply, her eyes flashing. "I could have bloody ki— Shit." She hung her head for a moment.

"You could have killed him for it?" Phil suggested, which wasn't what I'd been thinking at all.

Vi shook her head with a touch of impatience. "Not *Daddy*. I don't blame Daddy at all. Amelia had this way of getting people to do whatever she wanted. Well, *men*," she added, with a look of disgust for the whole cock-led lot of us.

Yeah. Given the way Mrs. F.-M. had had my sister by the short and curlies—and bloody hell, that was *not* an image I wanted to have in my mind—I reckoned it wasn't quite as simple as Vi had made it sound. After all, she'd managed to get me to make a right tit of myself in front of hundreds of people, and blonde hair aside, she really hadn't been my type.

"But I didn't kill her for it, either," Vi went on, her tone steely. "It's just a figure of speech and you know it. Who are you, anyway, Tom's fiancé? Police? You sound like it."

Not a bad call. Well done, that girl.

"Private investigator," he told her steadily.

Her eyes widened. "Who are you working for?"

"No one, right now."

I happened to know that wasn't strictly true—Phil's business was ticking along nicely, ta very much—but he was probably right to assume she wouldn't give a toss about any unrelated cases.

"Are you any good?" Her chest rose and fell, and she went on without waiting for an answer. "I want to hire you."

"To find out who killed your stepmum?"

Vi coloured. "*No.* I want you to find Mummy's necklace."

Phil and I exchanged glances. "I thought you knew it'd been found, uh, with your stepmum?" I asked cautiously. I mean, she'd literally just mentioned it.

She shook her head impatiently. "Not that one. The *real* one. The one Amelia had when she died was fake."

"Well, that puts a bit of a different complexion on things, doesn't it?" I said to Phil after Vi had left.

He nodded, petting Merlin thoughtfully. "Widens the field a bit."

"You reckon? I mean, it's got to look better for Vi and her dad, hasn't it? Not that, you know, I had them down for killing her, but well, it made it look personal, didn't it? And they were the only ones who could leave a necklace that valuable, uh, where they left it and know they'd get it back in the end."

"Maybe, but just how pleased do you reckon Vi would have been to find out her stepmum had sold Mummy's necklace and replaced it with a fake? Or Mr. Majors, for that matter?"

"Uh, yeah. Guess so. So you reckon that's what happened? Amelia sold the real bling?"

"Did I say that? Vi seemed pretty well informed about the value of diamonds, didn't she? It could have happened that way, though. I think we might want to start by having a look into Amelia's finances."

"'We'?"

Phil smirked. "Meaning me. But if you want to help, you could start by pumping Greg for information on her relationship with his boss."

"Hope you mean the bishop. I reckon her relationship with the bloke upstairs is something only she knows about now." I frowned. "Hang about, though. Is that even relevant? To the necklace, I mean. Which, in case you've forgotten, is what Vi's paying you to find out about. Not, you know, the murder of her stepmum, which she couldn't give a toss about."

He stared me out. "Maybe Amelia sold the necklace and gave the money to the church?"

"Yeah, 'cos she seems just the self-sacrificing sort who'd do that. Have done that," I corrected myself.

"There's more motives than altruism." He huffed. "Maybe she wanted to butter him up for something. Maybe he was blackmailing her."

"Maybe you're just making up excuses for trying to find out who killed her, instead of just playing hunt-the-necklace?"

Phil took a deep breath and let it out slowly. His lips were still quirked in an almost-smile when he answered. "Maybe I don't appreciate people dumping dead bodies on my bloke."

"Oi, I'm all right. Haven't even had nightmares about this one." That was technically true, so I didn't feel the need to cross my fingers behind my back or any of that bollocks.

The girl in the nightmare hadn't been Amelia; she'd been the little girl I found when I was a nipper. Still strangled, mind.

"Anyhow . . . I can't see us solving one crime without the other. The way that necklace—the fake one—was left on her body, that's got to mean something. Murderers don't do something like that unless the victim's seriously pissed them off."

"Well, not unless they're a complete nutter," I agreed. "You think it was personal, then?"

"Maybe. Or maybe she was trying to use it to pay someone off, which is why the financial question. I can imagine some people getting pretty nasty if they've been promised a rock worth several hundred grand and fobbed off with a handful of paste."

"What, like the bishop, you mean? No, seriously, I can't see what he's got to do with all this."

Phil shrugged. "It's just a gut feeling. Come on, it's not going to kill you to ask a few questions. See if you can find out anything about the other people Vi mentioned while you're at it."

"What, Sir Prancelot and Uncle Artex?"

"*Lance* and Uncle *Arlo* would be two of 'em, yeah." Phil stuck up the requisite number of fingers at me as a visual aid. "Talk to Cherry too. She might know something."

I grinned. "Got it. Now, are we gonna talk about that lot all night? 'Cos I've got a few alternative ideas for what we could be doing instead."

CHAPTER ELEVEN

I rang Sis up at work next day. "Wanna meet for lunch?"

"Mm, can't. I've got a meeting. I know, why don't I come round to your house after I finish tonight?"

"Let me guess—Greg's busy tonight, and you fancy having someone else cook you dinner?"

"Oh, well, if you're offering. That's very kind of you, Tom. Fish would be nice. Although not shellfish because of my—"

"Allergies, yeah, I got it. And you'll have what you're given and like it." I was already planning a trip to the fish counter at the local supermarket. There was a recipe I'd been meaning to try for trout done Thai-style I reckoned would be right up Cherry's street.

"Fine. I probably won't leave the office until six, is that all right?"

"Yeah, no problem. Just let yourself in if I'm out when you get there, I'll only be down the local shops." After a bit of a dodgy experience a few months ago, I'd asked Sharon at number twelve to hand me back my spare key, which had given the old tact muscles a real workout. We were still speaking, so I hadn't done too badly, and I'd given the key to Cherry. Hopefully I could trust *her* not to let any murder suspects in to lie in wait for me while I was out.

Now, you might be wondering why, seeing as I wanted to talk to both Cherry and Greg, I didn't just arrange to see 'em both at the same time. The answer is that Sis, when she's just with me, and Cherry, when she's on her best behaviour for the uprightly reverend husband-to-be, are two very different animals.

I mean, I'm sure she'll let her hair down once they're married. It wasn't anything that made me worry for the relationship, which I reckoned was pretty solid. Just, I could see her not wanting him to hear her speaking ill of the dead. And I had a feeling getting anything useful out of Cherry was going to involve quite a lot of speaking ill of dear old Amelia.

As it happened, a job went quicker than expected, and I was already back from the shops and in the kitchen when Cherry got in.

"Do I smell food? I'm *starving*," she greeted me with, padding into the kitchen in stockinged feet. I guessed she'd been wearing heels for the lunchtime meeting.

"Yeah, won't be long now. You want to put the rice on while you're here?"

Cherry backpedalled so fast I half expected to see skid marks on the kitchen tiles. "Oh, I don't want to get in your way. I just came in to give you this." She plonked a bottle of red on the kitchen counter. "I know we're having fish, but I thought we could drink it after the meal."

"Sis, I'm touched you think I give a monkey's what colour wine I drink with what. But yeah, after the meal is fine. I'll put it in the fridge, yeah?" I added just to wind her up.

Cherry glared. I grinned and bunged the rice on to cook myself.

The Thai trout went down a treat. Mildly spiced and delicately flavoured, it would, actually, have been a crime to drink red wine with it.

All right, so maybe I did care a little bit.

Cherry scarfed the food down like it was the best meal she'd had all week. I guessed she must have been cooking for herself again.

After we'd eaten, I opened the wine and poured a couple of glasses. Cherry took a long, deep swallow. Looked like she might be settling in for the night, so it was just as well I hadn't yet got round to filling up the spare room with junk again.

"Right, down to business," I said, putting my feet up on the coffee table. Cherry's tsk was so automatic I don't reckon she even realised she was doing it. "Tell me everything you know about Amelia Fenchurch-Majors. Apart from *She's dead*, 'cos I noticed that one already, ta."

Sis curled her legs up neatly on the sofa. "Where do you want me to start?"

"I dunno . . . Uh, what did she do for a living? Did she work? Or did she live off old Alex?"

"Well, she was one of these women who *say* they have a business but seem to have an awful lot of free time nevertheless." Not that Sis was bitter or anything. "She was an events planner, *apparently*, although if you ask me, she was more interested in interior design. She had plans to completely modernise their place in St. Leonards—had already started, actually. That driveway is all new since she came on the scene."

"What? No way. That farmhouse of theirs is listed, innit?" I was honestly a bit horrified. No wonder she hadn't been bothered about stomping all over those old wooden floors in her stilettos—by the sound of it, she'd been planning to rip 'em out anyway. "They've got rules and regs about that sort of thing. I had a job once on one of those old almshouses in St. Albans, the ones near St. Peter's Church, and you wouldn't believe the hoops they had to jump through just to get an extra loo put in."

Cherry gave a tight little smile. "Lance plays golf with the head of the planning committee. She'd have had *no* trouble."

"Yeah, who is this Lance bloke, anyway?"

"Amelia's *business partner*. Apparently." You could cut the sarcasm with a knife.

"You reckon he was a sleeping partner?"

Sis looked torn, but eventually admitted, "I don't *know* she was having an affair with him. And I only met him the once. But I wouldn't be surprised. Although goodness knows why she'd *want* to," she said with a hint of a shudder.

"Bit of a minger, is he?"

"No-o . . . There's just something *about* him. You'd have to see him yourself. And I could be wrong," she added virtuously. "Gregory found him fascinating."

"Your Greg finds roadkill fascinating. Did he reckon Lance'd look great mounted on the wall next to Mrs. Tiggywinkle?" Mrs. T. was, or rather had been, a hedgehog, personally taxidermied by the scarily reverend Greg.

"Don't mock. At least Gregory *has* an artistic hobby. When was the last time you did anything creative?"

I gave her a look. "Not half an hour ago, as it happens, and you practically licked the plate clean. So don't give me that, or you'll be cooking your own tea next time."

Give her her due, Cherry blushed. "Um. Sorry. I forgot. But please don't make fun of Gregory's choice of relaxation."

I frowned. "Why? Someone else been having a dig?"

"Oh . . . It was only Amelia, and only the once that I heard. But she said it to the *bishop*." Sis seemed upset, as well she might.

"Yeah, that was a bit out of order. Still, look on the bright side. She won't be doing that again."

Cherry snorted. "You're horrible." She took another sip of wine and visibly tried to straighten out her face.

"So what else can you tell me about Lance? What's his surname?" I sniggered as a thought hit. "God, I hope it's not Boyle."

"Don't be ridiculous. It's Frith."

I frowned. "That sounds familiar, somehow."

Cherry beamed. "You're thinking of the Scottish divination system, aren't you? It's quite fascinating to compare it with what *you* do, although it was much more ritualistic, of course." She paused. "You know, you really ought to experiment. Try taking your shoes off next time you use your thing."

"Uh . . . What? And seriously, *what*? Sis, for me to be thinking of your Scottish wotsit, I'd have to have *heard* of it at some point in my life, yeah? And what the hell have my shoes got to do with anything?"

"You know, *most* people would do some reading around their subject," Cherry said severely.

I'd never quite got around to telling her about the whole dowsing club fiasco. Partly 'cos she'd already left home when it happened and we hadn't been on all that good terms anyhow. But mostly 'cos it wasn't an experience I fancied reliving anytime soon.

"Oi, I read around it on Saturday. Much bloody good it did me." Reading. That sparked a thought . . . "Got it—Frith was the name of the bunnies' god in *Watership Down*, wasn't it? I remember you reading me that when I was little. You got your knickers in a twist 'cos I laughed at that bit where the rabbit tells Frith to bless his bottom."

"Well, trust you to reduce the favourite book of my childhood to its lowest common denominator."

"Anytime, Sis. Anytime." Funny, though. I'd had no idea I remembered that. God knows how old I'd been, although I reckoned it'd been before we'd moved out of London, so I couldn't have been more than eight. "I liked that book," I said, as it started coming back to me. "Fiver, the little one, he was the most important, wasn't he? Had all these weird visions and stuff that saved all their lives."

"I can't *imagine* why he was your favourite," Cherry said drily. "Although, come to think of it, I'd have thought you'd like Bigwig too."

I grinned. "Any similarities between my fiancé and a hulking big bruiser of a bunny rabbit are . . . probably best left unmentioned when he's around."

"Probably best left unmentioned when *I'm* around too." Cherry refilled our glasses.

When Phil got in around eleven, he found us both half-asleep in front of the telly, Cherry wearing an old pair of my pyjamas that looked almost as bad on her as they did on me. Although I s'pose Greg, if he'd been here, might have begged to differ. The wine bottle, needless to say, was empty.

Cherry twisted round in her seat to beam up at him. "Oh, hello, Phil. You missed a lovely meal."

"Save me any leftovers?" he asked, looking amused.

"Nah, sorry." If he'd wanted feeding, he should have said he was coming over. Not that I wasn't glad to see him. "Fish stir-fry thing. Wouldn't have kept. There's bacon and eggs in the fridge, though, if you're hungry." I shifted my legs.

"Don't get up. I'll just grab a sandwich." He disappeared, presumably to the kitchen. Unless he had some secret sandwich stash elsewhere in the house I was unaware of, which was pretty bloody unlikely on several different levels.

Cherry unwound her legs, stood up, and stretched. "I should head to bed."

"Big day tomorrow?"

She shrugged. "Just a day. Still, at least I won't have to get up so early, staying here," she added, brightening.

"Oi, no getting any ideas about moving in." It'd be the kiss of death for my sex life. "And don't forget to take your stuff out the machine." We'd bunged her work shirt in for a quick wash, together with any other bits and bobs she'd wanted to add—I'd carefully not paid too much attention.

Sis nodded and padded off. I heard her saying good night to Phil, then he appeared with a couple of beers in one hand and a plateful of cheese sarnies in the other, and plonked himself down next to me on the sofa.

I grabbed a sarnie. Well, it was only polite to keep him company, wasn't it?

"Cheers," I said, and took a bite.

Phil gave me a look that was darkly amused. "One of these days I'll add Tabasco sauce to the top one. That'll stop you."

"Nah, you love me too much." I was fairly certain he'd made extra on purpose anyway. He knew me pretty well by now. "So go on, what've you found out about dear departed Amelia?"

"Amelia Fenchurch-Majors was in business as a freelance events organiser, in partnership with Lance Frith."

"Yeah, Cherry was telling me about him. You met him?"

"Not yet. Got an appointment tomorrow." Phil hesitated. "He wants to meet you."

"Me? Why?"

"You found her, didn't you?"

"Yeah, but so what? God, I hope he doesn't want me to tell him about it." I felt a bit queasy and took a sip of beer to settle my stomach.

"Not sure. We only spoke briefly on the phone. Frith's been across country, sorting out some do at a castle in the Cotswolds."

"Huh. That's not much of an alibi. That's only a couple of hours from here. Maybe a bit longer, with summer weekend traffic, but not much."

"Agreed. What did your sister tell you about him?"

"Not a lot. Well, nothing concrete, anyhow. She reckoned him and Amelia might have been doing the dirty, and she thought there was something off about him, but she couldn't say what. Oh, and he plays golf with the head of the local planning committee, in case that turns out to be vitally relevant to solving the case."

"Christ knows, at this stage. So are you up for it? I'm seeing him for lunch tomorrow in the White Hart, at one. I told him you might have to work."

I thought about it. "Nah, I can make it. Might not have time to get home for a change of clothes, mind, but don't worry—the morning job's a dishwasher, not drains. Surprised he's okay with coming out our way, though, if he's based in St. Leonards. You'd think he'd want you to go to him."

Phil shrugged. "Maybe he's checking the place out for a function? At any rate, it was his suggestion." He huffed. "Maybe he's just the obliging sort."

"Okay, I'm trusting this bloke less and less the more I hear about him."

"He did sound pretty keen to meet you." Phil smirked. "That's suspect in itself."

"Git. So what else can you tell me about him?"

"Think I'll let you form your own impressions. Wouldn't want to bias you in advance." Phil demolished a second round of cheese sarnies in about three bites. I thought about nicking another but decided I wasn't peckish enough to bother. Which was just as well, really, as by the time I'd done debating about it, the rest had disappeared too.

I grinned. "Going for the record, were we? Never mind. I like a man with a healthy appetite."

Phil raised an eyebrow while chugging back his beer. I was duly impressed by his coordination. "Appetite for what?" he asked, putting the bottle down.

"Something a bit tastier than a cheese sarnie?" I suggested. Suggestively.

"Oh yeah? What's that, then?"

"Well, there's choccy biccies in the cupboard, if you fancy some," I teased him.

He gave me a look. "Serve you bloody right if I went for it. C'mere."

Things progressed nicely after that. Phil had my T-shirt off in under three seconds—there was one record he was definitely in the running for—and I wasn't doing too badly with his clothes either, despite the fact he'd cheated by wearing a shirt with buttons.

In fact, I won the race to get the other bloke's trousers undone, and celebrated by shoving my hand in Phil's kecks and wrapping it around his nice, hard prick.

He groaned. "Fuck me."

"Planning to," I panted, my own stiffie twitching as he grabbed my arse.

Which, of course, was the exact moment Cherry walked in.

"Tom, did you want a hot choc— Oh." She went as pink as her namesake. "Sorry. I couldn't sleep and— Sorry. I didn't realise you were staying over, Phil."

We scrambled apart like a couple of naughty schoolkids, holding our flies together and hoping nothing would fall out.

At least, that was what I was hoping. And I reckoned I knew Phil well enough by now to speak for him too. In certain circumstances, anyhow.

"Sorry, Sis," I started. "Didn't mean to give you an eyeful. We'll just—"

"Oh no, please. I'll just make my drink and take it upstairs." She gave us a soppy smile. "I really should get used to this, shouldn't I? After all, you'll be living together soon. Actually, Phil, I meant to ask you about that. There's a new barrister at my chambers who's looking for a flat—are you planning to rent yours out? I don't think she wants to buy, but if it's available to rent soon, she'd be very keen. Do you have a date in mind yet?"

Phil looked at me.

I looked back, a bit guiltily. "Uh, we haven't really talked about that yet, Sis."

"Oh." Cherry looked at us both, obviously confused. "I thought— Oh, well, never mind. I'll just leave you to, um . . . Good night."

She scarpered. Phil turned back to me, face still flushed and his hair all mussed up. He looked fucking gorgeous, and just a tiny bit uncertain. "Maybe we should—"

"I know just what we oughtta do," I told him, and shoved my hand back down the front of his kecks.

There was the sound of rapidly retreating footsteps, running upstairs.

Never let it be said my sis doesn't know what's good for her.

CHAPTER TWELVE

I got to the White Hart just after one the next day, to find Phil and our mutual dinner date were already in there propping up the bar with a couple of drinks. Phil was on the sparkling mineral water, so the whiff of gin as I approached them had to have come from Lance's glass.

Lance Frith was . . . Well. I could see what Cherry had meant when she'd questioned why Amelia would want to sleep with the bloke. He wasn't *bad* looking, mind. But he was just a bit . . . alien. He was a skinny bloke, and he'd dressed all in black, which could have been 'cos he was in mourning, but I was betting it was just his normal clothes. He was that sort of bloke. The look was completed with a bushy dark beard—very trendy—and big eighties-style goggly sunglasses—very not, especially indoors. His high forehead was creepily pale against all the darkness, and his full red lips the only spot of colour.

Round his neck, he was wearing a crystal divining pendulum. Was he taking the piss?

"Sorry I'm a bit late," I said, joining them. "Traffic." Actually it'd been the customer, who'd been a total git about the bill, but there was no need to go into all that.

"Not to worry," Phil said. "Lance, this is Tom."

Huh. So we were all on first-name terms already, were we?

Lance gave me a dreamy smile. "Tom. Poor Amelia told me all about you. I feel we have a connection already."

"Uh, it's great to meet you," I lied, taking his outstretched hand. It was limp, and I couldn't wait to drop it again. "Good of you to come so far out of your way."

"Please. It's hardly the other side of the country. I'm used to travelling for my work in any case."

"Shall we?" Phil gestured to the restaurant bit of the place.

We wandered over and hovered at the door until a waitress appeared with a handful of menus. It was the one who'd been on the bar the other night, so I gave her a friendly smile, and she dimpled back at me before leading us over to a table at the far end of the room.

Funny how you never think of German people having dimples. Swiss, yeah, or Austrian, but not German. What's that all about?

I took a seat near the wall, and Lance squeezed in next to me. Phil sat opposite.

"You're an events organiser, right? Think you might put something on in this place?" I waved my hand at the dark wood-panelled walls surrounding us. The last time I'd been in the restaurant here had been for Gary and Darren's wedding reception, now I came to think of it. That'd been an event and a half.

Lance's smile twisted. "I did have it in mind for a ghost-themed evening. I'm not sure I have the heart now. Tell me, are you sensitive to such things?"

"Uh . . . You mean, um, spirits? No. Sorry." Even as I said it, I realised I wasn't quite certain myself. See, me and Dave had sort of made the White Hart our regular meeting place, and I'd pretty much got used to how it felt here, but, well, there was definitely something I was picking up on. If I stopped ignoring it.

Hairs prickled on the back of my neck and my face must have grassed me up, as Lance leaned closer, his gaze intent through the smoky tan of his sunglasses. I had to fight the impulse to draw back, away from him. "But you do sense something here, yes? Tell me. How does it feel?"

"Dunno, really. Just . . . vibes." To say I wasn't comfortable with this was the understatement of the millennium. Weren't we supposed to be interrogating him, not the other way around?

Lance nodded, like he'd heard what I'd thought, which in no way made me feel any better. "You find hidden things, yes? And this is an old building. Fifteenth century, I believe. Are you aware of the wealth of superstition attaching to erections of this era?"

"Uh . . ." Not so much, no. And I was really wishing he'd get out of my face while using the word *erection*.

"All sorts of things have been found hidden inside the walls of medieval structures. Shoes, they're very common. Dead cats too."

Actually, that one sort of rang a bell. Not that I'd ever found any mummified cats in the course of my working day, thank God. Had to shift a couple of live ones off cisterns and out of airing cupboards before I could get to work, mind.

"Used garments," Lance continued. "And witch bottles."

I frowned, confused. "Which bottles?"

He nodded, which wasn't exactly helpful. "Typically, they contain samples of urine, and a pierced heart of some kind."

Lovely.

"Are you ready to order?" the waitress interrupted, the German accent subtly making it sound like we'd better be.

"Five minutes," Phil said firmly.

I was thinking it might be a fair bit longer than that before I got my appetite back, but I dutifully glanced at the menu and picked out the first thing that looked vaguely all right.

Lance was still ignoring his. "Did you know the Nether Wallop Cache was found to contain literally dozens of garments or garment fragments hidden inside the framework of the building, including hats, shoes, and underwear? So what does that tell you?"

I blinked. "Someone *really* didn't fancy doing their laundry?"

His face cracked into a beaming smile, which suddenly made him look a lot more human. "Quite possibly. But the usual interpretation is that they were there to protect the house from malign influences both natural and supernatural."

Okay, I was interested despite myself. "How's that work? I mean, dead cats, yeah, I can sort of see that one, 'cos of mice and witches and stuff. But somebody's old kecks? Were they hoping the smell would chase evil spirits away?"

"Nobody's quite sure. Shoes, now, it's well known you can trap the devil in them."

You could? How? Shove your feet straight in after? Wouldn't he jab your toes with his pointy stick?

Phil coughed. "Think the waitress is on the way back—you ready?"

Lance flashed me a conspiratorial smile and bent his head to his menu.

I tried to give Phil a look, but he was staring out into the middle of the room and didn't meet my eye.

We ordered—steak for Phil, risotto for me, and grilled fish for Lance, together with a bottle of pinot grigio. Not that I was planning on having more than the odd sip, and I didn't reckon Phil was either.

Phil waited until we all had a glass until he brought up the subject we were here for. "Can you tell us a little about your relationship with Mrs. Fenchurch-Majors?"

And there was a loaded question if ever I heard one.

Lance smiled, a wistful edge to it this time. "We met at university. We both studied history of art."

Really? Amelia, with her insatiable urge to modernise? The lecturers must have been terrible.

"We became firm friends, of course. And when we left, it seemed natural to go into business together."

"You were more than friends, though, weren't you?" Phil pressed. I gave him a sharp look. This was all news to me. "In fact, you were married, weren't you?"

Whoa. Okay, that put a whole new complexion on things. I couldn't help thinking of Dave's professional judgement that it was usually the spouse what done it.

Lance stared into his glass, twisting it between his fingers, a strange smile on his lips. "Oh, I wouldn't read too much into that. We were very young."

"Must have been hard carrying on working together after the split."

"Not at all. It was entirely amicable."

"And when she got married again?"

"I was very happy for her. Amelia deserved happiness."

Phil nodded, and there was a short break as the food arrived, which was probably just as well as (a) Lance was starting to look a bit narked about all the grilling and (b) it gave me a chance to get my thoughts in order.

It wasn't easy. I just couldn't imagine carrying on working with an ex as if nothing had happened. I mean, yeah, sure, keep your business and your personal life separate, but come on, people are human, aren't they? Not quad-core bloody CPUs with integrated graphics and Pentel umptium processors (Phil had been on at me to get a new laptop again, in case you're wondering). You're not going to stop feeling . . . whatever you feel about your ex, just 'cos it's 9 a.m. and time to start work, are you? Then again, I s'pose it's just like couples with kids, right? You keep the split amicable for the sake of the children?

'Cept, in that case, you'd only see the ex every once in a while, wouldn't you? Not all day every working day. I s'pose Lance and Amelia might've worked on different projects, but even so . . . And what the hell had Alex thought about it? Put it this way, if the Mysterious Cheating Mark had still been in the land of the living, I wouldn't have been too chuffed about Phil spending forty hours a week with him. Not that I don't trust Phil. Course I do. But feelings can be tricky little bastards.

"Does Alex know you and Amelia were a thing?" I blurted out. Then I shoved a load of risotto in my mouth in a classic case of shutting the stable door after Shergar's already made the one-way trip to the knackers' yard.

Lance paused, a restrained forkful of fish halfway to his mouth. There were two peas balanced on top. I was mesmerised, waiting for them to fall. "It was hardly a secret."

"No?" Phil put in. "I had to dig pretty hard to find out, myself. She never changed her name or went by *Mrs*. Did she wear a ring?"

A shrug. *Still* the bloody peas didn't fall. Had he glued them on with tartar sauce? "Occasionally. I didn't keep track. And why should she change her name? A rather medieval attitude, don't you think? Women are no longer *property*." The food made it to his mouth, intact, and I could breathe again.

I had another forkful of risotto. It was pretty good, but the rice was just a tiny bit undercooked. It's easy to do with risotto. Comes of being too worried it'll end up gluey.

"Some people like to change their name as a sign of love and commitment," Phil suggested.

"And some don't." Lance sounded a bit snippy. Defensive? "I don't even know why we're talking about something that was all over years ago." He put down his fork and took a large swallow of wine, which seemed like a good idea to me, so I picked up my glass to follow suit.

Phil waited until Lance had set his glass down again. "'Years'? That's interesting. According to my information, your divorce wasn't finalised until January this year. Only three weeks before she remarried, in fact."

CHAPTER THIRTEEN

I just about managed not to choke on my mouthful of wine. This was turning into an episode of *EastEnders*. Well, not exactly, seeing as no one had called anyone else a slag yet, but hey, we were only on the first course here. Plenty of time yet.

Lance gave Phil a frosty stare and fingered his pendulum. "That was merely a formality." He leaned over the table. Phil's turn to get a face full of Frith. "Tell me, have *you* ever been married?"

Yeah, no. Bringing up Phil's cheating bastard of an ex was well out of order. I put my fork down with a clatter. "I don't see what that's got to do with anything."

Lance turned my way, an eyebrow raised. "Interesting. No, my point is merely that anyone who's been married would know that a legal document has no effect at all on the feelings of those supposedly bound by it." He smiled, the git. "Amelia and I simply had better things to do than to place a high priority on the formal dissolution of something we already knew was over."

I glanced over at Phil. He looked away, his jaw tight. Christ knew what that was about.

"Obviously," Lance went on, "once Amelia became involved with Alexander, I was only too happy to expedite matters for her." He delicately lifted the skeleton from his fish and placed it to one side on his plate.

"Can you think of anyone who'd want to murder Mrs. Fenchurch-Majors?" Phil asked, a bit brutally, I thought.

Lance looked up from his plate, his eyes behind those daft sunglasses looking a bit moist, from what I could tell. "Of course not. Everybody *loved* Amelia."

This time, I did choke on my wine. "Sorry," I muttered when they both turned to glare at me. I pushed the glass over to the side of the table and decided to stick to water from now on.

"Disappointed suitor, then?" Phil suggested.

"I can't imagine who that might have been," Lance said dismissively. "Amelia had eyes only for Alexander. No, I don't suppose they'll ever find out who did such a terrible thing. It must have been someone who was mentally ill. She was simply in the wrong place at the wrong time."

That was interesting. It sounded like he didn't know about the necklace, then. Or maybe he just wanted us to think that? Okay, this was officially doing my head in.

Phil must have been thinking along the same lines. About the necklace, I mean. Not about it doing his head in. "Did Mrs. Fenchurch-Majors ever mention a diamond necklace to you?"

Lance frowned and fingered that bloody pendulum again. "Not that I recall. If you want to talk about jewellery, it's Arlo Fenchurch you need to see."

Phil nodded, like that wasn't news to him. "How did Mrs. Fenchurch-Majors get on with her stepdaughter?"

I was expecting another bland *Oh, she loved her, of course*, so was surprised when Lance gave a wry little smile. "I'm afraid she found her rather juvenile. So sad, a young woman of her age still acting like a spoiled child. A wasted life, by all accounts."

"I dunno," I found myself saying. "She seems to enjoy herself."

"But she contributes nothing to society. Amelia, now, she was a giver." Lance gave a sad little sigh and put his knife and fork together on his plate. "Tell me, was it very terrible, when you found her?"

Jesus, what did he expect me to say?

Not the truth. God, never the truth, when I'm asked this question by someone who loved the victim.

Course, it was equally possible he'd hated her.

I cleared my throat. "She was, well, I don't think she could have suffered much. I mean, it must have been quick." Sod it. I was having more wine.

Again, there was that rueful smile. "I'm sorry. You must have been asked that question so many times before."

"Uh . . ." Okay, yeah, it was sort of what I'd been thinking—but seriously, how many bodies did he reckon I'd found? "More times than I'd like, yeah."

"And of course it was terrible. Death is terrible." He took a deep breath, while I was still reeling from somebody actually *getting* it. Someone who wasn't Phil, at any rate. "And you must feel responsible, of course, because without you, she would never have been in that tent."

That . . . that hurt. Like a steak knife to the stomach. All the more so because I'd thought he was on my side. Which was stupid, and selfish, because at the end of the day, it had sod all to do with me, but . . . I'd been trying to ignore that queasy little feeling in my gut, all the worse because, frankly, I hadn't been able to stand the woman. "I . . . Yeah, I . . ." Shit. What the hell was I supposed to say? "Sorry."

Phil shoved his plate away, steak only two-thirds chomped. "If you've heard that much, then you know Tom had no idea where she was going. That was the whole bloody point."

Lance ignored him. He leaned in again with a look of concern on his face, so either my apology had been accepted or he hadn't actually blamed me in the first place.

Or he was just messing with my head, which I guessed was equally likely.

"I hope you haven't had trouble convincing the police? There can be a regrettable level of scepticism from officialdom, I've found, when it comes to dealing with anything out of the ordinary."

"No." I cleared my throat. "No, they, um, know about me and, you know, finding things."

"Really? And have you worked with them before?"

"Uh . . ." I glanced over at Phil, but he was no help whatever, the git. "Yeah, but I don't think I'm s'posed to talk about it."

"And if you did, you'd have to kill me?" Lance actually smiled. "Don't worry, I'm used to having to keep secrets. And not just what you'd think—surprise parties and the like. You'd be amazed how many people feel their events should be treated as if they're a matter of national security. But tell me, do they really *believe*?"

"Uh . . . Most of 'em, no. But I've got a mate on the force, and he knows I'm not faking it."

"That's marvellous. We need more people who are ready to be open-minded about these things." Lance nodded to himself. "And have you experimented with crystals?"

"You mean like that thing you've got round your neck?" I gestured at his pendulum-slash-pendant thing. It was a simple conical design in some dark stone, almost lost against his black shirt. Cherry had got me one for my last birthday, which was how I knew what it was, but the one she'd got me had been rainbow-coloured. According to the leaflet that came with it, each coloured stone represented one of the chakras. Seeing as it hadn't bothered to explain what the chakras actually were or why you'd give a toss about them being represented, I hadn't been all that impressed. "You had any luck with that?"

"I've had some success, yes. But—"

"Wanna show us how it's done?" I said quickly. I wanted to keep the conversation focussed on him, not me.

He gave a weird little smile. "Oh, I wouldn't presume."

The waitress came back at that point, which I was glad of because I was well confused by this conversation. "You have finished? You would like to see the dessert menu?"

That risotto had been pretty filling, actually. Either that, or I wasn't that hungry today. I snuck a glance at my watch to see how much time I had to play with, and realised it'd run out a while back. "Shit. Sorry. No, not for me, ta."

I looked at the other two. Nope, no takers there either. "Just a coffee," Phil said, and Lance asked for a herbal tea. "Tom?"

"No, actually I'm gonna have to go. Customer over in Harpenden—she gets a bit snippy if I'm late. Sorry," I lied through my teeth. Well, about being sorry. Not about the customer. You'd think she was the bloody Queen Mother, the way she treats tradesmen and other oiks, but at least she always paid prompt and was good for putting in a word for me with the neighbours. I'd got next door's bathroom refit and a couple of other jobs as well on her say-so, so keeping her sweet was definitely on my to-do list.

Lance stood up when I did. "Such a shame you have to rush off. It's been enlightening, meeting you." He held out his hand. I took it, expecting another limp grip, but he surprised me with a firm squeeze.

Then he didn't let go. "Before you go, let me give you my card. Perhaps we could speak again sometime about our common interest."

I hoped to God he meant divination, not Amelia Fenchurch-Majors.

Actually that was a lie. I didn't want to talk dowsing with him either. Mostly because I reckoned he knew far more about it than I did.

Still holding my hand, he reached into a pocket and pulled out an expensive-looking card case. The card he handed me looked pricey too, with his name embossed on the front.

"Cheers, mate," I said, just grateful he'd finally let go of me. I had a couple of my own cards in my back pocket, so I handed him one of those to be polite. It was slightly curved from where I'd been sitting on it and a bit dog-eared around the corners. It was probably time I ordered a new batch, to be honest, but I'd been waiting for the printers to have a sale.

Lance took it and placed it carefully in his wallet.

"See you later, Phil," I said with a nod, and legged it.

Mrs. T. in Harpenden was in a good mood that afternoon. I got two cups of tea and a slice of homemade fruitcake. It was pretty good, and I ended up asking for the recipe from her. She went pink and handwrote it for me, then wrapped up the rest of the cake for me to take home. Mr. T. doddered in from the garden, looking hopeful, to be told sharply there were Rich Tea biscuits in the tin if he *had* to spoil his dinner.

He doddered out again a couple of minutes later, looking sad. I tried not to feel too guilty.

CHAPTER FOURTEEN

We'd already arranged that Phil would come over for tea that evening, which seeing as he'd had a steak for lunch, I didn't feel bad about making just beans on toast.

Okay, I *tried* not to feel bad. Then I bunged some bacon under the grill when I heard him coming in the door. Well, I wouldn't want all those lovely muscles to waste away for lack of protein, would I? Pure self-interest, that's what it was. Honest.

"How'd it go after I left?" I asked, shoving some bread in the toaster as his size elevens clomped into the kitchen behind me. "Hey, did you ask Lance if he did murder-mystery parties? Gary went to one of those, and he said it was a right laugh, but I'm guessing poor old Lance wouldn't find it quite so funny these days." He wouldn't be the only one.

Phil just grunted.

"So go on, how'd it go? Get anything more out of him?"

"No."

It wasn't so much what he said but the way he said it that made me turn round to look at him. "What's crawled up your arse?"

He gave me a stony glare. "Next time we're with a murder suspect, you want to lay off getting all defensive on my behalf if he brings up something personal? Because one, I can take care of myself, and two, if he hadn't already known he'd hit a nerve, he certainly bloody well did after you jumped in on your high horse."

"Well, 'scuse me for trying to help."

"I don't need your help," he snapped, then sighed and rubbed the back of his neck. "Shit. Sorry. Just . . . I can deal with it, okay? You getting all uptight about stuff just makes it harder."

"Oi, I wasn't getting uptight."

"Yeah, right. Just like you're not now."

I gave the beans a vicious stir and slopped sauce all over the stove top. Bloody marvellous. "Just so we're clear, you wanna end up eating this or wearing it?"

"Jesus, I wish I'd stayed at home and ordered a bloody takeaway."

That was . . . I mean, Christ, I'd been joking. Mostly. I put the spoon down and turned to stare at him. "What the actual fuck? No, seriously, what?"

"Do we have to do this now?"

"Do *what*?"

Phil huffed and carried on glaring. "Talk about that smarmy git, all right? Does he *have* to be the first fucking thing you mention when I walk in the door?"

I stared at him, frowning in disbelief. "What? Are you *jealous*? Christ, you are, aren't you? I don't believe it. Okay, he maybe held my hand a bit on the long side when he said goodbye, but seriously, you'd think I'd been fondling his bollocks under the table or something."

"You didn't have to sit there for another half an hour while he went on about how bloody *fascinating* your talents are, and how much he'd like to spend some more time with you. Exploring your *common interest*." I swear he growled after he said that.

"No. You're right. *I wasn't fucking there.* So why the hell are you blaming me? I mean, Christ, I didn't like him much either, so why is it somehow *my* fault he got up your nose?"

Phil sort of deflated. "You didn't like him?"

"Seriously? That is an actual, serious question?"

"You seemed pretty bloody chummy at lunch."

"I thought you'd *appreciate* me putting the bloke at his ease. Make it easier for you to get him to talk."

"Oh, he talked all right. Wasn't about the bloody case, though, was it?" Phil turned away. "I've been trying for months to get you to experiment. Do something with your dowsing—find out how it works and how you can use it best. Then he turns up and you're all 'Wanna show me your crystal?'"

"That was to get him off my back! And I tried stuff with you, all right? It didn't work."

He met my gaze. "Because you didn't take it seriously."

"Yeah, well, you ever thought I might feel like a right prat, trying to channel some mystical sodding energies I know you don't believe in and I'm not sure I do either?"

Phil frowned. "How can you not believe in it? You know you're not faking it when you find stuff."

"Yeah, but . . . I just do it, don't I? I don't, I dunno, light a bloody candle and chant stuff with my shoes off."

"What have your shoes got to do with it?"

"I dunno, do I? Just something Cherry said. About Frith. The . . . thing. Not the bloke. It's some Scottish divination thing, which I reckon is why old Lance was so into it all. *Not* 'cos he's after a bit of rough with yours truly."

"What, he can't multitask?"

I glared at him.

"Joking, okay?" Phil ran a hand through his hair. "Look, I—"

He broke off and gave a quick, suspicious sniff. "Is something burning?"

I turned. Shit. There was a definite whiff of carbonising bacon in the air, and the smoke alarm started to screech. I switched off the grill quick and yanked the pan out to check the damage. The godawful noise stopped, and Phil came to look over my shoulder.

"Hope you like it crispy," I said with a shrug.

Phil reached around me to grab one of the least-burnt bits of bacon, hissing in a breath as he singed his fingers. "Still edible," he commented after taking a bite. "If you don't mind charcoal."

I salvaged another slice, breaking off the blackest parts and leaving them in the grill pan. "Could be worse," I agreed, my mouth full. I opened the window with my nongreasy hand. That bloody alarm would go off again if we didn't get the smoke out. Then I remembered the beans, and lifted the lid fatalistically. Yep, nice bit of orange sludge there. I'd need to clean that pan with a hammer and chisel. "Fancy that takeaway after all?" I suggested, too bloody knackered to start all over again.

Maybe it showed in my voice. Phil opened the fridge and crouched down to have a proper butcher's inside. "Got soup in the cupboard?"

"Yeah. Tomato or cream of chicken. And a couple of odd cans that were on offer."

"Tomato, then." He stood up, clutching a slab of cheddar and a bottle of beer, which he handed to me. "Yours. Go put your feet up. Even I can manage to heat up soup and do a bit of cheese on toast."

I opened the beer and took a swig. Jesus, I'd needed that. About to head into the living room, I paused. "Look, you've obviously had a crappy day. Wanna tell me about it?" I kept my tone mild.

Phil was silent a long time. Then he took a deep breath and let it out slowly. "Later, okay? Let's get you fed first."

"Worried I'll start biting your leg if you don't?" That was Merlin's latest trick, anytime he reckoned dinner wasn't coming quick enough. Speaking of which . . . "Oi, where've the cats got to?"

They'd been in the kitchen when I'd started cooking, drawn by the siren tones of the fridge door opening, but were now nowhere to be seen. I ambled into the living room and found Merlin pacing nervously on the windowsill while Arthur sat on the sofa, only the kneading of his paws on the cushions betraying he wasn't quite as laid-back about things as he was trying to pretend. I sat down to pet him. "Sorry. Mum and Dad having a domestic." Obviously, I saw myself as Dad in that little scenario.

Shut up.

I could tell Arthur had forgiven me already. He only clawed me lightly when I pulled him onto my lap. Might as well give him a bit of attention while I waited for my dinner.

The soup turned up with that gritty texture that means it's been overheated, and the toast corners were burnt. It was the best meal I'd had in ages.

I didn't tell Phil that. He'd only have thought I was taking the piss.

Arthur had stalked off, his dignity wounded by me trying to use him to rest my plate on. Merlin gave Phil's legs a quick sniff and a cheek rub, then carried on stalking twitchily while we ate in near-silence.

"Gonna tell me about it now?" I asked gently, when we'd finished.

We were sitting on the sofa, the telly with the volume down low, showing a darts match neither of us gave a toss about.

Pun not intended.

There was a long pause, then Phil huffed and spoke. "It was how it started with Mark, all right? He had a load of hobbies. Interests.

I wasn't working regular hours, so he'd find other people to spend time with. People he had stuff in common with, besides just watching the telly and all that. After a while, he just . . . stopped loving me. I wasn't enough for him. Not anymore. So these blokes he took to the art galleries and stuff . . ." Phil shrugged. "He started screwing them as well."

Jesus, what a bastard. "And he left you for one of the blokes he hooked up with?"

Phil shook his head. "No." He gave a bitter half laugh. "I left him, in the end. We had this row . . . Would you believe it, he couldn't even see what the problem was? Kept asking why I was getting so mad about him screwing other men when I'd never been that into him anyway."

"Well . . . had you? Been that into him?"

"I fucking loved him." Phil looked up at me, then, his eyes raw with emotion.

Something inside me snapped painfully at that. I told it to fuck off and die.

This wasn't about me.

Yeah, it said. That was kind of the point.

"Shit," Phil said, taking me by both arms. "I'm sorry. Just what you want to hear from your fucking fiancé, that, isn't it?"

"Nah, 's okay," I managed. "I mean, course you've had blokes you loved before me. Just 'cos I never . . ." I shut up then.

Phil's face had changed. "You? With the old Paretski charm? You must have."

I tried to laugh it off. "Short-arse crip like me? They weren't exactly queuing up at my door."

Too late, I realised what I'd said. Phil had paled. Him and his bloody guilt complex. "Didn't mean it like that," I added quickly. "Just meant . . . There wasn't anyone, that's all. Not anyone who really meant anything."

Phil's hands tightened on my arms, then relaxed just as I was about to mention the possibility of bruises. He moved them up past my shoulders to grasp my face in both hands, and kissed me.

Christ, it was like we'd been apart for a month. A year, even. His lips crushed mine, his fingers by contrast oddly gentle on my jaw. He tasted of melted cheese and charcoal, which went pretty bloody well with the beer I'd been drinking.

And of hunger. Definitely hunger. And I don't mean for more cheese on toast.

I didn't remember putting my hands on his waist. I was glad they'd managed to get with the plot without me, and decided a bit of positive reinforcement was in order, so I pulled his shirt up and out of his trousers. Yeah, skin was definitely better. I ran my hands up and down his sides, so warm and solid, and played a bit with his nipples, which were becoming more solid by the minute.

Phil kissed me again, one hand still holding my head while the other dipped down the back of my jeans to grope my arse. There wasn't a lot of room to play with, so it was just as well Phil's a determined sort of bloke. Then he made a noise of frustration into my mouth, which was hotter than you'd think, and let go with both hands so he could work on undoing my jeans. "Christ, Paretski, did you shrink these in the wash?"

"Nah, putting on weight from all these meals you keep cooking me." I grinned and lay back on the sofa to make it easier for him.

"Cocky sod, aren't you?"

Well, he'd be the best judge of that, seeing as he had my flies undone and his mouth almost on my dick. Then there was no more *almost* about it, and I groaned aloud at the sensation of him sucking me through the cotton of my kecks. "Christ, that's good." I felt hot all over, as if his breath on my stiff prick had been enough to tip me over from ambient temperature to *Jesus Christ, she's gonna blow*. Desperate for more, I scrabbled at my jeans until I'd got them and my underwear down past my hips. Then I stripped off my T-shirt for good measure.

Phil licked a stripe up my cock and rolled my balls with one hand, the other rubbing up and down my side like I was a startled horse that might bolt at any mo.

I could've told him there was absolutely no danger of that. Well, if my brain had actually been working, instead of short-circuited by pleasure, I could've. "Don't stop," I urged.

Phil looked up at me and smirked. "Sure you don't want me to try something else?"

"Like what?"

"Like this," he said, and sucked me down.

Fuck me. I gasped, struggling not to buck up into that gorgeous mouth of his, so hot and wet and fucking, fucking perfect. Phil's hand slipped down to my hip and held it firm—on my good side, which if you think was an accident, then you've never met Phil Morrison. I was panting, an arm thrown over my eyes because it was so fucking good, and then he started to alternate sucking with teasing my cockhead with his tongue, paying extra attention to that spot just underneath the head.

I lost it. Howling loud enough to bring half the neighbourhood round to complain about the noise, I came in a stream of shuddering ecstasy that seemed to go on and on. "Oh God," I breathed, and pulled Phil down on top of me for a spunk-flavoured kiss, squirming a bit at the pressure his iron-hard rod was putting on my frankly knackered cock.

"Kneel up," I told him at last. "Kneel astride me and wank yourself off."

Phil had his trousers off in two shakes of a lamb's wotsit. He did as he was told, settling his knees on either side of my chest, far enough up that I could get a hand on him too. I grabbed a handful of that magnificent arse and squeezed as I tugged.

"Come on me," I urged him. "Come on."

Washboard abs clenched as Phil's balls drew up. He groaned, long and low, and spattered me with hot spunk, on my chest, my neck, my face, and— "Oi, did you just jizz in my hair?" As I spoke, a dribble of spunk went in my mouth. I licked my lips.

Phil laughed. "Why, you got a hot date tonight?"

"Too bloody right." I grinned at him, totally, gloriously happy.

I tried to pull him down to kiss him again, but he resisted.

"Hang on a mo." He stripped off his shirt and used it to wipe up the mess he'd left on my face and chest. Then he lay on top of me, and we snogged like teenagers.

Well. Like teenagers who'd just had a really good shag.

CHAPTER FIFTEEN

We had to make do with a snatched bit of toast for breakfast, as we were running late. Well, we weren't when we woke up, but we definitely were by the time we managed to finally get out of bed. Fortunately, we were both in such a good mood by then neither of us gave a toss about breakfast.

"Are you coming with me to see Arlo Fenchurch this evening?" Phil asked, pulling on his jacket.

I glanced up from lacing my work boots. "Uncle Armpit? Wouldn't miss it. Unless, of course, you're planning to accuse me of trying to get off with him, that is." I grinned so he'd know I wasn't still pissed off with him about that.

Well, not *that* pissed off.

Phil gave me a look. "I never said you were trying to get off with Lance Frith. I may have said he was trying to get off with you."

"Oi, I was there, remember? There was a definite suggestion I was quite happy with the idea. And by the way, cheers for the ringing endorsement of my taste in men."

"Picky, are we?"

"Too right. Did you somehow miss those glasses he was wearing? And I'm not even talking about hanging a dowsing pendulum round your neck."

Phil shrugged. "Granted, he dresses pretentious, but there's nothing wrong with the bloke underneath."

"Sounds like I'm the one who should have been worried, then."

He gave me a serious look then, the sort that had me in mortal danger of melting into my boots. "You'll never have anything to worry about."

Sod it. I had literally nought point five seconds to get out the door, and I'd really wanted that second bit of toast.

But I wanted to snog my bloke silly more.

I made it to Mr. L.'s confusing country cottage (at some point, someone must have rerouted a lane, as the front door was round the back) only five minutes late. I don't think he even noticed. He was on the phone the entire time I was there—putting in a new loo, which turned out to be a bastard because the soil pipe had been a botch job—and didn't even hang up or put 'em on hold while he paid me. Needless to say, I didn't get the cup of coffee I was desperate for.

All in all, by the time I'd finished the morning's jobs, I reckoned I was well justified in calling up Gary and getting him to meet me for another pub lunch.

I know, I know. But, well, Phil had given me a lot to think about. And sometimes you need to talk stuff through to know how you really feel about it, yeah? And it was Friday anyhow, which made going to the pub at lunchtime practically obligatory.

This time, I'd picked the pub, so we met up at the Duck and Grouse. It's only up the road from the Four Candles, but streets away in terms of atmosphere, in my humble opinion. The sort of place that still has regulars who only go in there to drink beer and get away from the wife. I've got no idea where the wives go to get away from their husbands, but it's not the Duck and Grouse. The female clientele tends to be (a) young, single, and boisterous and (b) outnumbered.

I sank onto a barstool and had a squint at the menu while I was waiting for the barmaid to notice me. It was chalked up on a board on the wall, and hadn't changed for as long as I could remember, but you never know.

My vigilance was rewarded: I spotted a sneaky change from steak and kidney pie, chips, and peas to steak and *ale* pie, chips, and peas. I decided to play it safe and stick with a ploughman's. No point encouraging them in all this avant-garde bollocks.

The barmaid finished serving a bloke with a potbelly and a beard and ambled over in my direction with an unhurried tread. "What can

I get you?" She was middle-aged but dressed younger, with an air of having seen it all before and not being totally averse to seeing it all again.

"Diet Coke, please, love, and a vodka martini."

"For your invisible friend?" she asked with a smirk.

I winked at her. "He'll be here in a mo, and trust me, you won't be able to miss him."

Her smile broadened. "Now I remember you. You're Gary's mate, aren't you?"

"Guilty as charged." Gary might not come in here often, but it didn't surprise me one bit he was remembered when he did.

She sighed as she handed me my Coke. "Typical. All the best ones are either gay or taken."

"Hey, some of us are both," I told her, waggling my ring finger at her with a grin, because it was still a bit of a novelty to me and all.

"Congratulations," she said, and dialled the flirting down to zero as she mixed Gary's martini.

Right on time, the man himself turned up. He was on his own—presumably Julian had had a better offer. Date with the poodle next door, maybe? Course, that was never gonna work out. Well, not unless they stood her on a box.

"Is that for me? You're a lifesaver. I'm *parched*." Gary took a sip. "Mm. That's better. Now, are we eating? Silly question. Of *course* we're eating."

We ordered food (Gary braved the steak and ale pie) and took our drinks over to a table by the window. I shifted a potted plant over a bit so it wouldn't tickle my neck when I sat down.

"Stop fondling the ferns," Gary said distractedly, making himself comfortable with a faded velvet cushion. "Now go on, what's the latest crisis? Much as I'd like to think you simply invited me here for the pleasure of my company."

"Do you and Darren have common interests?" I asked, ignoring the guilt trip with the ease of long practice.

Gary gave me a smug look. "We are of one mind."

"Yeah, right. No, I mean, you do the bell ringing, yeah, and he does the Spanish classes and the Morris dancing—is there stuff you do together?"

The look turned pitying. "Well, Tommy dearest, when a man and another man love each other very much—"

"Oi, I'm not talking about you and him having sex!"

"Bloody glad to hear it and all," one of the older regulars muttered on his way past to the gents'.

Gary literally jiggled with stifled laughter. I glared at him and tried to pretend I hadn't gone red.

Seriously, they couldn't reopen the Dyke soon enough for my liking.

"I mean, like, hobbies," I explained, keeping my voice a bit lower this time, although God knows why. That horse hadn't just bolted, it was in the next county by now, sidling up to strangers in pubs and trying to sell them a set of used saddlery, one not very careful lady owner, sale due to change of circumstances.

"Does watching *Bake Off* count?"

I felt a twinge of envy. Phil was happy enough to watch 'em with me, but he just didn't *get* TV cookery programs. "No. Not the telly. Something you and him go out of the house to do on a regular basis."

Gary put on an obviously fake frown of confusion. "I thought we weren't talking about sex?"

"Eff off. Look, do you, or don't you?"

He shrugged so expansively his martini sloshed almost to the brim of his glass. "Not really, I suppose. But then, it's hardly healthy for a couple to live in each other's pockets."

That was rich, coming from him. The only reason people didn't think him and Darren were joined at the hip was that Darren's hips only came up to Gary's knees. "You don't reckon it's necessary, then? I mean, you know, there's all that bollocks about 'the couple that plays together stays together.'"

"And once again, I'd have to say I thought we weren't talking about—"

"Yeah, yeah. Right. No common hobbies apart from X-rated ones. Got it. Oh, cheers, love." The barmaid had come over with our meals.

"Sauce?" she asked, with a raised eyebrow.

Gary beamed at her. "Oh no, thank you, darling. I'm saucy enough already, aren't I, Tommy?"

Me and the barmaid exchanged *What can you do?* looks. "Bit of mayo for me, please," I asked, and started unwrapping my cutlery from the neat little napkin bundle it'd arrived in.

Gary took a thoughtful sip of his martini before doing the same. "What's brought this on? Has your young man been trying to drag you along on his mammoth-hunting expeditions?"

"Nah, it was just something he said about, well . . ." I stopped, not sure if I should say anything. No, better not. I took a bite of crusty bread and cheese.

"The ex?"

Bugger. I struggled to finish my mouthful and had to wash it down with a gulp of Coke. "Yeah, all right, but if you tell *anyone* . . . And that includes Darren, by the way."

Gary pouted. "I'll do my best, but you know how it is when you're in bed with the man of your dreams. Sometimes, despite your best efforts, something just slips out."

"Yeah, well, use less lube next time. I'm serious. If Phil heard I'd been telling everyone about him and that git he used to be with—"

"I'm hurt, Tommy. *I* am not everyone. But do tell. Is that how his previous entanglement withered and died—due to a lack of common interests?"

"Pretty much, yeah." I was *not* going to mention the cheating.

I gave Gary a sharp look in case he'd somehow managed to guess this bit of gossip as well, but he was busy stroking his chin and staring into the middle distance.

The old bloke came back from the gents'—I didn't envy his proctologist—and sent Gary a worried look.

"It's just so hard to think what you and Phil might have in common," Gary said at last.

"Cheers, mate."

"Apart, of course, from an outdated attachment to the aggressively masculine, which, while I have nothing against it per se, is not really *entirely* my area . . . Oh, I have it!" Gary sat up straight, a proud smile on his face. "Shooting."

"Shooting?" I echoed, my eyebrows chasing my hairline as a phantom pain shot—heh—through my arm. "Seriously?"

"Of course. Macho and violent enough for him, yet involving enough skill and precision to interest you. And, of course, with Phil preferring to cultivate an image as the strong, silent type, the headphones will be a definite bonus."

"I dunno. Doesn't he see enough violence in the day job?"

Gary gave me a stern look. "I was suggesting you shoot at targets, not actual people. I've heard gun clubs tend to take a dim view of that sort of thing."

"Ah . . . I dunno. I'll think about it."

"And in his line of work, knowing how to use a gun could save his life one day."

Okay, so that was a stronger argument. But . . . "Maybe he knows already? From the police?" Phil had been in the force six years, because apparently it was cheaper than going to private-eye school.

If, you know, there *was* such a thing as private-eye school.

"Was he in the police in *America*?"

Lacking a clean knife to cut the sarcasm with, I stuck up a finger. "No, but they have firearms units over here too, yeah? Some of 'em get training with guns, I know that much."

"So? Even if he did, maybe he misses it. I've heard a man can get quite attached to having something with that much power in his hands. Ooh, you know what? I've just had a really *radical* idea. Why don't you *ask* him?"

Screw the knife. You'd need a JCB to get through sarcasm that thick. I laughed. "All right, all right. I'll suggest it. Sometime."

Gary pouted, but let it go. "Any *other* family news to tell me?" His tone made it clear just which member of my family he was asking about.

"You mean Mike Novak?" I sighed. "Sod it. I'm gonna need another drink for this. Same again?"

"Ooh, yes please. But tell her it's an olive this time, not a cherry."

I got the drinks in—no olive for Gary, but they managed to dig up a slice of lemon for variety—and added a pack of ready salted to fortify myself.

"Well," I said, sitting down. "I've seen him a couple of times, but I dunno. It's just . . ." I waved my hands a bit, as if the words I wanted were flying around in the air between us and I just needed to catch them.

Then I told him.

CHAPTER SIXTEEN

It'd been . . . Christ, I dunno. I mean, what the bloody hell do you expect, meeting your real dad for the first time? Just . . .

I s'pose I'd thought there'd be some, I dunno, instant connection. That we'd get talking and somehow everything would make sense.

Like, say, my psychic so-called gifts.

I mean, I hadn't thought it'd be like I'd mention it, and he'd say, *Oh, yeah, that one: see, your great-great-great-squared-grandad married a gypsy girl and ever since then every firstborn son in our family is shit-hot at finding stuff and makes a killing as a plumber.* And then launch into a funny story about him as a nipper finding all the presents three days before Christmas.

Okay, maybe I'd thought that a *bit*.

But what'd happened was, I'd mumbled out a question about supernatural family gifts, which he'd interpreted as me thinking he'd come from Transylvania because all those Eastern European countries are basically the same to us ignorant Brits, which led to a geography lesson I really hadn't needed (okay, maybe I'd needed it a bit). By the time we actually got round to *my* gift, we'd been talking at cross-purposes so bloody long, it all came out sounding even more unconvincing than it usually does. Which, by the way, is another reason why I don't tell people about it, not if I can help it.

Mike—he'd told me to call him Mike, which was weird but also a relief, seeing as how I wasn't sure I could call him Dad without feeling guilty about, well, *Dad*—had given Phil this look. I was fairly sure it meant something along the lines of *Oi, you might have mentioned my long-lost son is in urgent need of care in the community.* Phil gazed back stonily, which probably translated as *No dissing the mental health of my intended, mate.*

Me? I'd changed the subject, pronto. Well, at least when you first meet the bloke who provided half your DNA, the one thing you're not short of is topics to ask about. (And topics to avoid at all costs, come to that.) I'd found out he'd gone back to Poland and got married to a lass from his hometown after having his fling with my mum. Was that normal? For Europeans, I mean? I knew one or two blokes who'd spent a summer visiting family in India or Pakistan and come back hitched, but I'd always thought that was like a religious or cultural thing.

I didn't like to ask if she'd been his girlfriend all along. Patiently waiting for him to make his fortune in England and come back to marry her, while he played away with my mum.

They'd moved to Bristol, him and the missus, and had a son. Just the one, which surprised me somehow, but I didn't like to ask. "Daniel, he is twenty-five now. He works in construction. Doing very well." Mike had showed me a picture of a fair-haired bloke who must take after his mum, looks-wise. Either that, or what was sauce for the gander . . . Nope. Not going there.

Mike snapped a picture of me on his phone. I wondered if he was planning to show it to Daniel, and what he'd think about me looking more like his dad than he did. I mean, he was my dad too, obviously . . . but it still seemed weird.

And the whole being Polish bit . . . See, as you probably already know, *Novak* isn't the way you spell, well, Novak in Polish. I mean, you say it the same, but it's usually spelled with a *w*. *Nowak*. I s'pose, if I thought at all about it, I just assumed he'd changed it to make life easier for himself, like changing Patschke to Paretski back around World War I when having a German name was a bit of a no-no. I mean, these days everyone and his dog knows Polish *w*'s are *v*'s, but way back in the mists of time around when I was conceived, it was probably either spend your life explaining spelling and/or pronunciation to ignorant Brits, or change the name.

Uh, no. Apparently that great-great-great-squared-grandad I'd been thinking about earlier had, according to family legend, actually moved to Poland from Austria-Hungary sometime around the Prussian War. (Or maybe *a* Prussian war. All this education was seriously doing my head in.) Mike even made a joke about it, said he'd had to come to this country to get his name spelled right. Then he pointed out that *Novak* was a name traditionally given to a bloke who'd moved into the area from somewhere else, so basically, no one had a bloody clue where my forebears had originally come from.

I could be anything. From anywhere. Christ. I'd thought I'd come away from meeting Mike Novak with more answers as to who I was, where I'd come from, and maybe even why I had this weird psychic so-called gift.

If anything, I had less of the bastards than before.

I'd made the mistake of trying to talk it over with Phil, after.

He'd given me a look. Seeing as we were in bed at the time, that involved turning over and pushing himself up on his elbow, which made me feel even more on the spot than I had done already.

"What?"

"You're just like my sister, you are."

"You what?" I was fairly sure the number of things me and Leanne had in common, apart from a moderate fondness for one Phil Morrison (which, if he didn't watch out, was liable to be getting more moderate by the minute), could be counted on the fingers of one fish.

"Leanne. Don't you remember her, back when we were at school?" He got that pinched look on his face he always did when talking of our mutual school days.

Course, I couldn't see a mirror from here. Chances were I'd got the same expression plastered all over my mug. "Not a lot, to be honest. She was a couple of years below us, wasn't she?" And yeah, some of the younger girls had had older boyfriends, but by the time she'd have been looking for one, it was pretty much common knowledge it wasn't girls I was after. Mostly, it had to be said, thanks to her big brother Phil spreading that juicy bit of gossip far and wide.

Yeah, I definitely had a pinched look on my face. I could feel the tightness of it.

Luckily Phil was back to staring at the ceiling now. "Used to be fat, didn't she? Got a lot of shit for it at school."

Oh. *Now* I remembered her. A vague picture of a mousey-haired girl bursting out of her school uniform who spent a lot of her time crying. I hadn't connected her with Phil, probably because I couldn't remember ever seeing them together. Still, how many teenage boys want to hang around with their not-so-little sister where their mates can see them? Yeah, kids can be bastards.

Case in point: you might have thought me and her would have a bit of fellow-feeling, seeing as we were the butt of most of the nasty jokes going around. Far as I could remember, we'd avoided each other like the plague, thinking (probably correctly) that if there's anything more fun to rip the shit out of than a podge or a poof, it's a podge and a poof who've chummed up together.

Phil carried on before I could sort out how to say yeah, I remembered her when he put it like that. "She used to reckon, Leanne did, if only she could lose weight, her whole bloody life'd be sorted. She'd get a boyfriend, all the girls would want to be her friend, and no one would laugh at her anymore. 'Cept then she did it, and you know what? She's still the same person with the same life. Just wearing smaller clothes. And yeah, a lot more boys fancied her. Trouble was, they were still the ones she could remember being pricks to her when she was fat."

"Yeah, but she's not in school now, is she?" I said, putting an arm around him and snuggling in closer. "I mean, she must meet all sorts now. People who never knew her back then."

He didn't respond. Not physically, I mean. "Yeah, and *now* if they don't fancy her, she's got nothing to blame it on, has she? And even if they do, she's gotta be asking herself, would they have been seen dead with her in the old days?"

There was an elephant in the room all right, and it wasn't bloody well Leanne. I pulled Phil and his guilt trip for the shit he'd put me through in high school a bit closer and gave them both a cuddle. "Oi. Water under the bridge, remember? Anyway, I thought we were talking about my dad. How'd we even get onto this?"

"*Because* what you were hoping for from meeting your real dad is exactly what Leanne was hoping for from losing weight."

"What, for more blokes to fancy me?"

Phil huffed a laugh. "No, and you know it. For doing one thing to somehow give you the answer to life, the universe, and sodding everything, all right?"

"Nah, that's forty-two. Everyone knows that." At least, they did if, like me and Phil, they'd recently watched Gary's DVDs of the eighties TV series of *The Hitchhiker's Guide to the Galaxy*. (According to Gary, it was an absolute classic and not to be missed, so when I gave the DVDs back, I didn't mention we'd stopped paying much attention fairly early on after a discussion about what you could do with two heads and three arms veered into X-rated territory with impressive speed.)

"Jesus, I was a fucking stupid prick when I was a teenager. C'mere." *Finally* Phil rolled over and hugged me back, one hand on my arse and the other stroking my hair.

"You want me any more *here*, we're gonna need another condom, just saying." I managed to get about a millionth of an inch closer, even so.

Gary listened while I went through my little spiel. About Mike Novak, I mean, not about what me and Phil got up to in bed or, for that matter, on the sofa in front of the telly. Not that Gary wouldn't be interested, mind. But I like to keep some things private.

Then he put his martini down thoughtfully. "Tommy, darling, you know I love you, but don't you think you're getting just a teensy bit obsessed with the whole who-am-I thing? Isn't it enough that you've met your real father? Do we have to go the whole ancestral-DNA route?" Gary pursed his lips. "Although that kind of thing can be fascinating. Did you know you share fifty percent of your DNA with a cabbage?"

"Speak for yourself." Then I frowned. "Savoy or red?"

"I've always thought of you as more of a brussels sprout, actually. But does it really matter if you get your work ethic and your little psychic thingy from your Slavic forebears, or if they're all your own work?"

I took a long swig of my Diet Coke, wishing it wasn't the middle of the day and I could've had a pint instead. "Ah, I dunno. Maybe Phil's right."

"Well, I wouldn't go *that* far." Gary reached over and patted my knee. Maybe he was missing Julian. "Never mind. We are what we are. So when do I get to meet the donor of your sperm?"

"Never, if you put it like that. I'll let you know, all right? And I'd better be off. The work ethic's starting to give me gyp."

"You should get that seen to. I had mine removed years ago, and I've never looked back."

CHAPTER SEVENTEEN

Me and Phil went round to see Uncle Arlo at six o'clock that evening, just as the skies were beginning to darken. Winter always seems so much closer when it starts to get dark before you've had your tea. I get mixed feelings at this time of year. Yeah, we're losing the long days of summer, and my hip definitely isn't a fan of colder weather, but there's something, I dunno, magical, if that doesn't sound too daft, about the nights drawing in. Maybe it's the kid in me looking forward to Christmas.

Or maybe it's just the thought of more time in bed with a certain six-foot private investigator. Yeah, that's probably it.

Fenchurch's Fine Fancies—and what kind of a name was that? It sounded like they ought to be selling overpriced, overdecorated cupcakes—was set up in, of all places, an old barn. It was down a winding, single-track country lane, the sort where you wonder if you should toot your horn when coming up to a corner, but always feel too self-conscious or, you know, too British to actually do it. In fact, the place was more like a series of connected barns, all tarted up, modernised, and set around three sides of a central courtyard with posh shrubs and big stone Buddha heads. The large plate glass windows, which I was guessing weren't original, were brightly lit and full of stuff for sale.

A pretty little necklace that looked like a daisy chain caught my eye—I reckoned Cherry might like it, and it's never too early to shop for Christmas, at least not for people whose allergies mean you can't fob 'em off with a gift basket of bath stuff.

Okay, so there's other reasons that would be a spectacularly bad gift for my sis. Still, no reason to rake over the past.

Then I saw the price tag and nearly fell into the shrubbery in shock. It wasn't the only piece with an unfeasibly large number of zeros to its name either. Even the silver stuff wasn't cheap, and claimed to be actually made of white gold, which I've never seen the point of. That and platinum. I mean, if you're going to pay top whack for a bit of bling, you want everyone to know it, don't you?

There was a *Sorry We're Closed* sign hanging in the door, which turned out to be locked when Phil tried it. He rapped sharply on the glass, and we waited.

I stretched, long and slow. "If no one answers, I vote we chuck a brick through the window and make off with the goods. Compensation for a wasted journey."

Phil huffed a laugh. "And this is the bloke who won't even take cash for a job under the table."

"That's different. That's professional ethics, that is."

"What, and burglary's all right because you're only an amateur? What are you, a modern-day Raffles?"

"Who?"

"Never mind. And just be grateful your mum never had a VHS player and a thing for Anthony Valentine. Looks like someone's coming," Phil added, but I'd already noticed the dark shape getting larger behind the *Closed* sign.

A second or two later, the door finally opened.

Uncle Arlo was not what I'd have expected from Amelia's brother. For a start, where she'd been whippet thin and brisk in her manner, he was well-padded and gave off a sleepy air, like a spaced-out teddy bear. He had heavy-lidded brown eyes and—most unlike Amelia of all—a mop of naturally silver-grey hair. To be honest, if I'd met them together, I'd probably have assumed he was her dad.

Then again, when you looked at the bloke she'd married . . .

He gave us a slow, considering once-over. "Ah. The investigator and the psychic sidekick. Come in."

Charming. Who was he calling a sidekick? Phil sent me a look, so I didn't actually *say* it.

"Thanks for seeing us, particularly at such a sad time. I'm Phil Morrison, and this is Tom Paretski," Phil said, putting out his hand. Uncle Arlo gave it a searching look for a mo, then shook it.

It didn't seem worth the bother of sticking out my hand for his examination. What with me only being the sidekick and all.

"Do come on through," Uncle Arlo said, in his ponderous way that made him sound twenty years older than he looked. He didn't seem all that sad, the git.

I mean, me and Cherry have had our ups and downs, but I'd like to think if one of us popped his or her clogs, the other one would be a bit less *business as usual* about it all only a few days down the line.

Then I thought about my big brother, Richard, who I saw almost never and didn't get on with when I did. Guilt rippled queasily in my guts. Nah, not all siblings were close.

Uncle Arlo led us through the sales area to the workshop, which was set in the final, and largest, barn of the three and smelled faintly dusty. Also metallic, but I'd been expecting that. The windows in this one were a lot smaller. There were around half a dozen benches, each with a semicircle cut out of the front as if for the comfort of some really fat bastard, which had a weird hammock thing set up underneath it. I s'pose it made sense, if you were working with diamonds and stuff. You wouldn't want half your year's salary disappearing through a crack in the floorboards.

No one was actually working there at the mo, but there were tools out on the benches. Racks of pliers with different shaped ends, magnifying glasses, and files of all sizes—the sort you file metal down with, I mean, not the sort you use to keep paperwork tidy. It looked . . . I dunno. Rougher than I'd expected, I s'pose, given all the dainty flowery stuff that came out of it. You see a bit of bling, you sort of forget someone actually had to beat and wrench the metal into shape in the first place.

I didn't get to gawp my fill, mind, as Uncle Arlo kept on going until we got through the workshop and into a tiny, windowless office. It was definitely a bit on the claustrophobic side with all three of us in there. Maybe that was the intention? There was only one chair in the room: the one behind the desk. Uncle Arlo took that, leaving us to make our own arrangements. I shifted some files—this time of the lever-arch persuasion—and perched on the edge of the desk just to pay him back. Phil stayed where he was and loomed, which a lot of people in Uncle Arlo's position would have found intimidating.

I was betting Uncle Arlo wasn't one of them. He leaned back in his chair and looked at us expectantly.

Phil coughed. "Mr. Fenchurch, as I mentioned on the phone, I'm looking into the disappearance of a certain item of jewellery that belonged to the late Mrs. Majors. Do you know the item I'm referring to?"

He didn't specify which Mrs. Majors, but then I s'posed either would do, really.

Uncle Arlo half smiled. "Well," he said. And stopped. There was a pause. I thought about drumming my fingers on the desktop, but Phil would only get tetchy with me. "I'm assuming you mean Amelia's diamond necklace?"

"That's the one. You're familiar with it?"

"Oh, absolutely. Yes." He stopped again.

Getting blood out of a stone would've been easier. And more fun.

Actually, scratch that. Getting blood out of Uncle Arsehole would've been more fun.

"Can you elaborate?" Phil asked.

Uncle Arlo glanced at me, his smile getting bigger. "Do I need to? Can't you just read my mind?"

"Not that kind of psychic," I said shortly.

"Oh, what a pity. I should think it would be so helpful in your line of work."

He was really starting to get on my wick. "I'm a plumber."

"Indeed? Good heavens. A psychic plumber. Well, well. Do the drains speak to you?"

No, but I was starting to seriously consider shoving him into one headfirst so he could have a nice old natter. I drew in a breath, but Phil beat me to it. "Mr. Fenchurch, I'm sure you have things you'd rather be doing. If you wouldn't mind just answering the question, we could stop wasting your time and let you get back to them."

Uncle Arlo quirked a lazy eyebrow. "Well, I suppose I'd have to say I'm *intimately* familiar with the item in question."

What, he'd shagged it? That was certainly how he made it sound. Definitely gave a whole new meaning to the name *Fenchurch's Fine Fancies*.

Phil folded his arms. "Mr. Fenchurch, did you, or someone who works for you, make a replica of Mrs. Majors's diamond necklace?"

Uncle Arlo's lips drew together in a disappointed pout, presumably because the carefully worded question was ruining all his fun. "Indeed."

I guessed that was a yes.

"And can I ask who commissioned the replica?"

Uncle Arlo steepled his fingers, stared at them a moment, then looked up and smiled. "Why, Amelia, naturally. That central diamond is worth close to half a million in today's markets. She was concerned about wearing it in public."

"In St. Leonards?" I couldn't help asking. "It's not exactly the crime capital of Britain."

I got a pitying look for my pains. Well, from Uncle Arlo at any rate. I didn't dare glance at Phil 'cos I reckoned it'd be a pissed-off one from him. "Amelia was a keen patron of the Royal Opera House, and of course her connection with the bishop led to a number of formal engagements."

In for a penny . . . "Were you and her close?"

Uncle Arlo blinked, and for a mo, his face looked saggy and old. Was it an act? "When she was a child, yes. She was much younger than I, of course. I was more of a father figure than a brother in those days. But when she grew up . . . Well. Who among us can say we're as close to our family as we'd like to be?"

Who indeed? Although, come to think of it, when I slung a glance at Phil, I realised he could probably tick that box.

Not that he was looking any too happy about it, mind. "What exactly was her connection to the bishop?" he asked, unfolding his arms and snapping out of it.

Uncle Arlo put his head on one side. "Didn't you know? She met him professionally. Her profession, not his, naturally."

Why *naturally*? Bishops got out and about a fair bit in the course of their holy duties, didn't they? As borne out by the fact I'd known Greg for months and only met his boss the once. If he hadn't been off doing whatever it is bishops do, where the bloody hell *had* he bogged off to?

"She organised an event for him? What kind?"

"Oh, I forget the details." Despite the sleepy air, I had a feeling Uncle Arlo never met a detail he didn't file away carefully under that artfully rumpled mop of silver hair.

"Back to the necklace," Phil said doggedly. "Did she give you any indication as to what she was planning to do with the real one? Once she had your copy, that is."

"I just assumed she would put it in a safety-deposit box. Majors doesn't have a safe at home. His sort never do."

"'His sort'?"

"Oh, you know. Old-fashioned. Entirely detached from the real world. Thinks keeping a shotgun in his study means he won't get burgled."

Alex Majors kept a shotgun? See, that's the trouble with the countryside. You think, yeah, Britain, gun laws, you're safe from being shot—then you find out half the homes this side of the commuter belt have an old shotgun knocking around somewhere that they got for "pest control" back in the 1950s.

Okay, maybe that's a slight exaggeration. But I'd prefer it if fewer murder suspects turned out to keep the things.

I wondered if old Arlo had one too.

"So Mrs. Fenchurch-Majors didn't tell you her plans?" Phil persisted.

"Didn't I just say that?"

"How long did it take to make the necklace for her?"

"Oh, not long at all. Yes. Less than a fortnight, I believe. A simple piece to copy, once one got hold of the central stone—the cubic zirconia for the surround, of course, I had already. I didn't charge her for the labour, naturally." He smiled. "In fact I didn't charge her at all. Dear Amelia. She was such a sweet little thing as a girl. Always so determined to get her own way. Much like her stepdaughter, in fact," he added out of the blue just as I'd started to feel a bit moved by the mistiness in his sleepy eyes.

"Did they get on well together?" Phil asked, poker-faced.

Uncle Arlo chuckled, apparently fully recovered from that little attack of emotion. "Oh, dear me, no. Couldn't stand each other. Two sticks of dynamite rubbing up against one another. Sparks and friction aplenty." He rubbed his hands together as if to demonstrate.

If you asked me, it was a weird way to think about your sister and your step-niece, but whatever floated his boat . . . And Christ. That was an image I really could've done without: Uncle Arsewipe perving to lesbian porn starring his relatives.

"Of course, Violet's devastated by her loss," he added, not even pretending to be sincere. Well, either that or he was just really, really bad at it.

"Of course." Phil gave him a direct look. "Do you get on well with your step-niece?"

"Naturally." He smiled sleepily. "She reminds me so much of Amelia when she was a young thing. And of course, I should in any case hold her dear for Amelia's sake."

Huh. That didn't exactly tie in with what he'd just told us about dear, dear Amelia hating the poor girl. And Christ, between him and Lance, they'd got me thinking about Vi as a teenager, not a grown woman who had to be pretty close to my age.

Maybe it was growing up rich that did it. Maybe, if you were rich, you could afford *not* to grow up.

Phil didn't call him on it. "Do you have any idea who might have wanted your sister dead?"

Uncle Arlo met him gaze for gaze. "I'm sorry—I thought you were here to ask about the necklace?"

"I'm looking into the possibility that the two crimes are linked." Phil kept his poker face.

"That's absurd. And surely, in any case, a murder investigation is a matter for the police?" His expression hardened. "I resent your implication that my actions in helping Amelia had anything to do with her death."

"Have you told the police what you've told us?"

"Of course," he snapped. The sleepy teddy bear had woken up fully now. And probably wanted his breakfast.

"They didn't mention that the replica necklace was found on her body?"

I froze—but yeah, Vi had told us that, hadn't she? So Phil wasn't dropping Dave in it.

"My sister was found in possession of one of her possessions? Dear me, how extraordinary." It was a good thing old Arlo didn't keep any potted plants in his office. They'd have withered and died at that tone.

Added to which, I might've been tempted to throw one at him.

Phil was made of stronger stuff. "Can you think of any reason why she'd have taken the replica of a very valuable piece of jewellery to a country fete?"

"I've no idea. Why don't you get the psychic sidekick to ask her? And find the real necklace, while he's at it—isn't that what he's famed for, and what you were actually hired to do? Now, if you'll excuse me?" Uncle Arctic's voice, as he stood up, could've cut diamonds.

I'd got to my feet when he did, which was just as well. A little bit of spit had flown out of his mouth and landed on the desk just where I'd been sitting.

"Look," I began, but Phil grabbed my arm.

"Thanks for your time, Mr. Fenchurch. We'll see ourselves out."

I waited until we were on the other side of the *Sorry We're Closed* sign. "Oi, why'd you stop me talking to him?"

Phil turned to raise an eyebrow at me as we walked briskly back to the car. A light drizzle had started to fall, and a few leaves drifted down from trees to complete the picture of autumn setting in. It was like someone had sneakily flicked a switch on the seasons while we were closeted in Uncle Arlo's windowless office. "Let me guess. You were going to give him a rundown of the actual psychic talents of one Tom Paretski?"

"Well, yeah. I don't want everyone thinking I talk to dead people. That's just creepy."

"And we need him to have this info because?"

"Because . . . 'Cos otherwise he'll have the wrong idea about me?"

"So why do you give a toss what he thinks? He's a murder suspect."

"Well, when you put it that way . . ." We climbed back into Phil's Golf, feeling a bit damp. "So what have we learned? Apart from that Uncle Arlo isn't as cuddly as he looks? And before you start, no, I didn't fancy him."

Phil stuck up a finger, but only briefly as he needed that hand to put the car in gear. "Fenchurch is running scared, and he knows the necklace and the murder are linked."

"He didn't seem to know they'd found it . . . You know. In her mouth." I blinked. "So it can't have been him."

"Or that's just what he wants you to think."

"Nah, it can't have been him. Why would he leave something at the scene which links him to it?"

"People don't always think logically after they've killed someone. Especially someone they love. Or hate, for that matter." He was silent a mo, slowing down to let an oncoming car pass. Bit winding, the lanes around here. "I spoke to the woman running the Cats Protection stall—remember, they were next door to the reptile tent? She reckoned she might have heard an argument going on in there, just before you found her."

"'Might have'?"

"She was talking to someone who was interested in signing up as a volunteer, at the time. She didn't hear what they said in the tent, only the tone, and she remembered thinking the tent ought to be empty, and maybe that was why whoever it was had gone in there to have their domestics."

"'Domestics'? Was it a man and a woman?" Because most people even nowadays tended to assume people were straight until proven otherwise, so chances were the thought wouldn't have occurred to her if they were both female voices. Or both male, of course, but I was betting one of 'em had to belong to Amelia.

Unless, of course, there had been two murderers, and they'd had a row? Say, for instance, over putting that bloody necklace where they'd put it?

"She wasn't sure. She was busy writing down this woman's contact details before she could change her mind about helping out. Oh, and the row might not have been in the tent after all. Could have been behind it instead. Or the other side of the hedge."

"I bet you were really glad you made the effort to look her up, weren't you?"

Phil half smiled. "Ties in with it not being premeditated, though. All helps to build up the picture."

I nodded. "Still looking a bit too pixelated for my liking, but yeah, I s'pose so."

"And there's another thing. You notice how the lack of any money changing hands over this replica necklace means there'll be no record of the transaction in Fenchurch's books?"

"So?"

"So we've only got his word for it she was the one who asked him to do it."

"But if he's lying about that, why admit to making it in the first place?"

"Staff. As in, he's got 'em cluttering up the place during normal working hours. Maybe one of them stumbled across him doing it? Chances are he even farmed out some of the work to one or more of them—or ordering that fake stone, at least."

"S'pose if you've got minions, you might as well use 'em," I agreed. "So what, you reckon someone else got the necklace made, swapped 'em out while Amelia wasn't looking, and then . . ." I frowned. "Someone got pissed off with her trying to pass the fake one off as real? D'you reckon she sold it? Nah, can't be—her and Alex were rolling in it, weren't they?"

"Alex, maybe. I haven't been able to look into his finances yet. But her? Not a chance. Her and Frith were on the verge of bankruptcy before she married Majors. His other wedding present to her was a bailout for the business."

"Huh. No wonder Vi didn't take to her. She can't have been too chuffed about the old man spending her inheritance on the new floozy."

"Yeah. Speaking of Vi Majors, I'm going to need to speak to her again. See what she has to say about her uncle making that necklace."

"You reckon she didn't know?"

"If she did know, I want to know why she didn't see fit to mention it."

I bit my lip. "Could've been her, couldn't it? If Vi *did* take the necklace when her stepmum thought she did—back when she called me in to find it—it could've been her getting the fake done."

"Maybe. She'd have had to have had reason for believing Fenchurch wouldn't shop her to his sister, though, wouldn't she? You're forgetting something else too. Mrs. Fenchurch-Majors called you in to find her necklace, right? And you got interrupted before you could find it—if it was even there. But she never called you back to have another go, did she?"

"Well, she had all the fayre stuff to worry about . . ." I wasn't even convincing myself. "Nah, if it really was worth three hundred grand or half a mill or whatever, she'd have had me turning that house upside down, wouldn't she? Unless it just turned up?"

"Or unless it was the fake one that'd gone missing. Worst-case scenario, she'd just have to ask her brother to do her another one."

"Yeah, but would he?" I frowned. "D'you think it cost much, making that fake? I mean, for the stones and all?"

Phil shook his head. "Cubic zirconia's cheap as chips. I looked it up online. There'd be the gold—or gold plate—but it'd still be peanuts compared to the real thing."

"Speaking of which—where the bloody hell is it? S'pose you've checked the local cash-for-gold place?"

"Among others. No, if she sold it, the big question is, what's happened to the money?"

"Been hacking her bank account?"

Phil smirked. "I've got my contacts."

We'd reached my house. "Coming in?" I asked as Phil pulled on the handbrake.

He nodded.

And before you ask, no, we didn't spend the evening going over the case. We spent it on the sofa with a takeaway and the telly.

What?

Everyone's entitled to a bit of slobbing around on a Friday night.

CHAPTER EIGHTEEN

Saturday, I had a couple of quick jobs to do—one of which, in the event, turned out to be a lot less quick than I'd been expecting—so me and Phil went our separate ways after breakfast and I didn't see him again until dinnertime. After which, I had to love him and leave him, although sadly without the *love him* bit, as I'd arranged to meet up with Dave for a few pints. His idea—I'd have thought the missus would have him on a short leash this close to her due date.

He barked out a laugh when I told him that, as we propped up the bar at the White Hart. "Short leash? I should be so bloody lucky. She wants it long enough to strangle me with."

I winced. "Cheers, mate. Really wanted to be reminded of that sort of thing."

"What? Oh, yeah, that."

"Yeah, that. Heard any more about the case?"

"Not a lot, no. Forensics have come up a blank—or, to be more bleedin' accurate, they found DNA from half of St. Leonards in that bloody tent. Lovely bit of blood under the fingernails—turned out to be all hers. Scratched her throat up, trying to get loose. That's the trouble with strangling. See, the instinct is to go for the thing round your neck, not the bastard what put it there." He took a deep swallow of beer. "Ah. Christ, that hits the spot. *And* the victim had shaken hands with just about everyone on that bloody field that day."

"She never shook my hand."

He grinned. "Maybe she was worried you hadn't washed it after the last bog you fixed."

"Oi, no dissing my personal hygiene. Nah, already had me right where she wanted me, didn't she? No need to waste manners on me."

Dave nodded slowly. "Makes you wonder, though. Who else did she have right where she wanted them—and how desperate were they to get out from under her thumb? Even in this day and age, there's a fair few men who don't take kindly to a woman having 'em by the balls."

I grinned. "Well, you've got me there. My balls are strictly off-limits to women. Although fair enough, there's only one man allowed to get his hands on 'em these days and all."

"Bloody hell, Paretski, you had to go there, didn't you?" Dave took a massive gulp of his pint. "Christ. Not enough beer in the world." He went to put his glass down, obviously thought better of it, and took another gulp.

"How's Jen doing?" I asked, taking pity on him.

"Pissed off. Past her due date. She's got another week and then they'll induce, and Christ, it can't come soon enough for either of us. She gave me my marching orders tonight—said if I ask her one more time if she can feel anything happening, she'll connect my dick up to the bloody TENS machine and turn it on full whack."

I grimaced. Electrodes and delicate areas: definitely not relevant to my interests. And one of my customers told me once about having a faulty TENS machine for her second kid's birth—Mrs. P. had switched the thing on and then turned round and accused Mr. P. of walloping her on the back. *"Kick like a mule, it was,"* she'd said. *"But they gave me a full refund and a £25 voucher when I took it back to the shop and complained."*

She'd smiled, like she'd found it a fair exchange.

Dave belched. "Your family all right?" he asked.

"Yeah, they're good. We're seeing Greg and Cherry for lunch tomorrow, over in St. Leonards."

"S'pose she'll be moving there after the wedding."

"Yeah, I guess so. Dunno what she's doing with her house."

Dave scratched his armpit thoughtfully. "Maybe she'll keep it. Don't they get kicked out of the tied accommodation when they retire?"

I frowned. "Never really thought about it, but yeah, I s'pose they'd have to be. Make room for the new bloke. Or lady, obviously. Huh. Maybe they have retirement homes for old priests?"

"Christ, they must be a laugh a bloody minute. Put me somewhere like that, I'd be queuing up for the one-way trip to Switzerland."

"I dunno." Despite never having been much of a God-botherer myself, I felt weirdly unable to leave the clergy undefended. "Greg's all right. And that new vicar in Brock's Hollow, you know, the one who's going out with Harry from the Dyke."

"And what the bleedin' hell's that all about? All the pretty girls that woman's had working for her over the years, and she ends up with a—" I never got to hear the rest of that sentence, as Dave's mobile rang, and he frowned. "Shit. That's the wife." He answered it and went pale. "You've gotta get me home. She's in labour."

Uh-oh. "Didn't you drive?"

"Yeah, but I can't *now*, can I? I've had four pints." That meant he'd had two before I got here. Unless he wasn't counting the round we'd just started, in which case he'd had three. "Be bloody marvellous, that, wouldn't it, if I get had up for drunk driving and lose my job the night my kid's born."

I looked regretfully at my almost full glass. "Come on, then. I've got the Fiesta out the back."

Dave wasn't happy about squeezing his bulk into my passenger seat. "Jesus, when are you gonna get a proper car?"

"Oi, it'll get you there." I pulled out of the pub car park through the narrow archway, taking it easy because it's blind both sides onto the main road. They'd built this place as a coaching inn, and I s'pose there wasn't as much traffic about those days. Also, it probably moved a lot slower.

"Yeah, but how soon? They come quicker the more you've had, and it's her third. Come on, get a shift on."

I turned right and headed up the hill. "There's a speed limit in this road, all right? You want me to drive faster, you lend me one of those flashing lights."

All the way there, I was thinking, *Christ, what do you do if someone has a baby? There was something about newspaper, right? You were supposed to wrap 'em in it like an order of cod and chips. Only probably without the salt and vinegar. And towels, or was that just if you didn't have any newspaper? Or was it the other way around? And boil up loads of hot water. That was what always happened in old films, anyhow.*

Dunno what they used it for. Maybe having a baby was thirsty work, and the new mum was always desperate for a cup of tea?

"You realise if I end up delivering this sprog, you're gonna have to name it after me," I joked weakly to Dave.

"If you end up delivering it, we'll have more to worry about than what we're gonna call it. Do you even know which end of a woman is which?"

"Oi, I'm not stupid. The baby comes out the end that *hasn't* got makeup on, right?"

"These days? You'd be surprised," Dave muttered.

"I even had a girlfriend once," I added without really thinking it through.

"I know. You told me. You were both six, and you only liked her 'cos she let you wear her Barbie slippers."

I'd told Dave that? Christ, I must have been drinking heavily that night. "I hope you've been treating that information as confidential."

"Worried someone might think you're gay? Anyway, far as I'm concerned, that does *not* qualify you to deliver a baby, all right? So get a bloody shift on."

I let the dodgy logic and the doubt in my abilities slide. He had stuff on his mind.

After all that, when we finally pulled up in front of Dave's well-kept semi in a much nicer street than mine, scrambled out of the car, and legged it to the front door, it was a bit of an anticlimax. We were met by Mrs. Next-door with her arms folded and bloodstains on her yoga pants, and told it was all over bar the shouting. "They're upstairs. Jen's fine and so's the kid."

"Blimey, that was quick," I said, as Dave took off upstairs faster than I'd ever seen him move, in a sort of loping waddle.

Mrs. Next-door shrugged. "Third baby." Then she grinned. "Don't think Jen was in a hurry to call Dave, either. He's been fussing round her like an old woman. Driving her mad, it was. Right. I'm off to get changed."

I half thought about sneaking off and leaving them all to it—this was a family time, and I wasn't family—but before I could make up my mind to get going, Dave appeared at the top of the stairs, holding a bundle of stained towels in a way that strongly suggested he wasn't just taking them to the laundry basket.

He came down the stairs a lot slower than he'd gone up.

"It's a boy." Dave's eyes were shining. "Look at 'im. You ever seen a kid so bleedin' perfect?"

He held out the wrinkled, still-bloodstained bundle for my admiration. Southgate junior took one look at my ugly mug and started to howl the place down.

"Great pair of lungs on him," I said, 'cos you have to in situations like this.

Dave cuddled him close, looking like the Michelin man holding a doll. "He's a fucking champ, this kid. Come on, let's get you back to your lovely mum. Cheers, Tom. I'll catch you in a day or two." The baby stopped crying, either recognising his dad already or knocked out by Dave's beery breath.

"I'll give you a call before we come round, yeah?" I called softly after him, feeling a bit shiny-eyed myself.

Just as I left, the midwife turned up. "You're too late, love," I told her.

"Everyone all right?" she asked briskly.

"Yeah, seems so. Little boy. Looks just like his dad." By which I meant, not a lot of hair, red in the face, and slightly worse for wear right now but basically okay.

"Did she deliver the placenta all right?"

"Uh . . . Really not my area. They're upstairs, yeah?"

I legged it.

Phil was still up—there was a light on in his top-floor flat. I parked on the street nearby and took the stairs two at a time once he'd buzzed me up.

"What happened to drinks with Dave?" he asked with definite air of expectation.

I grinned. "Just what you're thinking happened. It's a boy. Got a wail like a bloody banshee."

"Mother and baby doing well?"

"Far as I could tell. I mean, Dave brought the nipper downstairs to show me, so I'm guessing there weren't any medical emergencies going on."

Phil gave me a smile of the sort he never lets out in public. "Good to hear it. Fancy a drink to celebrate?"

"Uh . . . better not. I'm driving, and I already had a couple at the White Hart with Dave."

He shrugged. "So stay the night. The cats'll cope."

He had a point. "All right, then. What are we drinking? I was on beer at the pub."

"Beer it is, then." He grabbed a couple of bottles from the fridge, opened them, and passed one to me. We sat down on the sofa and put our feet up on the table.

I'd taken my boots off already. I'm not that much of a slob.

"Here's to Dave and his family, and especially the newest member," Phil said a bit on the formal side, raising his bottle.

"To the sprog," I agreed, and we both drank.

After all the excitement of the evening, I was yawning before I'd even finished my first bottle. Phil told me I might as well go to bed, which was fair enough, but then he followed me and proceeded to wake me up pretty thoroughly.

Not that I was complaining, mind, but I thought the logic was a bit lacking.

We lay there afterwards, catching our breath, and it struck me we'd never talked about it. I mean, I *thought* I knew what he'd say. He'd never brought up the subject, but there'd been hints, definitely. But I'd never asked him.

It felt like the right time, now. I rolled over a bit so I could look at him. "Do you think we'll ever . . . I mean, one day, do you think you'd wanna have kids?"

Phil stroked my hair and didn't speak for a moment.

I didn't hold my breath. Honest.

My chest still felt a lot easier somehow when he finally spoke. "Yeah. Yeah, I'd like to have kids. Not right now, but . . . Yeah."

"Good," I said, surprising myself by how much I meant it, and snuggled up closer. "And the moving-in thing, you want to do that, right? Move into mine?"

"Course I bloody do." He dropped a kiss to the top of my head. "You just tell me when you're ready, and I'll start packing. Tomorrow, if you like."

I knew he didn't mean *literally* tomorrow. He'd have to give notice to his landlord and stuff. And more to the point, I'd have to clear out the wardrobe so his posh suits and cashmere sweaters wouldn't get crumpled. But it was a nice thought. "Tell you what, we'll say Christmas by the latest, yeah?"

"By Christmas," Phil murmured into my hair, a smile in his voice, and Christ, it felt good to finally have it sorted.

I don't even remember when he turned off the light.

CHAPTER NINETEEN

We'd been invited over to Greg's for Sunday lunch, so after a nice long lie-in that got a bit energetic, we showered and then dashed to mine to feed two very irate cats. I thought Merlin would have my leg off before I'd managed to open the tin of cat food. Then I changed my clothes, and we headed off out to St. Leonards.

Cherry got a worryingly moist look in her eye when I told her about Dave's happy news. I wasn't sure if Greg noticed or not, and I wondered if I should warn him.

Nah, he'd find out soon enough if she was getting broody. Although whether it'd come to anything or not was a bit up in the air, at her age. Still, Dave and his missus had managed it, and they had to be older than my sis. And come to think of it, our own mum had been well past early forties when I'd made my debut appearance. So maybe Sis had genetics on her side, at that.

It was a weird thought. Me being an uncle, I mean. Actually, scratch that, it was *way* weirder thinking of Cherry being a mum. I wondered what Mum would think. She wasn't the sort who kept dropping hints about grandkids and knitting bootees on the off-chance, but I guessed she'd be pleased.

Still, carts before horses and all that. I bit my tongue to stop myself asking Cherry about it all while I helped her with the veg—Greg had a tendency just to roast *everything* if you left him to it, so Cherry had enlisted my help to try to keep the cholesterol count manageable. Well, that's how she put it. I had a suspicion she was more worried about not fitting into her wedding dress come February.

"I never asked you—how did it go with Phil's family?" Cherry asked, shifting cans and bottles around noisily in one of the cupboards.

"Bother. I was *sure* we had another jar of horseradish. It must be back at my house."

"Uh, yeah, I was meaning to ask you about that," I said, leaping on the opportunity to not answer her question. "Your house—what are you going to do with that after you and Greg get hitched? I mean, you're moving in here, right?"

"Oh yes. Well, actually, that was something I wanted to talk to you and Phil about. I don't want to sell, so the other option is to rent it out. But Gregory had quite a good idea—he thought perhaps you and Phil might like to live there. I mean," she added, turning pink. "Obviously we wouldn't expect you to wait until you're married before moving in. And of course we'd let you have it at a reduced rent. I haven't got a large mortgage, and as long as you cover that, it's fine."

Huh. That hadn't even occurred to me. Me and Phil live in Pluck's End? No question, Cherry's house was way nicer than we'd be able to afford any other way. Like Leanne said, it was dead posh round there. What would the neighbours think?

Heh. That was a selling point in itself. But it wasn't like I didn't have a perfectly good house of my own already. Okay, yeah, it was just a two-bed semi in Fleetville. But it was mine.

Course, it wasn't a *big* house. If me and Phil ever had those kids we'd talked about, it might start seeming a bit cramped. And Pluck's End was a nicer area for kids to grow up in, no question.

But all that was probably years down the line.

"Wouldn't you rather rent it out to someone who'll pay the going rate?" I hedged.

"Oh, the money doesn't matter," Sis said offhandedly.

Nice for some.

"It'd be worth it to know I had people in there I could trust not to wreck the place," she carried on.

Phil would probably jump at the chance to move somewhere a bit more upmarket than Fleetville. I wasn't sure why that thought gave me such a tight feeling in my chest.

Except . . . we'd *just* settled he was going to move into my house, and now it was all going to be up in the air again.

"Anyway, have a think about it, and let me know." Cherry frowned at a jar of English mustard. "This is nearly a year out of date. Do you think it matters?"

I unscrewed the lid and took a butcher's. Then I gave it a sniff. "Nah, I'm pretty sure it won't kill us. I won't tell if you don't."

Phil and Greg had disappeared by the time I made it out of the kitchen. Typical. I tracked 'em down in Greg's study, where he was showing Phil his latest taxidermy project. It was only a less-than-half-done wire frame at the mo, but it looked suspiciously birdlike.

"Oi, you didn't walk off with a feathered friend at the end of the fayre, did you?" I asked. "Or poison their birdseed?" I was joking, honest.

Mostly.

Greg guffawed, which was a bit on the ear-splittingly painful side in a room this small. "No, no. But the Swan Bottom people were most helpful in providing me with contacts, and by a fortunate chance, a specimen became available almost immediately."

"Pretty sure that's not how the bird would've seen it."

Greg looked guilty. "Ah. Perhaps not. Still, for the suffering, death can be a release."

I grinned. "You keep telling yourself that. Right, I think Cherry wants you in the kitchen."

Actually, her words had been more along the lines of *Tell him to stop showing off and come and* do *something*, but hey, I was pretty sure she'd have been mortified if I'd repeated them word-for-word.

"Lunch must be going all right, if she's let you out," Phil murmured, taking advantage of Greg's departure to pull me into his arms.

"Yeah, we'll probably survive it." Even with both of us fully clothed, I couldn't help smiling at the feel of his body pressed against mine.

Even the glassy-eyed stare of Greg's badger, who now had his own not-so-little alcove in the bookshelf, couldn't dampen the mood.

"So was this all just a lesson in taxidermy, or did you get anything useful out of Greg? About the case, I mean."

Phil huffed a laugh. "Greg reckons the bishop fancied Amelia."

I pulled back to stare at him. "He said that?"

"Not in so many words. He just suggested Toby might have 'experienced a moment or two of quiet regret' he hadn't met her before Alex Majors did."

I frowned. "You mean, when she was still married to Sir Prancelot? Huh. So Uncle Aardvark was telling the truth about Toby being her mate, not Alex's."

"Maybe. Or maybe Greg just heard the same story we did. It fits, though—Vi doesn't act like he's an old friend of the family."

"Nah, she seemed a bit creeped out by him, if you ask me."

We got called in to the dining room at that point, so I never got a chance to mention Cherry's house idea to Phil.

Ah, well. It'd keep.

For a while after we sat down to eat, the conversation was all of the *pass the gravy* variety. Well, once we'd disposed of the grace. Greg would probably get defrocked or excommunicated if he dared to taste his dinner without giving due credit to the bloke upstairs first. Still, at least he kept it decently short. Actually, this one was shorter than usual, possibly because my stomach rumbled loudly right in the middle.

What? It'd been a long time since breakfast.

"Tom? Toby asked if you'll be attending Amelia's funeral." Cherry looked like she had a bad taste in her mouth at the thought, but fair dues, she had just had a forkful of sprouts.

"Hadn't planned to," I said, just as Phil chimed in with "We'll be there."

We exchanged glances. He raised an eyebrow.

I shrugged. Fine. "When and where?"

"Tuesday at noon, in the cathedral," Greg answered. "Toby thought it would be appropriate, as she gave so much of herself to the diocese."

I had a sudden vision of Amelia literally giving herself to the bishop. On a silver platter. I just managed to hold back a snigger, so was saved from Cherry's disapproving look and Greg's sorrowful one.

"There will be a cold collation back here afterwards," Greg went on, oblivious.

"If old Tobe's the one pushing for her to have the big send-off," I asked, "how come the party's not over at his place? Come to think of it, where *is* his place?"

"Toby has a house out in the country. It wouldn't be suitable," Cherry said with a resigned note to her voice which suggested this wasn't the first time dear old Toby had managed to avoid having to do the mine-host bit by living somewhere *unsuitable.*

I frowned, trying to picture my work diary. If I rang up Mrs. M. and asked if I could come an hour early, it'd be doable, 'specially seeing as lunch was thrown in. Well, I assumed that was what Greg meant by *collation.* If not, I could always pick up a sarnie somewhere. "Yeah, I guess I can make it. What's it to Toby, though? Me going along, I mean."

This time, it was Cherry and Greg who exchanged glances. Clearly they had a different system of sign language than me and Phil, as I couldn't see what prompted it when Greg was the one who spoke. "Oh, Toby appears to have taken quite a shine to you, Tom."

I stared. "Yeah? How does he treat the people he *doesn't* like, then?"

Cherry made a weird snuffling sound.

I'm not saying it was a laugh, mind, but I'm not saying it wasn't either.

Greg sent her a gently reproachful look. She stared him out until he coughed and topped up her wine.

Go, Sis.

Phil, being Phil, just took advantage of the way the conversation had turned to the bishop. "Interesting man, your bishop," he said noncommittally.

Greg beamed. "Isn't he?"

"Don't suppose his duties leave a lot of time for a private life."

"Ah! Well, that's the interesting thing." Greg's eyebrows danced ponderously, like a couple of courting badgers of uncertain age. "The talk around Cathedral Close—although of course, one mustn't gossip—is that he's found himself a young lady. Certainly he's been spending more time away from his desk of late. All work and no play, as they say . . ."

It seemed weird to think of a bishop at play. "Hey, does he still wear the purple and the dog collar when he goes out on a date? Wouldn't that be a bit off-putting to the young lady?" Of course, maybe it was part of the attraction. I remembered how Greg and Cherry had met, and shot her a quick glance.

Her gaze was fixed firmly on her plate. But there was a definite pink tint to her cheeks, and I didn't reckon it was all down to the wine.

"Who's the lucky lady?" Phil asked Greg.

"Ah! Well, you see, nobody knows. Clearly someone who appreciates the value of discretion."

"Married, is she?" Oops. Just slipped out. But yeah, my Amelia-on-a-plate theory was looking good.

Cherry glared at me. "Don't be absurd. And for goodness' sake, don't go saying things like that where anyone *else* might hear."

Heh. Better not mention my *other* theory then, which was that *she* was actually a bloke. Old Tobes wouldn't be the first clergyman to spout fire and brimstone against homosexuals, all while getting his rocks off with them on the sly.

"Interesting," Phil said, and bunged a forkful of potatoes in his gob, the annoying git.

Cherry switched her glare to my intended. "Oh, come on. You can't just leave it like *that*."

Greg tried to shove an ecclesiastical oar in. "Now, if Philip isn't at liberty to say any more, we shouldn't press him."

"If he's not at liberty to say more, he shouldn't say anything at all. Should he, Tom?" Her gimlet stare switched back to me again.

I tried to ward it off with my cutlery. "Oi, don't drag me into this. But yeah, seriously?" I turned to Phil.

He smirked. "Word is, Violet Majors has also been seeing someone. And again, nobody seems to know who."

I frowned. "Whose word?"

"Polina Karwatsky."

"Who?"

"She's the Majors' cleaner." His expression got even smugger. "I don't just sit around in the office all day. I spoke to her Friday."

"Oh, is she Polish?" Cherry put in, which, yeah, had occurred to me but I hadn't planned to mention seeing as how it was completely irrelevant.

"Ukrainian."

"You kept that quiet," I not-quite-accused. And no, I wasn't talking about the girl's nationality.

He shrugged. "Didn't have a chance to mention it."

"While we're on the subject, Tom," Cherry said a bit louder than strictly necessary, leaning forward. She was going to get gravy on her top if she wasn't careful. "When are we going to meet your father?"

If she stretched her definition of *on the subject* any further, it'd snap and take someone's leg off. "Uh . . . Well, you know he lives over in Bristol, right? I mean, it's a long way at his age . . ."

Greg put down his fork. "I was hoping we might extend him an invitation to our wedding. After all, he is part of the family, albeit in a rather unconventional sense."

My knife fell from my hand. Greg was going to have to wash this tablecloth—or get Sis to do it for him, for all I knew—and serve 'em both bloody well right. "What? Hang on a mo. You can't do that. What about Dad?"

Cherry gave her fiancé an uneasy glance. "We've talked about it, and Gregory feels one shouldn't brush these things under the carpet."

"This isn't just not brushing it under the carpet. This is hanging it out the window for everyone to see and shouting 'Oi, look, dirty laundry here!'" I rounded on Cherry. "And you've changed your tune. What about the way you used to go on at me about not upsetting Mum and Dad? I don't know about you, but I reckon someone inviting the bloke I'd been cheated on with to a family do would bloody well upset me and then some."

I looked over at Phil, hoping for a bit of support here, but he was staring off into the middle distance doing moody-clam impressions.

Shit.

"Tom," Cherry said, her tone unhappy. "I know it's difficult, but Gregory and I . . . Well, we just thought it might be easier for you this way."

"*Easier*? How the bloody hell do you work that one out?"

"Well . . ." She cast a pleading look at Greg.

Her fiancé didn't leave her hanging. "We simply felt that it might be easier to introduce Mr. Novak at our wedding. Given that it is likely to be a rather larger affair than your own ceremony in the summer." Which was fair enough, seeing as pretty much the entire diocese was on the guest list for theirs. Greg's smile was kind and concerned. "There will be no need to spell matters out for those who don't already know. He can merely be introduced as an old friend of the family."

I swallowed. 'Cos they were right, weren't they? Not about having him at theirs first being easier, necessarily. Although maybe it would be, at that. It'd certainly be one major thing less to worry about when me and Phil tied the knot.

But about Mike Novak having to be part of my and Phil's wedding.

I mean, Christ, I'd been telling myself maybe he didn't have to come, that he'd understand it was for the best. But it wasn't like Dad didn't know about him being my real dad. Mike Novak would be the elephant in the room whether he was there or not—and God knows, I'd had no idea how I could break it to him he wasn't invited.

Or how I'd square it with my conscience afterwards. He was my . . . Well. Not my dad. But he was my father. Maybe I wasn't too happy with the way he'd buggered off and left when Mum told him to, but if I told him to piss off when it came to family occasions, I'd just be doing the exact same thing, wouldn't I?

Blood's blood, innit?

"More wine, Tom?" Greg asked, holding out the bottle of red and politely not mentioning the way I must have been staring into space for the last five minutes while that little personal epiphany unfolded.

"Uh, yeah. Ta."

"So anyway," Cherry went on brightly. "We were thinking you could bring him round for lunch one Sunday. But no hurry. Although it will have to be before December, obviously. Now, we're trying to decide what the ushers should wear. How would you feel about putting on a top hat and tails, Tom?"

It was just as well I'd already got gravy on the tablecloth. That way, I didn't have to feel guilty about the way I spluttered red wine all over it.

"You all right?" Phil asked as I drove us back to St. Albans. We'd taken my Fiesta, as it hadn't had a good run for a while now and had probably been getting itchy wheels.

"Fine." My hands tightened on the wheel.

"You don't have to let them steamroller you into having your real dad at our wedding if you don't want to. Or theirs, for that matter."

I didn't tell him he could have spoken up at the time. I had a fair idea why he hadn't.

"No, they're right. He should be there. I mean, at our do. I don't s'pose he really gives a toss about Cherry's wedding, but yeah, probably best to get the awkward stuff over with at their do, not ours." I took a deep breath. "And we should set a date. Start looking at venues, all that bollocks. Dunno why I've been putting it off, really."

Now, see, this is why I love my bloke. Instead of saying *You don't? It's been bleedin' obvious to me*, he just put a hand on my thigh and squeezed it gently.

"Oi, none of that," I told him with a weak smile. "You'll get me done for driving without due care and attention."

"Can't have that, can we?" Phil took a breath. "There's a place we could take a look at on the way back, if you want. I'll direct you."

Working out what sort of a place he was on about didn't tax the old mental faculties unduly, and I gave him a look. "Oh yeah? You been scouting out gay-friendly wedding venues on the sly?"

"Darren suggested it. Said he took a look when him and Gary were planning theirs, and it wasn't his sort of place but he thought I might like it."

Okay, so now I was intrigued. "Any word on whether I'm likely to go for it?"

"Just have to make up your own mind, won't you? Right. You want to take a right at the roundabout, then left down past St. Stephen's."

I tootled on down in the Fiesta. "Are we nearly there yet?"

"Yes. Now turn right."

"Oi, we're not going to your mum's, are we?" I asked, suspicious. "I know we said a small wedding, but I don't reckon her front room's gonna take more than a dozen, and that's if we squash 'em in like sardines."

Phil smiled. "No, we're not going to Mum's. Just keep going."

I kept going. Just as I was wondering if the housing estate was ever going to end, it did, and we were out in the countryside again. I was well confused. "Hang on a mo," I started.

"There it is," Phil interrupted. "Right here."

I turned down a tree-lined lane I really wouldn't have expected to find here—and there it was: a big old Georgian red-brick frontage with a wide sweep of lawn outside. The drive led us round the back, past what were probably really nice flower gardens in the summer, and even now weren't doing too badly, with a healthy-looking selection of shrubs.

I hadn't spotted any signs out the front that it was anything other than some posh bastard's country cottage, but here at the back it was obvious it was a hotel, with a nice-looking car park—and there's a phrase I never thought I'd need—and a discreetly tasteful sign proclaiming its four-star status. "Hang on a mo," I said again. "Isn't this gonna cost an arm and a leg?" I wouldn't be surprised if they asked for a couple of kidneys on top.

"Not if we have the wedding on a weekday. They do an off-peak deal. Sundays too, but I reckoned that'd be difficult for Greg and your sister. Park up, and we can take a look inside."

I parked. I was beginning to think Phil had put a bit more thought into this than just having heard the name from Darren. I wiped my palms on my jeans as I got out of the car. Christ, what if he'd set his heart on this place and I hated it?

We crunched over the gravel to the main door. Halfway there, a flash of colour caught my eye, and I turned to see a bright-red bridge over an ornamental pond, half-hidden by plants.

"Chinese garden," Phil said. "Thought it'd be a good spot for the wedding photos."

"Uh, if you've already booked the place, now would be a good time to mention it." I wasn't really joking.

"We're just taking a look, all right? If you hate it, that's no problem. We'll find somewhere else." He said it like he meant it.

Course, in his line of work, being a good liar can come in pretty handy.

I took a deep breath and pushed open the door.

Inside it was bloody lovely. The reception area was all rich, deep colours and dark wood panelling—actually, to be honest, it reminded me a bit of the White Hart. It was posh, no doubt about it, but it seemed comfortable too.

My mum would love this place, I realised. Cherry would *adore* it. It was just the sort of venue I reckoned she'd have gone for, if she hadn't been getting hitched in St. Leonards cathedral.

The young lady at the desk looked up and gave us a smile. Her name tag said *Sally*. "Welcome to Cottonmill Hall. Can I help you with anything?"

"All right if we take a look around?" Phil asked her. "We're trying to find a wedding venue."

"Oh, how lovely. For the two of you? Have you been together long?"

Phil nodded. "Nearly a year now."

"Fantastic. And did you have a date in mind? I'm afraid summer Saturdays tend to get booked up quite far in advance."

"We were thinking of a weekday. Maybe July?"

"Oh, I'm sure we'll be able to accommodate you, then. You'll find a lot of things much easier if you're not going for the traditional Saturday." Her smile turned conspiratorial. "And, of course, it's much better value for money. How many guests, roughly?"

"Probably no more than fifty."

Sally beamed. "Smaller weddings are so much nicer, I always think. Much more intimate and friendly." She was good, this girl. "Just give me one moment to get someone to cover for me, and I'll take you round."

She disappeared out back and returned a minute or two later with an equally bright and smiley young man by the name of Tim, unless his name tag was telling porkies. Tim congratulated us on our engagement, told us we wouldn't regret choosing Cottonmill Hall, and beamed happily as Sally led us away. Maybe they put something in the water round here.

"As you're having such an intimate celebration, you'll be able to use the conservatory for dining if you'd like to." She pushed open a door.

The room beyond was flippin' gorgeous. I mean, you think conservatory, you picture something small and hexagonal tacked on to the back of someone's semi, but this place was massive. It was light and airy, with a whole row of French windows that opened onto the gardens. I could just imagine it in summer, with the windows wide open and the curtains blowing in the breeze. At the mo, they had it set up with chintzy bamboo chairs and low tables, and there was a low fire burning in the grate at the end nearest the main building that gave it a cosy feel.

"Like it?" Phil asked, his voice low.

"Yeah," I said, unable to keep the surprise out of my voice. "Yeah, I do."

It was a bloody good thing it wasn't far to drive back to mine from the hotel. We'd left the place with a bundle of brochures, several pages of notes in Phil's notebook, and a provisional booking for July. I was in a bit of a daze.

I realised as I parked up I hadn't even asked Phil if he wanted to come back to mine. It was getting on for teatime now, although after our Sunday roast, I didn't reckon either of us would be hungry anytime soon. "Uh, sorry. Did you want to be dropped off at your flat?"

He laughed, the bastard. "Trust me, I'd have told you. Wasn't sure it was safe to leave you on your own right now anyhow." Then his face turned serious. "This is what you want, right?"

I guessed he wasn't talking about him coming in for a cuppa. "Yeah. Just . . . taking a while to get used it, you know?"

"If you think we're going too fast—"

"No. No, it's good. I'm good." I took a deep breath, wiped my hand on my jeans, and turned to look at him directly. "It's what I want. You. Me. Getting hitched. And the place is great. It's perfect. Good choice."

He looked grumpy. "It's not supposed to be my choice. It's supposed to be *our* choice."

"And it is." I forced a smile. "I really liked it. And you didn't pressure me into it, all right? Okay, yeah, Sally the sales fiend knew all the right buttons to push, but you didn't make me do anything I didn't wanna. Now are we gonna sit in my car all night, or are we gonna go inside and have a cup of tea?"

Phil smirked. "I can think of things I'd rather have. And we'd definitely better go inside for that."

So we did.

It wasn't until much, much later, when Phil had disappeared off back to his flat saying he had stuff to do and an early start on Monday morning, that I realised I'd forgotten to tell him about Cherry's offer of the house.

Ah, well. There'd be plenty of time for that.

CHAPTER TWENTY

had vaguely thought I'd just ring Cherry and tell her me and Phil had set a date for the wedding and picked a venue and all that guff, but it occurred to me she'd probably want a longer conversation about it than we tended to do over the phone. Plus I'd sort of left the Mike Novak question hanging a bit, and we probably ought to clear that up too. So when I gave her a bell Sunday evening after Phil had gone, I just arranged to meet for lunch on Monday.

Given that'd be two lunches with her in two days, my phone call left her clearly ready to combust with curiosity, which was a nice little added bonus.

Then it occurred to me I probably ought to have a word with the man himself before I started making all these plans involving him.

I looked at my watch. Still pretty early. He'd probably be in, and he wouldn't have gone to bed yet. I took a deep breath and called his number. As it rang, I had a moment's panic—it was a landline number, and chances were, the whole family would be home. What if his wife answered? Or his son—his *legitimate* son? Should I introduce myself? Had he even told them about me?

In the end, it was Mike's voice I heard. At least, I was betting Novak junior didn't have that trace of foreign accent I associated with his dad, having been born and bred here. Panic over. "Hello?"

"Uh, hi. It's Tom."

"Tom! It's good to hear from you. How are you? You're well?"

"Yeah, I'm good. You?"

"Ah, can't complain. My knees are giving me trouble again, but then, I'm old. What can you expect? How is that young man of yours?"

"Phil?" Like there was anyone else he might mean. "Yeah, he's good too. Actually, that was what I wanted to talk to you about. We've, uh, we've set a date for the wedding." I named it, trying to ignore the weird feeling in my stomach. "And, um, you're coming, right? I mean, if you want to?"

"Of course." Something about the slight pause before he said it, and the warmth when he finally did, told me he hadn't been counting on an invite. I felt a right git for almost living down to his expectations. "I wouldn't miss it for the world. And my boy, Daniel, is looking forward to meeting his brother."

I'd invited him too? Oo-kay. "Uh, yeah. Me too." I was. Honest.

"My Anna too. She can't wait to meet you." Well, that cleared up the question of whether he'd mentioned my existence. Hopefully it also meant they *hadn't* been a thing back when Mike and my mum had been doing the dirty. Oh God. If Mike's wife was coming to the wedding too, that meant she and Mum would meet. If they *had* been a thing back then, would she still bear a grudge after thirty years?

I had a brief, surreal, and frankly horrifying vision of Mrs. Novak grabbing Dad for a quick snog to get her own back and only just managed to stifle a nervous laugh.

We chatted a few minutes longer, mostly about all the extended family back in Poland who'd be sorry to miss the wedding (given what I'd read online about attitudes to gay people in Poland, I had a strong suspicion he was either deluding himself or just being polite), then said goodbye. Mike signed off with a promise to bring the vodka. Or possibly the wodka.

I had a feeling I was going to need it.

Monday lunch with Cherry went pretty much as expected. She was over the moon we'd set a date and suitably impressed with the venue. Turned out she'd been to a wedding there a couple of years ago—well, the reception had been there, anyhow. The actual wedding had been "a proper one, in church, of course."

Then she'd remembered who she was talking to, blushed, and apologised.

I had to laugh. "Never mind. Maybe we'll get Greg to give us a blessing, yeah?"

Sis looked doubtful for a mo, which I took to mean she wasn't sure how keen old Tobes would be about that sort of thing going on in his cathedral. Then her frown eased, probably because she'd worked out just how low the chances were of me ever actually bothering to try to arrange it.

"I'm quite surprised you went for Cottonmill Hall," she said, fiddling with her uneaten breadstick. Sis always wanted to meet for Italian when we had lunch, but she never ate anything there with carbs in it like pasta or pizza, which I'd always thought was the best bit of Italian food. Maybe it was some sort of modern-day Christian equivalent of the hair shirt.

Or maybe she just liked feeling morally superior to the rest of us all chomping down on our stodge.

"Why's that, then? Too classy for an oik like me?"

She flushed, meaning yes. "I just didn't think it was the sort of place you'd feel comfortable."

"Oi, I can do classy. What were you expecting—back room of a pub?"

"Pretty much, yes." She smiled. "Phil's been a good influence on you."

Huh. Did that mean I'd changed since me and Phil had got together? If I had, was that a good thing?

I was still worrying about it when I swung by Phil's office after my last job of the day.

You don't like to think someone's changed you, do you? Either it means you're not the bloke they fell in love with, or it means they took you on as a fixer-upper.

Course, if I asked Phil about it, he'd just think I was being daft. Still, maybe I could sort of edge around the subject . . .?

Sod's law, the decision was taken out of my hands, at least for now, seeing as I'd barely got in the door before it opened again behind me. "Alban Investigations?"

I turned to see a woman in her thirties wearing a frumpy business suit and frazzled hair. "Yeah, you're in the right place," I told her with a smile.

Hey, it's in my vested interest to keep my bloke's business ticking over nicely. Someone's got to pay for the champagne and caviar.

Or beer and bacon butties, as might be.

"Are you Phil Morrison?" she demanded.

I gestured to the man himself, who'd stood up behind his desk. "Mrs. Quinn? What can I do for you?"

"You can stop bloody spying on me, that's what." Her fists were clenched by her sides. They were also shaking just a little. I didn't reckon we were in any danger of her throwing a punch.

"Mrs. Quinn, I was asked to investigate your claim of identity theft. I'm happy to say the issue has now been resolved in your favour."

That caught her on the hop. "Oh," she said, in a small voice. "You mean . . ."

"You should be getting a letter in the post in the next day or so confirming debt collection proceedings have been cancelled."

"Oh." The wind was so far out of her sails, I grabbed the client chair and shoved it in her direction before she totally deflated and collapsed in a heap on the carpet.

"Cup of tea, love?" I suggested once she was safely sitting down.

"No . . . No, I'm fine. Thank you. So I'm off the hook? Completely?"

Phil nodded. Then he cleared his throat. "You might want to have a word with your ex-husband, however."

"Colin?"

"Or Christian, as he's been going by lately. Well, whenever he takes out a credit card, that is."

"I don't believe it." The tone she said it in called her a liar, and she stared at her hands, busy playing cat's cradle without any string in her lap.

"Divorce can be bitter," Phil said diplomatically.

Mrs. Q. looked up at that. "Bitter? I'll tell you what's bitter. First, having a name that makes everyone think you're a man, especially after that *bloody* book that's had everyone making bondage jokes the minute I introduce myself, and second, having someone bloody well steal it. Have you got any idea what that's like? I could kill that bastard."

I coughed. "Not a great sort of statement to be throwing around, just saying. You never know what's gonna happen."

"I wish it bloody well would." She looked up at me, her eyes teary with anger. "I don't expect you to understand. A name's more than a name. It's a symbol. It means *me*. He took my name, and he made it mean something . . . something *less*. Made it mean someone who doesn't pay their debts, who orders things they never intended to pay for. He ruined it."

I crouched down by her chair. "Look, love, you're more than just a name. Anyone who knows you would know you're not like that." Not that I'd know, to be honest, but after all she'd been through, she deserved the benefit of the doubt. "You could change your name tomorrow and you'd still be the same person. In fact, why don't you do that? Go back to your maiden name and forget about that bastard."

She gave me a trembly smile. "Should have done that a long time ago. Not so easy, though, is it? Even after everything the bastards do to you, you just keep hoping it'll all go back the way it was. You're right, though. Sod him."

She did stay for a cuppa after that, then we bid a fond fare-thee-well to the newly christened—or rechristened—Ms. T.

When I turned round after closing the door behind her, Phil was smirking at me. "So, names don't matter, then, Mr. Patschke stroke Paretski stroke Nowak-with-a-*w* stroke—"

"I'll stroke something in a minute, and not in a good way." I glared at him.

The smirk didn't fade.

Oh, fuck a bloody duck. I gave in and slumped down on the client chair, my head thrown back. "Fine," I told the ceiling. "Maybe, just *maybe* I was making a mountain out of a bloody molehill over this whole Mike Novak business."

Phil got up, walked around the desk, and swivelled the chair to face him. He crouched down and ran his hands up and down my thighs. "No you weren't. Not really. But there's worse things in the world than not being totally sure which country your great-grandad came from."

Yeah. I guessed there really were. Like having the bloke you loved turn out to be a bastard. "Did you keep hoping about Mark?" I blurted out, and wished I hadn't.

Phil's face turned bleak. "Really want to ask that?"

No. No, I guessed I didn't.

We headed off back to mine after that. The weather had turned a bit wet and windy—proper autumn squall—so I did bangers and mash for tea to warm us up a bit.

Any suggestions I might've wanted comfort food for reasons other than the weather are gonna get roundly ignored, all right?

Afterwards, we curled up on the sofa with some proper coffee and a couple of choccy biccies. Also a couple of sulky cats, annoyed 'cos neither of us had a hand free to pay them the attention that was theirs by God-given right.

There was nothing interesting on the telly, so after a while, I got to thinking. "You never said what you wanted to do about names when we get married, did you?" I said, making sure I was looking Phil right in the eye.

Yep. There it was. The expression froze. "We should talk about it," he said at last.

"Yeah, see, I was thinking." I took a deep breath. I was pretty sure I'd got this right. "We're both in business, and it doesn't pay to confuse people. And the way I see it, neither of us deserves to lose out financially just 'cos some people are tossers. So maybe we should stick with what we've got, yeah? Forget about the double-barrelling."

Phil's face softened. "Yeah. I reckon that's a good idea. If you're sure?"

I smiled. "Yeah. I'm sure."

After all, what's in a name? Really?

Phil put down his mug and slung his arm around me. Arthur was visibly Not Amused by this wanton display of skewed priorities, but he could suck it up and deal.

Then, of course, the doorbell rang.

"I'll get it," I said, seeing as (a) it was my house, strictly speaking, and (b) Phil was currently weighed down by around fifteen pounds of cat.

I opened the door, half-eaten choccy biccie in hand and still munching on my mouthful. And nearly choked.

It was Vi Majors, queen of the bloody annoying timing. She didn't look happy.

"What the bloody *hell* do you think you're doing?" She took down her umbrella, shook it briskly so that fat, cold drops of water landed all over me—*and* my flippin' biccie—and stomped past me into the hall without so much as a by-your-leave.

"Make yourself at home, love," I said sarcastically.

"Is that partner of yours here? Good." Clearly Phil was still in the living room where I'd left him. "I'm paying you to find a necklace, not a bloody murderer."

I made it into the living room. Vi had her fists clenched, squaring up to my Phil, who just stood there looking irritatingly calm—well, I bet it got Vi's back up—with his arms folded.

"What makes you think I'm not doing just that?" he asked.

"I spoke to Uncle Arlo today. He told me *everything*. He said you practically accused him of causing his sister's death."

"Oi," I said, narked. "That's not how I remember it."

Phil glared at me. Typical. There's no pleasing some people. Then he turned to Vi. "Miss Majors, I never suggested your uncle had murdered his sister. Just that the replica necklace was involved in her death. As you already know."

She actually threw up her hands and made a sort of truncated boiling-kettle noise. "Why would a fake necklace have anything to do with murder?"

Phil didn't answer her question, just carried on asking his own. "Were you aware that your uncle had made the replica necklace for your stepmother?"

Vi reddened. "Of course I was."

Was she lying? I couldn't tell.

See, *that*, now, that'd be a useful psychic gift to have.

Phil didn't give any sign he didn't believe her. "And you didn't think that information might be relevant to the investigation?"

Vi gave him the blankest look I'd ever seen. "Why on earth should I have? What the hell has the fake got to do with anything? I want you to find the *real* necklace."

I was watching Phil, not her, so I spotted it when the muscle twitched in his jaw.

There was no sign of it when he spoke, though. "Finding out the circumstances under which the replica was commissioned could give a valuable insight into what might have happened to the real necklace."

"Oh, that's bollocks."

"Miss Majors, you hired me to carry out this investigation. If you're not happy—"

"No, I'm *not* happy. Not in the slightest. In fact, I don't think I want to pay you anymore. You can just leave it. Send me a bill for your time so far. Or *don't*, actually, seeing as you weren't spending it on what I'd hired you to do." She wheeled round to give me a glare for no reason I could see. "You're just a couple of frauds. Both of you."

I was narked. "Oi, consultant to the coppers, here."

I mean, maybe I don't go around shouting about my psychic abilities, but I'm not gonna stand for people calling me a faker.

"Tom," Phil said warningly.

I shot him a glance, meaning *What?*

There was a nasty suspicion of an eye roll in the look he sent back my way. I didn't have much time to get annoyed about it, though, 'cos then Vi was stomping past me, catching me a hefty blow on the shoulder as she passed on her way out.

With her shoulder, I mean. She didn't punch me or anything. Luckily for both of us, I imagined.

I took an involuntary step backwards, a bit on the clumsy side, and winced as my hip complained.

"You all right?" Phil asked, at my side in an instant.

I frowned. "Course I am. I just trod awkward, that's all."

He huffed. The front door slammed loud enough to make me worry for the glass, so I guessed we were on our own again.

"Weather's getting colder," I offered. My hip always gives me more gyp in winter, as he well knows. The fact it was a balmy fourteen degrees today was neither here nor there.

Phil gave me a look. "Fine. You're fine. There's still a sofa over there with your name on it. Come on."

We trooped over to the sofa, Phil pointedly going first so I wouldn't have to struggle not to limp.

Okay, so he was nearest it anyway. So what?

Phil settled into one corner of the sofa, and I settled into a corner of Phil, with his arm round my shoulders and my feet up on the coffee table. And if you think people can't have corners, you haven't met my beloved.

"What do you reckon all that was about?" I asked, to get the conversation off the subject of my hip soonest. "Old Arlo put the frighteners on Vi? Or do you reckon she's covering for someone?" I thought about it. "Like, say, that secret bloke of hers?"

Phil shrugged. "Maybe. Or she just didn't like us upsetting him when he's already grieving."

"Why'd she care? He's not even her real uncle. Surprised they're even still speaking. I mean, the way he talked about Vi didn't sound like there was a lot of love lost between 'em."

"Probably doesn't say that sort of thing to her face, though."

"True." I thought about it. "That whole Uncle Arlo thing—think that means anything?"

He frowned, in that special way that generally means I have no idea what you're talking about and I strongly suspect you don't either.

"I mean, she's nearly thirty, right? Our age. If your mum remarried, would you call the new bloke's brother 'Uncle' anything?"

"No, but then I don't talk about my parents as *Mummy and Daddy* either."

"Yeah, when a woman that age talks about her daddy, it usually means something totally different. Think she's got one of them and all?" I grinned, and then had a light bulb moment. "Oi, you don't think it's the bish, do you? Her secret bloke? I mean, he's got someone secret too, hasn't he?"

Phil just looked at me.

"What?" I asked, pulling back to gaze at him properly because the nearness was making me squint.

"He's a bishop, not a Catholic cardinal," he explained patiently.

"So?"

"*So*, he's allowed to have a girlfriend. Why would they keep the relationship a secret?"

"Well, I could see Amelia getting a bit narked about it."

"Not anymore, she isn't."

"Okay, back to the rentboy theory. Or choirboy, I s'pose." That thought left a bitter taste in my mouth.

"Greg reckoned the bishop's seeing someone," Phil pointed out. "As in, spending time with them. Not just having an illicit fumble in the vestry."

"True," I said, relieved. "So are you gonna follow him? See what's what?"

"Maybe." There was that trademark Phil Morrison noncommittal tone again.

I slapped on the sarcasm with a shovel. "You know, if you think I'm talking bollocks, you could just tell me."

He smirked. "Don't like to keep repeating myself."

"Git."

"You wouldn't have me any other way," he said smugly, pulling me in tight again.

"Oi, I'll have you any way you like," I said, because, well, it's true.

CHAPTER TWENTY-ONE

S ay what you like about Amelia Fenchurch-Majors, she got a good turnout at her funeral. St. Leonards cathedral wasn't quite bursting at the seams, but there were a sight more mourners than I'd ever seen at any send-off not involving royalty. And that was without any strong-arming people to come along, unless she'd been doing it from beyond the grave.

Course, one or two of those present might just have turned up to make sure they actually buried her.

Not that I'd have included myself in that number, obviously.

Me and Phil had had a brief discussion about whether we still ought to turn up, given our current state of persona-non-grata-dom with Vi. Phil, though, was adamant the little matter that we'd been fired from working on the case wasn't going to stop him, and anyway, it wasn't like we'd be intruding on Vi's grief, seeing as she'd made it pretty plain she wasn't feeling any. So we went.

This being the Home Counties and not a Hollywood film, most people weren't in top-to-toe black, just wearing smart and vaguely sombre clothing, and there were definitely no posh hats with veils. I'd ended up wearing the suit I'd got for Gary's wedding. The grey was a bit on the light side, but it was easily the smartest outfit I owned. Phil, of course, possessed more suits than you can shake a tape measure at, and was in dark navy today.

The grieving widower was in dark grey, which was just as well with Vi hanging on his arm rocking a vivid purple frock. With black tights and heels, mind, so I s'pose at least she'd tried. Uncle Armband was in a navy suit like Phil, but several waist sizes larger and with exponentially more wrinkles. On his arm was a pale lady clearly in dire need of less stress in her life or, failing that, Botox. I couldn't put my finger on it, but for some reason, she really didn't look like she belonged there.

"Who's that?" I whispered to Phil.

"Mrs. Fenchurch. Elizabeth. Used to be a solicitor but gave it up due to ill health. For which read anxiety and depression."

"Yeah? Couldn't old Arlo give her something shiny to cheer her up?" I looked at her again and realised what had seemed odd about her. "Hang on, how come a jeweller's wife isn't wearing a scrap of jewellery?" She didn't even have the tiniest of studs in her ears. "Is that a funeral thing?"

"Could be. Pearls are traditional, mind."

I was already scanning the necks of the other ladies present. Yep, a fair assortment of pearls on display. I spotted my sister standing over by a display commemorating local soldiers who'd fallen in the Great War, their faces staring solemnly out from black-and-white photos, every upper lip as stiff as their uniformed spines. Cherry was wearing pearls, or at least what looked like pearls to my unschooled eye. For all I knew she'd got 'em out of a cracker. She caught my eye and smiled, so I waved.

And yeah, I realised that probably wasn't appropriate even before she gave me a scandalised look and turned pointedly away, ta very much.

Other ladies were wearing thin gold chains, some with crosses on, silver pendants . . . The usual, really, although I noticed nobody had on anything you'd describe as bling apart, of course, from our old mate Toby with his cross. Even Vi had on a restrained gold necklace. I wondered if it had been her mother's, and if so, whether it was a final, subtle *fuck you* to her dear departed stepmother.

The murmur of conversation all around us had a weird feel to it—too loud for a cathedral, but not loud enough for the number of people present. People were chatting, yeah, but they kept their voices low, and no one was joking or laughing. Somehow, though, you could tell it was just 'cos people knew how they ought to behave, not because they were genuinely cast down over Amelia's death. Every now and then someone would give a quick smile at something that was said, and then straighten their face out hurriedly.

Poor lady. Not much of a legacy.

"Come on, let's go and say hi to Cherry and Greg," I said, because people were starting to give me funny looks after all my staring at women's chests.

We wandered over to where they were standing, Greg in earnest conversation with a couple of little old ladies. The height difference and a slight case of dowager's hump on the part of one of 'em meant he was bent almost double in an effort to talk face-to-face.

Cherry was wearing a black suit that looked like she'd bought it for court appearances, and the world's clumpiest shoes. Greg, obviously, was in the usual dog-collar-and-black-suit combo he always wore for church affairs that didn't call for the fancy embroidered frocks he generally got to put on for special occasions.

We caught the end of Greg's conversation—something about vol-au-vents—and then the ladies scurried away. Greg gave us a suitably restrained and sombre smile in welcome. "Tom, Philip. So good to see you at this sad time."

He sounded so sincere I didn't have the heart to point out he'd seen us not two days ago, and we weren't any sadder now than we had been then. "Uh, yeah. Good turnout, innit?"

Cherry muttered something that sounded a lot like *Ghouls*, to which Greg didn't react. I was glad to see he'd already developed selective hearing.

"Indeed. Her energy and vision will be much missed."

Yeah, right. Some of those present had probably already given thanks.

A bright flash amongst all the dark colours caught my eye, and I turned. Lance Frith, who I'd assumed didn't own any articles of clothing that weren't black and would therefore be spoilt for choice, was wearing head-to-toe white. Weirdo.

I leaned in to mutter to Phil, "Christ. He looks like he's on his way to a cricket match. Or his own gay wedding."

Phil shrugged. "White's a mourning colour in some cultures."

"Yeah, but not this one." At least he'd left off the pendulum. He still stuck out like a gangrenous thumb in our conservative company. I wouldn't have been surprised if people thought he was taking the piss, turning up dressed like a ghost in a sixties' TV show.

Come to that, I wouldn't have been totally gobsmacked to find he *was* taking the piss. I just didn't know where I was with Lance, and I felt awkward as hell when he turned and caught my eye. He smiled and took a step in my direction like he was about to come over, but just then the organ started playing, and we all made a restrained scramble for seats. Phil and me found chairs near the back and managed not to scrape the legs too loudly on the floor tiles as we sat down. DI Sharp of the St. Leonards constabulary, who I remembered from the fayre kerfuffle, sat down at the far end of the row. Was he hoping the murderer had come along to gloat? Maybe he reckoned they'd be overcome with guilt in such Godly surroundings and blurt out a confession?

I nudged Phil. "Seen the representative of the law?" I whispered.

He nodded but didn't say anything. I looked back at the DI, saw he was staring straight at me, and looked away again quick.

Shit. Did that make me look guilty? I glanced back deliberately, to show I had nothing to hide, but he'd turned to the front by then, the bastard.

Despite taking place in a cathedral, the funeral was pretty much like any other I could remember. Toby's address from the pulpit painted a picture of a selfless, community-spirited woman I was pretty sure I'd never met and neither had he. The tears he had to wipe from the corners of his eyes were a nice touch, mind. Maybe he even believed what he was saying.

Or maybe we'd just cleared up the question of who Toby's secret lover was—sorry, had been.

I felt like a total bastard for being so cynical when Alex Majors got up to say a few words about his dead wife and was too overcome with emotion to actually get them out. To my total surprise, it was Vi who came to his rescue. I mean, not that I ever doubted she cared about her dad, but I was pretty amazed by the way she did it.

She stood up next to him, linked her arm in his, and said a few short words about her stepmum with no hidden barbs whatsoever. About how Amelia had brought joy back into her daddy's life after they'd lost her mum. Seriously, if you weren't in the know, you'd have thought they'd got on just fine. I took my metaphorical hat off to the girl and, glancing around, wasn't the only one. Even Uncle Arlo had an impressed look on his face.

It was him up next, and he managed a convincing portrayal of grief as he spoke about Amelia being more like a daughter to him than a sister. There was hardly a dry eye in the place, and even I was coming over a bit misty.

Then I glanced at Arlo's missus. She was paler than ever and staring straight-ahead, her lips pressed together in a tight line. I got the impression that not only was she deliberately not looking at Uncle Artful, she wasn't looking at *anything*.

What the hell was all that about?

Fortunately for the mob of mourners in general, and yours truly in particular, it turned out that a cold collation did indeed mean lunch, although it was all a bit on the dainty side. Apart from the vol-au-vents, which were massive, flaky, and stuffed to bursting with either coronation chicken or prawn cocktail. Despite the weird feeling of being in a 1970s time warp, they looked bloody delicious, but sod's law, I didn't dare eat one for fear of ruining my suit.

I caught a lot of interested glances from the so-called mourners, but at least no one had the bad taste—or maybe the nerve—to come over and grill me about finding the body, so at least I got to eat in peace.

Vi was still clinging to her dad's arm as he did the rounds of Greg's front room mechanically, thanking everyone for coming. When it came to my and Phil's turn, I got the definite impression he hadn't even registered who he was talking to.

After a while, Vi sat Daddy down with a plate of food I don't reckon he even looked at, and went to do the rest of the social stuff by herself. Phil went off to get some more vol-au-vents—he had ninja eating skills, the lucky git, and hadn't got so much as a stray flake on his lapel. I heaped a few more finger sandwiches on my plate, regretfully. Then I turned round to find myself face-to-sleepy-face with Uncle Arlo.

He raised a lethargic eyebrow. "No messages from our dear Amelia to relay?"

His voice was a lot louder than it needed to be, in my humble opinion, and several heads turned our way. "Uh . . ."

I was saved by the sound of Alex Majors dropping his plate, cutlery clattering as vol-au-vents somersaulted neatly to land facedown on the carpet. I winced. Cherry wasn't gonna be happy, having to clean that mess up.

Then again, she hadn't moved in yet. Greg could clean his own carpet.

"Daddy!" Vi ran over to her father, Lance Frith following her at a slightly-less-than-seemly distance, I noted with surprise. "Come on. Don't worry about that now. You need some peace and quiet." She led him away from the sad splat on the floor and out of the room.

I gave Uncle Arsehole a hard stare, which he returned with disinterest.

"How much longer do you want to stay?" Phil murmured in my shell-like, making me jump a bit as I hadn't noticed his return.

I looked at him, then at my newly laden plate. His had disappeared; presumably the vol-au-vents had all flown.

Phil rolled his eyes, grabbed two finger sandwiches off my plate, and shoved them in his gob at once.

Looked like we were on our way out, then. I grabbed the last two sandwiches and ate them, during the course of which they might have just happened to form a V sign as I held them up in his face.

One of the cathedral ladies tutted loudly.

Phil stifled a snigger.

We legged it for the door.

I wasn't best pleased when the plod collared me just before we could make it out of there, not least because quite a few heads turned at the sight, including Toby's and Uncle Arlo's.

"Mr. Paretski, might I have a word?" Sharp's tone was polite but steely.

"Dunno," I said with a laugh that might have come off just a tiny bit nervous. "Should I bring my lawyer?"

"No need for that." He smiled. It looked like something he'd practiced in front of a mirror. "You're not under suspicion. I just had a couple more questions I'd like to ask you."

I glanced at Phil. He didn't say anything. "Fine. Fire away."

"Actually, would you mind coming to the police station tomorrow? At three o'clock?"

Well, yeah, I would mind, as it happens, but there was definitely an undercurrent of sending the boys round if I didn't cooperate. Phil's hand on my arm tightened, so I guessed he'd noticed that too.

"I'll be there," I said, resigned. I'd have to see if I could do Mr. K.'s quote tonight instead, and fit Mrs. S.'s loo in during my now-to-be-nonexistent lunch hour.

"Think I should take Cherry along anyhow?" I muttered to Phil as we scarpered.

"What do you think?" If the look he gave me hadn't clued me in to what a bloody daft question he reckoned that was, his tone certainly would have.

CHAPTER Twenty-Two

So the following day, I had to drive up to St. Leonards—again—and make my way to the local nick, where I was shown into a boxy room with a window that looked out on a brick wall.

Some attempt had been made to make it look a bit less cell-like. Nothing was bolted to the floor, and there was even a plastic jug of water on the table and a stack of disposable cups. Just like this was an ordinary business meeting, rather than the sort of discussion where, say, people might expect things to get thrown at them. Cherry had bottled water in her office, which she presumably served to clients, although in her case it was in your actual glasses. I'd seen 'em.

Then again, some of her clients ended up in the nick, didn't they? Not a totally reassuring parallel, there.

Sis, by the way, wasn't with me. She had a paying client meeting already booked, and while she'd offered to try to rearrange it, she'd looked a bit doubtful and I hadn't liked to insist. After all, it wasn't like I was a suspect or anything.

I hoped.

DI Sharp shook my hand, thanked me for coming, waved me to a seat, and poured us each a plastic cup of water. He was a bloke a bit older than me, I reckoned, dressed in a grey suit that was just on the comfortable side of smart. His light-brown hair made him look a bit forgettable, but his eyes were, well, sharp.

A uniformed PC hovered on the periphery, in case I might be tempted to forget where I was.

"As I understand it," the DI said heavily—well, semi-heavily; he still had a good few years and several stone to go before he'd be punching at Dave's weight—"you're psychic, right?"

He didn't add the sarcastic finger-quotes. He didn't have to. His expression did it for him.

"Yeah, so?" Great. Now I was sounding defensive.

"So how come you didn't know the necklace was in the victim's mouth?"

I stared at him. "I *what*? Seriously?"

Sharp took a gulp of water, presumably to wash down unpleasant images, and put his cup down. Him being a bit on the heavy-handed side, the water sloshed and churned unhappily, much like my stomach right then. "You find hidden things. Or so I'm told. So how come you didn't know where that necklace had been stashed?"

"Uh, excuse me for being a bit distracted at the time. By the, you know, *dead body* I'd just tripped over."

"Ah, but it's not your first dead body, now is it?"

Cheers, mate. Thanks a fucking bundle. I now had a ghostly identity parade of all the deceased I'd been unlucky enough to stumble over through the years flitting through my head, all the way back to that little girl in the London park.

Although to be honest, even she'd been better than the one in the Dyke's cellar . . . I gagged, reached out blindly for my plastic cup of water, and managed to knock it over. "Shit." My eyes were watering from the effort of keeping my stomach contents in residence.

PC Peripheral hurried to mop up the mess. DI Sharp didn't turn a hair, but he did refill my cup for me, thank God.

I took a grateful sip, and the nausea receded. "Cheers," I said automatically. My voice sounded a bit rough, so I cleared my throat.

DI Sharp was looking at me expectantly.

"So, uh. No. Not my first. Be bloody glad if it was my last." I managed to give him a weak smile.

He didn't return it, the stingy bastard.

I rushed on to fill the silence. "See, when I'm finding stuff, I have to concentrate, yeah? Focus." I stopped, remembering that time in Phil's flat. I wasn't gonna mention it, but something in the DI's eye told me he'd noticed the pause. "Unless it's really personal, yeah? Then sometimes it shouts. But most of the time, I don't hear it unless I listen, you know?"

I could tell by his blank gaze he really, really didn't know.

"So that necklace... Well. And I wasn't, you know, really thinking straight. I mean. Yeah." Dead body. "So I didn't hear it."

There was a moment's silence. I bit my lip to keep from babbling on.

"So they speak to you, do they? The things you find?" he said at last, his voice flat as ever, but I wasn't fooled.

I stared at him. "Christ, no. I don't hear voices or anything. I'm not *mental*."

"Uh-huh."

"Look, talk to Dave Southgate, yeah? He'll tell you I'm not making this up or imagining it, whatever." A bead of sweat trickled down my spine and into my crack, where it itched like fuck.

Maybe I should've insisted Cherry came along after all.

Sharp just nodded. As if, say, he'd already talked to Dave and was just pissing me about. Not that I'm cynical or anything. "What *were* you looking for, in the tent?"

I took a deep breath. "I dunno. Forgot to ask her, didn't I? I mean, she was just s'posed to be hiding something." I shrugged. "It's ... it's not the thing that's important, yeah? Just that it's hidden, and *why* it was hidden. It makes the vibes different."

"So you wouldn't recognise this, then?" The DI signalled to PC Peripheral, who pulled an evidence bag out of a briefcase and passed it to him. Sharp held it out to me.

There was a yellow plastic duck inside. It had a number scrawled on the bottom in faded marker pen and a hook screwed into its smiley little head. Around its neck someone had tied a label with *For Tom* written on in biro.

I took it and swallowed. I could see it so clearly—Sis going over to ask Amelia to hide something. Adding my parting shot about avoiding the hook-a-duck stall with its paddling pool of water. Must have given her an idea about what to hide. She must have borrowed one—forcibly, if I knew Amelia—labelled it, hidden it. Maybe she'd even smiled as she did it. Thought it might raise a laugh when I dug it out and held it up to show the crowd.

I mean, Christ. God knows I hadn't liked the lady. But she just seemed so *human* to me as I pictured her doing all that. So real. So alive.

"Mr. Paretski?" Sharp said. Sharply. I realised I'd been sitting there staring at the thing like it was my long-lost cousin, now tragically deceased.

"Uh. Sorry. No. Hadn't seen it before. We didn't have a lot of time to set it all up, yeah? But, I mean, I know where it came from. There was a stall. Brownies, right?"

"Girl Guides," he corrected me, because apparently it was an important distinction.

He must have caught my look. "I've got daughters. You try suggesting to my eldest she's still in the Brownies, she'll have you with a tent peg." There was the actual ghost of a smile hovering around his lips. Then he stood up. "Right, Mr. Paretski. That'll be all for now. Thank you for your time."

"That's it?" I asked stupidly.

"Well, unless you'd like to have a look at the dripping tap in the gents' . . ."

I fixed the tap. It seemed like the polite thing to do.

I gave Phil a bell when I finally got out of there, just to reassure him I hadn't been read my rights and sent down for the foreseeable. "What are you up to?" I asked.

"Following some financial leads. You still in St. Leonards?"

"Yeah, just about to leave. Why?"

"How do you fancy giving the old Paretski charm a workout? If you haven't got a job on," he added. I was touched he remembered I actually had to make a living at this plumbing lark.

"Nah, had to cancel everything for the afternoon, didn't I? Could've been in there hours. Who d'you want charmed, though? You don't mean Frith, do you?" With Amelia dead and Vi hating us, I couldn't think of anyone else involved in the case who was likely to be susceptible to my dubious charms.

Phil huffed. "Not likely. Elizabeth Fenchurch."

Huh. I'd sort of forgotten about her. "Let me guess—you want me to ask her about him indoors?"

"Yes. Specifically, while he's *not* indoors. See if you can find out anything about his relationship with his sister and the Majors family."

"And where he might have been and who he was doing at the time of the murder?"

"You might want to be a bit more subtle about that." Phil sounded amused.

"Oi, subtlety's my middle name."

"You? You can't even spell 'subtlety.'"

"Course I can. I just don't want to right now, that's all. So, just to be clear, you want me to go poking my nose in about this case we're not actually employed on anymore?"

"That's the one. And don't forget to do a bit of psychic snooping while you're there."

"What, you reckon after he made the fake necklace, he might have forgotten to return the real one?"

"You never know, although my money's on whoever had it having sold it already. Cash is a lot harder to identify than stolen property. Unfortunately."

"Yeah? Would it be old Arlo's finances you're digging into?"

"Among others. Just see what turns up."

Phil gave me the address, and directions—apparently Arlo's gaff was so posh it wasn't satnav-able. It wasn't that far from Alex Majors's house, as it happened, on the same side of St. Leonards but just a bit further out into the sticks.

I found it without too much difficulty, despite almost missing the turn-in when I got there, it being just a gap in a line of tall trees that completely shielded the house from the lane. I whistled when I saw the place.

The Arlos—sorry, the Fenchurches—had a house just as expensive looking as old Alex's, if not more so, but that was where the similarity ended. Far from a listed building with more history than an entire box set of *Vikings*, this place looked like it'd been built yesterday from a kit that consisted entirely of plate glass and white-painted boxes. You could pretty much see right through it, which I suppose wasn't a problem if you had extensive grounds and no neighbours within a stone's throw.

Given all the glass, that last bit was probably just as well.

It was set in a bit of a dip, and I realised even if you chopped down all the trees, you probably still wouldn't see it from the road. Somebody was very keen on their privacy.

I didn't like it. Then again, there was zero chance I'd ever end up having to live in a place like this, so why worry?

I rang the doorbell and shuffled uneasily on the doorstep as Mrs. Arlo slowly made her way through the house to answer it, each of us in full view of the other the entire time. It'd be a bit of a bugger if you wanted to pretend you were out when someone called.

Today, Elizabeth Fenchurch was dressed in pale colours that washed her out just as much as the sombre clothes she'd worn to the funeral had. Still no jewellery. Her straight hair didn't exactly look *bad*, but it was definitely a bit flat as, to be brutally honest, was her figure.

"You're the one who found her," she said when she finally opened the door.

"Uh, yeah." I tried to work out how she felt about that, but she just seemed, well, not so much grief-stricken as generally depressed, if you ask me. And possibly doped up on something, from the way all her movements seemed to be in slow motion.

Then again, maybe she'd just caught the sleepiness from her husband?

"What do you want?"

Huh. Not so sleepy as all that, then. And fair question. "I was wondering if I could maybe ask you a couple of questions?" Too late, I remembered I was supposed to be charming her, and flashed her a smile.

I won't say she reared up like a startled horse, but it definitely seemed to make her nervous. I dialled it back sharpish. "Uh, sorry to bother you at this sad time," I added.

The trite phrase seemed to work where the charm offensive hadn't. Maybe I was losing my touch. "Come in," she said indifferently.

She led me through to the least cosy living room I'd ever been in. Everything was square or monochrome or both. It was like I imagined a waiting room in one of those Swiss clinics Dave had been talking about the other day.

I tried not to let it oppress me too much as we sat on a blocky sofa. Side by side, as all the furniture was facing the plate glass window overlooking the lawn. Handy, for the sort of family that doesn't want to look at one another any more than it has to. "I'm Tom, by the way. Tom Paretski. You're Elizabeth, right?"

She nodded, barely. "What do you want to ask?"

"Um, nice place you've got here," I lied. "Lived here long?"

"A year or two," she said, like she didn't care much either way.

"You and Arlo, you've been married for a lot longer than that, right?"

Liz shrugged. "Twenty years." She didn't sound like she cared a lot about that, either.

"Kids?"

"No."

Christ, this was hard work. Time for a new tack. "I know this is a bit cheeky, but I don't suppose I could trouble you for a cup of coffee?" I'd normally have asked for tea, but I reckoned she needed the caffeine.

She blinked and looked upset. "Didn't I offer you a drink?"

"Not to worry, love," I said quickly, but she'd already stood up and started walking off. Again there was this weird feeling she was just sleepwalking through life.

I followed her through the white living room past some white stairs to a white kitchen, the sort where anything that might have the bad taste to look like it had a practical purpose like a fridge or a cooker was ruthlessly hidden behind blank panels. No prizes for guessing what colour they were. It was all starting to make my eyes hurt.

And yeah, I took the opportunity to have a good listen to the vibes. There was something there, all right—in fact, there was more than one secret hidden in this house, but to be honest, all the trails seemed too faint to be anything important. There was a sense of shame to one of them, and another had mild annoyance with a whiff of guilt—put it this way, we weren't talking skeletons in closets. Not even the murder weapon the skeleton got done in by. It was probably all just the general stuff you got in anyone's house, like the secret stash of "medicinal" marijuana or the receipt for something you told him indoors only cost half as much as it actually had. That sort of stuff.

I tried not to look too disappointed. After all, if you really wanted to hide something, you wouldn't choose a flippin' glass house, would you?

Liz opened up a cupboard and took out a coffee machine (black, thank God). "White?" she asked, and I just managed to stop myself saying *God, no.*

"Yeah, ta. No sugar."

She set the wheels in motion, got some milk out of a fridge you wouldn't have known was there, and then we stared out of the window at the same view we'd seen from the living room. God, this was painful. "You like cooking?" I asked.

"Not really. Arlo tends to do all that."

So she didn't work, she didn't cook—not to be funny, but just what *did* she do? I mean, yeah, maybe she'd had to give up work due to stress or depression or whatever, but I couldn't see how sitting around on her own in this mausoleum all day doing sod all was supposed to make her feel any better.

"I like making salads," she offered, surprising me.

I was on that like white on, well, this house. "Yeah? I know a good recipe for warm salad with goat's cheese, bacon, and hazelnuts. Share it with you if you like."

For a moment she looked interested—then the veil dropped again. "Arlo probably wouldn't like it. It wouldn't be worth making it just for one."

Meaning her. Poor Liz. "Come on, love. Live a little. Like the ads say, you're worth it."

She almost smiled—and then looked away. The coffee was ready.

It was bloody good coffee, mind. I took a couple of very appreciative sips, and then noticed Liz was just sipping at a glass of water.

"Not a coffee drinker?"

"I'm not supposed to. It's bad for my anxiety."

"Yeah? You know what you want to do? Get a couple of mates together and have a spa day. I've got a friend who swears by 'em." I didn't have to mention his name was Gary.

Liz gave me a weird kind of half smile. "What did you want to ask me about?"

I guessed the socialising was over. "Did you and your husband make it to the Harvest Fayre? I'd have thought Amelia would've made sure you had an invite." And probably a stall to run, if I knew the late Mrs. F-M.

"I wasn't well that day. Arlo was going to go, but he was held up."

"Yeah? Where was that, then?"

She looked like she didn't want to answer. "Birmingham. He often takes trips up there. Trade," she explained with a shrug.

I made a sympathetic face. "Probably just as well in the circs. They were pretty close, weren't they? He told me she was more like a daughter to him—and I guess you too?"

The lawn got another good stare. "Amelia was grown up by the time I met Arlo. She was a lot older than she looked," Liz added, finally showing a bit of spirit even if it was of the spiteful persuasion.

"Uh-huh. Still, the big brother thing never really goes away, does it?" I was making it up wholesale now. God knows my big brother never came over all protective towards me.

Shrug.

Oo-kay. Time to try another tack. "Shame she never really got on with her stepdaughter."

Liz's mouth gave an odd twist, and she stared out of the window once more. "No great loss," she said so quietly I struggled to hear her.

Did she mean Amelia? Or friendly relations between her and Vi? "Have you had a lot to do with Violet Majors?"

"No." She put her glass down with a heavy *clunk* on the worktop.

I got the distinct impression I'd be getting my marching orders sharpish, so I hurried to ask another question. "How did—" I never got to finish, as the phone rang.

Liz picked up one of those cordless landline handsets. It was white. I was amazed she could find the flippin' thing around here. "Hello? Oh yes, fine. No. No, I haven't. No. The man who found Amelia is here. Yes, in the house. He came to ask some questions."

Shit.

"No, I— Oh. If you want." She held out the phone. "He wants to talk to you. It's Arlo," she added, as if I hadn't guessed that already.

I took the phone with a fair amount of foreboding. "Hello?"

"Tom. How kind of you to stop in to see my wife." His tone could have meant anything. Up to and including he really did think it was kind of me, but I wasn't betting on it. "I hope you haven't been placing her under undue stress," he carried on, in slow, deliberate tones. "She really isn't equal to it. Can I be crystal clear with you? Ambiguous and imprecise messages purporting to come from the beyond will not be well received in my house."

"Uh, really not my area, so no worries."

"Nevertheless. Would you pass me back to my wife, please?"

Fine. I handed Liz the phone. She listened for a moment, then looked up at me. "Arlo thinks you should go now," she said, her voice holding a faint hint of triumph, as if that settled the matter.

Which was odd in itself—did she think I wouldn't leave if it was only her who'd asked?

Still, message received and understood.

So I went.

All in all, it was on the late side of early evening when I started on my way home from St. Leonards. The skies weren't dark yet, but it was that stage of twilight when it's harder to see than in full dark, 'cos your brain reckons your eyes just aren't trying hard enough and your headlights have about as much effect as a kiddie's nightlight.

I should've given Phil a bell before I set off back, I realised. We hadn't made plans for the evening, and now I wasn't sure if he'd be over at mine, wondering whether to make a start on dinner (I hope he wouldn't get that desperate; I fancied something decent for tea) or back at his flat with his feet up and a microwaved ready meal on his lap. Or, you know, somewhere else entirely. I mean, it wasn't like he didn't have a life apart from me.

He might even have gone to visit his mum, although I personally wouldn't have bet my shirt on it.

I briefly considered pulling over into an upcoming lay-by to make the call. Very briefly. That would just be sad. Which was my main consideration, obviously, rather than the way the lay-by itself was shielded from the road by overhanging trees that cast it into gloomy shadow and looked well creepy. Not to mention, an ideal spot for a murder.

Then my phone rang, and I ended up pulling in anyway. It wasn't Phil, though.

It was Vi. "Yeah?" I said cautiously.

"Um." Her voice was uncharacteristically hesitant. Uncertain, even. "I owe you an apology. For being so rude the other night. Sorry."

Oh. "Uh, that's okay." I paused. "Does that mean you want to take back the firing-us thing?" Not that I was making any promises, mind.

"Um. Well, actually . . . Can you come over?"

"What? Why?"

"It's just . . . We've got a leak in one of the pipes, and there's water all over the floor, and Daddy's gone out for dinner."

"You're kidding, right? I mean, seriously?" Christ, she had a nerve.

"Look, I know it's a cheek, all right? But I'll pay you. I don't know any other plumbers—"

Why did that not surprise me?

"—and I'm really worried about the floors. They're going to be *ruined*. I mean, I've tried mopping up, but it just keeps *coming*."

Great. Those antique wood floors had probably thought they were safe now that Thoroughly Modern Amelia had popped her ironically retro clogs. "Have you tried turning the water off?" I thought about jamming the phone between my shoulder and my ear and setting off, but it'd be just my luck to get nicked for driving while using my mobile to talk to Vi bloody Majors.

"I don't know how."

"Have a look under your kitchen sink. There should be a tap there." Although in an older property like that . . .

There was a pause, enlivened by a few bumps and some heavy breathing. "There's *loads* of taps. Which one should I turn?"

I closed my eyes briefly, then opened them quick 'cos it was still pretty creepy and deserted in this lay-by. No sense in pushing my luck. "Just give all of 'em a go. Clockwise to close, yeah?"

There was a shorter pause. More heavy breathing. Some grunting. "It's really stiff."

I resisted the urge to say *That's what he said*.

"I'll have to put you down," she carried on.

More grunts.

Bang.

"Oh, *bugger.*"

Uh-oh.

Vi's voice got louder suddenly. I guessed she'd picked up the phone again. "It came off in my hand."

Flippin' marvellous. "I'll be there in ten," I said, adding a bit of a sigh in the hopes she'd appreciate she was messing up my plans for the evening something chronic.

Okay, so I hadn't actually had any plans. *She* didn't know that, did she?

"Just got to let Phil know where I'm off to, and I'll be on my way," I added, 'cos while I might be a sucker for an antique wood floor in distress, I'm not daft. Not that I really reckoned Vi had done her stepmum in, but there was no harm in letting her know Phil would know where I was and who'd called me over.

His phone, typically, went to voice mail, so I left a message, then pulled out of the dark lay-by, still miraculously un-murdered, and set off back to St. Leonards.

Chapter Twenty-Three

Vi looked severely frazzled when she opened the door of the farmhouse to me. "Oh, thank God. Come on in. It's this way."

She led me down the hall to a utility room, housing the boiler, a top-range washer and matching dryer, as well as an old-fashioned butler's sink for hand-washing. The last of which I wouldn't mind betting hadn't seen a lot of use since the demise of the first Mrs. Majors, and maybe not even then.

I didn't need my spidey-senses to locate the problem. Mainly because Vi had already found the leak herself and made a sad little attempt at stopping the leak with what had probably once been a very expensive scarf. It was right up by the boiler, on a junction, unsurprisingly.

She'd also thrown what looked like the entire contents of the family linen closet on the floor in an attempt to soak up the water. I'd have to scale the sodden pile to get at the leak, but first things first. "Right, let's get that water turned off," I said briskly.

The tap she'd broken turned out to control the water supply to the dishwasher. I hoped for the sake of any antique china in the house that she wasn't as ham-fisted with the washing up as she was with the plumbing. Then again, I *did* have a spare in the van.

I was planning to wait and see whether Vi was still apologetic after I'd fixed her pipes before I mentioned it, though.

First things first. I needed to locate the stop valve—which, to be fair to Vi, wasn't under the sink at all. Once again, my psychic gift was about as much use as that silk scarf had been at stopping the leak, but I eventually tracked it down near the front door, under a loose floorboard cunningly hidden by the welcome mat. I was just glad I didn't have to go rooting around for an outside stopcock in the dark. 'Specially seeing as a property like this might not even have one.

The stop valve turned easily, which was a relief. In a hard-water area, things seize up quick from the limescale and can be a bugger to get loose. It couldn't have been all that long since the last time they'd had a plumber round.

I'd expected Vi to go off and put her feet up while I got on with the work, but instead she dogged my footsteps and asked so many questions, you'd have thought she was thinking about a change of profession. (And yeah, all right, I made sure I didn't turn my back on her any more than I could help, especially with some reasonably hefty tools lying around. Like I said: not daft. Or suicidal, for that matter.)

Working the leaky junction loose was less effort than I'd have expected, given the age of the plumbing. I saw the problem straight away. "Blimey," I muttered, more under my breath than to Vi. "Never seen one that bad before."

"What is it?" Vi asked, poking her nose up to the pipe.

"Washer. It's corroded."

"Where? I can't see."

"Yeah, that's your problem, right there." The washer had corroded so much it literally wasn't even there anymore. "Don't worry—I'll just go and grab a spare from the van."

It was full dark when I got outside. Darker than I expected, I mean. It took a mo for me to twig that the security light hadn't come on. Houses like this? There's always a security light. It seemed a bit dodgy it'd chosen tonight of all nights to break down—but then, maybe it'd been down for months and they were just really bad at getting round to fixing it. I shivered and didn't hang about any longer than I had to, just grabbed the washer and a new tap head from the back of the van.

I was about to leg it back to the front door when it opened, light hitting me from inside. Vi stood there. "Why isn't the outside light on?" she asked, frowning.

"Search me," I told her. "Come on. Let's get this sorted."

I went back to the utility room, fitted the washer, tightened the join, sorted the tap under the sink, and turned the water back on before checking there were no more leaks.

By the end of it all, Vi was *still* frowning. "All right, love?" I asked, half my mind on totting up the bill and adding extra for the emergency call-out, not to mention the nerve.

Course, that could have been what her mind was on too . . . Nah. She wasn't the sort to get in a tizzy over a couple of hundred quid.

"It's just odd. I'm sure Daddy had a plumber in here only a couple of months ago."

"Yeah, thought you might've," I muttered distractedly.

"Yes, but you see, I'm sure that was a washer too. I wasn't here, but Daddy was talking about it at lunch on Monday. He thought the plumber he'd called in had ripped him off—that's why I didn't call him tonight."

I shrugged. "Old systems like this, you've got to expect them to need a bit of care and attention from time to time. And if the washers were the same age, it's not surprising they went one after the other."

"I suppose." She was silent for a moment. "I didn't just apologise to you so you'd come round and fix things. I do feel bad about what I said. I don't think you're a fraud. Lance has been explaining it to me. About how dowsing works."

"Yeah? Get on all right with him, do you?"

"Oh, you know."

Not really, love, but I didn't tell her that. "Good how him and your stepmum managed to keep working together after the divorce, wasn't it?"

"Oh, that was only ever a business thing. Their marriage, I mean."

I wondered who'd told her that. And how come she believed it. Seriously, who gets married for business reasons these days, apart from Mafia bosses?

"Right, love, here's the damage." I handed over my scribbled-out invoice.

She made a face. "I haven't got that much cash in the house. Do you take credit cards?"

"Sorry, no, but a cheque's fine. Or bank transfer."

"God, does anybody write cheques anymore? I'll pay you online." She peered at the small print at the bottom of the invoice, which is where I give details of my bank account, and fiddled with her phone for a couple of minutes. "Done. I can't believe you don't make everyone pay this way."

I tried to imagine some of my more elderly customers trying to get their heads around a phone banking app. "Long as I get what I'm owed, I'm not fussy. Right, cheers, love, and call me if you get any more problems, yeah?"

"I will. And thank you for coming, after . . . Well. You know. Are you all right to see yourself out?" She gazed sadly at the pile of soggy towels. "I need to load the washing machine."

"Think I can remember the way," I told her, and left.

I dunno why I felt so twitchy, walking back to my van in the dark. Maybe it was just 'cos I wasn't so used to the dark, what with autumn only just drawing in. I mean, I didn't hear a thing. Seriously, not a whisper. Certainly not any footsteps coming up behind me. It was dead quiet out there in the sticks, although I could just hear the odd car going down the main road at the end of the drive.

The only thing that happened was—at least, as I thought at the time—a spiderweb brushed my face. So my hand jerked up to brush it away, in case the spider was still in residence, because with that many legs at their disposal, they can flippin' well walk instead of hitching a lift on yours truly.

And then I forgot all about sodding spiders, because my hand was trapped against my face and someone was panting down my neck as they pulled a wire so tight around my throat it burned. My free hand flailed as I struggled. The bones of my tortured right hand dug into one side of my windpipe, a duller pain than the wire on the other side.

Christ. It was like I was giving a helping hand to my own strangler.

My face felt too large, my head too full. Some evil flying leprechaun was stabbing tiny knives into my eyes, and my vision went patchy-dark. There was the metallic taste of blood in my mouth. Shit, was this it? I struggled harder, my limbs wild. Christ, if I died now, Phil'd never forgive me. We hadn't even made it to the altar. I staggered—back, I think?—and tried to hit the bastard behind me who was trying to ruin my wedding.

I wasn't sure if I hit 'em or not—or if they hit me, or gave me a god-almighty shove—but all of a sudden, I was falling forward onto my hands and knees, gasping in precious air. God. I thought for a moment I was gonna chuck, but I managed to hold it in somehow.

Had there been footsteps? The sound of someone running away? I wasn't sure—but when I staggered to my feet, there was nobody there. Either my attacker had done a runner, or that'd been one bloody big spider. That spun its webs out of tungsten carbide.

I made this weird sobbing noise that might've started out as a laugh, and fumbled my phone out of my pocket. Dropped it. Thought *Fuck my life* as I got back on my hands and knees and gathered phone, case, and battery and clicked them back together. Staggered to the nearest wall and sat on the ground with my back to it, 'cos if my attacker came back for another go, I wasn't just dead meat, I'd been shrink-wrapped and put on special offer on the deli counter in Sainsbury's.

Finally managed to hit dial on Phil's number.

He picked up, thank God. "Tom?"

"Yeah." It came out as a whisper. "Need you."

"Where are you? Are you still at the Majors' house?"

I could hear sounds in the background—he was on his way already. I closed my eyes.

"*Tom*!"

Right. Hadn't told him where to come yet. "S'ry. Yeah."

"Are you in danger?"

"D'no."

Light cast a pathway to my left as the front door of the farmhouse opened. There was a Vi-shaped shadow bang in the middle. "Tom? Are you all— Oh my God!"

She ran over to me and crouched down to stare, wide-eyed, at my face. "Oh my God, what happened? Tom! Tom, can you talk?"

"Yeah," I croaked, and wished I hadn't.

"Oh God, oh God . . ." Vi carried on throwing a wobbly, then visibly pulled herself together. "Can you walk? Do you need an ambulance?"

Great. Just what I needed right now—more questions. I held up a hand, swallowed, and grimaced at the pain.

Headlights flared and got larger as a car came up the drive. Phil, thank God.

Except it wasn't. The figure that got out of the driving seat seemed grotesquely sticklike where I'd been expecting Phil's comforting bulk.

"Violet?" a voice called shakily, and I realised this was Alex Majors, home from his meal out.

He stepped closer and staggered to a halt. I thought for a mo we were going to have a second casualty on our hands. "Violet . . ." This time it sounded despairing.

Or maybe it was just my imagination, because Vi herself didn't seem fazed. "Daddy, thank God. Help me get him inside. Something horrible's happened."

Between me and Alex, I wasn't sure who was helping who back into the farmhouse, but at least Vi's arm was a sturdy aid, slung around my back. She took me into the kitchen and sat me down at the sturdy oak table, its surface scarred from the knives of cooks long dead.

Not that I was feeling morbid or anything.

Alex pulled out a chair with a tooth-grinding scrape on the stone floor and sat down a lot more heavily than I'd have thought he was capable of. He still hadn't spoken, apart from saying his daughter's name outside.

"Daddy, should I call an ambulance?" Vi worried, hovering at my shoulder.

I held up my hand again. All I wanted was my bloke. I mean, my throat hurt, my hand hurt, and I had a killer headache, but other than that, I was just a bit shaken.

"Should I call the police?" she went on, either oblivious or simply ignoring me.

Okay, that one was a little harder to argue with.

Shit. Someone had tried to *kill* me.

Nausea rose, and my vision went patchy for a mo.

"Tom? *Tom!*" A hand on my shoulder steadied me. "Oh God, shall I make a cup of tea?"

Christ. I wished she'd stop asking me all these questions and bloody do *something*. Then I heard the sweet, sweet sound of hefty fists banging on an antique front door. With a definite hint that if it wasn't opened soon, the door might not live to regret it.

Phil. At least, I hoped to God it was.

Alex had jumped a mile at the first knock.

Vi didn't look happy either. "Oh God, who's *that*? Daddy, can you go see?"

Alex took a shaky breath. "No. No, you should go, Violet."

She gave him a funny look, but went, leaving me and her dad alone in the kitchen.

Which was a flippin' fantastic time for it to occur to me that he'd arrived on the scene suspiciously soon after I'd nearly died. Say, just enough time for someone to leg it down the drive to a car they'd left parked down the road, get in, and motor up to the house like they'd only just got here.

I stared at Alex. He wouldn't try anything now, would he? In his own kitchen?

I mean, he prepared *food* there.

Then Phil burst in with Vi trailing after him, looking like he'd battled all the demons of hell to get here. "What the bloody hell's happened? Tom?"

He grabbed my shoulders and gave me a searching look. Whatever he saw didn't seem to reassure him. "Christ, Tom."

"'M okay," I croaked.

"The fuck you are." He turned on Alex with an air of quiet menace that threatened to turn extremely loud if he didn't get an answer he liked. "What the hell happened?"

"Daddy wasn't here," Vi put in, obviously not liking the implications. "Tom came round to fix a pipe, and someone attacked him when he left."

"You saw them?"

"*No*, but it's perfectly obvious what happened." Christ, she wasn't giving an inch.

Phil took a deep breath, then let it out. "Come on, we're getting you to hospital."

"What?" I whispered. "'M fine."

Which, obviously, I wasn't, but it was a hell of a lot easier than saying all I wanted was a hot drink and a cuddle, followed swiftly by bed, not to be prodded and poked by a load of strangers. If that was what I was after, I'd have gone on Grindr. And let's face it, next stop was gonna have to be the police—I didn't want to drag it all out any longer than I had to.

"No arguments. I mean it. Don't fight me on this one." Phil's voice and the look he gave me were intense, almost angry.

I subsided. If he was that bothered, I'd go with it. Still thought it was a waste of time—I mean, what were they gonna do? Send me home with a throat sweet and some painkillers, most likely.

Phil half lifted me out of my seat and kept his arm around me as we made for the front door. Alex and Vi didn't get a goodbye, but they did get a *"You'll be hearing from the police."*

He helped me into the Golf, buckled my seat belt, and generally looked like he wished he had a snuggly blanket and/or a whole load of cotton wool to wrap me up in. Worryingly, I wasn't sure if I'd have protested right then.

Phil spoke up once we'd got on the way.

"When I was a new PC, one of the sergeants told me about a domestic abuse case he'd been on years back—bloke tried to strangle his wife. Course, this was before the crackdown, all the emphasis on taking positive action. It was all 'Sure you want to press charges, love?' in those days. She didn't. She didn't want to see a doctor either. No one insisted." He huffed unhappily. "He went round to check on her the next day. She was dead. Internal injuries."

Christ.

"You don't mess about with strangling injuries. You could have a fractured hyoid bone," he went on. "Or larynx. Or internal swelling, or fluid in your lungs—"

I made a—hah—strangled noise and held up a hand. I got the picture, okay?

Then I closed my eyes and just tried to rest.

CHAPTER TWENTY-FOUR

Turned out I didn't have a fractured anything, or even water on the larynx, but the doctors insisted I stay in overnight anyway. After Phil's grim tales of domestic abuse, I wasn't gonna argue. To be honest, by then I just wanted to find the nearest bed, crawl into it, and sleep for a week.

Course, before I could get my head down, there was the plod to deal with.

I'd have preferred a visit from Dave Southgate, but he was still on paternity leave, so they sent a PC in a headscarf down from the local cop shop to take a statement. That was a laugh in itself. Not only did I have bugger all to tell 'em—yes, it was dark, no, I didn't see a face—I didn't have a voice to tell 'em it with, either. Lots of scribbled notes and failed attempts at sign language, while Phil glowered at the poor woman from the corner of the room. Of course, there was the obligatory question as to whether I had any idea who might want to shuffle me off this mortal coil sooner rather than later.

I glanced at Phil. He nodded, and filled PC Iqbal in about dear old Amelia and my part in her downfall. Her eyes got wider and wider—I was guessing murder was well above her pay grade. Phil suggested she liaise with the St. Leonards force. She sent him a look that strongly implied she was holding herself back from suggesting he go and teach her grandma to suck eggs.

Then she packed up her notebook and went off to liaise, and Phil kissed me on the cheek and left for what remained of the night.

Waking up in hospital is never a lot of fun. Then again, looking on the bright side, at least this time I'd been conscious when I came in and I didn't have a concussion. Still a bit of a downer, though, opening your eyes to bright lights, institutional green walls, and, lest we forget, a fair amount of actual pain. Especially when your subconscious has been doing its best to kid you all you have to do is roll over and get an armful of hot, muscular man.

On the plus side, said hot, muscular man was sitting in the visitor's chair by the side of the bed, which improved the looks of the place no end.

"Morning," I said. Well, if by *said* you mean *croaked like a bullfrog who'd just been gargling with rusty nails half dissolved in battery acid*, which was pretty much what I felt like too. I tried not to look too horrified at the sound. Phil was doing plenty of that for me already.

"Water?" he suggested.

I nodded, and he helped me sit up and take a drink.

And all right, yeah, I could've managed by myself, no problem. But sometimes you just wanna go with the TLC. 'Specially given how much it hurt just to swallow water.

"How do I look?" I rasped. That bloody hurt and all. I decided I was going to stick to whispers from here on out.

"Worse than last night," Phil told me, which wasn't encouraging. His expression wasn't either.

"Great," I whispered, and swung my legs out of bed.

"Are you supposed to be getting up?"

"Need to pee." There was no way I was arsing around with bedpans in front of my beloved. You've got to keep at least some of the mystery alive.

There was a bathroom just across the hall. Phil looked like he was having a hard time restraining himself from following me in, and I didn't reckon it was 'cos he wanted to get frisky or anything.

I did the necessary, washed my hands—carefully, as the right one had a vivid purple line of bruising across the back of it, which was extremely tender to the touch—and decided I might as well see how bad the rest of it was.

Christ. It was worse than I'd thought. I mean, I'd expected the livid bruising on my neck, and I wasn't disappointed, but that wasn't what stood out when I looked in the mirror. My eyes had bright red blotches staining the whites. One of them had almost no white at all. I looked like I'd got into the Halloween spirit a few weeks too soon.

"Jesus," I croaked out loud without thinking, and regretted it.

I hoped He wouldn't take it as a summons. He'd probably take one look and decide I needed exorcising. No wonder Phil hadn't looked happy.

As if on cue, there was a loud knocking on the bathroom door. "You all right in there?" Phil called.

Did he seriously expect me to shout back? I made him wait a mo until I could get to the door. Then I gave him a thumbs-up.

After that it was time for more poking and prodding, but they eventually let me go home. I was pretty happy about it until I remembered I'd had three jobs booked for today, so I'd be going home to a whole load of irate messages from customers I'd stood up. And it wasn't like I could call 'em and apologise.

Then again . . . After driving me back to mine, Phil was still doing limpet impersonations and looking like he wasn't planning to stop anytime soon, so I reckoned I might as well make use of him. I wandered into the kitchen to get the notepad I used for telephone messages and shopping lists.

Phil, who was putting the kettle on to boil, frowned. "Thought I told you to go and lie down."

I held up a hand, then scribbled down a quick note and held it up.

He squinted. "'Need to . . . call'? Can't read that last word."

I rolled my eyes. Come on, my writing wasn't that bad. I couldn't think of a way to mime *customers*, so I wrote it again in block letters.

"Oh. Right. Yeah. I can do that." He heaved a deep breath and held on to the kitchen counter with both hands. The kettle boiled and switched itself off with a click, and he flinched.

Christ. He really wasn't okay, I realised with a thud. He'd been all practical, at the hospital and on the way home—all focussed on me and what I needed. Now we were back, though . . . There were dark circles under his eyes, and he hadn't shaved.

I ripped off the top sheet of paper. *Want to talk?* I wrote. Then I put my arms around his neck and pressed us together.

I hadn't realised how much I'd needed the contact—but however much I needed it, Phil must've needed it more, judging from the way he grabbed me tight and held me even closer, a faint but noticeable tremor running through his whole body and into mine.

"I could've lost you," he growled. "If you hadn't got a hand under the cord—" He broke off, breathing hard. "You know how long it takes to lose consciousness when someone puts pressure on your carotid artery? Ten fucking seconds. All they'd have had to do then was wait. Another fifty seconds, they reckon, and there's almost no chance you'd make it."

Christ. I'd already come to the conclusion that this all pointed to a serious design flaw in the human race. It hadn't quite clicked just how close I'd come to being able to take my complaint straight to the man at the top.

Phil was still squeezing me tight, but I managed to push back far enough to look him in the eye. "I'm okay," I whispered. "Still here." God knows how reassuring it was, given the state of me, but he let out an incoherent sound and kissed me.

I must have made a sound myself at that—my jaw muscles being attached somewhere around the neck . . . Well, you get the picture. Phil pulled back and gave my face a tender stroke.

Then the overgrown macho bastard picked me up bridal-style and carried me up the stairs. I whacked him on the shoulder in protest.

But, you know. Not too hard. I didn't actually want him to *stop*.

He laid me on the bed so gently I could've been Dave's newborn kiddie. "Okay?" he asked, sounding almost as hoarse as me.

"Okay," I whispered, 'cos it's not that easy to nod when you're lying down.

Then he started to undress me.

I don't think I've ever felt so fucking *cherished* in my life. Every inch of me was stroked and kissed, like it was nothing short of miraculous. Maybe to Phil it was, right then. Despite the soreness from my injuries, I was still hard as iron by the time he made it down to my cock. I mean, Christ, I don't think anything short of decapitation could've stopped me getting hard at that point.

Then he put his mouth on my cock. I panted, although even *that* hurt, because it was so fucking good. His hand was on my balls, just where I like it, his other hand holding my hip. Not holding me down. Just . . . holding me. Everything faded but heat and pressure where I needed it most.

I came so hard I saw stars, ecstasy shooting out of me and into Phil's willing mouth. He swallowed every drop and carried on sucking until I pushed him off my oversensitised prick. I was pretty sure I had a Cheshire cat grin on my face.

It probably looked well creepy with the red eyes and the bruises, mind.

I gestured to Phil's cock, which was hard and dripping clear moisture.

He shook his head, the big daft git. "I'm okay."

I rolled my eyes at him. "C'mere," I whispered, and pulled him up to kiss me, ignoring the discomfort. I wrapped my hand around his hard prick and stroked it the way I knew he liked it, a little bit rough. Phil's mouth tasted of come, and I could tell he was holding back, trying not to hurt me. "C'mon," I breathed, stroking faster.

Phil groaned and came, hot spunk shooting over my stomach and chest. Then we cuddled up under the duvet and dozed for a couple of hours.

Course, it was a bugger getting the dried come off by the time we woke up.

I'd been expecting the police to either turn up at some time, or call me in to make another (written) statement. I was surprised when it was Dave who turned up—fortunately after me and Phil had made ourselves presentable.

"Christ, you look like shite," was his encouraging greeting, despite the shower I'd taken.

I frowned at him, raising an eyebrow as well in a bit of an awkward facial manoeuvre that was supposed to somehow convey *Shouldn't you be at home, knee-deep in nappies?*

Apparently Dave was a master of interpreting expressions. Who knew? "Jen's got her sister over, so I'm surplus to requirements anyhow. Thought I might as well come over and see what you've done to yourself this time."

I glanced at Phil. He shrugged. "I didn't tell him. Tea?"

That was to Dave, who said, "Cheers, mate," huffed, and eased his bulk onto my sofa. "After all the shit you've been mixed up in? Anything comes in with your name on it, they send it straight over to me. They know I like a good laugh down at the station. Anyhow, you remembered anything you didn't already tell 'em? Course you bloody haven't. Right. So they've been down to the scene, and this is what we can tell you."

Phil perched his arse on the arm of a chair. Looked like Dave was going to have to wait for his cup of tea.

"Whoever it was got you with a length of clothesline. Abandoned at the scene. Brand-new—probably fresh out of the wrapper just before they used it—and no fingerprints. Some DNA, but given the nature of it, we're working on the assumption it'll all turn out to be yours."

"So they went prepared," Phil growled. "Any indications it was the same assailant as Mrs. Fenchurch-Majors's killer?"

"What, apart from the bleedin' obvious?" Dave asked, echoing my thoughts exactly. He shook his head. "For the love of God, do *not* suggest we have two crazed stranglers wandering around the county."

Phil shrugged.

Dave turned to me. "How are you doing, anyhow?"

I shrugged. There was a right old shoulder workout session going on around here.

"Right. Any more thoughts on the person who attacked you? Was it a bloke?"

I nodded—then wondered what grounds I actually had for thinking that. I grabbed my notepad and wrote, *Think so but not sure. Taller than me, I think. Or same height.*

"You didn't notice the hands?"

I gestured to my throat, because honestly? I'd had a bit more on my mind at the time than whether my attacker had cleaned under their nails recently. Although . . .

Gloves, I wrote. *Thick ones. I think*, I added, as to be honest it was just a vague impression.

"Makes sense. Remember anything else about the gloves? Colour? Men's or women's?"

I shook my head. I mean, maybe if the hands themselves had been around my neck, I'd have had a better idea.

Course, in that case, having a hand raised when they'd attacked would've done me bugger all good and I'd like as not be dead right now. I swallowed. It hurt.

"Stronger than you, you reckon?"

Again, when I thought about it, I wasn't sure. They'd had me at something of a disadvantage, what with the whole strangulation bit and my right hand not being free. I did a wavy hand gesture.

"Notice anything like perfume? Aftershave? Smell of their breath from the curry they had for their tea?"

I shook my head.

Dave gave a heavy sigh. "So who've you been pissing off lately, anyhow? More than usual, obviously."

Phil cleared his throat. "We've been looking into the Fenchurch-Majors case."

"Course you bleedin' 'ave. Who's hired you?"

"The stepdaughter. Although she just wants her necklace back."

"Hers?"

"Miss Majors reckons it's hers, as it belonged to her real mother." Phil gave Dave a sharp look. "Technically, if Amelia Fenchurch-Majors still owned it at the time of her death, it should go to the person who benefits under her will. Although the family might be able to mount a legal challenge to that."

I scribbled down *Who benefits?* and was about to nudge Phil and wave it in his face, but Dave beat me to it.

"Come on, then, Morrison, you're obviously gagging to tell us who she left it all to. Whatever *all* is."

Phil dragged it out for another few tantalising seconds, the git.

Then he smirked and told us. "Lance Frith. And before you ask, no, that's not some old will from before she remarried, which wouldn't have still been valid anyhow. She made a new will after the wedding."

Dave scratched his crotch thoughtfully. "Wonder how many people knew about that? *And* whether it includes the grieving widower. Managed to dig out how much she had to leave?"

Phil nodded. "Not a lot, as it happens. Unless we count that necklace. There's the events business, but Frith would always have been the only person in a position to benefit from that. Not like they had a right lot in the way of assets. In fact, with her gone, it's questionable how much of a business is left anyhow. Frith's been putting up a good front, but while he's the one who did all the work, she was the one with all the contacts. Trouble was, it seems she had a nasty habit of making promises he wasn't able to keep. Asking around, I got the impression there's more than a few people who weren't all that satisfied with the services of Fenchurch & Frith."

"Yeah? Can't have been easy to work with. Although killing her might have been a bit extreme. Thing is, though, who'd want to off Tom? Why? Apart from the bleedin' obvious." Dave smirked, the git. Then he must have caught Phil's expression, and the smile dropped off his face so fast I swear I heard it crash on the floor. "Joking. Any chance of that cuppa?"

Phil was still giving Dave a dirty look, but he did get up and finally make the tea. I had a cup too, which seemed to go down slightly easier than the cup I'd had first thing, although I still wasn't looking forward to my next attempt at actual food. They'd given me thin porridge in hospital, which I'd only eaten half of as it really wasn't worth the pain to swallow it. While we drank our tea (and the other two had choccy biccies, the selfish gits), Dave regaled us with tales of the amazing antics of his son and heir, which mostly consisted of puking and pooping, although the peeing-during-nappy-change one was good for a laugh too.

"St. Leonards mob treating you all right, are they?" Dave asked, finally getting back to work.

I shrugged.

Dave made a dismissive huffing sort of sound. "Must be clutching at straws by now, poor sods. Two weeks after the fact and still no arrests? Not looking good."

Phil stood up abruptly and went to look out of the window.

I stared at him. Dave sighed. "Come on, Morrison, out with it. What's got your Calvin Kleins in a kerfuffle?"

Phil spun round, his face dark. "They're using him, aren't they? Tom. All that business at the funeral, making it so bloody obvious they reckon he's key to the case."

"What's this?" Dave was frowning too now.

"Sharp. Collared Tom in front of everyone and asked him to come for another interview. Which, by the way, turns out to be bollocks, seeing as all they do is show him a bloody rubber duck. Then, what happens? Vi Majors gets a conveniently timed leak and—" Phil broke off and gestured angrily in my direction. "They're using him as a bloody pit canary."

"Oi," I croaked. "Vi didn't do it. Me," I added, which, yeah, could have been open to different interpretations, but I was betting they got my drift.

She couldn't have attacked me, right? She'd been so concerned about me afterwards. I'd stake my life—hah—that was genuine.

Then again, an evil little voice whispered, *If you'd just tried and failed to kill someone, you'd be pretty worried about it and all.*

But…not to be sexist, but she was a girl. Maybe I'm not the biggest bloke around, but she could never have had a hope of overpowering me, could she?

I remembered the broken-off tap head and shuddered.

And there had been time, hadn't there? In between my attacker running off and her opening the front door. Maybe whoever had tried to kill me hadn't, as I'd thought, legged it down to a car parked on the main road and scarpered. Maybe they'd just nipped round the house and gone in through the back door.

But I'd just spent all that time with her. I'd have known if it'd been her slinging that cord around my neck.

Wouldn't I?

Phil was talking. "Have they checked out where the rest of 'em were that evening? Mr. Majors, Fenchurch, Frith…?"

Dave stood up, looking grim. "I think I'm going to have to have a little chat with our DI Sharp. I'll keep you posted. Tom, no going anywhere alone, right? Not even to take a piss. I'm sure you can find someone around here willing to hold your hand."

Or other bits, I scribbled hastily and held up for Dave's perusal.

Too hastily, apparently. Dave squinted, frowned, and gave up. "Whatever that said, I'm sure I don't wanna know."

CHAPTER TWENTY-FIVE

Vi Majors turned up at the house next, bringing a huge basket of pink and orange flowers all bound up with satin ribbon and guilt. No lilies, I noted with approval. I wondered if she'd remembered I had cats, or if it'd just been the luck of the draw.

"Oh God, you look awful," was her opening shot, proving she belonged to the Dave Southgate school of cheering up the ailing. "Are you all right? I've been so worried. I looked up strangulation on the internet after you'd gone, and there are all kinds of things you have to worry about."

Yeah, like getting arrested if you're the one who lured the victim over in the first place.

I didn't say it.

Phil folded his arms. "Who else knew you'd called Tom over last night?"

Vi made an exasperated sound, with accompanying hand flap. "Not you as well. I've been through all this with the police. *Nobody* knew, but for God's sake, *I* didn't try to kill him. Someone must have been following him and took advantage of the opportunity. It's the only explanation."

"Why?"

She stared at him. "Why what?"

"Why would anyone want to kill Tom?"

At least Vi didn't make any jokes about it. "I don't know. Maybe they think he knows something? Or . . ." She flushed. "Maybe they think he really *can* read minds or talk to ghosts."

Great. Maybe I should take an ad out in the paper or something: *Tom Paretski: His Limits.* I scribbled down *Family dinner—plumbers moan* and held it up for them to see.

Phil looked well confused.

Vi squinted. "Oh—that. You mean who was there when Daddy talked about that rip-off merchant? We all were, really. I mean, Uncle Arlo of course, and Lance, and Toby." She had a little twist to her mouth that suggested she'd have enjoyed her meal a lot more without the bishop's presence. "Oh, and Elizabeth Fenchurch, of course," she added dismissively.

I got the feeling a lot of the family were a bit dismissive about poor old *doesn't-rate-an-Auntie* Elizabeth. Including, I wouldn't mind betting, her own husband.

Phil coughed. "Want to fill me in on this?"

"Oh, it was the day before the funeral." The day she'd fired us, in fact. "We met up to talk about what Amelia would want people to say, that sort of thing. It was at the George Hotel—you know, that place not far from the cathedral? They do a very nice venison roast."

"And the plumbers moan?"

"That was while we were having coffee, I think." She flushed. "You see, well, somebody mentioned Tom. Wondering if he'd turn up to the funeral, and whether it would be in good taste."

Great to know my social graces or lack of 'em were a topic of after-dinner conversation. Although, on the other hand, I do get a lot of my work via word-of-mouth, and they say any publicity is good publicity.

"What exactly was said?"

She went even pinker. "I really don't remember."

Which I'd have laid money on (a) being a lie and (b) meaning nothing flattering to yours truly.

"And then everyone started talking about plumbers in general, and that was when Daddy mentioned the plumber he'd had round recently, and how he'd charged a fortune just to replace a washer. But he wasn't the only one. Everybody was chipping in with stories of dreadfully extortionate tradesmen."

Phil leaned forward. "Going back to when they were talking about Tom, who first brought up the subject?"

"I don't know." She stared us out. "I don't remember, all right? Look, I've told the police all this already."

Interesting.

"What was the tone of the conversation?" Phil went on.

Vi made a face. "Do I *really* have to go through it all again?"

Yep, I thought. Definitely twenty-nine going on fifteen.

Phil did his granite-statue impersonation. "Did anyone there seem particularly hostile towards Tom?"

"Oh no. Actually, Lance was defending you." She turned to me with an earnest look, apparently not noticing she'd just contradicted herself.

"Against what?" Phil had noticed, all right.

"Oh, Uncle Arlo's a total sceptic. He didn't mean anything by it," she added hastily.

"By what?"

"All the things he said about people who pretended to be in contact with the dead to prey on their relatives. Which is silly, because you haven't tried to prey on us at all, have you?"

I shook my head. It seemed to be called for.

She hesitated. "*Can* you speak to them? The dead? I mean, I'm not sure I want to hear what Amelia would have to say anyway, but, well, can you?"

I made a face I hope conveyed my meaning sufficiently.

Phil wasn't taking chances. "No. He can't."

Was that a sigh of relief on Vi's part?

"So anyone present could have got ideas from that conversation?"

"Yes, but ... You're not saying one of *them* tried to kill Tom? That's ridiculous. You might as well accuse *me*."

Phil's stare stayed stony, and Vi paled a bit.

"Can you tell me how many of them might have had access to your home that day?"

"Just what are you suggesting?"

Come on, love. You're not that dumb. Even I could work out what he was suggesting here: that someone had sneaked in, tampered with the plumbing, and then waited to see who she was gonna call.

And if DI Sharp hadn't come up with the same idea, he really ought to think about changing his name.

"Could someone have got in without you or your father knowing? Was there someone in the house all day?"

"Not all day. I took Daddy out for some fresh air. Just a drive in the country."

Huh. So no witnesses, I was betting.

"We were only gone an hour or so," she added defensively.

Phil nodded, which I reckoned was just his way of making her feel like she'd given away more than she knew. "Did any of the other people at that lunch have a key?"

"*I* don't know. Amelia could have given a key to anyone. It's not like she'd have told *me*." She paused. "Uncle Arlo was there, though. He came round to take Daddy out for a meal. To cheer him up. He was very low, poor Daddy."

"And they didn't invite you to go with them?"

"I didn't want to go," she snapped, then looked like she realised that'd sounded a bit off. "I knew they'd only end up talking business, anyway."

"They're going into business together?"

"Uncle Arlo wants to expand his business. Daddy's going to invest some money in it. I don't know exactly what it involves."

Huh. Seemed like when old Alex had married Amelia, he'd got the whole flippin' family as a bonus.

If by *bonus* you mean *millstone*.

"And the bishop? Lance Frith? Have they got keys?"

"Look, I don't know, all right? Why don't you ask them?"

Phil smirked grimly, which I wouldn't have reckoned was possible until he pulled it off. "I will."

Vi left soon after, probably feeling a bit narked her gracious visit to the afflicted had turned into an interrogation.

"Interesting about Alex Majors investing in Fenchurch's business," Phil said with the air of someone who knew something I didn't.

Trust me. It's something I'm pretty familiar with. I made *go on* gestures at him.

"That big house of Fenchurch's? Mortgaged for more than it's worth. He made a few bad decisions in business lately, and if he doesn't get a cash injection soon, he's going under big-time. His whole bloody life is built on sand."

Interesting, yeah—but what did it mean? I grabbed my notebook and scribbled, *Arlo killed Amelia for money?*

Phil shook his head. "All she had to leave was her jewellery. Even with the missing necklace, that wouldn't cover half of it. *And*, more to the point, he knew about the will."

I frowned. How did he know?

Apparently Phil could read frowns. "He witnessed it."

I covered up the writing in my notebook and mimed signing the bottom of the page, giving Phil a questioning look.

"What, Arlo Fenchurch, sign something he hadn't read?"

He had a point.

"Doesn't matter in any case. He knew he wasn't going to benefit. You can't, if you're a witness to a will. Legally speaking it makes any legacy to the witness null and void. So from his point of view, it'd make no sense to kill his sister. He'd want the connection to continue so he could get money out of her husband."

I let my shoulders slump. *Lance Frith?* I wrote, and drew a picture of a diamond necklace underneath it.

All right, I drew a wonky circle with a diamond shape underneath, with little lines coming out like sun rays to show it was bling.

Phil raised an eyebrow, which managed somehow to translate in my head as *There are newborn babies who can draw better than you can, Paretski.* Seeing as my eyebrows don't tend to be quite so eloquent, I just shoved a finger up at him.

He smirked, then turned more serious. "Maybe. Trouble is, where is it? If he was desperate enough to kill her for that bloody necklace, why hasn't he been after you to find it for him?"

I had a light bulb moment and scribbled down, *Lance + Vi in it together?*

"Which explains why you were attacked *because . . .?*" He sighed and scrubbed his face with his hands, looking suddenly tired.

I had another light bulb moment, although we were definitely talking lower wattage this time. *Alex did it? He has bling + doesn't want me to find it.*

"So he sabotaged his own plumbing so his daughter would call you in to the very house where he doesn't want stuff found?"

Oh, bugger it. I thought about throwing my notebook across the room, then had a change of heart and scribbled my final offer.

Toby=serial killer. Bish of Satan.

Phil laughed a bit grimly. "Maybe. Christ knows, I haven't got anything better."

Cherry dropped in on her way home from work. She looked upset to see me, but not particularly gobsmacked, so I could only assume Phil had ratted me out to her already.

In revenge, after several *Oh, Tom*s, I let him tell her the story of how it all went down. She had a pinched look on her face all through, but when he got to the end, she looked thoughtful. "Do you think you had a premonition it was about to happen, and that's why you raised your hand at just the right moment?"

What? "Nah. Spiderweb," I whispered. I *could* talk by then, but it made my throat hurt and came out sounding like a chain-smoking jazz singer after a three-week bender, so it wasn't really worth the bother.

"Spiderweb? Or *spidey-senses*?" The way she said those last two words, which by the way I'd never heard her utter *ever*, I half expected dramatic music to ring out from nowhere with a dum-dum-*dum*.

"Web," I whispered as firmly as I could, which obviously wasn't very.

"She might have a point there," Phil put in, looking interested. "Maybe your subconscious knows more than you do."

"Exactly." Cherry looked pleased. "You know, you ought to experiment."

Great idea, Sis. I'll just hire someone to try to kill me every other day or so and we'll soon have it all worked out.

I didn't say it, obviously. Not to spare her feelings. It just would've hurt my throat.

Phil smirked in my direction like he knew what I was thinking. "How are you getting on with that pendulum?"

I shrugged and gestured to my throat. Heh. At least it was good for getting me out of awkward questions.

"Oh—sorry. I shouldn't make you talk." The reprieve lasted all of thirty seconds before she was off again. "Have you had a chance to decide about the house yet?"

Great. I should have stuck with the pendulum after all. Phil frowned. "What house?"

"Oh, didn't Tom say? My house in Pluck's End. I thought you and Tom might like to live there after Gregory and I get married. I'll be moving to St. Leonards, of course."

Phil gave me a sharp look, which was well unfair given I wasn't exactly in a position to defend myself right now. "We've not had a chance to talk about it yet," he said, still giving me the evil eye.

"Well, no hurry, but obviously I need to sort out alternative tenants from March if you're not going to be using it."

He nodded.

Sis didn't stay much longer. Might've been the chilly atmosphere.

"Was gonna tell you," I whispered when she'd gone.

Phil huffed. It sounded exasperated but fond. Well, I hoped I wasn't imagining the last bit. "You think I'm worried about that now?"

Uh. Maybe?

Gary came round after dinner (soup, in case you couldn't guess). For someone who was supposed to be resting up and recovering, I was doing a hell of a lot of entertaining today. Not that I minded seeing Gary, though, particularly as he'd brought a large tub of ice cream with him, bless him. It was bloody nirvana on my poor throat.

He gave me a critical once-over as he sat down with his own bowl to keep me company. "Not loving the new look, Tommy dearest. Red eyes really don't go with your complexion."

No? I'd thought they toned in nicely with the purple bruising. Ah well.

He turned his narrowed eyes on Phil next. "What *have* you been leading our poor little Tommy into now?"

I scribbled down *Not his fault* and held it up.

Gary made an exaggeratedly doubtful face. "Killing Amelia, I can understand. She did have her moments of letting the inner bitch shine through. But why would anyone want to murder you?" He dug in to his ice cream as if he thought the answer might be at the bottom of the bowl.

Phil huffed. "All this misinformation the papers have been spreading about his talent. Maybe someone's worried he's been talking to the victim about who did her in."

Yeah. Maybe they wanted to send me over to join her so we could have a proper chinwag.

"Mm." Gary licked his spoon. I was fairly sure he wasn't making it look suggestive on purpose. "But does anyone really believe in all that? I mean, enough to kill somebody over?"

I shrugged and wrote *Safe > Sorry*.

"Is murder ever a safe activity? Obviously, I bow to your superior knowledge."

I rolled my eyes at him, but he had a point. If Vi had opened the door just a little bit earlier, she might have seen the whole thing.

Unless of course she was the one who'd done it, in which case she'd seen it all anyway . . . Nah. I just couldn't believe it. Not her.

Phil's spoon clinked against the side of his bowl. "Lance Frith is one of the faithful. Not so much Arlo Fenchurch, unless he's protesting too much. Not sure about Alex Majors."

Toby? I held up, more or less as a joke.

Phil gave me a look. "Plenty of atheists would say he already believes in stuff that doesn't exist. How far a stretch is it from God to ghosts?"

Gary nodded. "I've often felt something of a tingling in my bell tower. And, of course, a guilty conscience can make a man believe all kinds of things."

"You'd know," I tried saying. After the ice cream, it actually wasn't too bad.

"But are you certain, then, it was an inside job?" Gary went on.

I looked at Phil.

He *hmph*ed. "The attack on Tom suggests so. Although it's not totally impossible that Violet Majors is right, and he was followed to her house."

I shook my head. "I was halfway home. Stopped for her phone call. Did a U-turn. I'd have noticed." And yeah, it was *way* too early to give the vocal chords that much of a workout. I grabbed the tub of ice cream to fill my bowl up again before Phil and Gary scoffed the lot, the greedy gits.

Gary was giving me a pained look that confirmed my voice had sounded as bad as it'd felt. I glanced at Phil and wished I hadn't—he had that tightness to his jaw that meant he wasn't a happy bunny.

Shit. I grabbed my notebook. *Find out who nicked your hobby horse?* I wrote, and held it up in front of Gary's nose.

Gary's face lit up. "Ooh no, but it's causing a terrible scandal. The side is taking sides. Have you reconsidered giving it a little fondle?"

I shook my head.

"Well, if you change your mind, we'll be forever in your debt. The side is in turmoil. My poor sweetie pie says he hardly knows who to trust anymore."

I supposed trust was actually probably fairly important when you were dancing around waving bloody great sticks all over the shop.

"Now," Gary said brightly. "On to more cheerful things. A little birdie told me you two have finally set a date for the wedding."

He beamed at me expectantly. I nodded. Cherry must've blabbed.

Phil cleared his throat. "Second Friday in July."

"So much classier to marry on a weekday, I always feel. Although I must say," Gary carried on with a pout, "I'm wounded not to have been the first person you told."

I looked helplessly at Phil. "We haven't told the parents yet," he said, which was a better excuse than I could have come up with.

"And what about names? Your own, after the ceremony, I mean, unless there is some other news you've been keeping mum about? I do hope this isn't a shotgun wedding." Gary chortled. He and Darren were now cheerfully double-barrelled. Hyphenated for all eternity.

Well, hopefully.

"We're keeping our own names," Phil said shortly. "Look, I've got some paperwork to do, so I'll leave you to it for a bit."

He headed upstairs with his laptop. Phil finds Gary easier to take in small doses.

Especially when Gary's got a face on him like the one he was sporting right now. "Keeping your maiden names? Don't you think that shows a certain lack of commitment?"

I shrugged and wrote *Fine by me* in my notebook.

Gary arched an eyebrow. "The names? Or the lack of commitment?"

I gave him an eye roll. Then I wrote, It's what he wants, and I'm not bothered.

"Oh, sweetie," Gary said, his tone sorrowful. "You don't want to be the one who always gives in. It's a slippery slope, Tommy dearest."

I scribbled down, *I'm not.*

Gary just raised an eyebrow, the git.

Phil didn't say he was going to stay over that night, just hopped into bed with me as if he owned the place.

I can't say I was all that surprised, to be honest. Actually, for a moment there I was worried he'd taken Dave's advice to heart and really was intending to hold my hand while I went for a piss.

Course, if he moved in with me, it'd be our place, not just mine, and he'd be hopping into bed with me every night. Which, yeah, no cons there.

Just . . . I'd lived alone for years now. And yeah, he was round here a lot, but that wasn't the same as him having nowhere else to go.

Maybe it would be better to take up Cherry's offer? Start off fresh somewhere new? Somewhere bigger, where I wouldn't feel he was invading my space?

Christ, though, Pluck's End? I mean, don't get me wrong, it's lovely there. But would it be home, like Fleetville was? I felt like I belonged here. I knew the people in the local businesses, and, well, I fitted in. Would I fit in, in Pluck's End, with all the lawyers and the doctors and the retired bank managers?

Phil would, with his cashmere sweaters and his shiny VW Golf.

Everyone would think he was slumming it with me.

CHAPTER TWENTY-SIX

I felt a lot more chipper next morning, after a decent night's kip and a lie-in. My eyes were still a bit on the satanic side, and the bruises looked, if anything, worse than the day before, but at least my throat wasn't as sore. I wasn't planning on entering *X Factor* anytime soon, mind.

I could tell Phil was torn. He clearly wanted to be out and about tracking down whatever bastard had tried to break our engagement permanently, but he didn't want to leave me on my own. I had a feeling he was going to try to ship me over to Gary's to be babysat, and if that was the case, we were going to have to have words.

Probably written ones, in my case. But they'd be in all capitals.

"Feel up to a trip out?" he asked in the end.

"Yeah," I croaked, louder than I'd meant to. "Thought you'd leave me behind," I added in a whisper.

"Don't talk. You need to rest your throat. No. We're going to talk to Alex Majors about his plumbing, and having you along looking like that might loosen his tongue."

I grinned and grabbed my notebook. *You're sexy when you're ruthless*, I wrote.

It was a lie. He was sexy all the time.

Phil went off to make a couple of phone calls, and I set about making myself more presentable. With one of Phil's cashmere scarves round my neck to hide the bruising and sunglasses to hide the demon eyes, I looked like Lance Frith's less trendy cousin. Maybe I should grow a beard. I mean, I hadn't felt much like shaving this morning anyhow, so I already had a start on it.

I thought about mentioning it to Phil as we drove off in his Golf— he looked like he could do with a laugh—but although my throat was definitely better than it had been, I still wasn't keen on speaking when it wasn't absolutely necessary, especially when there was background noise around. Maybe I'd text him. Trouble was, he was driving. If I made him hit a lamppost, I'd be well embarrassed.

I fiddled about with my phone until I found the text-to-speech app and had an idea moment. I hit Play, and a robotic American voice asked, "SHOULD I GROW A BEARD?"

Well, it certainly got a reaction. Phil looked over, startled, the car swerved, and we almost *did* hit a lamppost. "Jesus, you want to warn me next time?"

I typed quickly. "SORRY."

"Christ. Can't you just learn sign language or something? It's like you've turned into Stephen Hawking."

I typed, WHEELCHAIR SEX. KINKY, which sounded all kinds of wrong in that cold robotic voice.

"No wheelchair sex. And no beards either." Phil squeezed my thigh. "I like you just the way you are."

"UNABLE TO SPEAK," I typed to cover for a stray bit of emotion that'd got in my eye.

Phil smirked. "Got it in one."

When he opened the front door of his farmhouse to us, Alex Majors looked to me like he'd aged a decade or two in the last day and a half. And he hadn't been in great shape to begin with. At this rate, we'd be going to *his* funeral by the end of the week. His long-limbed figure looked brittle and shaky, like a dead tree facing its final stiff breeze.

"Mr. Majors?" Phil said in his polite ex-copper voice. "We'd like to ask you a few questions."

I'd expected Alex to bluster and counter with a sharp request to know what we thought we were doing and why we weren't leaving it to the police. But he let us in without a word. Literally. It was a bit creepy, to be honest.

Maybe he was feeling guilty I'd been attacked on his property?

Phil coughed. "Perhaps we could sit down somewhere? Tom's not long out of hospital."

Well, if Alex hadn't been feeling guilty before, I was betting he was now. He nodded curtly and led us into the kitchen, maybe because that's where we'd sat the last time we'd seen him. Who knows? He waved us to sit.

Well, if we were going to make ourselves comfortable . . . I unwound my scarf and laid it on the back of the chair, then took off my sunglasses. Catching a sudden movement out of the corner of my eye, I looked up to see Alex staring at me in horror. Had he actually flinched when he'd seen me in my full glory?

There was an uncomfortable silence, which Phil broke by clearing his throat. "Mr. Majors, thanks for having us here. I'd just like to ask a few questions about the day Tom was attacked."

Alex blinked several times, as if he was processing it, then nodded sharply. All this silence from his end was starting to seriously creep me out.

"Is your daughter in?" It wasn't the opener I'd expected from Phil, but I guessed it was relevant. Alex might speak more freely without her in the house.

If, you know, he was planning on speaking at all.

After a pause that was just a little bit too long, Alex shook his head and finally spoke, his voice sounding almost as rusty as mine. "No. No, she's . . . out."

Out where? I wondered, but Phil didn't press him on it.

"I understand you had to call a plumber in quite recently. Can I ask you what that was regarding?"

He looked surprised to be asked about that. Hadn't the police asked him about it already? Or had they got the plumber's name from Vi and asked him direct?

Huh. I wondered if Phil had thought of that. And if it was going to be our next stop.

"A leak."

"Can I ask where, precisely?" Phil bored on.

In the metaphorical drilling sense, obviously. Nobody round that table was in any danger of falling asleep.

"It was . . . It was . . ." Alex stared at the kitchen wall like it might hold some clue to staving off his imminent nervous breakdown. He made a jerky movement, his arms pressing convulsively to his sides.

Then he let out a long breath. "It was me," he said in a voice that was almost calm.

"What was you?" Phil asked, barely controlled excitement in the way he leaned forward, like a greyhound that's just realised it could be rabbit time.

"I . . ." Alex cleared his throat. "I killed Amelia. And attacked Tom."

"Bugger me," I croaked.

Well, after that, it all got a bit official. Police had to be called—Alex, of all people, insisted—and statements taken.

Right at the wrong moment—just as they were loading a handcuffed Alex into one of the police cars—Vi rolled up in a racy little bright-purple Lexus I couldn't remember ever having seen before. Then again, if I had a car that expensive, I'd probably keep it locked up snug in a garage when I wasn't using it. Her worries about leaving it parked on my street didn't seem so unreasonable now.

Her eyes wide, she pulled on the handbrake, jumped out, and ran over just in time to see Daddy being driven off. I'd thought the plod might have taken pity on her and stopped to let Alex say a few words to his only child, but apparently compassion was in short supply today. Must be the budget cuts. They zoomed off down the drive, leaving Vi standing there, her fists clenched in frustration.

Me and Phil having already been locked out by the plod, we were in prime position to get the full blast of Vi's impotent rage, and she gave it to us with both barrels. "What's going on here? Where are they taking Daddy? What have you *done*?"

Phil was unmoved. "Your father's confessed to killing your stepmother and attempting to kill Tom."

"Why the *hell* would he do that?" she snapped.

Kill people? Or confess to it? I guessed she'd probably like an answer to both questions.

Phil confined himself to answering the first. "He said he realised marrying her was a mistake and he was worried Tom would give the police a message from her saying he'd done it."

As he said it, I tried to remember if old Alex had *ever* given any sign of (a) being anything other than devoted to the missus and (b) believing I spoke to dead people.

"But it's all a load of absolute *balls*," Vi insisted. "He didn't do it. I know he didn't."

I was pretty sure I agreed. I could remember how he'd looked when he'd come home to find me half-dead—that'd been genuine shock, that had. I'd stake my life on it.

Um. Probably not literally.

She rounded on me. "Tom? You're the psychic. You have to go to the police and tell them Daddy didn't do it. Tell them Amelia said so. Or . . . or tell them you've remembered something and it couldn't have been Daddy who attacked you."

"Look," I said, and cleared my throat. "I'm not making stuff up."

"But he didn't do it."

"Then it's likely there won't be enough evidence to charge him," Phil said flatly.

"But if he's confessed? I don't . . . Why would he even *do* that?" The anger was slowly turning to tears.

Phil looked a bit unnerved at the prospect.

I put a hand on her arm. "Look, love, got anyone you can go to?" It's not easy making a death-rattle sound comforting and sympathetic, which might have been why Vi shook me off.

She leaned against the wall of the house and put her head in her hands. Then she looked up, her tears drying, and she nodded. Without so much as a glance back at either of us, she half ran over to her little sports car, got in, and drove away.

Christ. I hoped she wasn't going to cause an accident.

Me and Phil got back in his Golf in a lot more leisurely fashion. "Think he did it?" I croaked as we set off.

"If he didn't do it, then he's protecting someone." Phil's jaw set. "Who do you reckon Alex Majors is willing to go to prison for out of that little lot?"

I stared at him. "Vi? But . . . No. Christ, no. Not her."

It made a horrible kind of sense, though. I mean, Alex had been floored by Amelia's death. He'd looked ill every time I'd seen him since.

What better to do that than knowing your only kid had killed the woman you loved?

But then why would Vi be so adamant he hadn't done it—surely it had to be in her best interest to let someone else go down for the crime?

Guilty conscience, because she'd never intended Daddy to take the rap? Or smokescreen, because it'd make people think she couldn't be guilty? Christ, this was doing my head in. "Who do you think she's gone to? Uncle Arlo?"

"You're talking too much. And maybe. My money's on not, though."

Yeah, I didn't reckon that wife of his would be any too welcoming. Who, then? "Lance? No, wait, he thinks she's a waste of space. Toby?" Christ, I could murder a warm drink.

"Might find out soon."

I gave him a look.

He smirked. "We're off to see Lance Frith now."

Apparently Phil reckoned he was on a roll. Maybe he was hoping Lance would take one look at us, say *It's a fair cop*, and hand over that flippin' necklace?

CHAPTER TWENTY-SEVEN

I dunno what I expected from Lance Frith's place. Probably some ultramodern new age hippy eco-house half covered in turf that looked like it belonged in Teletubbyland.

Turned out he lived in your genuine olde thatched cottage, in one of the villages around St. Leonards. It even had a suitably rustic name: *The Rowans.* As I followed Phil up the garden path, a black cat darted out from under the tarpaulin covering a car parked at the side of the cottage. Was old Lance taking the piss?

"Why's he not working?" I asked. It was just after noon on a weekday. If it hadn't been for the whole attempted-murder inconvenience, *I'd* have been working.

"Works from home. Told you his and Amelia's business wasn't exactly heavy with assets."

I hoped he didn't work in his pyjamas. They were probably covered in mystic sigils.

Not that I'd know a sigil if it jumped up and bit me on the bum, mind.

Phil rapped on the front door. After a wait that was definitely on the long side, given the size of the house—still, maybe Lance had been on the loo, or changing out of those magical jim-jams—the door opened.

Lance looked a bit flushed, but at least he was fully dressed. "Phil. Tom. So delightful to see you again." He was in all black again—maybe it helped him bond with the cat—but this time it was leggings, which if you ask me are just wrong on blokes, and a loose T-shirt. And sunglasses.

Maybe he had something wrong with his eyes? Say, the sort of thing that might make you botch a strangling job in the dark?

I mean, if that *hadn't* been Alex, obviously. Or Vi. Speaking of who . . . As Lance ushered us in, I looked around for signs of a female visitor—high heels by the front door, handbag on the hall table, lipstick smears on Lance's neck, that sort of thing.

Nothing. Was that a whiff of scent in the air? Yep, and it was coming from Lance.

Actually it wasn't bad. I wondered if Phil would like some for Christmas.

Not what we were here for, though. I *listened*—and nearly jumped out of my skin when Lance grasped me by the arm. "Tom, what a terrible experience for you. I'm surprised to see you up and about so soon. How are you?"

"Uh, I'm good," I rasped.

Lance winced. "Let me make you some lemon tea with honey. Please, come through."

The kitchen here clearly doubled as the dining room—the large, antique wooden table was all set up with hessian placemats. In the middle was one of those crystal things—geodes?—that's like a rock football on the outside and all geometrical lumps of gemstone on the inside. Well, half of one, at any rate—not much point having a whole one, seeing as how until you break it open and see what's inside, you might as well just have a pet rock. This one was amethyst, which I knew because it was one of the stripes on the rainbow pendulum Cherry had got me. I took off my sunglasses and had a proper look. It was well pretty.

Added to which, it'd probably make a good weapon against intruders—brain someone with that and they wouldn't be getting up in a hurry.

If I saw Lance's hand straying in that direction, I decided, I was legging it and taking Phil with me. I looked up and saw Lance staring at me, his mouth slightly open.

I flashed him a smile. "The eyes?" I croaked. "It's a whatsit."

"Subconjunctival haemorrhage," Phil helped me out with. "From strangulation."

Lance swallowed. "I'll put that kettle on," he said, and turned away.

It struck me, looking around at the rustic units and general lack of mod cons—he even had an Aga, for Christ's sake—that this was a weird sort of home for someone who'd been married to Amelia. Had she lived here with him before they'd split? Arlo's home seemed much more her style.

Was this place some kind of reaction to the breakup?

I was a bit dismayed to realise his lemon tea wasn't just your usual PG Tips with a slice of lemon instead of milk. It was your actual lemon herbal tea. Thank God he was adding honey so it'd taste of something besides boiled grass.

Then I remembered rule #1 of dealing with people mixed up in a murder: you don't eat or drink anything they offer you. Hah. Saved. Although when Lance put the tea in front of me, the aroma rising up from the mug was pretty darn tempting. Sod it. I wished I'd paid more attention to the box the tea bags came in. I contented myself with breathing in the sweet, tart, lemony steam.

Then I remembered some gases can kill you and shoved the mug further away from me.

Lance sat down with his own mug, and Phil cleared his throat. "Can I ask where you were on Wednesday night? From around 5 p.m. onwards?"

"Here. I was working on new material for the website." Lance drew in a deep breath and let it out slowly. "I wanted to put a tribute to Amelia on there, and of course all other references to her will have to be changed."

"You were doing that all evening?"

"A great devourer of time, websites, I'm afraid. I'm sure you both find the same."

Phil nodded. I kept quiet. Gary did my website, which is your basic shopfront one, no bells and whistles whatsoever despite all his pleading to give me the latest widgets and whatnots. Customers don't seem to trust a tradesman if the website's too slick. He'd agreed in the end, and even offered to put in the odd greengrocer's apostrophe and a few spelling mistakes, but I was fairly sure he was taking the piss by then.

"And you were on your own all the time?" Phil went on.

Lance stared at him coolly. "I'm afraid so."

"Do you often work such a long day?"

A faint frown appeared behind the sunglasses. "My plans for the evening were unexpectedly cancelled."

"Oh? What were they?"

"Private," Lance said snippily. "Really, I can't imagine you seriously suspect me of being the strangler. I know full well you've verified my whereabouts on the day of the fayre."

This was news to me, but then I s'pose it must be one of the hazards of the job—witnesses blabbing after you've grilled 'em.

Phil shrugged. "The police will have done exactly the same. Have you heard the latest development in the case?"

"Alexander's confession?" Lance hesitated, as if he wanted to make absolutely sure he chose the right words. "I find it very hard to believe that he would do such a thing."

Not, I noticed, complete denial of the possibility, like Vi. And hey, that news had travelled fast.

"Of course, his daughter's devastated," Phil went on, shrugging as if he didn't give a toss one way or another.

Lance looked away. "Yes. A terrible thing."

"Still, maybe it'll make her grow up a bit," Phil added. "God knows she needs it."

I gave him a sharp look. Callous, much?

Lance stood up so fast, his chair tottered and almost fell, only the counter behind it saving it. "I'm sorry. I'm afraid I have a client to deal with. But it was kind of you to come." His smile was so fake he ought to have had *Made in China* stamped on his lips.

"Not at all," Phil said politely as we both stood. "We can see ourselves out."

Lance watched us anyway, right up until he could close the door behind us, which was annoying as I'd planned to have another go at the vibes on the way out. I was pretty sure that had been Phil's plan too. I mean, he presumably hadn't brought me along *just* for my stunning good looks.

"That was weird," I muttered as we walked back down the garden path. "Him getting the hump over Vi."

"Not really." Phil smirked. "Getting any vibes off what's under that tarpaulin?"

I'd assumed it was just Lance being precious about whatever eco-friendly car he drove. I paused and *listened*—and found myself stumbling backwards.

Phil caught me with a steadying arm. "Whoa," I gasped.

That thing wasn't so much sending out vibes as it was setting up its own local fracking operation.

Someone ought to tell it that really wasn't a great idea in Hertfordshire, given all the recently discovered vast underground reserves of bugger all waiting to swallow up the unwary.

"Thought so," Phil said smugly, and lifted one end of the tarpaulin. Underneath was the unmistakeable bright purple of Vi's Lexus. To avoid all possible doubt, the number plate was clearly visible: V10 LTM.

Bloody hell. I was half-surprised I'd been able to walk past it earlier without getting a whiff of it—but then again, although the vibes had been strong, they hadn't felt *bad*, if you know what I mean. Not like someone's dirty little secret. And they'd gone completely now it was uncovered, so at least we could be sure there were no dead bodies hidden *in* the car, for example.

Or live ones, for that matter. I mean, you've got to think of every eventuality.

"Thought he didn't like her?" I said, as Phil let the tarpaulin fall back.

"Maybe he was protesting too much? Didn't want anyone to know they were involved, in case it was seen as giving him a motive for the murder?"

"So what's it mean?" I asked, once we'd buckled up back into the Golf.

"Not sure." Phil took a deep breath, staring straight out the front. "If it's what I think, I don't like it."

"What?"

"Lance Frith has a cast-iron alibi for the day of the fayre. Multiple witnesses—there was a problem with the electrics at the venue, so he had to be a bit more hands-on than usual sorting it all out."

Lance, dealing with electricals? Crystals and mystical energies seemed more his speed.

"But," Phil went on, "Vi's got no one who can vouch for where she was in those vital minutes when her stepmum was killed. What if they're in on it together? She calls you to the house, tells him it's his turn to do the dirty work, and then, because it's his first time and it's dark, or you get a tingle from your spidey-senses, whatever, he botches it."

Shit. Suddenly I was even more glad I was here with Phil instead of sat on my arse at home while he put himself in danger. But— "Alex wouldn't confess to save Lance."

"If Lance goes down, so does Vi. And maybe he doesn't know Lance is involved."

Well, to be honest, neither did we, for sure. "Could've been Vi both times," I said, though I didn't want to believe it.

Phil shook his head. "Just doesn't ring true for me. Too risky—you said you'd told her I'd know where you were and who'd called you out—and if she'd wanted to kill you, why not do it earlier, while you were busy fixing her plumbing? She could have strangled you while you were distracted, then shifted the body outside."

I shuddered. "I'd have known it was her," I reminded him.

He looked grim. "Not for long, most likely. You hungry?"

"Too right." Actually, what I really wanted right now was a drink. Say, a nice warm mug of lemon tea with honey.

Sod it.

We found a pub in the village that did food and grabbed a table. Phil ordered (soup for me; fish and chips for him, the lucky bastard) and brought the drinks over. My iced water went down like nectar from the gods, and the soup, when it came, wasn't bad either. I very nearly ended up wearing it, mind, having absentmindedly taken off my sunglasses and almost frightened the waitress to death.

"It's contact lenses, innit?" she said, her hand pressed to her ample chest after she'd got the food safely on the table. "For Halloween?"

I nodded. "Yeah."

"Ooh, you've even got the creepy voice. Oh, that's great, that is. Enjoy your meals."

After all that, I was kind of surprised I did.

"What's next?" I asked as Phil finished up his chips. I'd nicked one or two, but they were a bit on the crunchy side to go down smoothly.

"I'm taking you home. You need to rest."

"Bollocks. I'm fine." Thanks to the soup, it actually came out sounding reasonably human.

Phil gave me a half-convinced look. "Well . . . if you're sure."

"I'm sure." Still fairly normal. I was on a roll.

Heh. Soup and a roll.

"Then how about we go looking for some spiritual guidance?"

CHAPTER TWENTY-EIGHT

Toby's house in the country, only a hop, skip, and a jump away from Lance's place, was a bit disappointing, to be honest. I mean, bishops are supposed to live in palaces, right? Princes of the church and all that bollocks.

On current evidence, Toby's church must've gone republican.

It was a nice enough house, don't get me wrong: 1930s Georgian-style, with tall chimneys and a posh front door with a polished brass knocker. But it was just a house. He even had neighbours on either side. Granted, the high hedges meant old Tobes wouldn't have to risk actually catching sight of them, but they were there, nonetheless. Most of the front garden had been converted into a wide gravel drive, with curving flowerbeds and shrubberies to stop it all looking too bare.

We pulled up next to a stately dark-blue BMW with a fish badge on the back. I looked to see if he also had a sticker in the rear window proclaiming *Bishops do it in purple*, but sadly, no.

"What are we asking Toby about?" I rasped as we unbuckled. The soup was wearing off.

"That lunch, the day before the funeral. I've got a feeling about that lunch."

The doorbell was one of those electronic ones that are supposed to sound like something out of *Downton Abbey*, and never do. A short while later, Toby opened the door to us, beatific smile firmly pasted on his mug and eyes all a-twinkle. "Welcome. Do come in."

"Thanks," Phil said shortly, and stepped inside. "You've heard the news?"

Toby tilted his head to one side. "About . . .?"

"Alex Majors. He's confessed to killing his wife."

The eyes lost their sparkle, and the smile turned suitably upside down. "Oh my goodness. A sad business. Very sad."

We both nodded. I was itching to ask if he believed old Alex had done it, but I thought I'd better let Phil handle this his own way.

"Perhaps we could talk about it?" Phil suggested.

"Oh, by all means. Yes. Do come through." He seemed genuinely flustered by the news—then again, I'm sure Greg's told me more than once that a lot of the church is theatre. Maybe Toby was just a good actor.

As he led us through a spacious hallway and a cosy sitting room, out to a comfortably large conservatory out the back, I got a strong sense of déjà vu. Just like at Uncle Arlo's, everything was white—but somehow, in this house, it *worked*. I couldn't put my finger on exactly why, but I reckoned it was something to do with how Arlo's gaff was all straight lines and corners, whereas this place was mostly curves. Still, the similarities were too strong to ignore. Had Amelia somehow had a hand in decorating both places?

Or was I reading too much into it? Maybe the local Homebase had just had a sale on white paint.

The conservatory was set up as a dining room with a six-seater table in the middle, but with a comfy-looking bench all around the perimeter of the room—one of those ones where you can lift up the cushioned seats and there's storage underneath. Excellent place to stash a body, I found myself thinking, and was glad when we sat down at the table.

It was bright enough out here to keep my sunglasses on. I took them off anyway.

Toby stared. "My goodness. You look positively demonic. How are you?" he added belatedly, like he'd only just remembered he was supposed to be caring.

"'M okay," I muttered. So much for him having taken a shine to me.

All right, I'd never believed that. Interesting, though, that he didn't look surprised. He'd clearly heard *that* bit of news.

"Can I get you anything? Tea? Coffee?"

"No, thanks," Phil said politely. "We've just had lunch."

Seemed like he didn't want to give Toby time to relax.

"As you wish. May I ask how you know about Alex's confession?"

"We were there."

"He confessed to *you*?"

Phil nodded. If you ask me, Toby looked a bit miffed at that. Maybe he'd expected Alex would've chosen someone more suitable to unburden himself to, like a man of the cloth.

Specifically, purple cloth.

"And I take it there is no doubt as to his veracity?" Toby added, sounding hopeful—although I wouldn't have liked to say what exactly he was hoping for.

"That's in the hands of the police now."

"Dear me. I must arrange a visit to him." Toby folded his hands as if in prayer, and even closed his eyes briefly. Wasn't there a bit in the Bible about how you shouldn't be really obvious about praying just so's everyone would think you were dead holy? I couldn't remember it exactly, probably because I hadn't paid as much attention in Sunday school as I should have. Then again, it'd been over two decades ago.

"In the meantime, I was wondering what you could tell us about the lunch you attended with Alex Majors the day before his wife's funeral?"

Toby blinked. "Really? I'm not sure what use that's likely to be."

I cleared my throat. Ow. "Okay if I use your loo?" Might as well take a butcher's around the place while we were here, right? And it wasn't like I was going to be any more use out here.

"Of course. By the front door, on the right as you go out."

"Cheers." I went out through the sitting room into the hallway, closed the door behind me, and *listened*.

Blimey. The Force was strong with this one, all right. The trail was blinding bright, with faint strands of guilt almost hidden under a blaze of religious fervour.

I shuddered. Christ. Had it been Toby who'd tried to kill me? *Thou shalt not suffer a witch to live*, Sodom and Gomorrah, and all that vicious Old Testament stuff? The trail led to a small room that was set up as a study. I glanced behind me nervously (and pointlessly: that door from the sitting room had a creaky hinge and I'd have heard it open) and slipped inside. There was a desk with a computer and wall-to-wall shelving full of files, but it was one of the desk drawers that was blazing bright like a heretic on Bonfire Night and calling out to me like a siren. I tried the handle.

Locked.

I looked in the desk tidy. There was a small key nestling in the paper-clip tray, and when I tried it in the lock, it turned. Toby, Toby, Toby. If I switched on his computer I'd lay odds I'd find his password was *Password*. Well, that or something like *Jesus Christ*.

My heart thumping, I pulled open the drawer. What was it gonna be? Secret membership of that weirdo church in America that hates homosexuality? Details of pray-away-the-gay camps he was planning to set up in Britain? The first thing I saw was a year-old edition of *Church Times*. I shifted that aside impatiently—and hit pay dirt.

A colourful booklet with a montage of happy, smiling priests and nuns on the cover, and at the bottom, the words: *Converting to Roman Catholicism: A Guide for the Ordained*. Underneath it, I found another, less glossy booklet—*The Road to Rome*—and, slipped neatly inside its front cover, letters between Tobes and Cardinal someone. Long letters, and lots of them, in spidery handwriting, because apparently this was something you didn't dare trust to your hard drive.

I didn't have time to decipher a lot of the letters, but I caught several mentions of meetings to discuss the faith. The skirt he'd reputedly been chasing? Was bright crimson and came with a matching skullcap.

I couldn't help it. I snorted out a laugh. *This* was Toby's deep, dark secret? He was defecting to the pope's lot? Just to check, I listened again.

Nothing. Not a blip. Which meant not even a porn stash. Apparently, for all his faults, Toby really was as holy as he was painted.

I shoved everything back the way I'd found it, locked the drawer, and replaced the key. Then I trooped back into the conservatory. Toby looked up. "Ah, at last. I was becoming a little concerned about the state of your colon. I trust you're feeling better now?"

Yep. Holy, maybe, but still a git.

Phil raised a questioning eyebrow. I shook my head minutely, and he stood up. "Well, we won't keep you any longer. Thanks for your time, Bishop."

Tobes nodded graciously.

"What did you find?" Phil asked as we buckled ourselves back into his Golf.

I grinned. "You're not gonna believe it. He's turning Catholic."

"That's it?"

"Yep."

Phil drummed his fingers on the wheel. "And there was nothing else?"

"Nope."

Phil sighed. "I think we need to talk to Violet Majors again. Tomorrow," he added firmly, with a stern look in my direction.

"Yes, Mum," I said, and tried not to look too relieved.

Honestly? I was cream crackered. Takes it out of you, this detecting business.

Okay, so maybe it was really down to the getting-strangled bit.

CHAPTER Twenty-Nine

"You're sure you're up for this?" Phil asked for the umpteenth time the next morning.

"Course I am." My throat was feeling a lot better today, after an early night and a breakfast of eggs lovingly scrambled by my fiancé. I'd asked for fried, but he'd said he reckoned scrambled would be better for my throat, which I took to mean he was still finding the yolk thing a bit daunting.

All right, he could have been telling the truth, but I know what my money was on.

"Anyhow," I went on, "I need to get the van back, don't I?"

Seeing as Vi had already seen me in all my bruised, red-eyed glory, we weren't relying on the element of surprise today. Phil had called her and asked if it was okay to come round to the Majors' farmhouse to see her.

Apparently there had been a telling hesitation at that point, which suggested she'd spent the night at Lance's place. Interesting. And depressing. I didn't *want* it to be those two, but it was looking more and more likely.

She'd agreed we could go round at eleven. I was totally fine about it until we actually got there, and then it hit me. I could have *died* here. Right over there, by that tub with a shrub in it that needed pruning. I took a deep breath.

"Sure you're okay?" Phil asked again.

I flashed him a smile. "I'll live."

Phil's expression was grim. As if, say, he was brooding on how close that'd come to being a lie. "Come on then, let's do this. But if Frith is in there too, we don't turn our backs on *anyone*, you got that?"

I nodded. No way on this earth would I have let him go in there on his tod.

We knocked.

Vi opened the door to us dressed in bright red, which seemed in poor taste. Then again, maybe she was trying to lift her spirits. She certainly looked like she needed cheering up. "Come in. This is all so horrible. Daddy's still locked up like some kind of criminal, although they must know he couldn't have done it."

She sounded like she was trying to convince herself. Then again, maybe she was just hoping nobody else would be convinced?

"Is Lance here?" I asked bluntly as we wiped our feet and walked on in. The wooden floor in the hallway was looking a bit sad from its soaking a couple of days ago, and I could see the water marks stretched into the living room.

She blushed. "No. Why would he be here?"

"Just checking." Still hoarse. Okay, so my throat wasn't *that* much better.

"Nobody's here but me. And now you two." She gave me a look. "Oh, for God's sake. You can't possibly think *I'm* a danger to a couple of strapping men."

I was touched she'd included me in the *strapping* category.

"You don't seriously think *I* tried to kill you?" Vi went on. "I brought you *flowers.*"

"Yeah. Cheers, love."

She frowned at me. "Should you be speaking so much? You still don't sound very good."

"Miss Majors," Phil interrupted. "Can I ask you about your relationship with Lance Frith?"

"What relationship?" she snapped back way too fast to be convincing.

I cleared my throat. Ow. "Gonna take another look at the plumbing."

Phil glared at me. "Not on your own."

I glared back. I was a strapping bloke, all right? Vi said so. Then I sighed. "Fine."

We all trooped into the utility room. It was looking a lot drier than the last time I'd seen it, although there was still a pile of wet towels on the floor. I guessed Vi had been too busy to catch up on the laundry. "That's it," I told Phil, pointing out the offending junction. He had a look; tried to loosen it with his fingers. Failed.

Hey, when I tighten stuff up, it stays tightened.

I hadn't really expected to see anything that might give us a clue as to who'd done the tampering, and I didn't. Still, for completeness, I thought I might as well check out the stop valve under the floor. "Catch you up," I said, as Phil and Vi filed back out towards the living room—Vi first, 'cos Phil's not daft. "Gonna check by the front door."

We already knew no one was lurking there.

Phil turned. "Just a mo." He trotted down the hall and stuck his head in the kitchen and the dining room. "Fine."

They disappeared into the living room while I peeled back the rug and lifted the floorboard.

The valve was still there, but no answers. Of course, if Vi had sabotaged her own plumbing, would she have let it get so bad? Would she have bothered to pretend she didn't know where the stop valve was while water was pouring out onto her floors?

Maybe, I supposed, if she wanted to play up the I'm-so-helpless thing and make it seem less likely she'd been the one to cause the problem. I was still staring into the hole in the floor when I heard a key turn in the front door, barely audible over the sound of voices from the living room. Had the plod let Alex go?

I looked up to see Uncle Arlo walk in.

Well, that cleared up the question of whether he had a key or not. I stood up quickly, wishing I'd brought in a monkey wrench or something equally hefty. He didn't seem surprised to see me, which bothered me.

Then I told myself not to be so daft. "Looking for Vi?" I asked, feeling uncomfortable under the weight of his steady gaze.

Finally he spoke, his voice quieter than I expected. "Well. I must say you look the part now. Positively possessed."

"They're in the living room," I said shortly. "Her and Phil."

And I'd be bunging the floorboard back in place and joining them sharpish. I know they say *the more the merrier*, but I'm not sure that really applies to murder suspects. Arlo nodded, gave me another searching look, and padded slowly past in his soft-soled shoes. As he did so, I got a faint metallic whiff, as if he'd spritzed today with eau de workshop.

Then it clicked. When I'd been attacked, I'd thought I'd tasted blood. Except there hadn't *been* any blood. My mouth had been open, gasping for breath. I hadn't bitten my tongue or my lip or anything like that.

And it hadn't been a taste. It'd been a smell, only I'd been too preoccupied at the time with almost dying to notice the distinction.

The metallic smell, not of blood, but of Uncle Arsehole's workshop.

I couldn't stop a sharp intake of breath. My veins filled with ice as I stared at Arlo—and he wheeled to stare straight back at me.

He knew. Christ, he knew.

"Phil?" I croaked, but it wasn't sodding loud enough. The murmur of voices coming from the living room didn't falter.

"Oh, you don't need Phil," Arlo said quietly, walking towards me with an unhurried tread.

I unfroze and darted past him—or tried to. A massive weight hit my thigh, and I went down hard. My hip screamed, the pain so bad I was winded by it.

He'd rugby tackled me, the bastard, and now his weight was pinning me, the metallic smell stronger than ever. I tried to wriggle out from underneath him, but, Jesus, he was twice my size. I drew in a shaky breath to have another go at calling out for help—and then his big hand was over my mouth, covering my nose as well.

Christ. He was insane. There were two other people in the house. He couldn't mean to—

Suddenly I could breathe again. It wasn't good news. As I gasped for air, he grabbed my head with both hands—and banged it hard on the wooden floor.

My vision went. I heard a distant voice calling, "Phil? Tom's fallen."

Next thing I knew Phil's face was all I could see. "Tom? *Tom?*"

I tried to speak. Something I had to tell him . . . Then I saw the blurry shape of Arlo behind him. "Arlo," I gasped.

Phil turned, thank God. He threw up an arm as something came down—cried out when it hit, and fell on top of me. Christ. Arlo had the loose floorboard. He was swinging it again.

The bloody stupid *bastard* on top of me was trying to shield me with his body. I tried to shove him off, get him out of the way, but my arms were made of limp spaghetti.

Fuck it. Adrenaline kicked in, and I made a superhuman effort to twist my body, rolling us over, me on top.

Who needs an intact skull, anyhow?

There was a *bang* like the end of the world.

Phil swore and pushed me off him.

I blinked. Arlo had fallen back against the front door clutching his side. His shirt was blossoming red stains that spread from beneath his hands.

I looked behind me to see the barrel of a shotgun with Vi Majors on the other end of it, her hair wild and her bosom heaving. She looked like some kind of primeval spirit of the hunt. I half expected to see a parked-up chariot pulled by monstrous foxhounds. "You *bastard*," she screamed. "I can't *believe* I used to have sex with you!"

Arlo? She'd had sex with *Uncle Arlo*?

What about Lance?

This was doing my head in worse than the floor had.

Suddenly weak, I lay back on the floor again, misjudging it badly and almost knocking myself out completely. To be honest, I'd have been just as glad not to have to listen to the constant stream of obscenity spewing from cuddly old Uncle Arlo, most of it directed towards Vi. But then again, *Ow*.

"*Tom!*" Phil's voice was louder this time. I really wanted him to let me rest, but he insisted on pulling me up into a sitting position. He wasn't gentle, which I realised after a mo was because he was only using one arm.

Shit. "Phil? Your arm?"

"I'm okay."

He wasn't. "Vi?" I croaked. She was just standing there, gun raised. Would it still be loaded, or had she shot the lot?

Did I feel lucky?

"Miss Majors, please put the gun down," Phil said in what I like to think of as his copper voice.

Vi blinked and seemed to realise what she was doing. Or, more specifically, what she'd just done. "Oh my God." She put the gun down shakily on a side table, where it snuggled up to a photo of her dad with his arms around Amelia and a big smile on his face. Her hands crept to her mouth. "Oh God."

Phil struggled to his feet, which I was pretty sure he'd have found a damn sight easier if he hadn't insisted on holding on to me the whole time. "We'd better call an ambulance," he said with a definite grudging note in his voice, and grabbed his phone.

"Must be crazy," I gasped. "Witnesses."

Phil turned to me. "Probably planning to frame Vi for it somehow. Just like the other attacks."

A chill ran over me as I worked out what that would have meant.

He'd been planning to kill Phil too.

Christ.

"Me?" Vi sounded indignant. "He was blaming *me*?"

Dear old Uncle Arlo let out a string of obscenity that, roughly translated, indicated that if he had his way, his darling step-niece would die a withered old hag in jail, the stupid, useless, fat lady-part. Not that he actually used the word *lady-part*.

Still, to be fair, she had just shot him in the gut.

"So," I said to Vi, trying not to fall over. "You and Uncle Arlo?"

CHAPTER THIRTY

"He just seemed so . . . Oh, I don't know. Fun."

Really? Arlo Fenchurch?

We'd moved to the sitting room, me and Vi, leaving Phil to watch over Uncle Arlo and make sure he didn't bleed out on the antique wood floor before the emergency services got here or, more to the point, take advantage of the fact he was leaning against the front door and make a break for freedom.

Phil was favouring his right arm, which I hoped to God wasn't broken, but insisted he was up to it and would yell for help if he changed his mind. He'd refused Vi's offer to reload the shotgun for him. He hadn't *said* that was because he didn't have a clue how to use it . . . but I was starting to seriously consider Gary's join-a-gun-club suggestion.

Vi had found me a bag of frozen peas wrapped in a tea towel to hold against the lump on my head. I'd managed to prop 'em up on the back of the sofa and was using them as a pillow. It wasn't all that comfy, but it had the big advantage of taking zero effort on my part.

"And it was exciting," Vi carried on. "You know, meeting in secret. He'd pretend he was taking a business trip up to Birmingham, and we'd meet at a hotel. Just like a proper, old-fashioned affair. He's very old-fashioned in lots of ways, really. He has this way of really making you feel like a lady."

Couldn't say he'd ever made me feel like one. "What about Elizabeth?" I had to ask.

Vi rolled her eyes. "She's just so . . ." She waved her hands and made a sort of *ugh* noise. "They haven't slept together for *years*."

Right. Because no cheating husband in the entire history of the world ever told porkies about *that*.

"Look, I felt bad about her, okay?" Vi insisted, maybe sensing she was losing her audience. "But Arlo would've divorced her years ago if she hadn't been ill. He was just too kind-hearted for his own good."

Seriously?

Vi must've caught my expression. Her face fell. "Oh God, he was lying to me, wasn't he?"

"Based on the evidence? Probably." I closed my eyes briefly, felt like I was drifting off, and reluctantly opened them again. "You see him the day of the fayre?"

"No." She shrugged. "I was supposed to, but I rang him and told him I thought we should stop seeing each other. He said we should talk about it, but we never did. Everything got a bit forgotten when Amelia died."

On her side, maybe. I was betting not on Arlo's. He struck me as something of a vindictive bastard.

"Why'd you dump him?" I asked. I mean, she hadn't *known* he was a murderer.

Well, potential murderer, at that point.

"It was . . . He had a bit of a temper, you know? It made me feel uneasy. And, well, I'd been spending some time with Lance—he was helping me with my business ideas. I mean, I didn't really *have* any ideas, but he's so full of them. I was a bit resistant at first, but, well . . ." She blushed as she smiled. "We're seeing each other now. He's really keen on everyone reaching their full potential. So inspiring."

I wondered if she'd still think that if she'd heard the way he'd spoken to us about her. Then again, hadn't his main criticism been that she was wasting her potential? "Why'd you keep it a secret, you and Lance?" Her and Arlo's little bit of adultery, yeah, she wouldn't want to brag about that, but Lance?

She stared at me. "Daddy was in *mourning*. I didn't want to be *insensitive*."

Uh-huh. "And neither of you twigged it might look a bit suss, meeting in secret after a murder?" I took another sip from the glass of water Vi had got me. Talking too much, again.

"But we didn't do it," she said, like miscarriages of justice were something that only happened to other people. She shook her head. "But why would Uncle Arlo kill his own sister?"

"Not sure. The necklace?"

"Maybe." She bit her lip. "Are you *sure* it was Uncle Arlo who killed Amelia?"

"Pretty sure. Think he'd risk jail to protect anyone else?" Then I frowned. "How," I began, and coughed. Vi topped up my glass of water from the jug on the table. For someone who'd just shot a bloke, her hands were pretty bloody steady. Then again, the wound looked far from fatal, more's the pity. "Cheers. How did Arlo know we were gonna be here?"

Vi looked away. "Um. Well, you see, he called me while I was with Lance. He asked me to let him know if I had any more contact with you."

"What?" My voice cracked. "You mean you told him I'd be here?"

"Well, *I* didn't know he was going to try to kill anyone! He said he just wanted to talk."

Jesus.

I was glad to hear the sirens at that point.

It was a long, long time later before me and Phil got to go home, what with all the police and paramedics who all wanted a piece of us.

Alex Majors got home before we did—apparently they hadn't charged him with anything yet, seeing as Sharp had been on the ball enough to smell a rat in his sudden confession. Alex seemed a bit bemused to find us in his house, but I reckoned he didn't much care about anything other than being back home with his surprisingly non-matricidal daughter.

"Oh, Daddy," Vi said, giving her dad a fond but exasperated look as he sat next to her on the sofa, still wearing the rumpled clothes he'd been arrested in. "How could you possibly have thought *I* killed Amelia?"

He clutched her hands. "Darling, I'm so sorry. So very sorry. I didn't want to believe it. But I realised, after the marriage, how much you resented Amelia. I . . . I didn't do things very well. I should never have given her your mother's necklace. I . . . I loved her very much." He hung his head for a long moment, and when he looked up again, his eyes were wet with tears. "I hoped you would one day warm to her. I prayed you would. But then she died, and Arlo . . ."

He didn't finish.

"What about Arlo?" Vi demanded for all of us.

"He seemed so kind. So regretful. He said he couldn't stand to see me nurse a viper at my bosom." Alex had to stop for a mo and take a few deep breaths before he could carry on. "He took me in completely. He told me he saw you going into the tent. Where Amelia was . . . Where it happened. And then when Tom was attacked after you called him here . . ."

Christ. It must have seemed to confirm it. But . . .

Vi beat me to it. "How did Uncle Arlo manage to get here before you? Hadn't you only just left him when you came home?"

"No." Alex ducked his head again and shook it gently. "I visited the garden of remembrance at the cathedral on the way home. It was Arlo's suggestion. He said it would help me find peace."

Bloody hell. It had damn near helped *me* find peace and all. Of the *Rest In* variety.

I wouldn't mind betting Arlo had been the one to bring up the subject of plumbers in general, and one Tom Paretski in particular, at that prefuneral lunch, as well. Still, that wasn't important anymore, seeing as we had him bang to rights. And at least his diversion of old Alex had come with a built-in time limit. I mean, there's only so long you can stand around in the dark being all remembrance-y, which was probably all that'd persuaded Arlo to scarper instead of having another go at yours truly and doing the job properly that time.

"What *I* can't understand," Alex went on, "is how he could be so heartless as to try to blame *you* for poor Amelia's death."

Vi blushed like a beetroot and glared at me and Phil as if daring us to say anything about her quasi-incestuous little fling. And while we were on the subject, what was with her still calling him Uncle Arlo, even after she'd shagged him and he'd tried to frame her? That was well weird, that was.

Phil coughed. "Probably because of the hold it would give him over you. I imagine he was hoping your association would be very lucrative for him."

Yeah. Nothing to do with Arlo being a vindictive bastard who couldn't stand Vi dumping him. Nothing at all.

"What if Vi hadn't called me in that night?" I asked as we drove back home in Phil's Golf. I'd had to leave the van there after all, what with the borderline concussion and general shakiness. Just as well Phil's arm had turned out to be just bruised, not broken, or we'd have been leaving the Golf to keep it company and getting a taxi back to mine. I noticed he rested his hand on his leg as much as he could. "What if she'd just looked up the nearest plumber on her phone?" I had a nasty thought. "I mean, it was dark out, and he came at me from behind. Christ, some poor bastard could've ended up getting strangled instead of me."

Phil gave me a look. "Because it's not like your average plumber has his name all over his van in big letters? Like, say, one Thomas Paretski?"

"Oh, shut up. Okay, so he wouldn't have killed the wrong bloke. He still wouldn't have got his grubby mitts on *me*."

"Then he'd have tried something else. Maybe tried to lure you out some other way that couldn't be traced back to him—borrowed someone's phone, maybe, or found a payphone." Phil huffed. "Maybe he'd just have asked Vi to call you over for him."

Christ. Yeah. "Must've been pissed off when it didn't work. After all that effort, with the plumbing and the security light and all."

Phil looked thoughtful. "Maybe. On the other hand, he had it in for Vi Majors, didn't he? Probably got a kick just from picturing her alone in the house with gallons of water pouring onto the floor. Anyhow, you're talking too much."

"Nah, 's fine."

"Really? That frog in your throat's so big it should have its own TV show."

God, I was *so tempted* to make a crack about romances with pigs.

Nah. Phil might not have been a copper for a few years now, but he's still a bit sensitive about stuff like that. I glanced over at him and saw he had this half-amused, half-resigned look on his face, as if he'd somehow developed his own psychic talent and had just read my mind.

Hey, I'd had two attempts on my life this week. I reckoned I was entitled to a bit of paranoia.

The cats gave us their version of a hero's welcome when we got back to mine—Arthur gave me a quick sniff and then stalked off to check what he'd left in his food bowl, while Merlin sat down next to Phil on the sofa and started licking his bum.

Merlin's own bum, I hasten to add. Not Phil's. Nobody gets to lick that except me.

I grinned. "Think the honeymoon period's over with you and him."

Then I realised that was *another* thing we were gonna have to talk about. The honeymoon.

Phil put his good arm around me and pulled me in for a kiss. "Don't sweat it. Plenty of time to decide about that."

See? Telepathy.

Just as we were about to ring for a takeaway prior to getting a *very* early night, my phone rang.

"Have you heard the news?" Cherry breathed down the line.

"Uh, the news in general, or some particular news?" I asked cautiously. I didn't reckon Arlo's arrest would've hit the headlines yet, and if she hadn't heard about it, I really wasn't feeling up to filling her in right now.

"The news about Toby. He's *resigned*."

Oh. That. "Yeah? They say why?"

"Oh, he's becoming a Roman Catholic or some nonsense. But don't you see? With him resigning and the dean retiring due to ill health—"

"Greg's going to have a lot more work to do?" I said to wind her up.

"Don't be obtuse. It means a vacancy—two vacancies—and he's the man who knows the diocese best. This could be his big chance."

"Yeah? Well, fingers crossed." Then I grinned as a thought struck. "Know what else it means?"

"What?"

"You're short a bishop to marry you come February."

There was a silence. Then, "Oh, *bugger*."

I cracked up. "Language, Sis."

CHAPTER THIRTY-ONE

Next day being Sunday, me and Phil were able to have a good long lie-in without any guilt whatsoever, followed by a cooked breakfast I reckoned would keep us going until dinnertime. When the doorbell rang soon after we'd finished eating, I made sure I had a good look at who it was before I opened the door. I didn't want any *more* pics of yours truly appearing in the local press.

It was Dave. And he'd brought company. He squinted at me. "Oi, you still concussed?"

"Depends," I said cautiously.

"Nah, I'm not taking any chances. Your bloke here?"

Phil answered that one by coming out into the hall. "All right, Dave?"

"Peachy. Cop a hold of that." He handed over a kiddie car seat containing a snoozing Southgate junior. "Just bung him down somewhere—*gently*. He ought to sleep for a while yet."

Phil took Dave's son and heir with his good arm, as the proud father wiped his size thirteens on the mat. "I could murder a cuppa," he said pointedly, in my direction.

I gave him a look. "Does your Jen know it's bring-your-kids-to-work day?" My voice was finally getting back to normal, thank God. Well, ish.

"Work? This is just a social visit, this is. Anyhow, Jen's knackered, poor cow. Says it's a bloody sight harder doing night feeds in your forties. We're letting her sleep. You put that kettle on yet?"

"What did your last slave die of?" I muttered, already on my way to the kitchen.

"Well, it wasn't from being bashed on the head by a murderer, you daft git."

"Oi, if your lot did their job properly, he wouldn't have been running around bashing heads in the first place, would he?"

Dave rubbed his neck. "Yeah, well. Words have been had with a certain DI Sharp, that's all I'm saying."

"I'm touched."

"Not by me you bloody won't be. Nah, don't bother with the fancy stuff. Just gimme a mug of PG Tips."

I put Cherry's present of a tin of Fine Old English Breakfast (stainless steel infuser included) back in the cupboard and got out the tea bags. There's a lot to be said for undemanding mates.

Me and Dave got back into the living room with our three mugs of tea to find Phil with the kiddie seat on the coffee table near him, rocking it gently and staring at the sleeping sprog with a silly smile on his face.

He stopped as soon as he saw us looking, and coughed. "Got a name yet, has he?"

Dave beamed. "Lucas. Luke for short. And you can shut it with the Star Wars jokes, all right?"

"Never crossed my mind," I lied through my teeth. And started wondering where I could get hold of a stuffed Yoda for the nipper. And a Wookie. Maybe an Ewok or two.

Dave parked his arse on an armchair with an *oof*—from both him and the chair, I reckoned—and took a gulp of tea. "Christ, I needed that. One thing Sharp and his crew did right, mind. They found that necklace you were supposed to be tracking down. Missed a trick there, didn't you?"

"Why? Where was it?"

"Arlo Fenchurch's house. Well, most of it was. Shame about that big diamond in the middle. Gone walkies, hadn't it?"

Huh. "I could've *sworn* there were no strong trails in that place." I felt a bit off-balance. Uneasy. I mean, not that I ever *asked* for this gift, and God knew it'd caused me enough grief over the years, but I wasn't sure I was happy to think I might be losing it.

Dave chuckled. "Psychic satnav on the blink, is it? Sure you updated your maps recently?"

Then again, I thought with a rush of relief, that trail at Toby's had been loud and clear and bright as anything. Nah, I still had it.

Phil frowned. "Maybe there was something messing with the vibes? Surprised he'd hide it there, though. Why not in the workshop with all the other jewellery?" The frown cleared, and he nodded to himself. "No, it makes sense. Go on."

Dave and me exchanged glances. "Come on, Morrison. Share with the class."

Phil gave us an innocent look, as if he was surprised we hadn't worked it out ourselves.

Totally fake. I know my bloke.

"Fenchurch knew we'd be paying him a visit at the workshop," Phil said. "And maybe he believes in your talent for finding stuff, and maybe he doesn't—although if you ask me, a man who makes that many digs about it is trying too hard to convince himself it's all bollocks—but anyhow, he shifts what's left of the necklace to his house, thinking better safe than sorry. Chances are, he doesn't think a lot of it at the time. It's strong emotions you sense, right? And he reckoned he was pretty safe. 'Specially as he wasn't expecting a home call soon after." He flashed Dave a look. "Sharp wasn't after Arlo, was he?"

"Thought it was young Violet, didn't he? Apparently Fenchurch managed to make the hints subtle enough he couldn't be accused of actually saying she did it. You know the sort of thing. Character assassination, making sure Sharp knew how much she hated Amelia. What with them having been involved, he'd have had plenty of ammunition. No need at that stage for him to actually tell an outright lie about what he'd seen or heard." Dave shook his head.

"So the trail wasn't that strong." I reckoned we'd wandered off the main track here. "Yeah, that could be it. Why didn't he melt it down, though? That would've got rid of the problem for good."

Dave leaned forward. "Again, we're guessing here, 'cos since he's got himself all lawyered up, Fenchurch's lips have been sealed tighter than a tick's arse, but maybe he'd planned to put in a new stone and swap it back at some point. Once he'd got the money he needed out of old Majors. He wouldn't wanna get rumbled some point down the line and mess up a beautiful friendship. All the necklace was for was to keep the business up and running and looking good until the brother-in-law had signed on the dotted line."

Phil huffed a laugh. "So it was like a payday loan?"

"The interest rate's always a killer, ain't it?" Dave chuckled. Jedi junior stirred and snuffled, and Dave rocked the car seat a few times. "Oi, settle down now, settle down. What he hadn't planned for was his sister finding herself a bit short and trying to sell the thing."

I frowned. "Was that before or after she got me in to look for it?"

"Must've been after," Phil said with a fair amount more certainty than I reckoned he had any right to. "Arlo walks off with it and starts making the fake, she notices it's gone and calls you, then sometime after that he plants the fake back. She reckons Vi's had enough of playing silly buggers, congratulates herself on getting out of paying you a finder's fee, and takes a trip down to her friendly neighbourhood diamond merchant."

Okay, so it all sounded pretty plausible.

"*Course,*" Dave went on with a subtle hint of *Who's telling this story?* "The minute said diamond geezer has a good look at it—and yeah, we've tracked him down and got a statement—he knows it's a fake. He tells her, she goes ballistic, and—guessing again, although it's backed up by a few things Fenchurch let slip in hospital—confronts big brother about it at the fayre."

"That was the argument the cats lady heard?"

"That's what my money's on. Amelia demands the real thing back—and the kicker: she threatens to tell Alex Majors that Fenchurch has been carrying on an adulterous affair with our not-so-shrinking Violet if he doesn't deliver. Trouble is, Fenchurch *can't* deliver, seeing as how he's sold the main bling already and spent the cash on shoring up his business. Fenchurch sees his lucrative arrangement with Alex Majors about to come to an abrupt end and, because he's an entitled bastard with a nasty temper and an even nastier line in misogyny—"

"—brings his sister to an abrupt end." Phil's smile was grim. "After which he's got free rein to carry on ingratiating himself with Majors, being a comfort in his hour of grief, all that bollocks."

"And fingering Vi," I added.

They stared at me. I might have flushed.

"Not like *that*. I mean, making everyone think she did it." Including her dad, poor bastard.

"Yeah. Gives Fenchurch a hold over Majors and, as an added bonus, lets him get back at the ex for dumping him."

"Well, only if he actually told the police she did it. And if he did that, he wouldn't have a hold over her dad anymore, would he?"

Phil snorted. "His sort? Probably gets his jollies just from knowing he can bring someone's world crashing down."

Yeah, I'd been worried about that. "Is Vi going to get charged with anything for shooting the bastard?"

Dave shook his head. "What, the bloke what killed her stepmum, seduced her, and tried to frame her for murder? Anyhow, it *seems* she didn't know it was loaded, and she only meant to threaten him with it. Never meant to shoot anyone, honest, guv."

I stared at him, visions of Vi the Avenging Fury dancing in my head. "And you believe that?" Especially the bit about her using the word *guv*.

He chuckled. "Don't matter what I believe. Sharp's satisfied, so who am I to argue? You *want* the girl to go down for shooting that turd?"

Well, when he put it like that . . .

There was another snuffle, then a tiny cry, which rapidly turned into a full-on wail from the direction of the padawan in Pampers. Dave unstrapped him from the car seat and picked the little mite up in his big hands, smiling fondly. "Oi, now, we'll have none of this, my lad. Anything you say *will* be taken down and used in evidence against you."

I shot Phil a worried glance. "Think he's hungry?" I asked Dave.

"Nah, he's just making sure we haven't forgotten he's here, aren't you, champ?" Dave patted the tiny back a few times, and the crying subsided. "Want to hold him?" he asked me out of the blue.

"Uh . . . Thought you were worried about concussion?"

"Just stay sitting down and you'll be fine. Here you go." He bent down to hand me Southgate junior and laughed. "Christ, don't look so bloody terrified. They're harder to break than you think."

They were? I was having trouble believing it, desperately trying not to hold on either too tight or too loose. This kid weighed less than Merlin. He probably weighed less than Merlin's *dinner*.

"Put him up against your shoulder. He likes that."

Slowly, carefully, I lifted the kid up, holding his tiny head 'cos even *I* knew that much about babies. He snuffled warmly into my shoulder, smelling of nonbiological washing powder and the barest hint of wet nappy. He didn't cry again. I could hardly believe I was holding an actual little person.

I *certainly* couldn't believe he'd got half his DNA from Dave.

I glanced over at Phil, and the way he was looking at me made my chest go tight. The poker face had slipped, and he was blinking a lot faster than he normally did.

Then Dave burst out laughing, the insensitive git. "Better watch out, Paretski—looks like your bloke's got his heart set on a shotgun wedding."

With my hands full of our nation's future, I couldn't make the rude gesture I wanted to.

Luckily, Phil did it for me.

Gary and Darren popped in to see us midafternoon. We'd actually been supposed to be going for a pub lunch with them that day—Darren knew a place out Berko way that apparently did a great Sunday roast with all the trimmings—but given the events of the day before, we'd cried off, giving minimal details.

So naturally, Gary wanted to hear the full story from the horse's mouth, as they say.

Speaking of which . . . "Any news about your hobby horse?" I asked, as we lounged around in my living room, Phil having given them the short 'n' snappy version of events.

He was better at that than I was. Came from writing case reports, I reckoned.

Gary raised an eyebrow. "Oh, that? Yes, it all came out last night in the pub. In vino, as they say, veritaserum."

"Veritas," Phil corrected.

Gary gave him a look that strongly suggested Phil could take that and shove it up his (verit)arse. "*Anyway*, as I was saying before I was so rudely interrupted, it turned out that a certain lady who shall remain nameless but is, however, *not* Mrs. Hobby had been harbouring a secret desire to emulate Catherine the Great."

"You what?"

He sighed. "Russian monarch? Famed for, shall we say, a somewhat excessive fondness for our equine friends?"

"You what?"

This time I got the full eye roll. "Horse fucking, darling. Horse. Fucking."

Darren sniggered, then shook his head solemnly. "We get a lot of that."

I stared at him. "Horse fucking?"

"Nah, Morris dancing groupies. Women what get all excited when they hear the jingle of a man's bells. Me, I have to beat 'em off with a stick."

I swallowed. He was winding me up, right?

Right?

"And the dent?"

Gary shrugged. "Hobby didn't specify. One can only speculate that the equipment didn't, alas, live up to its reputation."

I gave him the side-eye. "If you're telling me he keeps a giant papier-mâché cock under that cloak... Seriously. I don't wanna know."

Later—much later—me and Phil were pottering around the kitchen, conspicuously *not* talking about tiny babies and their mysterious ability to turn grown men into mush. Arthur was keeping a beady eye on us from his favourite perch on the top of the fridge while Merlin sniffed at his food bowl and then flashed me an outraged look at its continued emptiness.

"Funny things, cats, aren't they?" I mused. "I mean, they get more attached to places than to people, don't they? I read somewhere that moving house—for people, that is—is supposed to be as stressful as getting divorced. So for cats, yeah, it's gotta be even worse, poor little furry sods." God, it felt good to be able to get whole sentences out without feeling like I'd been swallowing sandpaper.

Phil gave me a look.

"What?"

He smirked and put his arms around me. "You don't want to move, do you? Take up your sister's offer of the house. You want to stay here."

Now I felt like a git. "No, that's not what I meant. Seriously. Look, I've been thinking about it. You want to move, don't you? I mean Cherry's house is way bigger than mine, it's in a nicer area—"

"Further from the office."

"You could get a new office out there. Get a better class of client."

Phil laughed. "Because everyone who comes knocking on my door wants all their neighbours to know about it."

"Okay, so you keep the office in Hatfield Road. It's not that far to drive in every morning. Cherry's been doing it for years. And me, obviously, I can work anywhere."

"But it's not what you want. Is it? You'd rather stay here."

Christ. I couldn't lie to him. "I'll get used to it. I know it's what you've always wanted—somewhere better than where you grew up." Aspirational, that was my Phil.

"*Tom.* Yes, I want something better than I grew up with. I've never made any secret of that. But . . . it's a state of mind as much as anything. It's about believing you deserve a good life just as much as some bastard born with a whole bloody canteen of silver in his chinless gob. And yeah, maybe I didn't always realise it, but I don't need the big house with the fancy postcode."

He stopped, smiled at something, and stroked my hair. "I don't need any of that stuff. Not as long as I've got you."

Funny, I'd thought my throat was better now. But here I was, getting all choked up again.

Only in a much, much better way this time. "Me too." My voice came out hoarse, so I coughed and said it again. "Me too."

Explore more of *The Plumber's Mate Mysteries*:
riptidepublishing.com/titles/series/plumbers-mate-
mysteries

Dear Reader,

Thank you for reading JL Merrow's *Blow Down*!

We know your time is precious and you have many, many entertainment options, so it means a lot that you've chosen to spend your time reading. We really hope you enjoyed it.

We'd be honored if you'd consider posting a review—good or bad—on sites like **Amazon, Barnes & Noble, Kobo, Goodreads, Twitter, Facebook, Tumblr,** and your blog or website. We'd also be honored if you told your friends and family about this book. Word of mouth is a book's lifeblood!

For more information on upcoming releases, author interviews, blog tours, contests, giveaways, and more, please sign up for our weekly, spam-free newsletter and visit us around the web:

Newsletter: tinyurl.com/RiptideSignup
Twitter: twitter.com/RiptideBooks
Facebook: facebook.com/RiptidePublishing
Goodreads: tinyurl.com/RiptideOnGoodreads
Tumblr: riptidepublishing.tumblr.com

Thank you so much for Reading the Rainbow!

RiptidePublishing.com

Also By JL MERROW

The Plumber's Mate Mysteries
Pressure Head
Relief Valve
Heat Trap
Lock Nut (coming May 2018)

Porthkennack
Wake Up Call
One Under

The Shamwell Tales
Caught!
Played!
Out!
Spun!

The Midwinter Manor Series
Poacher's Fall
Keeper's Pledge

Southampton Stories
Pricks and Pragmatism
Hard Tail

Lovers Leap
It's All Geek to Me
Damned If You Do
Camwolf
Muscling Through
Wight Mischief
Midnight in Berlin
Slam!
Fall Hard
Raising the Rent
To Love a Traitor
Trick of Time
Snared
A Flirty Dozen

ABOUT THE AUTHOR

JL Merrow is that rare beast, an English person who refuses to drink tea. She read Natural Sciences at Cambridge, where she learned many things, chief amongst which was that she never wanted to see the inside of a lab ever again. Her one regret is that she never mastered the ability of punting one-handed whilst holding a glass of champagne.

She writes across genres, with a preference for contemporary gay romance and mysteries, and is frequently accused of humour. Her novel *Slam!* won the 2013 Rainbow Award for Best LGBT Romantic Comedy, and her novella *Muscling Through* and novel *Relief Valve* were both EPIC Awards finalists.

JL Merrow is a member of the Romantic Novelists' Association, International Thriller Writers, Verulam Writers and the UK GLBTQ Fiction Meet organising team.

Find JL Merrow on Twitter as @jlmerrow, and on Facebook at facebook.com/jl.merrow

For a full list of books available, see: jlmerrow.com/ or JL Merrow's Amazon author page: viewauthor.at/JLMerrow

Enjoy more stories like
Blow Down
at RiptidePublishing.com!

CPSIA information can be obtained
at www.ICGtesting.com
Printed in the USA
LVHW041804081118
596436LV00003B/649